Arenas & Monsters

DOMINIC N. ASHEN

4 Horsemen
Publications, Inc.

Arenas & Monsters
Copyright © 2023 Dominic N. Ashen. All rights reserved.

4 Horsemen
Publications, Inc.

4 Horsemen Publications, Inc.
1497 Main St. Suite 169
Dunedin, FL 34698
4horsemenpublications.com
info@4horsemenpublications.com

Cover by Oxford
Typesetting by Autumn Skye
Edited by Tilda M. Cook

This is a work of fiction. All characters, organizations, and events portrayed in this novel are either products of the author's imagination or are used fictitiously.

Library of Congress Control Number: 2022947612

Paperback ISBN-13: 979-8-8232-0089-9
Hardcover ISBN-13: 979-8-8232-0090-5
Audiobook ISBN-13: 979-8-8232-0087-5
Ebook ISBN-13: 979-8-8232-0088-2

Table of Contents

Dedication:

To my David, a good friend, a great boy, and my biggest fan.

Chapter 1

"Have you gotten used to the bad jokes yet?"

"Can you really get 'used' to bad jokes? I have learned to tolerate them," I jokingly reply. "I take it he has always been like that?"

"Oh yeah, since we were kids." Michael nods his head next to me as we walk. "And then he always makes that stupid face of his."

"Oh, I am *quite* familiar," I tell the man, just before we both break into our best impressions of David's trademark wide, toothy, I-just-told-a-terrible-joke-and-am-so-very-proud-of-it grin.

"Alright, that's enough," the man we are mocking says from his spot ahead of us, turning around and continuing to walk backward. "*You* stop encouraging him," he says, pointing at me before aiming his finger at his brother. "And *you're* just jealous 'cause I'm the funny twin."

"I thought you were the hot twin?" Michael asks flatly.

"It's a heavy burden, but I'm both," David answers solemnly, before turning his face back and grinning, making me snort a laugh.

"That's not even a joke!" his brother groans.

We are only three members of a group of ten (eleven, if you count my wolf companion, Sona) that have been traveling north together for the past nine days. We are an eclectic bunch, though most of them are human, the three exceptions being an orc (me), an elf, and the aforementioned wolf. We have passed through a few small settlements on our way to the village of Rakatune, which we should reach the day after tomorrow, but our ultimate goal is Manamequohi, a city that lies much, much farther north.

Michael is David's non-identical twin brother. He is just a hair's breadth shorter than David; I would estimate at somewhere around 1 ¾ meters in height. He is also a little stockier, with medium-length curly brown hair, compared to David's which is short, straight, and black. He has a mustache, along with a good amount of stubble, as he has not quite gathered the courage to attempt shaving without a mirror yet. They share the same bright green eyes, along with many other facial features, which makes it easy to tell that they are related.

Since leaving Pákannon ten days ago, the two of us have been making it a point to talk and get to know each other. Before that, he and I were having a bit of trouble seeing eye-to-eye on some things, namely his brother's homosexuality and relationship with me. Though to be fair, David says that he was not exactly aware of it himself until I awakened something in him. Of course, all of the issues between me and Michael could have been solved if David had simply *told* his brother what was going on, but that is not how my pup works.

For all of his complaining, I know the smile he wears under that grin is genuine. It is important to him that Michael and I are getting along. He spent those first few days stressing over his brother discovering his secret, all while watching the two of us continue to antagonize each other. Though I maintain that most of the antagonizing was on Michael's part. In any event, we have become fast friends since, largely through telling stories about David.

The area we are walking through at the moment is lightly forested on our left and right, several dozen meters from our path. Off in the distance to our left are the Emerald Hill Mountains, a tree-covered mountain range that extends north to south almost the entire length of the eastern coast of Avural Ug'dol.

"I think we might need to take a break soon," Adam, the team's leader, comments from the front of the group.

"It's too damn hot," Elisabeth, who prefers to be called Liss, complains from her place next to him.

She is not the first person to complain, and I do not blame her. Though the first day of summer was only weeks ago, we are already feeling the effects. With the sun high in the sky, it is *hot*, and with no nearby trees to offer any shade, finding an area with enough shade to wait until the midday sun passes would be a worthwhile endeavor.

"Maybe we can find a place in the trees to have lunch and wait out the heat." Adam looks to our left, already thinking of the same idea.

"Yeah." Liss nods her head. "Let's see what's around the next bend."

Adam is a good man and someone I have gotten to know well in the time since meeting him. A natural and charismatic leader, he attended the Northlake Academy of Knighthood alongside David and Liss. The three of them left together, each for their own reasons, though all were at least somewhat related to a general distaste for how the academy was run. He has blue eyes, short blonde hair, and I do not mind telling you, a very nice body. His height falls somewhere between mine and David's, and I'd say the same is true for our muscles—though my pup is doing his best to catch up. Though at one time they evidently had very similar builds, these days David's body is more suited for speed than outright strength.

I hold an equally high opinion of Elisabeth. She is only slightly shorter than Adam, and from what I have gathered during sparring sessions, her physical prowess is an equal match for his. She has brown eyes and short, red hair, a style she chose more out of practicality than anything else. She is a stoic woman who takes her work seriously, and I have come to appreciate her perceptiveness and attention to detail. She is also the only person to have taken an active interest in hunting with me—though I usually make David come with us as well.

As we near the bend and pass over a small hill, I can hear good news in the distance before we see it: a river. A refreshingly cool one from the looks of it, though that may be the temperature and humidity talking. It flows eastward down the mountain before turning and bending to the north. Its sight gives everyone a small burst of energy, everyone walking just a little faster.

"You wanna...?" Liss asks the unneeded question.

"Oh yeah, that's where we're going," Adam says with a nod of his head, leading us toward the watery banks.

We set up camp a short distance from the river's edge, behind a rocky outcropping that, while it may not provide complete cover from the road, should at least work for our belongings. It is more a collection of bags and backpacks than a camp, but it suits our current purposes. I grilled our extra fish when making breakfast this morning and stored them in my magical satchel, so they should still be warm when I retrieve them from the knapsack once we are finished swimming.

"Will our stuff be safe here?" Liss gestures to our collection of things.

"I don't see why not, but just in case," Piper, Michael's fellow student at the Elven Institute for Arcane Studies, says with her hand extended toward the items. Her eyes and hand glow purple before a similarly colored pulse of energy extends out from where she has aimed, bathing our items and then us in the light. I have seen this before—an alarm spell. "There. Now if anyone comes near here who *isn't* us, we'll know about it."

"I'll do ya one better," Riley, a druid and Michael's other friend (though not a fellow student), says while making the same gesture, a similar effect taking place with green-colored energy. "That'll keep away any unwanted animal visitors as well." He crouches down, looking at Sona. "Except o' course you, little lady." He tips her an invisible hat.

"You *have* been doing that every night to keep bugs away from camp like I asked, right?" Piper asks the druid, finished with spellcasting.

Riley looks at her for a beat of silence, then looks like he is lost in thought for another. "Yes," he finally says, flatly.

Piper narrows her eyes at the obvious lie. With her black hair and dark complexion, I initially thought she might be from the same region the institute is located, Alkebulan, but her accent is distinctly from Albion. The woman is a sorcerer compared to Michael's wizard, which means she has naturally gifted abilities allowing her to detect and analyze the presence of magic. She can also alter aspects of her own spellcasting, making spells larger, last longer, or as she is more want to do, adding small flourishes like changing their color. She has been extremely polite and a capable teammate, but I would be lying if I said her personality was not a bit...haughty. I once overheard Elisabeth refer to her as "high-maintenance."

Riley is unruffled by his friend's glare. He has red hair and fair, freckled skin, and an accent that originates from the Eire, which if I'm not mistaken is a nation located on the same island as David and Michael's home country of Lutheria. The man has been extremely friendly and jocular—and I'm not positive, but I think he may also have flirted with me a number of times. He is also a spellcaster, though not a student at the institute as he is a druid, meaning his magic falls under the natural category rather than the arcane. He met Michael and Piper while passing through the institute on his druidic pilgrimage and was working with them on a secret project that led to all three of them joining us two weeks ago.

The "secret project" is one that they had been working on for over a year and sounds far-fetched even to me—and I witnessed it happen: teleportation. Together, these three were able to utilize ancient elven monuments, a special type of crystal, and some incredibly complicated spellwork to discover a way to teleport between monuments across the globe. The attempt that led them to us was actually their first—and also something of a mistake. They had intended to only travel a short distance from their school, but they somehow traveled halfway around the world instead, to the monument we just happened to be visiting at the same time.

We are still unclear as to how that happened, as the only thing that links our groups are David and Michael. By traveling so far, Michael's group burned through all of the "fuel" needed for the teleportation spell: reponiam, a dark, smoke-colored crystal that can be used to store spells and other forms of magical energy. On top of that, as they were conducting this "experiment" under the cover of night, they arrived with only the items and clothing they had on them at the time. Manamequohi may be one of the only places we will be able to acquire the amount of reponiam needed to cast the spell that will take them home.

With our makeshift camp set up, most of us start to strip down. Given the weather and seeing as some of our group were stuck here with quite literally only the clothes on their back, most of us have been dressing as lightly as possible while still keeping defense in mind should something unexpected happen. We have already faced a group of bandits on the road once, which is the same reason we want to keep our possessions out of sight. For the more physical fighters, this means leather armor over some clothing and underbreeches, while the spellcasters are wearing robes over lighter armor, if they wear any at all.

Most of us strip down to our underclothes, with a few electing to leave on an additional layer. The men go shirtless, while Liss leaves her top half wrapped, and Piper has no qualms about displaying her brassiere. The two more modest members of our group, Corrine and Tsula, only remove their outer robes, happy to dip their legs into the cool waters, while Riley does the exact opposite, jumping into the river completely naked. Not to be outdone, David follows suit, the two skinny dipping while the rest of us either shake our heads or blush and look away.

Corrine is one of the original members of the group, meaning I met her at the same time I did David, Liss, Corine, Nate, and Adam—when I arrested them for trespassing and assault. Looking at her, you would never suspect she spent two months behind bars, but I am sure she did not expect to end up there herself. She is the shortest member of the group at around 1.6 meters in height with blonde hair somewhere between medium and long tied into twin ponytails on either side of her head. She is fairly soft-spoken and reserved and refers to herself as a missionary but is also a cleric or priestess—a divine spellcaster. While her magical talents mostly lie in healing, she has also proven herself to be capable in matters pertaining to the undead, and I suspect there may be more to her story than she has let on.

Tsula is technically the newest official member of our group, though she initially joined us only hours before Michael, Riley, and Piper's sudden appearance. She is a young elf woman from Pákannon with naturally tan skin and long black hair tied in a single braid that is often thrown over her left shoulder. "Young" is a relative term as she is technically older than me at the age of forty. However, because of the way aging works for those with elven ancestry, she ages much slower than most other species, both mentally and physically. This puts her closer to our other teammates, who are all in their early twenties, while I am thirty. She is the cousin of my good friend Nylan Adcaryn and a fledgling wizard in her own right, though I have only seen her in combat a handful of times now. She does not even carry a weapon, something I have implored her to remedy at the next village with a weapons shop. She is also very shy, especially when she is made the focus of attention, but as she has spent more time with us, she has grown more outgoing.

With two of our number already floating in the center of the river, the rest of us wade in slowly as we adjust to the cool temperature. The summer sun does little to heat the running water. Shady trees line the banks, and farther downstream, I can see a lodge built by a colony of beavers. It is a peaceful setting, and soon enough, those of us who wish to are enjoying our time in the water, relaxing, talking, even attempting a few short swimming races. It is a nice way to spend the afternoon together. Sona even joins in, jumping into the river and splashing about, though she leaves before long, shaking her wet fur dry before laying in a sunny patch of grass.

"Hey." David swims up to me excitedly after besting Adam in a race. "Didja see me win?"

"I did." I chuckle at his eagerness for approval. "Are you enjoying yourself?"

"Yep." He nods happily. "How about you?"

"Very much so." I lean forward, lowering my voice so only David hears. "Any recent nightmares?"

"No, Sir." David shakes his head. "Not since a few nights ago."

David is the original reason we are headed for Manamequohi, and my main reason for being a part of this group at all. When I first met him, he was a loud, impulsive, overly dramatic troublemaker who seemed to actively enjoy causing me undue stress. He is still most of those things, but the main difference is that now we are a couple, and all his flaws only seem to make me love him more.

He is mine, and I mean that in every sense of the word, though not everyone in our group is aware of that detail. After their arrest, David attempted to earn his and his friends' freedom by challenging me to what he thought was a fight to the death. Instead, when he lost, he became my possession, literally. Though I have many regrets regarding this event and the way I treated David in those early days, meeting and having him in my life is not one of them.

The nightmares I am asking about are the result of a series of terrible acts that occurred... Spirits, it was not even a full month ago, though it feels like it has been much longer. That night, three and a half weeks ago, there was a mutiny among the V'rok'sh Tah'lj rangers. A cult of fanatics seeking some unknown power captured myself and David and a few others, brutalizing us for information. Finally, in an act of brave stupidity (my words), David threw himself into harm's way to save our friend, Nylan.

And then he was killed.

But, as David has joked to his brother, "It didn't stick." Before the cult members had a chance to regroup, David was alive, awake, and looked very, very angry. He saved many lives that night, including my own, but the memories he was left with are fuzzy at best and traumatic at worst. Hence the nightmares. We still do not understand how he was brought back to life, but we are starting to uncover answers, and Manamequohi should hold more. We know that the sword used in the ritual and the temple it took place in are connected to Olympian myths of old, and so may David's rebirth.

"That is good to hear." I offer him a small smile. "I hope that continues."

"Me too, Sir." David nods before his eyes lock onto the riverbank behind me, going wide. "Is that a frog?" he whispers.

I turn my head to look. "I think so?" I am confused by the question, but before I can get an answer, David has leapt toward the bank, capturing the creature in his hands before it can leap away.

"Yes!" David hisses in a low voice, holding his captured prey in front of him.

"What are you going to do with that?" I eye the amphibian warily.

"Do you remember when I said I wouldn't make fun of your fear of heights because it's not funny when it's something that really bothers you?" He looks over at me slyly.

"Yes?" I do not like where this is going.

"That rule doesn't apply to siblings." He grins evilly, then scans across the river for his brother. "Hey, Mikey!"

"What's up?" Michael turns around toward his brother, who is already headed in his direction. "What are you..." His eyes fall on David's clasped hands. "What's in your hand?"

"Nothing," David replies innocently, still walking closer. "A new friend."

"David..." Michael takes a step backward, then another. "This isn't funny, David."

"Aww, c'mon. He just wants to say hi!" David holds his hands out in front of him. "I bet he could jump from here to—"

"*GLACIO!*" the brown hair wizard calls out, pointing the index and middle fingers on his right hand at his brother and firing a beam of frost-blue light. The water surrounding David begins to freeze, crackling as it hardens. Before he can react, David is stuck in a small glacier, an iceberg in the middle of the river. I immediately hear a cackle that is distinctly Liss-sounding come from behind us.

"S-so...c-cold..." David's hands are shivering, the frog held within leaping to freedom and causing Michael to flail backward, his eyes darting through the water to catch where it has gone.

"Not to say that wasn't deserved," I start, quickly crossing to reach David, "but could you please defrost him before hypothermia or frostbite start to set in?"

"Right, sorry." My words shake Michael from his frog search. "*Calefacto.*" He waves one hand toward his brother, the ice quickly melting.

As soon as he is "free," David leaps onto me, wrapping his legs around my waist.

"COLD!" I shout in surprise as his ice-cold groin meets my stomach. "*Nargol's Tusks*, David, warn me!"

"Help, need warm," David mumbles incoherently into my neck, still shivering. Somehow, this boy has the ability to be both infuriating and endearing at the same time. Or "infuradearing" as he or his brother might say.

Oh dear. I appear to be losing my mind.

"If you're gonna fuck in the river, at least go farther downstream!" Elisabeth jokes as David siphons off my heat, displaying his shivering middle finger.

"Do that again, and I'm leaving you as a David-sicle," Michael warns.

I spend the next few minutes helping David's lower half warm up, rubbing my hands along his legs, thighs, and rear. His front is still firmly lodged against my own, warming up as well. Once he stops shivering, he allows me to lower him from my waist and stands, still close enough to leech heat. I am just about to ask Corrine to ensure he didn't incur any frost-related injuries when Sona begins to growl.

"Well, aren't you two *cute*?" A voice has all of us turning and looking toward the riverbank holding our belongings, seeing what looks like a young man, no older than a teenager, standing in front of them. He turns and looks at the growling wolf, smiling arrogantly. "Oh, calm down, I'm not hurting anyone."

"Who are you?" Adam is the first to act, already walking toward him.

"Just a traveler, like you." He looks between us all with a feigned innocence in his eyes.

"What do you want?" I ask next, not trusting him. More than the obvious, there is something about him that is *off*.

"I suppose that depends on what you all have here." He begins to look down at the objects around him. "Ooooo! A spacious satchel." His hands move to grab my bag by the straps.

"Hey!" David shouts, already rushing to exit the river. "Put that down!"

"Or what?" the boy taunts, just before turning and running into the forest with an almost supernatural quickness. Sona quickly takes off after him, barking loudly.

"Get back here!" David shouts as he rushes off to pursue him as well—completely nude.

"David, Sona, wait!" I call after both my pups as I start to give chase as well in nothing but a wet loincloth.

I am not nearly as fast, but I am no slouch—I was Ranger Captain, after all. I manage to keep the three in my sight, Sona and David slowly gaining ground on the thief. Sona is closer, but just when I expect her to start nipping at his heels, the boy turns around and blows a white powder from his hand into the air behind him. Sona has no choice but to run right through it, no doubt inhaling as she does. Her movements start to slow until she comes to a stop, her body swaying and then falling to the ground. *Some sort of sleeping powder.*

Before I have a chance to warn David, the thief does it again, aiming for him on his other side. I curse myself as the cloud hits him the way it did Sona, expecting him to react the same way. Instead, I hear what sounds like an angry growl, right before David starts to run even *faster.* The boy hears the same growl and turns, looking back in surprise before desperately attempting to escape his pursuer.

It is a pointless exercise, David tackling him into the ground a few moments later and sending my bag flying to the side. The two bodies tumble on the ground, the attempted burglar fighting to break free of David's hold. Coming to a stop, I hear another growl as David slams him into the ground on his back, pinning him by the shoulders. He struggles in his grip, looking up at him irate as I finally catch up.

"What *are* you?" He looks at David closely, right before I see one of his pinned hands turning, opening palm face up to release a bright flash.

I barely have time to close my eyes and shield myself from the worst of the light attack, but David takes the full brunt to his face.

"Aaahhh!" he cries out as he falls to the ground on his back, hands moving to rub at his blinded eyes.

"David, it is alright. I am right here." I press one hand to his chest, my eyes busy looking through the forest for any sign of our would-be bandit.

"What happened? Who was that and why can't I see?" David's eyes look around at the trees and sky above us, unfocused.

"Not who—what. He was *omi'kan*. Fay." At least, that is what I believe, given what we witnessed.

"He's a fairy?" David confirms.

"A *jogah*. A type of forest nymph," I explain as I help him to stand. "He used his fae-magic to put Sona to sleep and blind you before *turning invisible and running off like a coward!*" I shout the last part into the open forest, hoping he can still hear me.

"Where's your bag?" David attempts to look around. "Why can I still not see?!"

"It is only temporary, but Corrine or Riley can assist if it does not wear off soon." I look around, spotting my bag lying against a tree. "My bag is here."

"Phew." He relaxes slightly as I help him to walk over to it. "Are you sure he didn't take anything?"

"It would be extremely unlikely," I tell him as I throw it over one shoulder while he hangs onto the other. "Without knowing what is inside, the only way to retrieve anything without wild guessing would be to turn the bag inside out. That would cause *all* of its contents to spill out."

"Then I stopped him!" David smiles proudly to himself.

"Yes, you did," I say with a chuckle. "Now come. We need to help Sona."

I aim us at where Sona lies sleeping, people already walking toward us in the distance. Elisabeth and Nathaniel, from the looks of it, were both clothed but still visibly wet. Liss has something bundled in her hands, and the two meet us at Sona's unconscious body.

"Here." Liss tosses the bundle to David, which turns out to be a pair of pants.

Unable to see, David feels the clothing hit his side, his hands flailing as he manages to grab one pant leg before it hits the ground. "Thanks."

"What happened to them?" She points between David and Sona.

"I believe our assailant is a member of the fair folk," I tell them as I kneel next to Sona.

"Shit, really?" Nathaniel comments, trying to look anywhere except David's naked form.

"Yeah, he blinded me with a magic flash," David starts as he struggles to pull on the pants blindly, hopping on one leg, "right after he knocked Sona out with some fairy dust."

"Fairy magic is the worst," Nathaniel complains. "'Fairy dust isn't even real! It's just ground-up potion ingredients."

"Looked pretty real." David sounds skeptical.

"Woodland fay have the ability to 'activate' the properties of magical plants," Nathaniel starts to explain. "When you make a potion, you have to activate the ingredients, usually with magic or some other kind of magical ingredient. Fairies can do that all on their own, so they just dry out and crumble up some hypnograss and then *boom*, sleepy-time fairy dust. It's like making a potion without the actual potion."

"And because of that, it is little more than a magical poison." And seeing as I am a low-level, nature-aligned spellcaster myself, I should be able to wake Sona up on my own. I place both hands on the sleeping wolf's side.

"*Ikma'lota.*" As I cast my spell, my hands start to glow a dim forest green before Sona's body does the same, processing the sleeping weed much faster than it would on its own. She starts to stir, and I move back as she stands on unsteady legs.

<*Thief!? Where?!*> She growls as she looks around, offering a weak bark to the trees around us.

"Gone. But we stopped him," I attempt to soothe the confused canine. "Thank you for your help."

She sniffs the air, looking around warily as she regains her senses. She offers a few more barks of warning to the forest but otherwise accepts my explanation. With one pup healed, it is time to fix the other. Ready to help David back to camp, I stand, and when I do so, both Liss and Nathaniel's eyes move to my waist, Nathaniel's going wide as he quickly looks away, blushing, while Liss has no trouble meeting my eyes, looking very amused.

"Guess I should've brought you something to cover up with too," she jokes, and I look down to see that the thin, white fabric of my underwear is doing very little to hide the green contents within, especially when wet. *Shit.* "You two can walk behind us."

We make our way back to camp to find the rest of the group gathered around our belongings. Some people are still drying off or getting dressed while others are inspecting their things to ensure nothing else was taken. Adam sees us approaching as he finishes pulling his shirt over his head and walks to meet us.

"Did he get away?" He looks at us, disappointed.

"Yeah, but we got our stuff back," David responds in his general direction.

"That's good, at least." Adam steps closer, inspecting David's unfocused vision. "What's with your eyes?"

"He blinded me with magic," David answers flatly. "Can someone point me at Cory?"

"Over here, David," the priestess answers cheerfully. With David handed off, I retrieve my own clothing.

"Hey! Get away from there!" In the middle of pulling on my pants, I stop to see Nathaniel shooing Sona away from his bag, which she had been sniffing at quite intently. She scampers away, offering an annoyed huff in the mage's general direction before laying down in the grass once more.

Nathaniel is the final "original" member of David's group that traveled together across the ocean from Lutheria, landing on our shores only a month before our first meeting. He is just about as tall as David, though much lankier, with messy brown hair and perpetual stubble. He is something of a polarizing figure; while an adequate spellcaster and team member, his personality can be somewhat lacking. He is similar to David: perpetually snarky but lacking the charm that allows my pup's humor to land better. While he seems to lack much formal training, he has proven to be exceptionally knowledgeable when it comes to magical creatures. He and Liss are also in a relationship, though it seems to run hot and cold at any given moment.

That makes Sona the eleventh and final member of our group and a somewhat unofficial one. She is a young female wolf with a beautiful black coat. We met purely by chance, just before we arrived in Pákannon. We had stopped on the road for a brief lunch and were in the middle of some sparring when we heard a yelp of pain coming from the forest. Tracking it to the source, we found poor Sona with her paw caught in a bear trap. Corrine and I were able to work together to calm, free, and then heal her, and I assumed that would be the end of it. Then a few days later, when the ten of us were facing down the threat of an *ukte-na*—a giant, deadly snake—she reappeared, attacking and distracting the serpent to give us time to regroup and slay it. After that, I realized that we had bonded—a magical connection formed between a natural spellcaster and an animal. The bond connects us, allowing us to communicate and understand one another with more than just words. So far, it has been a wonderful partnership.

"I don't get it. How'd he get through our alarms?" Adam asks once everyone seems to have settled.

"He was a fairy," Nathaniel answers him.

"Oh, bloody hell," Piper grouses.

"What's the big deal about fairies?" David asks the mages.

"The way fairies use magic... *See* magic, is different from us," Tsula answers next. "It's almost like a different type of magic altogether with its own set of rules."

"And they're not exactly the most forthcoming bunch, so there is very little we actually know about it," Nathaniel adds, normally the one to have more information on a topic like this one.

"They love their damned loopholes," Piper complains, crossing her arms. "I'll just have to make sure my next alarm spell doesn't have any."

Our time swimming may have been ruined, but we still need to eat lunch. Once our bellies are full of fish, we pack up and return to the road. Though we are on guard after our riverside encounter, the rest of the afternoon is thankfully uneventful, and when the sun begins to set, we find a nice place along the road to set up camp.

With the tents stood up and the campfire roaring, we settle in for the night. Several alarm spells are cast, ones that the casters insist will cover creatures of fay origin as well. Dinner is a simple one of trail rations, but I will do some hunting in the morning. That should hopefully keep us fed until we reach Rakatune. After a little more talking and relaxing, everyone begins making their way to their tents to turn in.

David and I lucked out tonight, pulling the first and second watch shifts respectively, and while we would normally take advantage of the time alone, our thief from earlier in the day has us on edge. Or at least it has David on edge as he spends most of the first twenty minutes pacing in a circle around camp, eyes locked on the perimeter. After I point this out to him, he finally takes a seat next to me, rolling his eyes. An hour later, nothing has happened, and my shift is over. Corrine is already exiting her tent to replace me, and David has another half-hour before Riley replaces him.

"See you in a bit," I mumble against his lips as I kiss him goodnight.

"I don't get how you can sleep when that guy is probably still out there, waiting to steal our stuff again," he grumbles back.

"I have you to keep me safe." I ruffle his hair, amused at the paranoia. "Goodnight, David."

"G'night." He gives me a less-grumbly kiss before I leave him.

I enter my tent, undressing before crawling into my bedroll. It has been a long day, several of them in fact, but if the worst I have to worry about tonight is another attempted theft, I will take it. Closing my eyes in the darkness of the tent, I lay my head back and drift off into unconsciousness.

David and I are running in a forest. Running from...something. Wait, what are we running from? How did we get here? I look over to David on my right, who looks panicked as he dodges between trees. With my eyes no longer watching where I am going, my body slams into a tree ahead of me, and I bounce off, falling to the ground.

"No!" David rushes to help me stand, pulling me to follow him. "Come on, we have to hurry! He's almost here."

"Who? Who is almost here?" I resist his tugging, needing an answer.

Before I get one, a different sound fills the air, the sky turning dark as David looks around in fear. Music, like chimes, or bells, or maybe a music box of some kind. But the notes sound wrong, the pitch off or distorted. And it seems to be coming from all around us with no clear source.

"It's too late," David whispers. "He's here."

"I don't understand, who—"

Black tendrils erupt from the ground around us, breaking through the earth and wrapping around our limbs and torsos. Before we have the chance to fight back, we are lifted into the air. As I hang there, I see another tendril reaching for the sword on David's back, pulling it from its scabbard as it raises David even higher. As they hold his limbs away from his body, I realize in horror what is about to happen, unable to do anything but scream as the sword is plunged into David's chest.

I wake with a shout, one loud enough to wake David who was asleep next to me, and possibly the rest of camp. After looking around in a panic, I realize in frustration that I was having a nightmare, and I pound the ground with a fist. *Dammit.* That is what I get for tempting fate right before bed.

Chapter 2

"...and then we were grabbed by a bunch of tentacles?"

"Tendrils."

"What's the difference?"

"I think tentacles are specifically the body part of an animal." David and I pause our discussion, and even Sona looks at Liss, who shrugs. "Nate talks about that kind of stuff a *lot* when we're alone."

"Regardless, yes, we were both grabbed," I continue recounting last night's nightmare. "Then we were lifted into the air—"

"And I was stabbed again," David finishes for me.

"Yes," I respond with a sigh. "You were stabbed again."

It is late afternoon, Solisday (it is important to keep track of the days when out in the wilderness), and the four of us are hunting for dinner, or at least attempting to. After waking several people last night with my nightmare-induced scream, I managed to fall back asleep with some unease. Thinking on the nightmare only briefly after waking in the morning, my attention was immediately drawn to other matters, namely trying to find something for breakfast.

That hunt was not successful, leading to a breakfast of trail rations. We then had a fairly quiet and uneventful day of travel, especially when compared to yesterday. David somehow managed to not bring up my nightmare at all until *right now*, which for some reason, he has decided is the best time to talk about it. It is not that I am trying to avoid it, but the timing is very inconvenient.

I have no problem talking about my nightmares, though I would like to point out that *he* still feels shy enough to want privacy when discussing his own. Since getting him to open up about them, he has gone out of his way to ensure neither of us is keeping anything bottled up. Which is honestly fantastic, and I will have no problem talking about it *after* we are finished hunting. Truthfully, I am not giving the bad dream that much weight to begin with. I am unclear as to where some of the imagery came from, but I am self-aware enough to know that the base cause is my mind reliving David's violent death.

"So what do we do?" David asks as if there were a simple solution.

"Maybe talk about it when we're not trying to sneak up on dinner?" It would seem Liss is having the same issue I am.

David huffs in response, but the point seems to be made and we finally have silence. As our group has grown in size, hunting has become less and less convenient. You cannot feed ten people on just a few rabbits. I have been considering hunting something larger, like a deer, but that comes with its own issues, the main one being storage. My spacious satchel can fit a lot, but even that has its limits. There is also the matter of waste—in my culture, it is considered disrespectful to not use every part of your kill. Beyond the meat to be butchered, inedible organs and ligaments can be used for fertilizer, fur and bones used for clothing or decoration—everything has a use.

It might work if we found a deer small enough, but there is no telling when or where we might run into one. In the interim, I expect us to lean more heavily on fishing to feed ourselves on the road. There's not much in the way of game that falls into a size category between the two. Nothing except maybe feral livestock and a few large birds—

As if on cue, Sona growls, right before I hear a gobbling sound in the distance—the call of a *lum'tik'bra*, or as David and Liss call it, a turkey. I could easily make a meal for ten with a bird that size, two if I stretched it out with a stew, and the feathers could be sold to a fletcher or used as spell components. With a plea for continued silence and a signal to follow, Sona and I lead the others toward our target.

One successful hunt later, the four of us begin the walk back to camp with our dead fowl in tow. I stop with David and Sona in a small clearing along the way to butcher and clean the bird while Liss continues on, as this is not a three-person job. David has been somewhat squeamish in the past, but seeing as hunting will be an almost daily part of our lives for the time being, he has been trying to push past it.

We finish a short while later (there were so many damn feathers to deal with), and after washing up, we return to the camp proper so I can get started on dinner. I will have to make sure to refill my water canteens as it takes most of what I have to fill the pot I place over the fire. I add the meat and other spices while David slices vegetables and other ingredients to add as the water comes to a boil. Sona lounges in the grass next to Riley, who happily pets through her fur, and while we work, I can hear some of the others discussing what sounds like magic.

"The spell functions very similarly to featherfall," Michael explains to Tsula, the two looking through Michael's spellbook.

"I see that." Tsula nods her head. "It looks like you increased the weight-reduction portion of the spell exponentially."

"Right," Michael agrees. "I couldn't make it *completely* weightless because—"

"Because then whatever you cast it on would just float away," Tsula finishes for him.

"Exactly." He gives her a bright smile. "But by making them *near*-weightless, and adding a little bit of force underneath—"

"—you can suspend the target in mid-air," Tsula summarizes, sounding fascinated. "It would be forced to hover there, like an aerial snare."

"I haven't used it in a fight yet, but that's the idea." Michael is clearly pleased that the girl he is infatuated with is finishing his sentences. "So far, all I've really done with it is use it to move things from one dorm to another when I was given a new room at the institute."

"That still sounds like an ingenious way to use a spell like that," Tsula assures him.

"Thanks." Michael smiles, suddenly bashful.

Overhearing some of the mages discussing their magical prowess has been a common occurrence over the past week and a half. It makes sense, seeing as the mages in our group outnumber the non-mages six to four, seven if you count myself, though my abilities are nothing spectacular. We have only seen combat a handful of times since the majority of them joined, but they have been invaluable team members each time.

Michael, Tsula, Piper, and Nathaniel are arcane casters, all of them wizards (though Nathaniel and Tsula are untrained) with the exception of Piper, who is a sorcerer. That means their magical abilities fall under what most people would think of as "traditional" magic—creating lights, detecting magic, and conjuring bolts of arcane energy. Michael and Nathaniel both carry walking sticks as weapons, though I know at least Michael's doubles as a spell focus. I have seen Piper wielding a wand on occasion, though she seems to prefer using her sorcerer magic to summon arcane weapons like a whip, and as previously mentioned, Tsula does not currently have one. Ideally, none of them will ever have to use their weapons in a fight, but you can never be too careful. Especially with our track record of bandits, giant snakes, and ghosts.

Corrine is a divine caster, while Riley is a natural caster, like myself. That makes the two of them the team's healers, with Corrine edging out the redhead in raw healing power, as well as having some manner of power against the undead. As its name would suggest, Riley's magic lends itself more to the natural world, things like animals, weather, and elements. My own magical talents are nowhere near as strong as his. Both of them wield wooden walking staves, though again when it comes to combat, they have mostly relied on their magic.

The rest of us are all wielding a sword of some sort (two, in David's case) and have also had fairly extensive combat training. Given the dangers we have faced on the road so far, we have tried to impart some of our skills onto the others with the occasional sparring session, to middling results. Physical combat is not for everyone. The mages are known to engage in some training of their own, practicing spells and using trees or rocks as "target practice."

"Would you like to try it out?" Michael asks, looking from Tsula to a small pile of rocks.

"Absolutely," she agrees, standing and offering him a hand to do the same.

Still standing by the fire, I stir our dinner stew as I watch the two wizards approach the rocks. Each of them selects a larger rock, separating it from the others and taking several steps back. Nodding to Tsula, Michael goes first.

"*Pendere!*" Michael lifts his hand in front of him, palm face-up, and a moment later, the stone is hovering in the air.

"Very nice," Tsula compliments. "*Leriana!*" After doing the same hand movement, her own target floats up just like Michael's.

"There's something I don't get," David starts, directing his incoming question to his brother as he dumps his chopped potatoes into the pot. "Why can two people say different things but still cast the same spell?"

"Because the words themselves aren't what's important," Michael starts to explain. "It's about the intent behind them."

"Michael and I tend to use Elutian incantations," Piper adds, having exited her tent just a few minutes ago. "But that is only because that's the way they are taught to us at the institute. It's a dead language that is the root of many others, so it's easy to pick up while still sounding different enough from regular speech."

"Aye, and I use Old Eirish, 'cause that's what they taught at my druid circle," Riley says from across the fire.

Explaining the inner workings of magic, particularly Michael to David, has also become a common occurrence. Though he has a tendency to brag, there is genuine interest on Michael's part to impart this knowledge to his twin brother. David once told me that Michael used to help him with a lot of his schoolwork, and he would in turn sometimes allow his brother to "experiment" on him with new spells or potions.

"Now, there are some really high-level spells that require you to be precise with what you say, and how you say it," Michael continues, lowering his stone back to the ground. "You have to watch for things like your rhythm or inflection or even the time of day or star position. But for *most* spells, what you say is more like a trigger word than anything else."

"So the words don't actually matter?" David oversimplifies.

"Not exactly." Michael pauses to consider the next part of his explanation. "It's hard to explain, but you can sort of...feel the energy around you. Casting spells is done by making that energy do what you want."

"The first few times you cast a spell, it's a bit like solving a math, physics, and chemistry equation in your head, all at once." Piper takes a seat by the fire, waiting for dinner to be served. "You have to know the science behind whatever it is that you are trying to do so that you can use your magic to make it happen. I can only really speak for arcane spellcasters, though."

"It is similar for natural spellcasters as well," I jump into the conversation to add my own information. "Perhaps not quite as scientific, but you must still know the basics behind how something works in the natural world for your spell to work."

"Aye, at the druid circle, I had to study things like weather patterns and how water is formed, or what happens when the temperature changes rapidly," Riley lists some examples for me. "Even my shapeshiftin' has stipulations. I can only change into animals I've actually spent some time with. All their muscles, bones, organs—the more different they are from a human, the more difficult it can be."

"Divine spellcasting is basically the same as well," Corrine, as the only divine caster in our group, adds. "Especially when it comes to healing. The more you know about how the body works, the better you can direct your healing energy to the parts that need it most."

"Aren't you also kind of asking someone else for help when you cast a spell?" Liss asks from her seat next to Piper.

"There is a 'prayer' aspect to my spells, yes." Corrine nods confidently. "Some people say that gives you some wiggle room when you cast because even if you don't know all the specifics, God does. But I don't really like to assume things will just work out like that before I start casting."

"Did they teach you about biology at your church school?" I ask Corrine, curious about her schooling as she does not speak on it much.

"Some, but I had to seek out a lot on my own, too," she admits, and I am not surprised. Corrine is a follower of the God of the Albionian Church, also known as Yahweh or the God of Abram, and from what I have learned and witnessed myself, they do not consider science and the divine to mix well.

"So what if it's a spell you've cast a bunch of times?" David continues with his inquiry. "What changes?"

"It's like muscle memory," Piper answers. "Once you know how to do something, it's just a matter of repeating it. Like Michael said, the 'incantation' is really more of a trigger—a way to help your mind quickly recall all of those specifics."

"Really powerful casters don't need to use them at all; they can cast everything silently," Michael adds. "But even when you *do* use them, the actual specifics of the word being said are kind of irrelevant. I can literally just say 'fire' and cast a fire spell." As he says this, he holds a hand in the air, a flame bursting from his palm when he says the word "fire."

"I think I get it," David says while biting his lip, likely fibbing at least a little.

"Don't worry. I'll explain it again later," Michael knowingly tells his brother.

Finishing up dinner, I think more about my own magic. It is not something I make use of very often, typically only in emergencies or when it is something that only I can do, and with Riley here, that is very unlikely. The most I have used it lately is with Sona, first when using it to calm her so we could free her from the bear trap she was caught in, and then again when I realized the two of us had formed a magical bond, which was out of either of our hands. Now we "talk" with magic every day.

Once the cooking is finished, David helps me pass out the bowls. I pour the remaining stew into a large soup canteen my father Rurig gifted me, and thanks to the way my satchel works, it should be just as hot when I retrieve it in a day or two for leftovers. After everyone has finished their meal, we settle in for the evening, some people reading books by the fire while others tend to their weapons or armor.

I might pull out a book a little later myself, but there are other things I think I would rather do first. Like David. I glance over at him, pleased when he returns my knowing look with a sly smile, before glancing off into the forest. We wait about fifteen minutes for our food to settle before David stands, exiting camp as nonchalantly as possible. I give it another minute before I follow, as aware as ever that we are likely fooling no one.

I walk until the fire is just a small light in the distance when something leaps at me from behind a tree. Something with black hair, green eyes, and a hungry mouth. David smashes our lips together in a kiss, pushing me back against the tree's trunk. I allow myself to be manhandled, bringing my hands to his waist and pulling us together.

As silly as it is to me that we have to sneak off for this sort of thing at all, I keep that opinion to myself. David was already nervous about having sex in camp *before* his brother teleported halfway around the world and joined us. His feelings on the topic can vary from day to day (namely based on how horny he is versus whether or not he is willing to put on clothes and leave our tent), so it is something I am gently getting him to grow more comfortable with.

And, if I am being honest, I do not exactly mind having sex in the middle of the forest. It is a little thrilling.

I deepen our kiss as I lean back against the tree, my hands wandering from his sides to his rear. I growl into his mouth when he bites at my lips, squeezing his ass roughly and grinding our crotches together. I press my face tightly against his, the threat of sharpness from my tusks making him whine.

David's own hands roam over my chest and down my stomach, coming to a stop on my crotch, where he squeezes me through the fabric of my pants. After gently stroking a few times along my length, his fingers move up to untie my belt. Then he unbuttons my pants, sinking to his knees on the grass.

Once my cock has been freed from its confines, he leans forward, nuzzling and placing wet, open-mouthed kisses against my skin. He slides his lips along my shaft until he reaches the top, using his hand to pull back my foreskin and lick over the head. I groan softly at the warm tongue swiping over the sensitive skin.

I growl, fisting one hand in his hair as he starts to take more of me into his mouth. Looking down, I watch David's hand start to wander to the growing pouch of his crotch, stopping before it reaches its target. *Good boy.* I close my eyes, leaning my head back as the warm heat envelops me, David letting out a muffled moan around me.

"I swear that's hot every time I see it." Adam's voice surprises me enough to almost slam my head back against the tree.

"*Dude.*" David sounds exasperated, sitting back on his heels after almost choking himself on my cock. "You *cannot* sneak up on us like that!"

"Sorry, I didn't want to interrupt," Adam sheepishly apologizes.

"Gotta put a fuckin' bell on your or something..." David grumbles before turning back to my prick.

"Yeah, you seem really upset," Adam jokes at his friend's eagerness.

"You wanna get your dick sucked or not?" David challenges after pulling off a second time. "We've got a time limit."

I laugh softly into the air, shaking my head at their antics. "If you both are quite done." I replace my hand on David's head, guiding his mouth back to my shaft.

If I do not seem more put off by Adam's sudden appearance, it is because this is not the first time this has happened. That was almost two weeks ago during the Summer Solstice celebrations on our final night in Pákannon. After a night of dancing, I surprised David by inviting Adam back to our room, where the three of us enjoyed quite the nice evening together. Since then, we have gotten together a few more times, mostly quick dalliances in the woods like this one.

I realized David's attraction to his friend not long after I joined them. It was actually rather adorable, almost like a schoolyard crush, and it was something he did not even seem to be fully aware of. He thought at first that I might be jealous or upset by this information, but he really did not need to worry. I mean, I find the man plenty attractive myself but feel no reason to be threatened by him. Especially as, once the two of them moved past the awkward beginning stages, their friendly camaraderie started coming through during sex. Adam is obviously interested, but I can still sense some hesitation when he seeks us out. Whether that is because of a lack of experience or because he is hesitant to "use" his best friend like both of them actually want, I am not sure. Either way, I am in for a good show.

Following my minor admonishment, Adam comes to stand next to me, unbuttoning his fly and pulling out his cock. David's eyes wander to the peach-colored prick as it comes into view, twitching lightly in the air. He reaches up to wrap a hand around it, stroking lightly but keeping his focus on me in his mouth.

After a few more moments of sucking, he pulls off of me and switches over to Adam, swallowing most of his length down in one stroke. My still-wet appendage hangs in the air only centimeters away, and I cannot help myself and lightly slap it against David's cheek. He looks up at me with playful eyes before he starts stroking me as well.

We switch David back and forth like this, something he has done a few times before. He keeps his hand on whomever is not currently occupying his mouth, though his attention is still firmly on who is. I feel my cock give an involuntary lurch at the sight of David's nose buried in the golden forest of hair surrounding Adam's base, eager to have him buried in my own.

"Sir," David starts, catching his breath after pulling off of my cock for a moment. "Can I touch myself?"

"Yes, you may. Good boy." I smile at the request, glad that he remembered before groping himself without permission.

David lets out a happy groan of approval as I re-enter his mouth, taking his hand off of Adam to undo the front of his own pants. He quickly pulls the pouch of his underwear to the side, his cock springing into the air, already fully hard. It has been several days since he was last allowed to masturbate. It is not a new rule, but one that has become more prominent since starting our journey.

I am not particularly upset by the thought of David pleasuring himself. It is just one of the ways I like to exert my control over him—and one of the few still available to me while we are in mixed company. David enjoys it just as much as I do, which is why we make such a good pair. The terms for a relationship like ours where I come from are *avakesh*, which is the submissive and owned partner, and *kavan*, which is the dominant and owner.

That is why David calls me Sir and defers to me, while also being paranoid about the others (namely Michael) finding out. I have already explained that our relationship did not begin on the best terms, but that does not mean I do not still treasure his submission each time he offers it to me. I also do not mind telling you that the boy looks *damn good* in a collar, cuffs, and little else.

Now happily working his own cock, David continues to bob up and down on both of ours. With his attention divided, his technique does start to get a little sloppy, though that is not necessarily a bad thing when it comes to oral sex. Each time he switches between us, he also switches hands, trying to stroke both himself and the person not in his mouth at the same time. It is rather amusing watching him attempt to keep up with three different rhythms, and eventually he just gives up and leaves us to take ourselves in hand.

I am happy to take over some of the work for him. The next time he moves from Adam to me, I grip him lightly by the hair. Holding him in place, I start to snap my hips forward, fucking my cock into his mouth with short, shallow thrusts while he remains stationary on his knees. David's cock gives a lurch as soon as I grab his hair, and his hand speeds up once I start to thrust.

Taking a cue from me, Adam does the same when David is passed back over, holding his head firmly in place while Adam fucks his cock in and out of his mouth. David's lips are swollen and red, and a small amount of drool escapes from the corners of his mouth. I can hear little else over the cut-off moans and gurgles each time Adam's cock pushes all the way in his throat. Fuck, I think I am almost ready to cum.

"I am getting close," I announce, rapidly fisting my own cock.

At my warning, Adam releases David, who turns back towards me. I quickly grab the back of his head, plunging my cock back into his oral depths, humping into David's face fast and hard. It takes less than a half-a-dozen strokes to push me over the edge, pulling David all the way down on my cock and cumming with a cut-off growl.

David does his best to swallow, trying to keep up with the load I am pumping directly into his throat. It has been a few days, so I know it is a large one, and I am unsurprised when I hear a choking noise from below as it becomes too much. When I am done and finally pull back, a trickle of white rolls down his spit-slick chin, whatever remains of my load that he was unable to swallow.

I lean back against the tree to catch my breath as David does the same on his knees. His beard may be a mess, but the hand on his cock has not slowed down once. He does not even need to be told what to do next, turning to Adam, who is also working his own prick. David kneels up and opens his mouth, ready for whatever the blonde may need it for.

"Work my nuts," Adam orders, pulling David toward his crotch.

Adam continues to swiftly fist his cock while David worships the man's testicles as requested. My pup drags his tongue over the fuzzy peach-colored orbs, sucking each one into his mouth. Adam keeps a tight grip on the back of his head, holding him against the base, David's nose pressed against the man's skin. All the while, both men continue to pump their cocks, each chasing their own orgasm.

"Gonna cum." Adam is the first to cross the finish line.

He pulls David away from his balls, holding him in place only inches from his prick and still-moving hand. Adam's eyes are closed, his face screwed up in concentration as David kneels with his mouth open. Then his hand slows down, and I see his cock pulse, just before shoving the head into David's mouth. He continues working his hand up and down the shaft as he unloads.

David manages to swallow everything, though he still has my seed drying on his chin. His eyes are shut as he kneels on the forest floor, hand still moving in a blur over his cock. Knowing he is so very close to the edge himself, I reach a hand out and stroke it through his hair—before grabbing a fistful and tugging sharply. The sudden pain makes David gasp, and a second later, he unleashes his own cum all over the forest floor.

I pet through his hair gently as he comes down from his orgasmic high, leaning against me with a worn-out smile. Once he is no longer floating, I help him to stand, watching as he brushes the grass and dirt from his knees. He grimaces as he stretches his legs, sore from having spent so long in one position. Still, when he opens his eyes, they are filled with the sleepy warmth that only comes after good sex.

"*Fuck*," Adam breathes out as he tucks himself away. "Thanks. I needed that."

"I think we all did," I agree with the sentiment, rebuttoning my pants.

"Yeah, that was good," David adds a little goofily.

"Uh..." Adam grimaces slightly as he takes in David's face. "You're gonna want to clean up before we get back to camp."

"You think?" David rolls his eyes, lifting the front of his shirt up and cleaning his face as best he can with the back of it. It leaves a small wet spot on his stomach, but other than that and his red eyes, there is no other immediate evidence of our activities. He should be okay to make it back into camp without anyone noticing. *As long as they do not look too closely.* Cleaned up as best we can, we start to walk in the direction of camp.

"Uh-uh." David stops, pointing at Adam. "You gotta wait back here for a few minutes. It'll look weird if we all come back into camp together."

"Seriously?" Adam is nonplussed by the demand.

"Yes, seriously." David crosses his arms in front of him. "In fact, walk that way some. I don't even want it to look like we came from the same direction."

"Fine." Adam rolls his eyes, turning to the right to put some distance between us.

"Do you really think your brother might notice a detail like that?" I question my pup, wondering if he is not being a little overly careful.

"I don't know, and I don't really care. I can deal with my brother pretending to not know that I'm going out into the forest to fuck you." David points at me while calling out the ridiculous motions we are all going through for some reason. "But I can't *also* deal with him pretending to not think that I'm fucking Adam, too."

Chapter 3

I wake up the next morning after a nightmare-free night of sleep. As we are only a few hours out from Rakatune, we skip breakfast, intent on getting a large lunch once we arrive. Tensions are still a little high after our fae-related run-in two days ago, but the rest of our morning is uneventful, and eventually, the trees give way to grassy plains with Rakatune visible in the distance. The open fields of growing crops are a welcome sight, and we should reach the city proper by late afternoon.

This is where I need to part with Sona, at least temporarily. While I trust her to not attack anyone in the city and would even be able to communicate as much to her, other people will not feel the same. They will only see a wild animal—which she is, no matter how magical. I will make it a point to seek out a leatherworker in town to see about having a collar fashioned. Symbolic as it may be, it will at least put some of the minds of others at ease, assuming Sona will be okay with wearing one.

"We will meet you in the forest north of this village tomorrow," I tell her as I kneel down, scratching behind her ear. "When the sun is high in the sky."

<Forest. North. High sun.> She "repeats" with a bark. *<Friends stay safe.>* With a final yip, she takes off into the forest, likely already thinking about hunting her dinner.

"Why do those houses still look so small?" David asks about the structures that are no longer distant, yet do not seem to be growing any larger.

"Why do you think, David?" Michael asks in response.

"It's a village of *halflings.*"

Michael is correct. Rakatune is a small village, and not just in respect to its population or geographic size. Founded and primarily inhabited by halflings known as the Rakan, the vast majority of its buildings are suited to people of their stature. While I know of several dwarves and gnomes who are happy to make a home here, other, larger species can have trouble finding a place to fit in. I am able to see clear over the roofs of many of the homes and older structures we pass as we enter.

The road that runs through the village is a busy one, so many of the public accommodations are housed in larger, more accessible buildings. Some of them have obviously been altered over the years to increase the size of their walls and ceilings as traffic to the city has increased, a few having features like two differently sized doors or windows at different heights. Agriculture is the city's main and really only export, the bulk of it shipped by cart to nearby trading posts and villages like Pákannon rather than sold in their own marketplace.

Unlike V'rok'sh Tah'lj and Pákannon, Rakatune lacks any sort of perimeter wall. There are plenty of fences to protect the vast swaths of farmland, but I suspect larger walls would only get in the way. Other than seeing the occasional guard patrolling the streets, I cannot speak much on the city's defenses, but the people here seem to enjoy a quiet, peaceful life.

The inn is thankfully a building suited for travelers of our size, though I do have to duck to make it through the doorway. While visitors are not uncommon to Rakatune, we still get a few looks from other patrons due to the number of people we have traveling together. I let Tsula assist Adam in negotiating with the innkeep for our rooms as she is more familiar with the local dialect than myself.

"Alright, we lucked out and they have six rooms, but they all only have one bed," Adam informs us, keys in hand. "So who's getting to sleep solo tonight?"

"I don't mind sharing with someone," Corrine offers first.

"I can share with you," Tsula quickly agrees.

"I'm certainly not going to complain about getting a bed to myself for the night," Piper happily accepts their decision.

"Which means you're with Adam, Firecrotch," Liss tells Riley with a smirk, while Nathaniel stands behind her, too busy looking through his bag to notice the exchange.

"Right back 'atcha, Coppertop," Riley responds with a tip of an invisible hat.

"Alright then, see everyone in the morning," Adam says as he hands out the keys.

Everything divvied up, we all make our way to our rooms, all of us on the same floor. Like most of the village, this is a single-story building, as there are obvious impracticalities to managing a multi-story structure unsuited for your own personal height. David and I's room is small, even by non-orc standards, but the bed looks comfortable regardless. Putting our bags by the wall, we begin to remove our outer layer of armor, eager to get to the dining room for lunch.

The architecture of the inn and the rest of the village reminds me in many ways of home. Here, buildings are constructed by first planting saplings along the boundary of the structure. As the trees are grown (usually with the assistance of magic), they are bent into shape, forming the structure's frame. Cut wood is then patched on over the frame, forming the walls and a round dome-like ceiling.

We do things similarly in V'rok'sh Tah'lj. Most of the lumber used in construction is not typically cut by traditional means but is instead pulled from the ground while still living, and then shaped and preserved with magic, bark and all. Even our furniture is manufactured that way, giving it a very unique look. My stepfather Jarek works in a tree nursery and carpentry shop doing exactly that. The items here seem to be a combination of that style and traditional carved wood.

Once we are as unpacked as we need to be for the night, David and I exit our room for the dining room, where most of the others already are. The room is filled with round tables, none of them large enough to seat all of us, so we split ourselves between three. Lunch is venison stew, a common dish to serve in this area, though there are more vegetables in this batch than I care for.

After we finish eating, we still have a lot of daylight left, so some of the group decides to venture out into the city and take care of some necessary affairs before we leave in the morning. We need to restock some of our supplies, and a city this large should have a weapon and armor shop we can stop by as well.

After asking the innkeeper for its location, I decide to make the weapon shop our first stop. The past week or so being relatively quiet means that virtually none of our equipment requires any repairs, but Tsula is still without a weapon. She has never owned one before, so David, Michael, Piper, and myself have volunteered to assist her in picking one out. With the other three in tow, I lead the way.

The shop is not located far from the inn as it is one of the more frequent stops of those just passing through the city. It is a small building, and I do not just mean the outside—though I do have to duck again under the doorway to enter. The inside is equally small, and the inventory a little lacking. There are only a few different racks of weapons, along with a couple of mannequins wearing armor.

Most of the items for sale also appear to be too small, for me at least. Obviously, the shopkeeper's main clientele are their fellow halflings, so most of the weapons and armor are made for someone of their size and stature. Most non-halflings would not have much of an issue wielding any of these, but at least personally, my hands are too large to grip most of them comfortably. And armor is out of the question entirely.

"Here we go," Michael announces when he spots some staves on one of the racks.

"Oh..." I can tell Tsula is a little overwhelmed already by the selection. "Which one should I pick?"

"That is up to you, dear," Piper answers.

There are about a dozen staves on the rack, divided into two categories. The first are traditional quarterstaffs, straight and the same width throughout, well-balanced at each end. The other half are more ornate, walking sticks with decoratively carved handles, most likely intended to be used by a spellcaster.

"You could really fuck someone up with one of these," David tells us as he picks up one of the martial staves and tests its weight.

"I, uh..." Tsula stares wide-eyed as David begins to twirl and spin the staff in his hand.

"I am not sure Tsula's skill level is quite there yet," I give the girl an out.

"Show off." Michael rolls his eyes at his brother's antics. "You'll most likely want one of these. They're customizable."

Michael reaches for one of the walking staves, this one with a handle that appears to be an owl. At a closer glance, the owl's eyes appear to be recessed, and there are similar notches elsewhere along its "body." Not notches, sockets.

"Aww, that carving is rather cute," Piper coos at the wooden bird. "And there are plenty of slots for all sorts of charms."

"And look!" Michael grasps the top of the owl, showing that it actually screws apart, revealing a hollow compartment. "You can fit a spell focus in there."

"Oh wow," Tsula comments as she takes it in.

"You *sure* you don't want one like this?" David tosses his choice from hand to hand. "I could teach ya."

"I think, uh, these are more my style." Tsula gestures to the caster-staves. "Thank you, though."

"I guess you could still do some decent damage with that owl," David adds absentmindedly.

"Regardless of your choice, we will be able to help teach you how to use it to defend yourself," I clarify.

"Thank you." Tsula nods with a smile.

She ends up selecting one with a turtle for a handle, facets all along the pattern of its shell. As we are headed up to the shopkeeper to pay, the leather armor catches my eye again, and I remember my need for a collar for Sona. I do not see anything like that on display, but it cannot hurt to ask.

"Excuse me," I call for the man's attention after he has finished with Tsula. "Do you take custom orders for leatherworking?"

"I do." The halfling nods. "What are you looking for?"

"A dog collar." I gesture to my neck. "For a fairly large dog."

I hear a snort from behind me that sounds like David. *The last time I bought a collar was for a pup of a different variety.*

"Yeah, I might have something that could work." The halfling pauses, thinking. "Did you have a color in mind?"

"Something dark. Black or brown." I will leave any other specifications up to him.

"Just a minute." The man steps into the back, returning with a long strip of dark brown leather. "How is this?"

He holds out the strip for me to take a closer look at. It is large, more likely to function as a belt than a collar at this size but could easily be cut. I stroke a hand along the top, feeling the soft and supple skin.

"This would be perfect," I tell the man, who looks pleased to have the order.

After giving him a rough estimate of Sona's neck measurement, he asks me to return in half an hour when he should be finished. We negotiate a price of a single gold piece, which is generous, but given the speed in which he will be completing the order, it still feels fair. I leave the man five silver as a deposit, the other half to be paid when I return to pick it up.

The four of us exit the shop, intending to continue our shopping excursion. Our next stop is to the market so we can refill our other supplies, and we see some of the others there doing the same. As I said before, they are largely an agricultural-based people, so I make sure to tell David to select some of the fresh produce they have on display. Though the Rakan are more vegetarian than most others, they also have access to livestock, which allows me to replenish my meat stores, though at a bit of a markup.

By the time we are finished, it is about time for the collar to be ready, so I return to the weapon and armor shop with David while the others return to the inn. The completed item is exactly what I needed and well worth the rest of the payment. Now I have to hope that Sona will not mind wearing it, which I will find out tomorrow.

With nothing left to do, and the evening drawing closer, we walk back to the inn. We spend some time in the common area with the others, going over our travel plans and other things. In addition to the occasional magic lesson, another topic of discussion that comes up from time to time is speculation on David's connection to the myths covering the walls of the Temple of Zeus—where he was killed and resurrected.

There was an inscription around the rim of the sacrificial bowl, which according to the archaeology report, was a fragment of a larger inscription on the wall. *"When the Fates are blind and the gates are closed, only blood spilled in sacrifice can restore the strength of the gods. Oceans will split where the caged abyss bleeds and goats will fight eagle as the wolves' maws grow wide."*

After David was once more breathing, there was such rage radiating off of him. He was different, and I do not just mean mentally or emotionally. He was faster and stronger as he leapt around the room to take his revenge. Even when he was finished, he was not himself, even speaking a different language at one point. So when combined with the line about blood and sacrifice, there is some assumption that it must be about him.

"So why are we not using the 'D' word? Demigod, right?" Liss looks to Corrine, who nods in approval.

"Demigods are the children of gods, and our dad is *definitely* our dad," Michael tells her. "We get told we look like him all the time, especially David."

"If it weren't for the green eyes, Grandpa said I coulda been dad's twin when he was younger," David corroborates.

"But isn't that what the other stories on the wall are about?" Nate points out next.

"*Some* are," Michael concedes. "But not all of them. It also doesn't really make sense. I mean, demigods are all super strong and have all sorts of other powers."

"Hey, I'm plenty strong," David defends himself.

"Yes, you are." I pat his leg in a soothing gesture. "Because the 'burst of strength' that seemed to overtake David only happened *after* he died, in addition to vanishing once the moment had passed, I may have to agree with Michael."

Not that the thought hasn't crossed my mind. I have spent a few late evenings by the fire, wondering just what happened to my pup that night. It is not even that night alone, there have been several times in the past when I have wondered if there isn't more about him than meets the eye. I have seen him climb walls like an acrobat, his body has gained a large amount of mass in a very short time, and just two days ago, he withstood a full blast of fae-powered sleeping dust. I can still remember the frustrated "*what are you?*" our attempted thief spoke, wondering the same thing as the rest of us.

After that conversation, we have dinner, which turns out to be the same thing as lunch. After eating, we retire to our rooms, all of us eager to spend at least one night sleeping in a bed before another few days of tents and bedrolls. Once back in our room, I clean up in the bathroom while David sits on the bed. Bathroom is generous; Rakatune does not have widespread plumbing like V'rok'sh Tah'lj or even a magical shower and toilet like Pákannon.

Things here are much, much simpler. There is a small wash basin on a stand and a shower that is at least similar in shape to those in Pákannon but lacking the ability to make the water hot. All the water is pumped by hand, my arm already sore from using the rusty water pump outside. We also have a chamber pot, but we have been encouraged to instead use one of the outhouses.

"Looks like the day's almost over, Sir," David says in a sing-song voice as I exit the bathroom. "Know what that means?"

"What?" I ask skeptically.

"It means I managed to make it an entire day without earning any spanking demerits." He grins wide.

"The day is not over yet, pup," I challenge, chuckling.

"Oh no, Sir, I am going to be on my *best* behavior the rest of the night." To make his point, he kneels down in front of me. "Is there anything your slave-boy can do to help make your night better?"

I am torn between wanting to invent a reason to spank him and wanting to take him up on his offer and see how far I can push him. I look around our room. The walls are fairly thin, so we will need to be careful about noise, but small as it may be, it certainly beats a tent. No reason not to take advantage while we can.

"Strip, and kneel by the bed," I order, already reaching for my shirt.

We watch each other as we undress, our eyes moving to each newly revealed piece of skin. His shirt unbuttoned, he slides it off of his shoulders, revealing his lightly furry and muscled chest underneath. The golden scar across his sternum stands out, centered and angled slightly to the right. Despite the darkness attached to its creation, I must admit it makes him look sexier.

Our pants come off next. While I lay mine over the back of a chair, David shimmies out of his and kicks them off to the side. For once, I do not correct him, instead stepping forward and pulling him against me. I capture his mouth in a kiss as my hands roam over his body, all the way down his back to cup his ass. Taking advantage of our added privacy for the night, I see that he has changed into a different pair of underwear—a red jockstrap. While I normally enjoy picking that out for him, traveling means needing to be alert and prepared, which sexy underwear does not always allow for. I am also certain his brother's head would explode if he ever saw him in one.

David's own hands scratch down my back with the blunt of his nails before grabbing my own loincloth-clad rear end. Ready for the next phase of the evening, I tear our mouths apart, looking at David with hungry eyes. I put my hand on his chest, growling and pushing him backward onto the bed...only to immediately grab him by the shoulders when I realize his head is going to hit the wall.

"That was close," he jokes nervously, staring up at the wall only inches from his head.

"Very," I say with a sigh, pulling him back up to stand.

My immediate plan ruined, I satisfy myself with more kissing, pressing my body against David's while we stand together. His cock pushes out against the pouch of his underwear, a wet spot on the head pressing into my inner thigh. I can feel my own length doing the same to him, fighting against its fabric confines.

David's hands, at first rubbing along my back and arms, move to the front, dipping between our two bodies. He grasps my cock through my underwear, squeezing it briefly before stroking slowly up and down the shaft. I growl into his mouth, feeling myself pulse in his hand, which makes him squeeze me again.

Daring to take charge, he moves one hand to my hip and pushes me to turn around. I decide to humor him, allowing him to flip us so he is now facing the bed. He presses against my chest, urging me to sit while kneeling at the same time. Hitting the small bed—which is not used to someone of my weight—causes me to bounce a little higher than intended, and the top of my thigh smacks right into David's chin.

"Spirits, I am so sorry. Are you alright?" I look down at David's bent-over form, my hands hovering just above his head which is shaking in...laughter?

"I'm okay." He looks up, rubbing his jaw and looking amused. "Let's try that again."

Taking hold of my thighs, he spreads them apart as he shuffles between them. His hands move to tease my encased cock before he leans down to mouth at it through the fabric. His fingers dip into the top of my underwear, tugging them down and freeing me from their confines. My length twitches involuntarily as he lowers his face to nuzzle against the root of my cock, inhaling my scent.

He slides his mouth up the length of my prick, leaving a trail of wet kisses in its wake. Wrapping his lips around the head, he twirls his tongue slowly around the ridge before lowering himself to take in more of the shaft. I groan low when I feel myself hit the back of his throat—and then push inside as he swallows me down even farther. He almost manages to make it all the way to the base before he's forced back by his gag reflex. Catching his breath and looking at my slick shaft with determination, he nods to himself and tries again.

I fist one hand in his hair as chokes himself once more on my cock, growling when I feel his tongue working against the bottom of my shaft. I keep my grip light, following his head as it bobs up and down. When he finally pulls off with a gasp, his eyes are watery and his lips swollen, but he still looks hungry for more. Standing, he reaches for my bag, retrieving his cleansing charm and the oil we use for lubricant.

Holding the charm to his stomach, he stalks back toward me on the bed, oil in hand. I move up the mattress, watching him climb on to follow. As he straddles my hips, I move backward a little too fast, my head banging against the headboard. Then I overcorrect, moving forward too fast and slamming my forehead into David's. After a hiss of pain from the both of us, we devolve into a fit of giggles.

"We *have* done this before, right?" David groans, laying his head on my shoulder.

"I could have sworn, but I am starting to question that myself," I reply, rubbing my forehead and staring at the ceiling.

"Okay, one more time," David says as he sits up, still straddling me.

Uncorking the bottle of oil, he pours some out into his hand before closing the bottle and tossing it to the side. He reaches behind himself, the slick hand wrapping around my cock. Once he's finished with me, his fingers move from my cock to his hole, where he stretches himself in preparation. Happy to continue following David's lead, he grabs my cock once more, taking aim as he lifts his hips and sinking down when he finds his target.

We both groan happily as my thick length is enveloped by his tight heat. My hands automatically move to grasp his ass, squeezing both cheeks as my hips push upward in an attempt to delve even farther. One hand on my shoulder, David leans over to kiss me while his hole adjusts to the size of its intruder.

David rocks his hips, sliding himself up my cock before sliding back down. Pushing up from my shoulder and sitting up straight, he starts to ride me, slowly lifting and dropping himself on my cock. As he sets a rhythm, I drive my own hips upward, meeting him halfway and helping him to bounce a little higher on the next stroke.

It is a good position for trying to keep the noise down. Other than the bed squeaking, the only other sounds are coming from the two of us. The only thing I would prefer would be to have a mirror behind David—I like being able to watch my cock disappear inside his body.

David begins bouncing faster on my lap, both hands flat on my chest for extra leverage. I watch his face carefully, looking for signs of an impending orgasm. Once he starts to bite his lip, I know it cannot be far. Only a few moments later, with a muffled grunt, he pushes himself *all* the way down, grinding his hips in a circle as his hole pulses when he finally cums dry. With a happy sigh, he slumps over my chest, a satisfied smile on his face.

"Oh? Are we done?" I question my dozing pup.

"Suddenly very sleepy," he lies with his eyes closed.

"And what happened to my eager slave?" I grab his ass in my hands again, squeezing when I ask.

"He's sleepy too," he teases before lifting back up, his hips following the movements of my hands.

He starts to ride me once again, this time with my direction at the helm. I grip his flesh tightly, using my arms to pump his body up and down my cock. David's cock is heavy in its pouch, lightly thudding against my stomach each time he slips back down. David's face screws up in concentration as another orgasm nears, biting into his wrist to muffle his moans when it washes over him.

I savor the feeling of his hole pulsating around me, holding him down against my hips before I start to fuck upward with purpose. The tight heat is pushing me toward my own finish line, squeezing me each time I bottom out. At the speed I'm going, I can feel my testicles slapping up against his skin with each thrust. Then I'm cumming, and they draw up tight as I unleash the first volley into David. I quickly pull him down by the thighs, burying every bit of myself and holding him there as I grit my teeth and struggle to not growl.

His work done, David lowers himself back to my chest, panting heavily. I am catching my own breath, our skins slick with sweat. As he tries to move into a more comfortable position, I attempt to slide down the bed so I can stretch out my legs—only for my feet to hit the board with an audible *thunk*.

"I am starting to miss the tent," I muse as David snorts a laugh against my chest. *Perhaps I should just throw the mattress onto the floor...*

We disentangle our limbs and our crotches, taking a moment to stand and stretch. After we clean off, we are both back on the bed, curled somewhat awkwardly around each other on the small mattress. The room is warm, and I consider opening the window, but I am feeling just comfortable enough to not want to get up again.

"Are you ready to talk about that nightmare you've been avoiding, Sir?" David pokes me in the chest as he asks.

"I have not been avoiding it." I roll my eyes. "But yes, we can talk about it."

"It doesn't freak you out?" he questions my nonchalance.

"It's not that I am undisturbed," I start to explain. "I just already understand the root issue of their cause."

"What's that?" he asks next.

"Guilt," I answer simply.

"Guilt about what?" He pulls back and leans up on an elbow, meeting my eyes.

"You." I stroke a hand down his side. "Your death. Being unable to protect you. Surviving when you did not." *And perhaps a few other reasons.*

"But I *did* survive," he tries to reason.

"You did not make it out unscathed," I point out.

"Neither did you," he counters.

"I did not say it was a rational reason." I shrug one shoulder. "The subconscious mind rarely is."

"Well, I don't blame you for my death," he consoles, attempting to pull us closer.

"I am glad to hear it," I respond honestly. "I suppose I need to stop blaming myself." My own words, as well as a few things spoken earlier give me pause. "David... You know I do not *really* think of you as a slave, right?"

"Even though I technically am?" As he "jokes," he pulls at the chain collar locked around his neck—my collar.

"I mean it, after everything that happened with Redwish, and the ritual, and my own poor decision making, it is important to me that you know that," I try not to plead.

"Of course, Khaz," he reassures me. "I know that's not how you think of me. At least not all the time." He winks.

"Good," I tell him, kissing him on the forehead and trying to use his smile to smother any lingering guilt, at least for now.

With our libidos sated, and the night only getting later, we prepare to turn in for the evening. After turning off the lantern, I spoon David from behind, throwing my arm over his waist. With both our legs curled, we fit comfortably on the center of the bed. Kissing the top of David's head, I drift off to sleep, wondering what tomorrow might hold.

Chapter 4

The next morning I am in the inn's dining room with David enjoying a late breakfast. Once again, the meal does not seem to be all that different from the previous one, but I stow any complaints. I am actually looking forward to cooking again once we are back on the road. Elisabeth and Nathaniel are both sitting with us, the four of us eating our meal in comfortable silence.

"So, you guys try to fuck in those tiny beds last night?" Liss asks us bluntly, causing Nathaniel to choke on his tea and turning David's face red.

"We did," I answer with a laugh, ignoring the way David kicks my foot under the table. "It caused no less than three separate injuries, in fact."

"Uncomfortable as shit, right?" she continues with a grin. "I almost put the mattress on the floor. Made me actually start to miss screwing in a tent."

"I said the same thing!" I have really come to enjoy Liss's frank nature, though both of our men seem to only want to sink lower in their chairs.

We manage to finish our meal without any further embarrassment. We have our rooms for another couple of hours but will likely leave before then. Almost all of our group is here eating; we will just need to gather our belongings. As I look around the room and start to work out a plan for the day, my eyes fall on a table in the corner and my whole body freezes.

"What is it?" David asks, noticing my change in posture as I try to settle as calmly and nonchalantly in my seat as I can.

"You noticed them too, didn't you?" Liss asks me, wearing a wry smile as her eyes briefly move in the direction of the corner table.

"Noticed who?" Nathaniel asks, already gearing up to look around the room.

"Stop," I tell him flatly, leaving no room for argument. "It is very important that neither of you visibly react to the information I am about to share. You *especially* cannot start looking around the room. Do you understand?"

Both men nod imperceptibly, Nathaniel even raising his empty teacup to his mouth to mime drinking.

"It appears we are being followed," I say, Liss confirming with a slight nod.

Sitting at the table in the corner that none of us are currently looking at are two men that look very, very familiar. I first saw them in Pákannon in the dining room of our last inn. They stood out a little more then, their clothing not quite matching the local fashions, but they appear to have corrected that issue. Were it not for the fact that there are only a handful of other people our stature here, I might not have noticed them at all.

"We are?" I can feel David grow tense, and I reach over to squeeze his thigh and calm him.

"Possibly. There are two men sitting at a corner table that I saw in Pákannon," I explain, still speaking low. "Now, we *are* traveling the most direct route from Pákannon to Maname, so it is entirely possible they are merely traveling the same way we are, but the timing is very suspicious."

"I saw them in Pákannon too," Liss adds. "Caught 'em looking over at our table once or twice. They've been doing the same thing here."

"What do we do?" Nathaniel asks, too afraid to look up from the table at all.

"I may have a plan." *Or at least the beginnings of one.* "In a moment, I am going to go talk to Adam and ask him to follow me to our room. After we leave, David will go to Michael, Piper, and Riley, and do the same."

"What about us?" Liss asks about her and Nate.

"You two will remain here and keep an eye on them," I tell her. "Six of us in one room is already risky, but they will definitely notice if all ten of us go missing. I will explain the plan to the rest of you once we are on the road. Other than that, just act natural. Do not alert Tsula or Corrine yet."

"Right. Natural." Nathaniel moves his hands to rest on the table for a moment, before resting them on his thighs, looking distressed. "What do I normally do with my hands?"

"Who do you think they are?" Adam asks after being brought up to speed in my room with the others.

"Could they be working for Redwish?" David's voice grows worried.

"It is possible," I admit as that is what my mind first thought of as well.

"Even if they're not, I don't like that *anyone* is following us." Adam crosses his arms. "You said you had a plan?"

"One that involves taking a slight detour," I start to explain before turning to the assembled mages. "But it is dependent on how skilled Michael and Piper are with illusions."

"Pretty good, depending on what you need," Michael answers.

"I need believable facsimiles of David and Riley." Both casters' eyes go wide. "They do not need to speak or do anything more than walk next to us. Is that possible?"

"Difficult, but possible," Piper confirms. "I cannot promise that someone looking closely enough wouldn't be able to tell."

"That is fine. We just need it to appear that all ten of us are leaving here together." I want us to appear unaware of their presence for at least a little while longer.

The two spellcasters split up—Michael with David and Piper with Riley respectively. After studying their target's faces for a moment, they both begin to cast a spell, stepping back and holding their hands out, palms upward. A second later, two mirror images are standing in place, making both men's eyes go wide in surprise.

"Whoa." David sticks out his hand, passing harmlessly through his duplicate. "This is weird."

"Speak fer yourself." Riley gives his a once-over. "Always knew I was good lookin'."

"How long can you keep them active?" I ask, taking in their appearance. Small things like freckles are not quite the same, but the important details are there.

"With concentration...maybe a couple of hours?" Michael offers.

"That should be enough." I nod my head.

"Why do you need them to make illusions of the two of us?" David points his thumb between himself and Riley.

"Because while Adam and I are gathering the others to leave, you are finally going to climb out the window." I look toward the closed window, the rest of the plan clicking into place.

After everyone finishes retrieving their belongings (and nearly forgets to grab David's and Riley's), we exit the inn as a group of ten, at least as far as anyone watching is concerned. Once we are far enough away, Adam and I do our best to explain the plan to the others, keeping the information light enough so as not to give anything away to our stalkers.

While we were gathering our companions and their belongings, Riley and David climbed out of the room's window and exited the town ahead of us, going west instead of north as originally planned. While out there, the two of them were to make contact with Sona. Between the time she has spent with me and David and Riley's druid magic, they should be able to communicate that I want her to stay with them, rather than seek me out. Given the canine's proclivity for sneaking around, the lack of her presence should hopefully go unnoticed.

David is also skilled in the art of sneaking around, something I (and several other rangers and officers) can speak to from personal experience. I chose Riley to accompany David because, in addition to staying camouflaged, he will be able to signal us with his abilities without alerting anyone else. The forest on either side of us is thick enough to provide cover and should not hinder their movement.

Their goal while in the woods is to watch and wait, first for us to exit the village and then for anyone who might be following us. On the off chance that I am wrong and those men are not in fact after us, then wasting a few hours is the worst thing we have to worry about. We will double back, turn north, and make up the lost time over the next few days. But my gut is rarely wrong about these things.

I have no idea how close the two men are or how they might be tracking or eavesdropping on us, which is why there are two stiff if not unconvincing illusions walking with us. It has been an hour since we left the inn, and I can see the strain on Piper and Michael's faces as they concentrate. Then a crow flies overhead, cawing once as it crosses from right to left. That is Riley, and our signal; the single caw means we *are* being followed, and his direction means they are in the forest on our left.

"Adam," I call out to the man at the front of the group, "can we stop here for a moment? I want to do some hunting before the day gets too hot."

"Sure, we can set up camp for a minute just up there." He points just ahead, following my lead. "I might even join you."

"Excellent. Liss, perhaps you would like to join us as well." *We might be laying this on a little thick.*

"Sure." Her subtle eye roll tells me she shares that sentiment.

We each grab our weapons and turn toward the forest with myself in the lead. Because of my magical bond with Sona, as long as we are not too far apart, we are able to magically sense each other's presence. While she remains with Riley and David, I can use her to pinpoint their location in the forest—which should also lead us to where our stalkers are hiding.

The forest is as silent as we are as we move forward, weapons in hand. My eyes and ears are scanning ahead of us, unsure of who or what we might find first. If it is David and the others, we will need to keep up our charade until we can subdue the men following us. I can feel us drawing closer and closer to Sona, and just when I expect to catch her slinking out of the brush, sounds of a struggle on our right have us turning.

Hanging from the tree branches is one of the two men, his body wrapped in vines of thick moss. He curses as he flails in the air, his movements only making the flora wrap around him tighter. Another fight can be heard on our left, and two bodies burst through the foliage before wrestling on the ground.

"Will you stay down?!" David growls as he tries to hold the man in place.

The man swears at him in Pákagi before shoving him off and jumping to his feet. David does the same, pulling a sword from his back and pointing it toward the man. The man is ready for a fight until he looks around and sees that he is surrounded by Adam, Elisabeth, and myself, with his companion still hanging from a tree. He is distracted when Sona makes herself known, growling at his back, causing the man to yelp in terror. This allows David to move in and knock his feet out from under him with a sweep of his leg, quickly pouncing and pulling his arms behind his back.

"Were there any problems?" I ask as Riley steps out from his own hiding spot.

"Not sure if this one is capable of anything," Riley starts, gesturing to the man on the ground that Liss and Adam are helping David to restrain. "But that one's been usin' magic to spy on us. Heard him tellin' his friend everything you all were saying." Riley points at the man wrapped in vines, his mouth covered and hands restrained to prevent further spellcasting.

"They left town not long after you did and went right into the forest," David explains as he makes his prisoner stand. "They made sure to keep their distance. It didn't look like they were doing anything *but* spying."

"Which means they may have been listening in on our conversations for weeks," I determine, stepping up to the man David and Liss are holding. "Who are you working for?" The man only stares at me, a stubborn look in his eyes.

"Let's get back to others," Adam decides as Riley lowers the ensnared man. "We can see what we can get our new friends to tell us there."

We search both men after removing their weapons, two short swords. Other than a wallet and some camping supplies, the only thing of note we find is a two sets of anti-magic bracers, likely intended for us. After ensuring both men are adequately restrained with their hands behind their backs and the mage still gagged, we push them out of the forest and toward our makeshift camp. They exchange a look with one another but are otherwise stoically silent. Once the others see us approaching, relief is visible on Piper and Michael's faces.

"Oh thank god," Piper exhales, the fake Riley at her side vanishing into nothingness as the fake David does the same near Michael.

"You caught them!" Corrine says with some cheer.

"Why were they following us?" Tsula follows up with concern.

"Not sure," Liss explains as she maneuvers her captive through camp. "They're not talking yet."

"Tie them both over here, please," I request, pointing at two trees.

"They're all yours." Adam stands back with the others after the men are tied in place.

"Who are you working for? Why have you been following us?" I direct my questions more to the ungagged man, for obvious reasons. He rolls his eyes in response, pushing me to repeat myself a third time. "*Who are you working for?*"

"You sure you don't want to try asking my friend?" He gestures with his head to his gagged companion.

Sona's sudden bark has the man flinching back, and I remember how he reacted to her in the forest. I am not above exploiting someone's fears in that way. With a quick whistle, I call her to my side, where she starts to growl. The effect is immediate, the man quaking in his bonds.

"Do *not* make me repeat myself a third time," I warn, the threat of an angry canine hanging in the air.

"The Blackbriar Guild!" the spy reluctantly spits out, and I do my best not to look taken aback.

"What is the Blackbriar Guild?" Adam asks me, watching the man attempt to cower.

"Mercenaries and bounty hunters. Very, *very* well trained. They are known for taking on extremely difficult or long-term contracts," I explain. Even outnumbering them, the fact that we were able to capture two Blackbriar mercenaries is no small feat. I also know that there is more to what the man is telling us. "Who took out the contract with the guild? Was it Naruk Redwish?"

The man only shrugs with a smug look on his face, flinching once again when Sona barks in displeasure at his "answer." "I really don't know! They don't tell us that sort of information—only our instructions to complete the contract."

"Do you really think it could be Redwish?" David asks from my other side.

"What did they have you doing?" My mind reels with the possibilities. "Were you just sent here to spy, or were you waiting for the opportunity to attack us? Who are the bracers for? Are you here to capture David or steal his sword?"

"Calm down. We're not after your little pet or his sword." The man scoffs, rolling his eyes.

"Then what *are* you after?" David steps forward to ask.

The man once more falls silent, and once more Sona does not like this, growling and crouching into an attack stance. "Alright, I'll tell you. Just call off your damn beast!"

A muffled noise of displeasure makes its way out of our other captor at this outburst, glaring at his now eagerly talking friend.

"If *you* want to get your face chewed off, go right ahead," he responds with a glare of his own.

"Sona, down," I instruct, her growl stopping as she sits upright.

"We're after a mage," the mercenary starts. "They stole something valuable from a former employer who wants it back."

"Mage?" We have *six* of those in our group. "Who? What is the name?"

"We weren't given a name." He shakes his head. "Only a description. Wizard, male, medium-length brown hair with unkempt facial hair. Like him." He nods just behind me in Michael's direction.

"Unkempt?" Michael's hand moves up to his mustache.

"You could use a trim," David tells him with a pat on the back.

"Michael is not our only brown-haired wizard." As I speak, all of us collectively turn to face the mercenaries' intended target: Nathaniel. The man has already put some distance between himself and the rest of us and is looking around nervously as he clutches his shoulder bag to his chest. He looks ready to bolt.

"I swear if you make us chase you, I will make sure you regret it," Elisabeth warns through gritted teeth. "What did you *do*?"

"I-I can explain!" Nathaniel stammers, still holding tightly to his bag.

"So *start*!" Liss growls, stomping toward him.

"Wait!" Adam calls out, hand in the air. "Not that Nate doesn't have a lot to explain, but maybe we shouldn't have him do it in front of the bounty hunters that have been stalking us? Especially when *we* don't know what *they* know." *He makes a good point.*

"When was the contract offered to the guild?" I turn on my heel, returning to my interrogation. "And what other information *were* you given?"

"Other than the description, not much." The man shakes his head. "The contract came in maybe three months ago. We were told our target landed at Freeport sometime in late Piscea. We followed a trail up and down the east coast but lost track of them somewhere west of Holbrooke."

"How long have you been following us, exactly?" I take a threatening step toward the bound man. "How did you find us to begin with?"

"The guild has scouts everywhere," he explains, ignoring the unhappy groans of his fellow mercenary. "When your group was spotted heading north along a road to Pákannon, we moved to intercept you. We assumed we had found our target until there were suddenly three *other* mages with you one day. The contract also neglected to mention anything about an over-protective orc with an undead slave or your mutt."

"*Undead?!*" David takes offense to the not-entirely-inaccurate description.

"*Slave?*" Michael notices the much more disconcerting portion of the statement.

"I think that is enough," I declare, deciding we have the information we needed.

Wanting to shut the conversation down before they say anything else I would rather Michael not hear, I gather my own magic and use it to cast a silencing spell on the area, pushing out with my hands and shushing the air. As silence falls all around us, I gesture for those gathered to follow me away from the two mercenaries—including Nathaniel, whose upper arm is being held in a vice-like grip by Elisabeth.

"That should keep them from hearing us or anything else," I explain once we are far enough away. I position myself on the opposite side of Nathaniel, allowing me to keep an eye on both him and the mercenaries. The group closes in around Nate in a tight circle, none of us looking happy, but Liss wearing the angriest expression.

"They've been tracking us for months," Adam says with a groan. "*Why?* What did you steal, Nate?"

"*Start talking,*" Liss grits out, squeezing his arm even harder.

"Oww! I-I will!" The mage struggles in her grip, reaching for his bag with his free arm. "Let me just—"

"He's going for something!" David pulls his sword out at the perceived threat.

"Wait, please!" Nathaniel pleads, hand still in his bag. "It only just hatched." *Hatched?*

Very slowly, Nathaniel's shaking hand lifts out of his bag, cupping something in his palm. Some sort of creature, small in size, a combination of pink and tan, and shaking like a leaf itself. It looks like a bird of some sort at first glance, but then I notice that its lower half is covered in juvenile scales, like a lizard.

"What is it?" Tsula asks what we are all wondering, as we gather in a tight circle.

"Gallucockus Rex..." he starts to explain, hand still shaking. "...a baby cockatrice."

"A *what?!*" Michael jumps back.

"Can't those things—" Adam starts.

"Kill you with a glance," I finish, looking warily at the small creature.

"It can *what?!*" David's eyes go wide.

"Okay, yes, they *can* do that, but it's just a defense mecha-nism," Nathaniel defends, pulling the hatchling to his chest. "They don't have the ability to do that until they're almost two years old, and this little guy can't even open his eyes yet."

"*Yet!*" Michael emphasizes.

"How did you get a baby cockatrice?" Adam demands an explanation.

"Well, it wasn't a baby when I got it..." At Adam's glare, Nate's posture shrinks once more. "I used to work for someone who was very rich. He was a collector of magical things: weapons, artifacts, creatures. I was hired to look after that collection—specifically the creatures."

"Like some kind of magical zookeeper?" Corrine asks, still looking closely at the tiny creature.

"Basically." Nathaniel nods his head. "It was a pretty great job. Demanding, but I liked it, a lot. Enough that I over-looked some of the more questionable ways my employer came into new items to expand the collection with."

"So you had a cushy job working for some rich dickbag looking after his pets," David growls. "What did you do to get *mercenaries* sicced on us?"

"I'm getting to that!" Nathaniel snaps. "One day, my employer came to me with something new for the collec-tion: an egg. A cockatrice egg. I figured it was going to be raised alongside his other creatures, but he thought keeping something like that around would be dangerous. You can train them and use magic to dampen the effects of their powers, but he didn't want to risk it. So instead, he wanted me to hatch it, raise it until it was old enough for its eyes to come into their powers...and then kill it. All he wanted was the eyes." His voice drops to a whisper.

"So you stole the egg and ran," David concludes, his voice softening at the revelation.

"I swear—I didn't think he'd chase me all the way across the ocean," Nathaniel continues. "The plan was to find someone who would be able to take care of it, or at least a place where I could release it into the wild. I thought I'd have months before the egg hatched, but then we got arrested."

"You mean *you* got us arrested," Liss corrects, still gripping his arm tightly.

"Yeah," he agrees with a sigh.

"When you were taken into custody, there was no mention of an egg in your belongings," I point out. "Nor can I imagine that it would actually survive all that time in our custody."

"Cockatrice eggs look just like round stones and are just about as durable," he explains. "I knew it would be alright on its own. I just started to get nervous that it might hatch without me the longer we were in jail."

"*That's* why you were getting so antsy during my last few visits!" David states with realization.

"And why I have caught you paying so much attention to your bag as of late," I add.

"The egg hatched four days ago. It's just... It deserves as much of a chance at life as anything else does." Nathaniel's head hangs as he clutches the tiny thing to his chest. "Not to just be raised and killed for its useful parts."

The anger drains out of me, instantly feeling pity for the small shivering creature in his hand. I think many others feel the same way, anger draining away. Everyone except Elisabeth, whose face remains stony. The grip she holds on his upper arm grows tighter as she eyes Nathaniel suspiciously.

"Who were you working for?" She grits her teeth as she asks.

"...Richard Calvinson," he barely mumbles out.

"Are you fucking kidding me?" She angrily pushes him away into the middle of the circle. "Fucking *Calvinson?!*"

"Who is Richard Calvinson?" I ask, seeing varying degrees of realization on the others' faces.

"A very, very rich man," Adam answers.

"Yeah, like rich enough to be involved in all kinds of fucked up and illegal shit," Liss growls as she steps toward Nathaniel. "Rich enough to make a person *disappear*. Why didn't you tell me?"

"...Because I knew you wouldn't forgive me," he croaks out, defeated.

While I can understand being upset at your lover being involved with underhanded people, Elisabeth's anger still seems misplaced. A glance around reveals the others are feeling just as confused as I am, though David and Adam are wearing the awkward grimaces of someone who knows what is the matter. Liss only has murder in her eyes.

"I say we hand him over to them," she states flatly, crossing her arms. *That was fast.*

"Whoa, maybe we should talk about this first?" Adam feels the same way.

"What's there to talk about?" Liss stubbornly responds.

"I'm not saying what he did was great," Adam starts, "but I'm not sure handing him over to *bounty hunters* is the right thing to do either."

"Bounty hunters only following us because *he* led them to us," Michael points out.

"Right, and if we give them what they want, they leave us alone." Liss crosses her arms. "Problem solved."

"I dunno." David sounds reluctant. "I can't believe I'm saying this, but I think I'm with Adam. I don't think we should hand Nate over."

"Really? *You?*" Liss is incredulous at my pup's empathy. And so am I.

"I mean..." David looks at Nathaniel for a moment. "That little thing he stole is pretty cute, and I'm pretty sure if we hand him over, we have to hand it over, too." *There it is.* I mentally sigh.

"Unbelievable." She rolls her eyes, thinking the same thing for different reasons.

"We still have to do *something*," Corrine tries to get us back on track.

"Right." Adam wipes a hand down his face. "Khazak, what are the chances of...*convincing* them to help us?"

"Ya mean bribin' 'em, right?" Riley clarifies, having remained silent up until now.

"Yes," Adam admits with a sigh. "Could we maybe pay them or something and get them to cancel the contract?"

"It is unlikely." I shake my head. "The Blackbriar Guild is not known for backing out of their deals."

"W-what if we asked them to say he's dead?" Tsula speaks up suddenly with a dark if not reasonable idea.

"That might work," I consider. "It will be expensive, though."

"We can at least try," Adam reasons.

"Not to interrupt," Piper calls for our attention, then points to the bounty hunters struggling in their bonds, "but we may want to try that soon. They certainly aren't looking any happier the longer they we have them tied up."

"Might as well make an offer now," Adam decides. "Keep an eye on him." He points at Nathaniel as the two of us walk back toward the mercenaries.

"No problem," Liss scoffs as the others follow me and Adam.

"How much is the contract paying?" I ask after dismissing the silencing spell.

Both men only glare in response.

"Fine." I sigh. "How much to get you to report back that your target is dead?"

"Ha!" The ungagged man throws his head back to laugh. "More than you can afford. Not to mention all the extra that was promised for bringing him and whatever that thing he stole was in alive."

"There goes that idea," Adam groans.

"Just give up now. You said it yourself—we aren't known for breaking our contracts," he tells me with a sly grin. *Wait, how did he—?* "I can read lips."

"Alright, I've had enough of you." Corrine suddenly steps between the two of us. "*Caecitas!*"

The man suddenly shouts in surprise, his eyes looking around wildly. "Hey! Where did the light go?"

"What did you do?" I ask the woman.

"Made him temporarily blind," she says loud enough for the man to hear her. "And I can make him deaf and mute too if he wants to keep it up." I must admit, I enjoy Corrine's darker side.

"So what are we doing, Adam?" David asks our leader now that we seem to be out of options.

"I don't know, but we need to get moving," the blonde says after running his hand through his hair. "It's not safe to stay on the roads, especially if people are after us."

"Are we...bringing them with us?" Piper asks for clarity.

"I am not sure we have any other option at the moment," I state with a sigh.

"Yeah." Adam nods. "At least until we can think of a plan."

"You won't get away—"

"*Mutus!*" Corrine shouts before he has a chance to finish.

"Thanks, Cory," Adam says with a tired smile. "Let's make sure they're secured and get a move on. I really have a bad feeling about all of this."

"What about him?" Liss shoves Nathaniel forward.

"I guess that depends on him." Adam steps forward, meeting him halfway. "Anything else you're not telling us?"

"I swear, that's everything." The now-timid wizard hangs his head.

"Alright then, let's get going," Adam tells him confidently.

"That's it? You're just going to trust him?" Liss asks angrily.

"No, but if he runs, then he is officially not our problem anymore." Adam looks the man dead in the eyes. "Understand?"

"Yeah." He shakily nods his head. "I-I won't run."

"Good." Adam nods confidently.

"*Great*," Liss grounds out, turning to face away from the group.

Adam and David both look on with regret in their eyes but say nothing. *There is something I am missing here.* After securing our (hopefully temporary) prisoners, we march down the road ahead of us, arms still tied behind their back and Corrine's threats hanging in the air. Multiple eyes are also on Nathaniel, though none more than Elisabeth, who seems determined to monitor his every move. Whatever history she has with this "Calvinson," the man seems to be powerful enough to fracture our group from across the sea.

Chapter 5

With our prisoners in tow, we continue onward to our next destination—which should still be Manamequohi. We rejoin our original path after making a *long* circle around the outskirts of Rakatune, not wanting to explain to the townspeople why we now have two bound men with us. The two of them are in front with Adam and Elisabeth, who are keeping them on a literal short leash. Nathaniel is up there as well, unbound but still being closely watched.

An awkward silence has settled over the group, both at Nathaniel's revelation and the fact that we are holding two men against their will. Granted, they were *spying* on us and likely about to attack us, but we may have a hard time convincing anyone else to take our side. The man chasing after Nathaniel for his theft lacks any jurisdiction across the ocean, but not many people like to cross the Blackbriar Guild.

This man, Richard Calvinson, sounds like a powerful and well-connected individual—just like Councilman Murbank. I know from personal experience how dangerous someone like that can be. I have never seen Liss react so strongly to something before. I have seen her annoyed, but never that angry. Whatever this man did to her must have been terrible for her to have turned on Nathaniel like that.

So bad that I spend the next hour wondering what it might be until my curiosity finally gets the better of me.

"David," I ask as he walks on my left, keeping my voice low. "Can you tell me more about this Calvinson character? Or at least his connection to Elisabeth?"

"Uh..." He looks nervously ahead at the back of Elisabeth's head, biting his lip. "Alright, I can't really go into a lot of detail, but it has to do with her family."

"Are they related?" That might explain it.

"No," he whispers with a shake of his head. "Some of her family used to work for him. Some of them still might, I think."

"You know, if you're going to talk about me, you might as well just ask me yourself," Liss calls out from the front of the group, and I mentally curse myself.

"I am sorry, Liss," I apologize after catching up to her in our procession. "I was not trying to speak about you behind your back."

"It's fine," she responds with a sigh. "I probably owe most of you any explanation after all that anyway."

"Only if you are comfortable," I offer, knowing full well she will do it anyway.

"Like David said, I've got family who works for him," she starts, speaking loud enough for the rest of the group to hear her. "Three of my older brothers: Brian, George, and Thomas."

"What do they do for him, exactly?" I am very curious what a man like Calvinson has people doing.

"Different things." She shrugs. "Brian is the oldest— eight years older than me—and he's kind of a meathead. He calls himself an 'enforcer' but he's just the guy's muscle. Acting like a bodyguard, intimidating people who owe his boss money, *hurting* people who won't pay up or fight back. That sort of thing." She sounds bitter as she describes him.

"George is the second oldest, and not even a full year younger than Brian," she continues. "He's a smuggler. He moves all kinds of illegal shit for Calvinson all over Lutheria and beyond. Drugs, weapons, and even supposedly *people*." She shakes her head in disgust. "They both got involved when they were around seventeen years old. Never really told the family what they were doing, just that Mr. Calvinson had hired them to help around his estate. That went on for years, and they always seemed to be doing great. Or maybe I was just too young to realize what they were actually up to."

"Thomas—Tommy is what I called him—is fifth in line, and only two years older than me." She holds up two fingers. "He had just finished school and was looking for work, so he asked if they'd be able to help him get a job with Calvinson too. He wasn't strong or athletic like them, but they told him that wouldn't matter. That's when I started to learn what was really going on."

"Because Tommy told you?" Piper, who I did not realize has been listening intently right behind us, asks.

"Not exactly. Tommy and I were close, and I could tell something was wrong, but he wouldn't tell me what it was. I kinda had to...force it out of him." I can easily picture a teenage Liss strong-arming her slightly older brother. "He still wouldn't give me all of the details, not about everything, but he told me about what Calvinson was really like, and what Brian and George were really doing. Whatever the guy had *him* working on, all I knew was that it involved a lot of money. Like a *lot*. Enough to make Tommy nervous, either about where it was coming from or where it was going."

"What did he do?" Tsula asks next, also listening just behind us.

"At first, nothing. But eventually it became too much for him." Her voice starts to get more somber. "He wanted to quit. Said he was going to talk to Brian and George first and see if they could help him with Calvinson the next day."

"What happened?" Piper chimes in this time.

"I don't know." She shakes her head. "He never came home. Brian and George did, though. Told us that he chickened out on quitting and ran away instead. Said they saw him get on a carriage headed out of town. Thank god no one believed them. It started a huge fight. I thought my dad was going to kill them when they refused to tell him where Tommy was."

"But what happened ta Tommy?" It is Riley's turn now.

"We went to the constable, but as far as the city is concerned, he's still missing." She is back to sounding bitter. "That was almost two years ago. My parents and siblings and I turned over every stone we could looking for him since. Missing persons posters, private investigators, hell, it was part of why I joined the knight academy. Still, nothing."

"Maybe there's a chance he's still—"

"He's gone," Liss cuts off Corrine with finality. "My other brothers haven't shown their faces around the house since, and good riddance. Fuck them and anyone who would work for someone like Richard Calvinson." She spits out the last part of her sentence in Nathaniel's direction, making him flinch.

The rest of our travel for the day does not go smoothly, thanks in no part to the two bounty hunters who have no interest in helping us get to our next destination. Given the amount of time we have already lost thanks to our detour, we elect to skip stopping for lunch, eating as we walk. Still, we make very little progress and end up stopping for the night not nearly as far along as we should have been.

The temporary solution for holding our temporary prisoners involves tying the both of them to the trunk of a tree. Seeing no reason not to, I lock the anti-magic bracers on their wrists, ensuring their magical prowess remains neutered. When the discussion turns to dinner and feeding them, there are a few among us who think we should let them go hungry for the night, though Adam and I both feel that would be unnecessarily cruel. No need to get more on the guild's bad side than we already are.

Both men have rations in their packs, some sort of hardtack and jerky, but as they are both restrained, one of us will have to feed it to them. Nathaniel volunteers, likely to work his way back into our good graces, but Elisabeth immediately accuses him of trying to work *with* them to escape and says she will do it as well to keep an eye on him. I am not sure I understand her logic, but it gets the job done.

While the two of them are being fed, I work to prepare dinner for the rest of us, which is just the remaining still-warm turkey stew I prepared before entering Rakatune. As the bowls are passed out, everyone is too uncomfortable with the presence of these strangers to really talk. Eventually, it becomes too much, and in addition to replacing their gags, we cover their eyes with makeshift blindfolds and fill their ears with wax earplugs Piper had purchased in Pákannon. Just to be safe, I ask Sona to keep watch, the black-furred wolf finding a spot of grass to lay in as she monitors her new chargers.

With our privacy somewhat regained, people begin to relax and speak more freely. The discussion still veers clear of any of our more pressing matters—like our prisoners and what we are going to do with them. Instead, we talk about lighter subjects, like food and the small and rather adorable creature Nathaniel is caring for.

"What do they eat?" Tsula asks, the two of us sitting with the man and his pet.

"Yes, I am not exactly clear on whether its diet is more like a reptile's or a bird's," I add. The two are not that dissimilar, but I could see it going either way.

"Kind of both?" he confirms, looking down at the creature running around the small "arena" he has created with his crossed legs. "He's still too young to need to worry too much. He'll be fine for now with some grass and bugs or worms for protein."

"He? Is it a boy?" Tsula looks down at the small hatchling. "Does he have a name?"

"Oh, no, sorry. It's still too soon to be able to sex them." He reaches down, petting a single finger over its head. "I hadn't thought of a name yet. Wasn't originally planning on giving it one... I didn't want to get too attached."

It appears like it may be too late for that, though it is hard to believe something so small will grow into something so deadly.

"Well, as adorable as that thing is, it's getting late," Adam announces as he stands. "I'm about ready to head to bed. Nate, I think you're bunking with me tonight."

"Right," he confirms with a sad nod. While I am sure the change in sleep arrangements is largely due to his split with Elisabeth, I cannot also help but think Adam also wants to keep a close eye on the flighty mage.

After the watch assignments are divided up (two at a time, to keep an extra set of eyes on the mercenaries), each of us that isn't on duty makes for our own tent. With a final scratch behind the ear, I tell Sona goodnight, knowing she will keep her own watch on our prisoners while sleeping outside. Then David and I crawl into our tent and lay down for a few hours of sleep before we are up for our shifts.

It is a few hours later when my alarm stone goes off softly in our tent, signaling David's turn at watch. I have another hour before it is my turn and toss and turn for a bit. After twenty or so minutes of being unable to so much as doze, I mutter a "*fuck it*" to myself and decide to get up and start my shift early, joining the voices I can hear murmuring outside.

"I'm surprised to hear *you* of all people defending him," I overhear Elisabeth by the fire.

"I'm not defending the guy," David defends himself. "I'm just saying, I'm surprised to see the switch flip so fast. You've been together a while now."

She scoffs. "It's not like we were serious."

"I know I am new to the group, but it seemed fairly serious to me." I announce my presence as I approach.

"Hey," David greets me. "Can't sleep?"

"Not at the moment." I shake my head as I take a seat. "How long had the two of you been together, if I may ask?"

"Barely four months." She tries to sound nonchalant.

"It was closer to five," David corrects.

"Okay, but for two of them we were in jail and separated from each other," she points out in return.

"Well...it's not like either of you were seeing anyone else," David reasons.

The scoff and slight eye roll we get in response tells me David may not be right about that.

"Wait, *were* you seeing someone else then?" David asks, confused, and I'm not even sure if he's pieced together that the prisoners were all segregated by gender, meaning if she did, it wasn't with a man.

"Don't worry about it," is all she says. "None of that matters anyway. He lied to me about something he knew I would never be able to forgive him for."

"Isn't that kind of why he hid it from you?" She looks at David like he just stole her last piece of bacon. "I'm not saying the dude doesn't suck for what he did, but I get why he didn't say anything. It's not like he could undo any of it, and obviously telling you would have just pissed you off. Even if he wasn't trying to get in your pants, I could see him keeping it to himself just to keep things cool with the group."

"Yes, but as you said, that does not excuse what he has done, least of all dragging the rest of us into his mess." I think of the small hatchling in his possession. "Even if his intentions were good, he has put the all of us in danger."

"Yeah, but you have to admit that baby bird-lizard is pretty cute," David tells me.

"So you *are* defending him?" Liss rolls her eyes.

"No," David says with a frustrated chuckle. "Look, I never really got what you saw in the guy to begin with, but you did see *something*, right?"

Elisabeth sighs and contemplates her next response. "Do you know why I left the academy with you and Adam?"

"I mean, I figured it was for similar reasons." David shrugs. "That you were tired of dealing with all the dumb bullshit."

"Yeah, but the 'dumb bullshit' I was dealing with was a lot different than yours," she starts to explain.

"What do you mean?" He looks puzzled.

"Well for starters, do you know how many of my instructors used to hit on me?" She counts on her fingers. "Mr. Thomason, Mr. Baker, Captain Burkhart..."

"They *what*?" David is taken aback. "But they were your *teachers*. Most of them are like twice our age!"

"No shit," Liss deadpans.

"That hardly precludes someone from being a sexual harasser." The power dynamics alone would make even the smallest flirtation suspect.

"What... What did they do?" David hesitates to ask.

"It was mostly the things they'd say. Making comments about my appearance, calling me things like sweetheart, asking if I was single." She sighs as she relives the memories.

"Captain Burkhart actually grabbed my ass once. I almost punched him in the face, but I didn't want to risk a night in the dungeons."

"I might have taken that risk, were it me." *The man sounds like absolute trash.*

"So what *did* you do?" David bites his lip. "Did you tell anyone?"

"Other than warning a few of the other female cadets, nothing. Who was I going to tell?" She frowns, staring at the fire. "That was another problem. Other than a few captains and like *one* sergeant, there are exactly *zero* women in positions of power at the academy or in the Order of Lutherian Knights at all."

"That is unsurprising to hear," I say with a sigh. "I am sorry you had to deal with that."

"You're both acting like this is *normal*." David seems flabbergasted by our attitudes.

"Because it kind of is?" Liss gives him a shrug.

"Even as progressive as we are in V'rok'sh Tah'lj, I witnessed sexism firsthand on numerous occasions." Especially in the fields of law enforcement and the military. "When I became Ranger Captain, I had my hands full just trying to stamp it out in my own department."

"Thanks to the other girls, I knew I wasn't the only one this was happening to. I joined the academy because I wanted to make something of myself, and when I realized I was never going to go anywhere as a knight, I wanted out." She nods her head. "When Adam talked to me about leaving, I couldn't agree fast enough."

"That's still bullshit," David grumbles. "But...what does this have to do with Nate?"

"So, when we first met Nate, he hit on me almost immediately." She laughs a little at the memory. "Like, literally in the same tavern he joined the group in. I told him no, that I wasn't interested, and do you know what he did?"

"What?" We are both on the edge of our seats

"Left me alone," she states simply. "He didn't make me feel bad, didn't keep hitting on me, didn't try to change my mind. I mean, I caught him staring a couple of times, but he treated me just like anyone else on the team."

"Wow, Liss, that's—"

"Pretty pathetic, right?" She cuts him off, shaking her head. "I should have higher standards than 'listens to me when I say no.'"

"I was gonna say it sounded kinda nice," David offers with a small smile. "I *do* know that guys can be real creeps when it comes to asking women out. I've had to step in a few times when a dude in a tavern wouldn't back off some poor girl."

"Yeah." She relaxes when she realizes neither of us plan to chastise her. "There was just something about it that made me like the guy, and as time went on and he didn't change, it grew. Two weeks into the boat ride, I went to his room, knocked on his door, and told him I was interested."

"I remember talking about that with Adam the next day," David comments.

"Yeah. It was pretty great at first." Liss nods to herself. "We had weeks to get to know each other on the boat. I told him about the academy and why we left, about how screwed up my family is, and all about Richard Fucking Calvinson. And he sat there and acted like he didn't know a goddamn thing." Her voice turns bitter by the end of her statement.

Neither of us knows what to say, her anger at the man justified.

"Alright, pretty sure my shift is up." She stands after a moment of silence. "I'm headed to bed. See you in the morning."

"Goodnight." I offer a small wave

"G'night, Liss." David does the same.

As she enters her tent alone, I feel David reach for my hand and squeeze.

"There's not any deep, dark secrets you've been keeping from me, right?" David half-jokes in a low voice.

"Not that I am aware." I smirk at the silly question. "What about you?"

"Nope." He shakes his head. "You know all the deepest and darkest."

"I hope we keep it that way." I lean over to steal a kiss.

Our watch shift together is entirely uneventful. We would normally be a little more relaxed, maybe even find some way to pass the time, but the pair of mercenaries tied to a tree right next to camp make that difficult. Even if they are blind and deaf at the moment, that they spent so long following and observing us is an uncomfortable thought. As the minutes pass, however, that uncomfortable thought seems to recede further and further into our minds until eventually David is straddling my lap as we sit on the forest floor kissing. At least until we hear the sound of a tent flap and freeze, turning to see Adam emerging.

"Sorry, didn't mean to interrupt." He takes in our slightly surprised forms.

"Phew." David slumps over in my lap. "I am really glad it's just you."

"If you don't wanna get caught making out, maybe don't do it right in front of everyone's tents?" Adam looks at us with a raised eyebrow.

David flips his middle finger toward Adam, grumbling to himself as he climbs off my lap.

"So I take it that it's been quiet?" He nods at the bounty hunters.

"Nothing to report," I tell the man, standing and brushing off my pants.

"Good." He sighs as he takes a seat on a log. "I'm not sure I can take any more stress today."

"It has felt like a particularly long day," I commiserate.

"We've got one person on the team feeling completely betrayed by another, who has endangered *all* of us because of his secrets." He gestures to the two bound men. "And I still have no idea what to do about *that* mess."

"I have been trying to think up solutions myself." *Not that I am having much luck.* "With the influence the Blackbriar Guild wields, we are going to have a hard time convincing any potential law enforcement to take them off our hands. Our best option might be to find someone traveling south and then pay them to take the men as cargo, only releasing them from their bonds at the end of the journey."

"Wow, that's cold," David comments in surprise.

"It is a temporary solution at best," I downplay the idea. "It does nothing about the contract they have for Nathaniel, and our actions are likely to only gain their further ire— more than we already have for essentially holding two of their number hostage."

"At least we're feeding them?" David scratches the back of his head nervously, looking at the sleeping men.

"Khazak's right. All this does is buy us more time." Adam groans, running a hand through his hair. "Any ideas for a more permanent solution? Other than handing over Nate."

"Anyone know how to fake someone's death?" David asks, only half-joking.

"If we can make it to Manamequohi, Nathaniel might be able to request sanctuary." I am trying to remember exactly how the rules of the location functioned. "They have very strict non-violence laws and do not permit the guild to operate within their borders. That won't necessarily stop them from trying or from retaliating against the rest of us in revenge."

"At least it's something," Adam responds with a sigh. "Now we just have to find someone to bribe to take them off our hands. And then probably find some new work because that is going to completely drain our funds."

"I can cover the bribe," David offers, holding up a hand. "I still have a lot of money left from working with Khazak for two months."

"Thanks. We'll try to figure out some way to get Nate to pay you back." Adam sighs again. "Maybe I should have listened to you and turned him down when he first asked to join. How did I become the group leader anyway?"

"It was your idea to leave?" David shrugs.

"I know I have only been with you a few weeks, but you have been doing a good job from my standpoint." *Even if it took some getting used to at first.*

"Thanks, but it doesn't always feel like it." I can still see the stress lines on the young man's face.

"Hey, you've kept us together after a month-long boat ride, two months in jail, *and* one of us dying and coming back. You're doing awesome, man."

"I don't think I can take credit for the resurrection, but thanks." Adam throws an arm around his friend's shoulder.

"Alright, unless there's anything else, my watch shift ended when Adam got up, so I'm going back to bed." He stands and points at our tent. "G'night."

"Night, David." Adam gives a short hug.

"See you in the tent," he says before bending down to kiss me on the lips.

"See you in a bit," I tell him as he enters, leaving Adam and me alone.

"So, you were a leader for a long time, right?" Adam asks once we are alone.

"I was Captain for five years before leaving," I inform him.

"Ever deal with anything like this?" he asks next.

"Are you referring to the two people fighting or the mercenaries chasing us?" I try to lighten the mood.

"I mean like Liss and Nathaniel," he clarifies with a small laugh.

"Problems between personnel were common at the ranger station," I admit with a nod. "Sometimes it might be due to a romantic entanglement, sometimes people just did not like each other, but having to change someone's shift times, or even move them to the opposite station, was not an uncommon solution. Though neither is really an option here."

"Right, we're stuck together." Adam sighs.

"All you can do is whatever you think is best for the group." I squeeze his shoulder. "I meant it when I said I think you are doing a great job, but I am always here if you need advice or to talk."

"Thanks, Khazak," he tells me with a smile.

We sit there in a comfortable silence for another ten or fifteen minutes when I hear someone finally starting to stir in the tents. When I look to my right, I see a mop of red hair sticking out of a tent flap as Riley exits. Though he is here to relieve me, he still looks half asleep, so I give him a few minutes before standing and saying my goodbyes.

"Goodnight gentlemen," I give them both my leave. "May your night continue to be quiet and uneventful."

Both men wish me a goodnight as I enter the tent I share with David. Already falling asleep, I quickly strip out of my pants and shirt, crawling into the bedroll behind him. Tired from the long day, I sink into a peaceful slumber, my body curled around David's.

Then I hear a loud crash outside.

Chapter 6

I wake up quickly after the crash, already assuming the worst. I can hear Sona growling before she gives a bark of warning, sensing her anger from here. Then there's another crash, and what sounds like yelling and struggling, and then finally a scream.

"David, wake up." I shake him by the shoulder.

"Huh?" He sits up, looking around blearily.

"Get your clothes on. We are under—"

Something strikes the top of our tent, heavy enough to smash through the tent poles and bring the entire thing crashing down on us. David and I struggle against the leather and wood, fumbling in the dark to find the exit. I manage to get my hands on one of our swords and use the blade to tear a hole in the leather, allowing us to crawl out of the collapsed tent.

The camp is in chaos, with multiple fights taking place around the dying campfire. Before I can rush to anyone's assistance, something slams into my back and sends me tumbling forward onto my face. Flipping myself over, my attacker stands over me, a large human wielding an equally large club that he no doubt just used to destroy my tent.

"Stay down." He holds the weapon in both hands as a threat.

"Get the hell away from him!" David surprises the man by leaping onto his back and wrapping an arm around his throat.

The man drops the club as he struggles with David, grabbing at the arm around his neck and reaching behind him in an attempt to pry off his assailant. I kick one of my legs hard against his ankle, tripping and sending him to the floor as David releases him and rolls out of the way. Ignoring the pain in my back, I stand and reach for the man's weapon while handing my sword to David. Lifting the club with both hands, I bring it down on the man's leg with a sickening crunch. He screams as he is hobbled, at least until he can be attended to by a healer.

Adam and Elisabeth are the only two of our companions still fighting. The rest are on the ground struggling in metal cuffs—more anti-magic bracers. I also see that our two prisoners are no longer bound to the tree, deducing that our new attackers must be other members of the Blackbriar Guild. That must have been why they had been following us for so long: they were waiting for backup. I try to count, but it's difficult with all the action. *Six, maybe seven?* Off to the side, I can see another mercenary brandishing his sword at Sona.

"Run!" I shout, doubting that they have any intention of taking her alive like the rest of us.

With an annoyed growl and an angry bark, she reluctantly takes off into the woods. I know she wants to help, but she cannot do that if she is dead. The human who was about to attack her looks like he wants to give chase until one of the other mercenaries puts her hand on his arm.

"Let it go." She looks off in the direction Sona ran. "We got what we came for." She holds up her hand, and I can just make out the baby cockatrice sitting in her palm. Then she takes notice of us.

"Watch out for those two, Kez," one of the two men we had tied up warns, still picking wax out of his ear. "They're trouble."

"Oh really?" She holds out her hand for someone else to take the creature as she approaches us. "This doesn't have to be difficult. Are you sure you don't want to come along peacefully?"

"Why don't you ask your friend with the broken leg?" David nods behind us at the large man still groaning in pain.

"Have it your way." Her hand moves to grab the axe strapped to her back.

David and I are wearing little more than our underwear, each brandishing a weapon that is not our own. *I knew sleeping near-naked was a mistake.* She stalks closer, and I dig my bare feet into the ground, ready for a fight—when suddenly, David and I are both tackled from behind by three others—one on him and two on me.

"Dammit, let me go!" David shouts on my left as we are both wrestled to the ground.

"That was too easy," the woman, Kez, says with a laugh.

"Get this asshole off me, and I'll show you fuckin' easy," David growls.

"Threats don't really hold a lot of weight when the person throwing them around is in his underwear." She leans over us with a smirk.

"Says the cowards who had to attack while were sleeping," I spit out, still trying to buck the weight off my back.

"You know, we don't have to take *all* of you alive. Keep it up, and I can always hurt one of your friends. Maybe one of the girls who looks about ready to piss themselves in terror?" She throws her thumb back in their direction, the fight draining out of me at the threat. "I owe you a little payback for what you did to my guildmates."

"They were going to attack us first!" David throws back at her. I hear a distinctive *click* sound as a pair of irons are snapped onto his wrists.

"Uh, Kez?" a female voice belonging to someone on my back says hesitantly. "None of the cuffs we brought are big enough to fit this guy."

"So use rope," Kez answers with an eye roll. "Get these two with the others. Pim, take a look at Rax's leg and get him fixed up. Boz, Tak, and Dot, go get the carts. And somebody relight that fire. I want to look through their stuff before we load it all up."

"You already have your target. What exactly are you planning on doing with the rest of us?" I ask while rope is retrieved and wrapped around both my wrists.

"We'll probably let most of you go, after bringing you back to guild headquarters and confiscating your belongings as restitution for all the trouble," she states as a matter of fact. "But *you* two..." She turns to one of the men originally stalking us. "This *is* them, right?"

"Yeah, that's the orc and his slave-boy." The man nods his head. "The one who they say died and came back to life." *How much do they know? How long were they following us, exactly?*

"You know, you hear people talking about an orc traveling the countryside with his recently-resurrected slave, and you wonder if you might be losing it." She looks between the two of us. "But after these two started saying the same thing in their reports, I just had to see for myself."

"You still did not answer the question." I narrow my eyes.

"Well, I figure there must be *someone* willing to pay a good price for the two of you, at the very least for information." She shrugs. "And if not, then I'm sure we'll be able to find some other use for you."

"Fuck you," David grits out.

"Aww, come on. You of all the people here should already be used to the idea of being owned by someone else." She mockingly reaches out to pat him on the head, which he shakes off. She turns once more to one of the two men we captured. "I can't believe you actually got caught by these people."

"I'm telling you, they're trickier than they look," the first man complains again.

After the fire is relit, David and I are moved to sit with the others. Everyone is in various stages of undress, still in sleeping clothes, or at least underwear. Most are also wearing a look of stress, fear, or both.

"What happened?" I ask, unsure of who was on watch when the attack took place.

"They got the drop on us," Riley admits with a sigh. "Piper and I were on duty. We didn't even hear them 'til they were shoving us to the ground. Sorry, everybody."

"Do not beat yourself up too badly," I reply, looking around at the mercenaries and our destroyed camp. "We never stood a chance."

Counting the three Kez sent off, I count eight bounty hunters total. Half of them are human, along with two dwarves, an elf, and a halfling. Even outnumbering them, our group is not even close to being as well trained, on top of them having the element of surprise.

Kez, one of the humans, seems to be the leader, at least of this mission. From the way she speaks, I could also see her holding some position of importance in the guild, but I have no knowledge of their inner workings. She is a tall, muscular woman, with short black hair, brown eyes, and a naturally tan complexion.

To my left, *three* horse-drawn carriages come down the road before being brought to a stop next to our camp. Each is pulled by two horses, the carriages made of wood and painted a solid black. The only window is on one of the back doors, small and barred, no doubt so that the bounty hunters can avoid scrutiny over the "goods" they are transporting. The three drivers dismount, opening the doors on the rear of the carts before rejoining the others.

We watch as the mercenaries pick through our destroyed tents, pulling out our weapons, bags, and any other belongings they can find. Almost everything gets thrown into the back of one of the carts, except for things like clothing, bedrolls, and the tents themselves. Kez allows the others to take care of this "grunt work," content to sit by the fire and coo at the now doubly stolen hatchling.

"You know, I really can't blame you for stealing this thing." She strokes a finger down its back. "It's adorable."

"You can't give it to Calvinson," Nathaniel pleads. "He's just going to raise it until he can kill—"

"I'm not really in the business of telling clients what to do with their possessions," she cuts him off, then turns to the other mercenaries. "Are you almost done?"

"Yeah, I think we got everything," a female dwarf—Pim, I think—responds.

"Get this lot loaded onto the other two carts. I want to be halfway to the guildhall by sunrise." She walks over to Nathaniel, grabbing the front of his robe and forcing him to stand. "Except you. You get to sit with me." She grins evilly.

The rest of us are split into two groups before being shoved into the back of one of the other two carts. I am placed with David, Michael, Tsula, and Riley, each of us with our hands still tied behind our backs. Two of the Briars sit at the reins of our cart, one of the humans we originally caught following us and a dwarf, visible through the open front door. A quick check of the rear door shows that they are locked, the window covered by a wooden slat that is also locked into place. Outside, I can sense Sona not far from us in the forest, moving when we do, no doubt tracking us.

I should have known that once word of our "adventure" had reached Pákannon, it was only a matter of time before the rumors spread elsewhere. I take a seat on the floor with the others and sigh. Things are silent at first, and I am reluctant to break that silence given that anything we say will just be overheard. There is also a small amount of awkwardness, given that me and David are still only wearing our underwear. *At least David did not sleep in a jock.* There is also the matter of everything that was just said regarding our "unique" relationship.

"So..." Michael is the first to say anything, speaking low. "What was with all that 'slave' stuff everyone kept talking about? That's twice now."

"I don't know, man." David shakes his head. "Just some weird stuff they're saying. Ignore it. It's nothing."

Michael stares blankly at the obvious lie.

"Look, is right now *really* the best time to talk about this?" David glares at his brother.

"Why, are you all busy or something?" *Who in spirits—!?* We all turn to this new voice and are equally surprised to see the face of our thief from three days ago staring back at us.

"*You!*" David grits out angrily.

"*Ssshhh!*" I hiss, looking toward the front of the cart, surprised when neither of the men in front so much as glance behind them.

"Oh don't worry. They can't hear us right now." The fae looks over his shoulder at the same men. "We need to work fast, though. Turn around."

"Why are you helping us?" I narrow my eyes. *What is he playing at?*

"I like you more than I like them." He crouches down at my side, pulling a knife with a stone blade from his pocket.

"Plus, I need your help, and you can't do that if you're stuck in some cell somewhere. Now turn around."

I cock an eyebrow, but nonetheless allow him to cut through my bonds.

"What about the rest of us?" Michael asks, turning and wiggling the metal anti-magic bracers around his wrists.

"Can't help you there. Iron." *One of his kind's few universal weaknesses.* "But lucky for you, the guy with the keys happens to be driving."

He points toward the front, where through the door I can spot a ring of keys sticking partially out of the pocket of the man holding the reins. They are also made of iron, which explains why he needs my help. However, I am not a skilled pickpocket—unlike him, I am sure. *Not that we have many options at the moment.*

"How exactly do you want to do this?" I ask, still rubbing my sore wrists.

"I'm going to put them both to sleep, and you're going to pull them back here while I take the reins," he explains his plan. "Your cart is the one in the middle—so you need to be quick because if the lady driving the cart behind you notices anything weird, we're gonna be in trouble. She *reeks* of anti-magic wards."

"But not anti-fairy wards?" David counters.

"Not many people think of those." He sticks out his tongue. "Now get ready. Oh, and uh... You might wanna cover your noses and mouths and maybe...don't breathe for a little bit." He reaches into his pocket again, his hand filled with "dust."

"I am ready." I move into a crouching position.

"Good." He nods, before tiptoeing toward his targets. "*Sleepytime,*" he whispers, leaning forward and blowing the dust between the heads of the two men.

There are two brief sounds of confusion, before both men slump over—and only one of them toward the middle of the cart. I rush forward, grabbing the other by the shoulder before his face has a chance to meet the road. I breathe a sigh of relief, pulling both men back as our new "friend" takes a hold of the horses.

"What now?" I question as I fish the ring of keys from the pocket of an unconscious man and begin the process of unlocking everyone's restraints, as well as the lock on the back door.

"One of you is a druid, right?" he whisper-asks over his shoulder.

"That'd be me," Riley answers, awaiting his turn.

"Great. The cart in front of us is holding four of your other friends." He leans the side and points forward. "You and me are gonna move up there so we can unlock them next."

"Th-then what?" Tsula asks, doing her best to mask her fear.

"Then I guess we try the same thing on the last one?" He shrugs. "Might be tough though. That lady in charge is driving, and she sees everything. I swear I thought she almost saw *me* earlier tonight, and I was invisible!"

"How long have you been following us?!" David demands.

"I dunno, like five or six days? I haven't been with you the *whole* time." He waves off the concern. "You two are *way* too noisy when you have sex in the forest."

I sigh while David groans at the unnecessary revelation.

After everyone is uncuffed, we attach those same cuffs to the two men who were driving, in case they wake up. David insists on interlocking their arms to make it as difficult for them as possible, and I find it hard to disagree. We lay them both on their sides at the back of the cart, before I give keys over to Riley, who morphs into a small, red fox, a smattering of white freckle-like spots along its tail and belly. He takes the ring of keys in his mouth and pads toward the front of the cart.

"Good choice," the fairy tells the fox before turning into one himself.

The reins drop to the wooden seat, and I quickly grab them before they have a chance to slide off. I crouch awkwardly in the seat, paranoid that my height might be visible over the top of the carriage. Riley joins the jogah-turned-fox on the seat next to me, following him as he hops forward onto the backs of one of the horses before leaping off onto the road ahead and quickly scampering under the cart ahead of us.

A second later, David slides into the seat beside me, clearly wanting to avoid having to talk or even look at his brother at the moment. That is a problem I have not even begun to think about dealing with. We are both still shirtless, and the cool night air is causing our nipples to peak and harden. However, all either of us can do is stare at the cart of ahead for a sign that Riley and the fairy-boy are finished.

"It's fucking cold." David crosses his arms over his chest.

"You could always take the clothes off of the unconscious human." The dwarf is unlikely to be wearing anything that will fit either of us.

I can see him consider this, and then look behind us, when he gives a sudden yelp of surprise. Then I hear a second yelp from farther back and turn to see the reason: the fairy has returned.

"How are you doing that so quietly?!" David demands to know, before turning to his brother. "When *you* teleported, it was like the sun exploded."

"That's because I'm not teleporting."

"That's because he's not teleporting," Michael and the boy answer in unison.

"I'm turning invisible, moving, and then becoming visible again when I'm where I want to be," he states plainly.

"*Why?*" David remains skeptical.

"Because it looks cool?" he answers as if that should be obvious.

"Whatever." David shakes his head in the seat next to me. "Did it work?"

"Yes!" he answers affirmatively. "The good news is the druid is unlocking your friends as we speak."

"Good news implies the existence of bad news," I say wearily, still keeping the reins steady.

"Yeah..." I can hear the fae's voice trail off. "I kinda... ran out of sleeping dust."

"You *what?*" Michael sounds exasperated behind me while I can only groan.

"I managed to sneak your friend in with the keys, but I didn't realize I was out until I tried to use some on the guards in front," he defends, poorly. "But come on, there's only six of them and nine of you. Ten if you count that wolf that's been running alongside us in the woods. You can handle that, right?"

"They have all of our weapons, our armor, and are *still* holding one of our friends hostage," I point out, almost surprised when David does not correct me on "friend."

"Yeah, but you have most of your mages back," the fairy shoots back. "You telling me you guys *can't* handle it?"

"We can handle it," David challenges, then looks at me. "...Right?"

"I might have a plan brewing," I admit, nodding my head. "What kind of weapons were those men carrying?"

"Um, it looks like a pair of daggers," Tsula responds. "And...another pair of daggers."

Wonderful. I sigh. "Alright, I am going to need you to return to the front and pass along a message. David—get dressed."

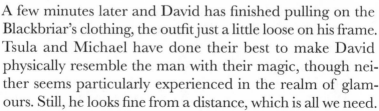

A few minutes later and David has finished pulling on the Blackbriar's clothing, the outfit just a little loose on his frame. Tsula and Michael have done their best to make David physically resemble the man with their magic, though neither seems particularly experienced in the realm of glamours. Still, he looks fine from a distance, which is all we need.

After ensuring he is ready, I hand over the reins and slip into the back, moving all the way to the now-unlocked rear doors. David slows the horses, pulling them to the right along the road as we come to a stop. Shouts of confusion comes from the cart behind us as the cart in front continues on for some distance until doing the same.

As soon as we are stationary, David hops off the cart and dashes to the forest on the left, just as planned. Soon, the sounds of someone vomiting can be heard coming from the forest, complete with a splashing effect provided by a water flask—Michael's idea. After some noises of disgust, there is nothing but silence.

"Vuk?" Kez calls out. "Go see what's wrong with him," she orders one of the other Briars to investigate.

"Vuk?" the woman, the other dwarf, repeats as she approaches the forest. "Is that—?" There is a *thud* as David's fist connects with the woman's face, and then the sounds of a struggle as he wrestles her to the ground to lock her in the set of cuffs he took with him.

"What the hell..." *That is Kez again.* Crouched by the doors with Michael and Tsula, I listen for one, two, three pairs of boots to hit the ground... *NOW!*

I kick open the doors, allowing Tsula and Michael to exit first, firing off bolts of arcane energy at the three Briars. While one of them—Rax, the man whose leg I broke earlier—is struck in the back and is knocked to the ground, the other bounces harmlessly off of Kez, as if she is wearing an invisible suit of rubber. It ricochets into a tree, exploding in a small burst of force.

Michael and Tsula are readying their next spells, but I am still without a usable weapon, forcing me to keep my distance. I can hear more fighting sounds ahead of us as the other half of our group deals with their own two guards. While Rax picks himself up from the ground, Kez and her companion turn to face us. He is a halfling and a mage, already preparing a spell of his own. The three of us leap out of the way of his arcane missile, spooking the horses of the rear cart when they explode too close. At the same time, David exits the forest holding a sword and whistling for Kez's attention. *Thank the spirits, a real weapon.*

"*Pendere!*" Michael calls out, scooping both hands up and lifting the halfling into the air.

"*Verancha!*" Tsula follows up, punching out with her fist and hitting the man with enough invisible force to knock him through the air and into a tree behind him.

With one of them down, it is only Kez and Rax, with me and the mages on one side and David on the other. Then I feel a familiar presence as Sona exits the woods to my left, growling angrily. While Kez only digs her feet deeper into the ground, her friend is starting to look nervous.

"Oh, *fuck* this." The bear of a man throws his club to the ground and runs in the opposite direction—right past a confused David. "You said this was going to be an easy jo—AAAHHHH!"

Before the man makes it very far, tree roots spring from the ground and wrap around his body. They squeeze him as he screams and struggles, sinking him partially into the earth and holding him in place. A second later, the back doors on the first cart finally open, the rest of our companions exiting and moving to join us near Kez.

"This doesn't have to be difficult," I mock as we circle in on her. "Are you sure you don't want to come along peacefully?"

A short while later, all of the Blackbriars have been restrained and loaded into the back of a single cart. Nathaniel and the hatchling have been freed, and we have retrieved what remains of our belongings. Sadly, that does not include our tents, sleeping rolls, or clothing. Those of the Briars wearing something that actually fit were stripped, but I still find myself temporarily pantless until I retrieve another pair from my bag.

We have commandeered the other two carts for our use, which hardly makes up for the missing items and kidnapping but should help speed along our travel. After double checking the locks on all of the cart's doors, I walk around to the back and slide open the small window slot on the back door, a pair of angry eyes already there to greet me.

"Now, we have left you some rations, but you will notice that only two of you have your hands tied in front," I start to warn. "I suggest you remain kind to them."

Kez's eyes narrow, but she and the others say nothing.

"David." I gesture for him to follow as I walk around to the front of the cart.

"What do you want me to do?" He is still adjusting the ill-fitting clothing.

"Destroy the cart's wheels," I tell him as I start to undo the horses' saddles.

"What?" He looks between me and the cart, confused.

"Destroy the wheels," I repeat. "And load some of the pieces into our cart, so they won't be repairable, either."

"...Okay." David pulls his sword, the Harpe, from the scabbard on his back.

The blade, allegedly made of adamantine, can supposedly cut through anything. It makes quick work of the wooden wheels, the cart slumping to one side as David makes his way around to all four. By the time he has finished and is moving the pieces, I have both horses untied and am leading them away. I point them in the direction of Rakatune, and with a quick slap on the rump and a little push of magic, I send them galloping down the road. Horses like that should have no problems finding shelter, and more likely, a new home. I return to the back of the cart once I am satisfied with our hobbling of their transportation.

"Are you *serious?*" Kez asks, no doubt realizing what just happened.

"So sorry, would you like a bucket, too?" I taunt. "We must have left ours in the *camp you destroyed.*"

"You know this won't hold us for long, right?" Her eyes narrow in the slot.

"Yes, I do." I nod and then close the slot. "Which is exactly why I feel *no* remorse for leaving you here."

"This isn't over!" she calls through the door as I turn and walk away with David.

"Nice job, everyone." The fairy grins as we rejoin the others. "I knew you could do it."

"I still don't understand why you're helping us." It is Adam's turn to be confused with the boy.

"I *told* you. I need your help with something." He rolls his eyes again.

"But *what?*" Liss sounds annoyed.

"It's complicated. I'll explain it to you when you get there." He waves off the question and then points behind him. "Just keep heading north along this road."

"Are you coming with us?" Corrine asks next.

"Spend a few days riding around with all of you in a cramped cart?" He makes a face of disgust. "Thanks, but I'll pass and meet you there."

"*Where?!*" Liss demands.

"You'll see when you get there!" He throws his hands up as he shouts back before vanishing into nothingness once more.

"Who the hell was that?" Nathaniel can be heard asking.

"No idea." Adam shakes his head. "So, just to be clear, we didn't just sentence eight people to a slow and painful death by locking them in a broken-down cart on the side of the road two weeks into summer, right?"

"They will be fine," I assure him. Mercenaries of their caliber are very, very resourceful. "In fact, I would not be surprised if they were out within the next few hours, so we really need to leave as soon as possible."

"Right." Adam nods his head before turning to the others. "Pick a cart and get on; we gotta start moving."

"Are we going to help that fairy boy?" Piper asks as we start to climb in.

"I don't know." He shakes his head. "Our plan is still to make it to Maname. We'll just have to see what the kid wants when we catch up to him.

The group splits into two. Riley and I elect to take the reins as we are the most attuned with animals. The horses do not look weary, but they have not rested much and we are going to have to push them for a little longer. Michael thankfully does not join me and David, which is one awkward conversation I am happy to avoid for a little longer. Instead, we get Adam, Piper, and Liss, along with Sona who spends the first twenty minutes standing on unsure legs in the back. A little later and David is taking the seat in front next to me, pressing against me suggestively.

"Are you...turned on right now?" I ask with slight hesitation.

"Maybe..." he responds shyly. "What? It's hot when you get all mean and angry. Like when you're gonna spank me for something *really* bad."

I can only laugh at that description, shaking my head. "Well, I hope you can hold onto that for a few days because they are going to be long, and we are not going to have many opportunities to stop."

Chapter 7

"<Khazak?>" **Ragnar groggily answers the door.**

"<Good afternoon, friend.>" I immediately feel guilty for keeping him up. *"<Could I come in for a moment? I need to talk to someone.>"*

"<Of course, come in.>" He steps back and holds the door open for me. *"<Nylan was just telling me about your visit a few hours ago.>"*

"<I apologize, I know it is early and you must want to sleep.>" His shift would have only ended a few hours ago.

"<Last night certainly was interesting.>" Ragnar chuckles as he takes a seat on the couch next to Nylan.

"<Did something happen?>" Nylan asks me, worried. *"<Did he try to escape again?>"*

"<No, nothing like that. Though he is the reason I am here to talk again.>" I think back to everything David revealed not even an hour ago. *"<If what he has told me is true, then he was deceived into fighting me.>"*

"<What do you mean?>" Ragnar sits up straighter.

"<Advocate Redwish was the one to explain the Ritual of Steel & Thunder, but David tells me that he neglected to reveal the actual consequences of losing.>" A conversation I have admittedly only heard one side of.

"<He had no idea what was supposed to happen if he lost?>" Nylan's eyes are wide.

"<None.>" I shake my head with a sigh.

"<*I am not certain what the man's goals were, but I must admit that when Redwish came to give me David's challenge, I felt pressured to accept.*>" I start to run the conversation back in my mind. "<*Not that it was difficult after he played into my anger and frustration over the temple attack perfectly. Dammit.*>" I feel my anger rise once more as I realize his manipulation.

"<*What did he think was going to happen when he lost?*>" Ragnar circles back.

"<*Death, apparently.*>" I shrug.

"<*And he still wanted to do it?*>" It is Ragnar's turn to look shocked. "<*I cannot decide if that means he is crazy or has really big balls.*>"

"<*What are you going to do?*>" Nylan avoids making any obvious testicle-related jokes.

"<*I am not sure.*>" I shake my head. "<*Speak to Redwish, for one, if not to find out his reasoning, then at least to ensure this does not happen again. But I cannot undo what has already been done.*>"

"<*I guess that explains why he has been fighting so hard.*>" Nylan frowns.

"<*Not to say that this is not terrible, but it does seem like he got a better deal than he originally thought,*>" Ragnar points out. "<*Being stuck with you rather than dying.*>"

"<*I am not so sure about that.*>" I sigh, ready to get to the difficult part of what I wanted to discuss. "<*Since this began, I have had many questions regarding how David even came to be aware of the Ritual of Steel & Thunder, let alone issue a challenge for it. Yet not once did I attempt to learn the truth.*>"

"<*You said yourself that you were probably being manipulated too,*>" Ragnar tries to defend my actions. "<*He also attacked you and agreed to try to kill you.*>"

"<*There are other ways David could have been punished for his crimes.*>" I shake my head again. "<*The way I have been treating him, the things I have forced him to do... Even if he knew full well*" *what may have been coming, does that make it any better? What kind of person am I to continue treating him like that?>"*

Ragnar and Nylan both look at each other in silence, unable to answer aloud.

"<Spirits, if he had not given in to me after the battle, I would be no better than a...>" I cannot even bring myself to say the word. "<I have to let him go.>"

After David's brief conversation with Michael, bound in the back of the cart, the memories of our early relationship resurface as we ride through the night and well into the morning. I released David not long after leaving Ragnar and Nylan's home, removing his collar and moving him into my spare bedroom. It was only the next day that *he* convinced *me* to give things another chance, though he only suggested our relationship as a temporary arrangement at the time. Neither of us expected things to come this far.

While I hear the occasional snore behind me, most of my "passengers" find it difficult to sleep, and I doubt those who can are sleeping well. I am not sure I would be able to if I tried, my mind too focused on the mercenaries we left behind and the potential dangers that lie ahead. Our plan for getting Nathaniel to Manamequohi for safety may now apply to all of us. *I need to speak with Adam about our next steps.*

"Hey, want me to take over?" Right on time, the blonde man pokes his head out from the back. "You look a little tired."

"No, thank you," I answer with a small shake of my head. "We need to stop soon anyway and let the horses rest. There should be a small lake coming up on our right."

"That sounds good." He nods, taking a seat. "We can take a break and refill our water."

While we managed to recover most of our rations, few of us have had a chance to eat. I would normally be happy to spend our break hunting for our lunch and dinner, but time is something we are short on. Every minute not on the road is a minute closer to the Blackbriars' inevitable escape, when they will no doubt begin coming after us again. So dried venison jerky and salted walnuts it is.

"Have you given any thought to what we will do next?" *Not that there are many available options.*

"Yeah, I was thinking Nate might not be the only one who needs to declare sanctuary when we reach the city," he tells me, having come to the same conclusion.

"I am afraid it is either that or get on a boat to a place very, very far away," I confirm with a sigh.

"No, thanks. Did that last year," he replies, referring to the boat journey he and the others took from Lutheria. "Although, I guess we could have Mike and the others teleport us somewhere, right?"

"That might work." Though I hope it does not come to that. I can only imagine writing a letter home, explaining why I am a fugitive. Which my twin sister Ayla will no doubt find a way hold over me to our parents. *I can see her smirking already...*

We reach the lake about an hour later, pulling both carts into the grass. Riley and I are thankfully not the only ones who have experience handling horses, all three former knights-in-training assisting us as we untie them from the carts and lead them to the water's edge. We can stay here for an hour, maybe an hour and a half, but I would not want to risk any longer.

I may have to ask Corrine and Riley to heal the horse's fatigue with their magic. It is not as good as actual rest, but it will have to do until tonight. Though a few of us take the opportunity to try to nap, we are still far too close to danger to consider setting up camp. My eyelids are already heavy. *I may have to ask Corrine about helping with my fatigue as well.*

The others are taking the opportunity to rest at the lakeside, some even sticking their feet in the cool waters. Nathaniel, clutching the baby cockatrice to his chest, takes a seat in the grass, creating a closed circle with his legs and allowing the chick to run around between them. Piper, Tsula, Corrine, and Riley cannot help themselves and coo at the creature as it runs around the arena made of Nathaniel's lower limbs. Meanwhile, Elisabeth stands off to the side, glaring at the back of her ex's head.

"David, Khazak," Michael calls for our attention. "Can I talk to you? Privately?" He gestures toward the forest with his head.

David looks at me before answering with a nod. "Sure."

We hand the horse reins to the others, following Michael as he leads us into the tree line, far enough in that we can speak without being heard. I think David and I both already know what this is about, but that does nothing to quell the small amount of dread and anxiety growing in my stomach. I am not sure there is any explanation that will satisfy the wizard.

"So." Michael leans back against a tree. "You gonna tell me what all that slave stuff was about now?"

"I told you, Mike. It's nothing." David tries to shrug off the question. "It was just a joke. A dig to get under our skin."

"It didn't seem like just a joke." Michael shakes his head. "Not the way they were talking about it. People who didn't even know you."

"I'm telling you—it's nothing." David starts to sound frustrated.

"I know when you're lying!" Michael rolls his eyes. "Plus you basically confirmed it when you said you didn't want to talk about it when we were still tied up. His complete silence isn't helping either." He points at me.

"I am just allowing David to—" I start to defend.

"Decide which version of the real story he's going to tell me, so you can back him up?" He looks unimpressed as he pinpoints my plan.

"Oh my god, why do you even care?" David goes on the offensive. "I told you, it's nothing. You know how we met."

"Not any of the actual details," Michael points out.

"The details don't matter!" David throws his hands up in frustration

"The more you refuse to tell me about them, the more it seems like they do!" They are both starting to raise their voice.

"Maybe we could all calm down for a moment?" I tentatively ask.

"*We are calm!*" they both yell at me in unison.

"Clearly." *Why does there have to be two of them?* "David, I think we should tell him."

"Yeah, David. Just tell me." Michael's tone is anything but helpful.

David looks at me, betrayed, before glaring at his brother. "Fine. Do you remember how I told you that after we were arrested, I tried to get us all out?" Michael nods. "I did that through a loophole in one of their laws."

"Not a loophole," I correct. "Just an old provision that is intended to be mostly ceremonial these days."

"How convenient." Michael huffs.

"So first off, you need to keep in mind that the guy who gave me all this information, our 'lawyer,'" David makes air quotes, "is the same guy who stabbed me in the chest."

That seems to get Michael's attention. "Redwish?"

"Yeah. I wasn't exactly polite to him or...anyone else in the city. He only told me about the 'provision' after some curses and insults," David continues. "Which probably explains why he didn't tell me everything. He said it was an old ritual, where I could issue a challenge to the person who captured us—Khazak—and if I won, we would all go free."

"What happens if you lose?" Michael is quick to question.

"Well, he didn't tell me, exactly." David sounds a little embarrassed by this, but I know firsthand how manipulative Redwish could be. "But I *thought* it was a fight to the death. The winner goes free and the loser...dies."

"If someone is challenged, do they have to accept?" Michael asks next.

"No, why?" David is confused, but I see where this is going.

"Because if it *were* a death match, what incentive would I have had to accept?" I answer for Michael. "I was already free."

"Look, I wasn't exactly thinking straight at the time," David defends, glaring at his brother a second time. "I was a little more concerned with trying to get me and my friends out of jail."

"Fine, so then what *actually* happens to the loser?" Michael refocuses the conversation.

"Well..." David starts to stall.

"If the challenger wins, nothing." I decide to just get it over with. "They are set free. But if the challenger loses... they become the personal property of the victor."

"*Personal property?*" Michael immediately turns on me in anger. "As in you would *own* him? Like a *slave?*"

"Yes." I nod in shame. "More or less." *The finer details on what exactly being an avakesh means would be lost on him and, in the end, would not matter.*

"That's what that fucking collar is about!" Michael's anger grows. "So you knew that and *still* accepted the challenge? *Why?!*"

"I did not expect to...keep your brother." The words feel heavy on my tongue, my guilt growing with every syllable. "I originally planned to send him back to his cell, to serve out his sentence with the others."

"So why didn't you?" He does not let up. "What made you change your plans?"

"Hey, did you miss the part where I thought it was a fight to the death?" David tries to redirect his twin's attention. "I tried to kill him. I almost fucking did!"

"Yeah, but you *didn't*," Michael points out, still glaring at me. "So, what happened? You saw my brother and changed your mind when you decided you wanted to *fuck* him?"

"What the fuck, Mike?!" David gets right in his brother's face. "Don't fucking talk to him like—"

"David, stop." I reach out and pull him back. "I agree with your brother."

"You do?"

"You *do*?" Both of them are confused, more so David.

"You know I have many, many regrets regarding how we met." I lower my head in shame. "The decisions I made then."

"You were being manipulated by Redwish too!" He now tries to defend me.

"He may have lied to get me to accept your challenge, but to your brother's point, I still knew what I was accepting." These are thoughts I have wrestled with a number of times. "What I planned does not matter because I did not follow through with it. Instead, I forced myself on you."

"You did not—"

"I got lucky." I cut him off quickly. "*Very* lucky that you were attracted to me."

"Was he, though?" Michael tries to step between us.

"What?" David is as confused as I am by that statement.

"As far as I'm aware, up until he met you, my brother liked girls," Michael continues, trying to stare me down.

"That is a bit of an oversimplification." My tolerance for his attitude is starting to wear thin.

"It's also not true!" David sidesteps him to give us both some room. "I might not have known it, but trust me, I was definitely into guys before I met Khazak."

"Or that's just what he made you think." Michael shakes his head to himself.

"How would I even—?"

"So now you know how I think better than I do?" David counters angrily.

"Why are you even defending him? He agrees with me!" *That does not mean you have to be smug about it.*

"Because you're acting like he's some kind of a monster!" *That is one word for it.* "Maybe I fought it at first, but I still liked everything that happened!"

"Do you even hear yourself?!" The others likely can, considering their volume. "That's not how it's supposed to work, David."

"Because *you* have so much experience with relationships?" He pokes his brother angrily in the chest.

"I know they don't usually start with one person becoming the property of the other!" Michael bats the hand away.

"He is right, David." *At least when it is done unwillingly.* "It does not matter that in the end you enjoyed what happened. I did not give you a choice. I simply took you."

"So what I feel about it doesn't matter?" His voice goes cold, and I worry he is missing my point.

"That is not what I'm saying." *His brother is not helping me word any of this correctly at all.*

"I don't know what you're saying!" He's not just angry but hurt. "I know things started off badly, but I thought we were past that, that we were okay. I like what we are. What we have. I *love* you."

"I love you, too." I reach for his shoulder. "I am not trying to invalidate your feelings."

"I am!" Michael pushes between us again. *Alright, I think I am just about done with this.*

"Oh my god," David grits angrily at the sky before looking at his twin. "I can't believe I have to explain this to you, but you don't get to tell me how I feel! Nobody does!" That last part feels like it is also directed at me.

"I'm not telling you how you feel." Michael rolls his eyes. "But you've known this guy for what, three months? I've known you your *entire life*. Do you really think he knows you better than I do?"

"That is not what this is about." I shake my head as the man twists his brother's words.

"Why are you even still wearing that collar thing?" Michael's eyes go to the metal chain around David's neck.

"Because I *want* to," David grits out, refusing any more of an explanation than that. *Not that Michael deserves one.*

"How does this seem like a normal relationship to you?" Michael throws his head back in frustration. "Even if you ignore the part where you're both guys!"

"Well then, I guess it's a good thing that you're not a part of *my* relationship, huh Mike?" David gets right in his brother's face before turning toward camp and speed-walking out of the forest.

I follow after him, not having anything more to say to the other man. This is not how I wanted that conversation to end, but I don't think it will be possible for Michael to act reasonably when he is so emotional.

"So you're just gonna run away again, just like before." Michael's words give us both pause as we reach the tree line, allowing him to catch up and stand in front of David. "Will you stop and listen to me for a second?"

"Why? You don't want to listen to me." David tries to push past him.

"I'm just asking you to think about it," he implores. "We grew up together, and not once did you ever talk about anything like this. I never saw so much as a hint of it—and I shared a bedroom with you for *eighteen years*. Isn't it possible that you only started feeling these things after he forced you to start liking them?"

"*No*, because that's *not what happened*." David growls in his face. Near the shore, the others are trying not to notice us.

"I am getting a little sick of this argument." I almost feel as though I'm not allowed to defend myself, but his suggestions are bordering on offensive, not just to me but to David.

"I don't give a fuck what you're sick of," he sneers at me.

"Don't fucking talk to him like that!" David shoves his brother again in my defense.

"Why do you keep defending him?!" Michael shouts.

"I'll defend whoever I fucking want to!" David shouts back. "Did you ever stop and think that maybe I didn't contact you for a reason?!"

"What are you talking about?" Michael attempts to hide how much that statement hurt him.

"You treat me like a fucking idiot!" David's shouting continues. "I know I'm not the smartest guy in the world, but you act like I don't even know my own fucking thoughts. You decide that there's a problem and how you're gonna fix it without ever talking to me about it! You won't even *listen* to me half the time, just like you're doing now!"

"I'm not... I don't..." Michael looks at me disdainfully. "What do you see in him anyway? How could you pick him over me?"

"He is not picking anyone over anyone," I tell Michael with a frustrated sigh.

"Well maybe he should!" Michael challenges. "Seriously, David. Him or me?"

"Don't do this, Mike," David warns coldly.

"Why? Because you don't want to hurt his—"

"Because I'll pick him!" David cuts his brother off.

"What?" Michael is clearly taken aback. "Why would you pick this dick over your own—"

"Because he's not the one making me choose, asshole," David finishes, quickly cutting his brother off again before once more walking away.

"You can't just run away from me like everyone else!" Michael taunts.

"So are you mad that I left or just mad that you don't know me half as well as you think you do?" David spits out over his shoulder. "How about you just *fuck off*, Mike?"

"For the record, I would *not* make you choose," I try to lighten the mood as I follow.

"I'm still mad at you, too." He looks forward as he tells me, but at least he is still talking to me.

I barely register the footsteps before Michael roars in anger, just as he tackles David from behind, the two falling to the ground in a blur of anger and frustration.

"Michael, David, stop!" I yell in a vain attempt to end things before they go any further.

Lakeside, I hear a shout of surprise from either Corrine or Tsula as the two men wrestle on the ground. When there appears to be no sign of things stopping, the others draw closer and gather around the two in a wide circle. Limbs fly in all directions as the two grown men roll around in the grass and dirt, still arguing.

I hesitate to call it a fight given that neither man is using anything even resembling their full strength. If they were, I doubt David would allow Michael to even attempt to stand up, and Michael would have blasted David halfway through the air with his magic. No, this feels juvenile and childish. *Just like the fights you used to have with Ayla.*

"Why do you have to be such an asshole!" David growls while pinning down his brother's arms.

"I'm an asshole?! You're the asshole!" Michael shakes his wrists free before shoving his brother off of him. "I'm just trying to look out for my *brother!*"

"By accusing my boyfriend of being a monster and tricking me into being gay!" David jumps back on Michael, wrapping an arm around his neck.

"He already agreed with me! Why are—!"

Both men are silenced as a deluge of water crashes over both of them, courtesy of Riley, who has used his magic to cause a large spout to shoot out from the lake. As the brothers are soaked by the cold water, they split apart, their angry words reduced to sputters.

"Are ya boys done?" Riley asks the two still-fuming brothers.

Michael growls in frustration as he stands, his clothes soaked through. "Whatever! Fuck this." He points at Adam. "And fuck you too, Adam. This is more shit you knew and didn't tell me about." He stomps off toward one of the caravans.

"So... Have a good talk?" Adam tries to joke as David picks himself up.

"I'm getting changed and taking a nap," David states wearily, heading for the opposite cart his brother climbed into.

"Sorry," Adam apologizes as I watch my pup leave.

"I am sorry as well," I say with a sigh. "Especially to the rest of you for having to witness that."

"That was certainly...interesting," Piper comments.

"I-I think I'm going to go try and talk to Michael," Tsula decides, heading for his cart.

"Thank you for ending that before things got any more out of hand, Riley," I commend the druid for his quick thinking.

"No problem. Used to have to do that at home when our dogs would fight." Riley looks at the two carts. "You think they'll be alright?"

"I hope so." Otherwise the rest of this journey is going to be a headache.

Chapter 8

After Michael and David's fight, we remain by the lakeside for another twenty minutes, long enough for the horses to get their fill of water. Riley and Corrine use their healing magic to rejuvenate their spent energy, but I can sense their reluctance when we lead them back to the carts. We just need to make it until nightfall, then we can set up camp and rest properly.

There were some slight changes in who was in which cart, and I am now riding with David, Corrine, Riley, and Elisabeth. Sona is still with us as well and has gotten more comfortable, periodically sticking her head out of the front at my side. I am still at the helm, as much as for my skill as to give David some space. He has been "napping" since the lake, still processing how he feels after our conversation with Michael.

I know why he is upset, or at least I have a good idea, but until we actually have a moment where we can be alone and talk, there is not much I can do. Honestly, I could use some time to think myself. It is difficult to put concerns about a relationship into words without upsetting the other person, particularly when they involve things that are at the foundation of that relationship.

His know-it-all sibling twisting everything I said did not help in the slightest. The man barely knows half the story yet feels free to tell both of us how it played out. Not to mention his ridiculous notion that I have somehow "turned" David into a homosexual.

The worst thing is, part of me is worried he may be right. Not about David liking men—that is just stupid. But everything else he said, the things he accused me of, are things I have thought about myself.

Am I a monster? I did not used to think so, but the more people call me that, the more I think about the past, and the more ashamed I am of my actions. Ashamed of other people knowing about them. I barely even told my own friends and family all of the details, knowing they would not sound nearly as good as they may have in the moment.

Michael and I had been getting along so well too...

"Hey." Liss takes a seat next to me, coming up from the back. "You doing alright?"

"I am fine," I confirm with a weary nod.

"That was a pretty big fight." She looks behind her into the cart. "I know it was mostly between the two of them, but you seemed fairly involved."

"You could say that," I start, sighing. "Michael wanted more information about the way David and I initially...met."

"Oh." The single word says it all.

"As you can imagine, he was not a fan," I continue. "Though I maintain that his response was a *bit* of an overreaction."

"It was a lot," she agrees with me. "I think that runs in their family. But you know..."

"Yes?" I already have an inkling of what she is going to say next.

"I can't say I didn't think that differently when I was sitting in that cell back in V'rok'sh Tah'lj," she admits. "None of us knew what had really happened to David. All we had to go on were stories being told by the guards, and no offense, but it seemed like most of them *barely* spoke Common. The things we were hearing didn't exactly sound nice."

"I apologize for that." Honestly, my officers should have known better than to be gossiping like that, especially in front of arrestees, but I suppose I did not know them as well as I thought in the end.

"Honestly, if it weren't for the fact that I've seen the way you two are with each other literally every day, I might feel just how Mike does." She seems almost reluctant to admit this. "We all might."

"That is alright," I assure her. "I actually understand that. That is what good friends *should* feel. I actually thought Michael was making some very good points, which is why David is upset with *me*."

"Because you agreed with what he was saying?" She looks at me skeptically.

"That, and the subject matter on which we were agreeing." I sigh wearily. "David does not like that I have doubts about our relationship."

"What kind of doubts?" From the way she says it, I know she is thinking about her own recent relationship troubles.

"Doubts may not be the right word." I gather my thoughts before continuing. "As I said, I understand why you all would feel the way you did when you first learned of me. The way David and I first became involved... I have many regrets regarding my behavior. I made a lot of mistakes."

"Can't disagree with you." She shrugs. "Though like I said, none of us are holding it against you."

"I am thankful that David does not hold them against me either." *Though perhaps he should, in some ways.* "I cannot take back anything I did, but I can ensure that my actions do not cause us further issues down the line. I have experience in this area, and I only want to *talk* about it, but David does not want to hear it."

"Yeah, he's always been pretty bullheaded," she says without a hint of irony about her own stubbornness. "You're a patient guy."

"It is something I am learning to work around." *And not just with him.* "Tell me... Are your feelings toward Nathaniel still the same?"

"Why would they be any different?" she answers, prickly as a pinecone.

"Well, most of the rest of the group seems to have...if not forgiven him, at least lessened their anger toward him." While still resentful of the trouble he has caused us, I understand the man's reasoning.

"Well I haven't." She confirms her stubbornness. "And I'm not going to."

"Tell me, thievery and bounty hunters notwithstanding," I start with several caveats, "if he had told the truth about his former employer, what would you have said when he joined the group?"

"I never would have let him join to begin with," she answers quickly.

"So perhaps he kept it from you in the hopes that you would see that he was not as bad a person as you might have otherwise thought?" *Not that it makes it any better.*

"Not possible," she states flatly. "You can't be a good person and work for Richard Calvinson."

I don't know the man, so I don't have a response to that, but I can see Liss silently turning my words over in her head. I am not sure why I am trying to defend Nathaniel; I have no real stakes in their relationship. Perhaps I am just feeling sympathetic for the only other people in the group having relationship problems.

"...The baby cockatrice *is* cute, though," she tacks on, begrudgingly.

We ride for several more hours, not stopping until after sunset to set up camp. Seeing as we are missing many of our belongings, "camp" is sadly little more than the few bedrolls we took from the Blackbriar's set up around the fire. Once we have the carts in place and the horses secured, I finish our fortification by asking the mages to cast an illusion spell to hide the camp altogether—something we did in V'rok'sh Tah'lj to disguise the ranger encampments patrolling the forest.

After ensuring our campsite is concealed, we settle around the small campfire. I see most people going through their belongings, taking inventory of what they need to replace and what they still have. Thankfully, I know that everything in my magic satchel is safe, though it does remind me...

"Sona," I call out, looking for the wolf as I reach into my bag. "Would you like to wear this?"

<*What is?*> She pads up to me, sniffing the leather collar I hold in my hands.

"Sure, you ask the *wolf* before you force a collar around its neck..." I hear Michael

mumble to himself.

"A collar." I think about the best and simplest way to explain this. "It will...let others know that we are friends."

She looks at me silently before stepping forward and lowering her head, allowing me to attach the soft brown leather to her neck. I thread the strap through the buckle, ensuring it is not too tight, scratching her behind the ear when I am finished. She shakes her head, testing the feel and weight, but overall seems content to wear it. I was right about the color; it can barely be seen in the light of the fire.

"Are you hungry?" She should be, after spending most of the afternoon on the cart.

<Food!> She happily barks.

"Go find your dinner," I send her off. "Make sure to stay hidden."

<Stay hidden.> She huffs once before turning and taking off into the forest.

With one of them taken care of, my thoughts move to my other pup. We have not spoken since the lake, but his brother's mumbled comments have me thinking I should at least try to finish my conversation with David. I spot him deciding on a decent plot of grass to spread out a bedroll, on the opposite side of the fire as Michael.

"David." I can feel Michael's eyes on my back as I approach his twin. "Do you think we could talk?"

He looks up at me, unhappiness still in his eyes, but he nods. "Yeah, okay."

The two of us exit camp in the same direction as Sona, away from the road. We walk until we are far enough away that our voices will not carry—and I am taking raised voices into account. I hope this discussion is a calm one, but with all the tension of the past few days, anything is possible.

"So, what did you want to talk about?" David asks, leaning against a tree and staring at the ground. "The way you regret having ever met me, or the way my feelings about our relationship don't count?"

"That is *not* what I said, David." It is a struggle not to roll my eyes at the histrionics. "And you know that."

"I don't know nothin' about nothin'," he grumbles, petulantly crossing his arms.

"It was difficult explaining myself with someone speaking so negatively about us in the conversation. My words came out sounding harsher than I meant them." I try to appeal to his romantic side, closing the distance between us and tilting his chin up to look at me. "I never meant to invalidate your feelings, and I certainly don't regret having met you. I love you very much, and what we have is very, very important to me, David."

"Except for the parts where I wear your collar or call you Sir." He tries to look away.

"And what gives you that idea?" I turn his face back toward me.

He says nothing, still frowning and not quite meeting my eyes. Seems he is going to need proof. I suppose I have been neglecting my duties a little given all the recent secrecy. I quickly take both his wrists in my hands and pin them to the tree above his head. He looks shocked, though still says nothing.

"When I ask you a question, I expect an answer, *boy*." I decide to lay it on thick.

"I..." He hesitates, though to be fair I did not *actually* expect an answer.

"Last I checked," I take his wrists in one hand, using my other to pull the collar out of his shirt, "this marked you as mine. Now, despite what anyone else may have to think or say, I have no intention of taking this off. Do you *want* me to take it off?"

"What?" His face screws up in a flash of anger. "No!"

"Do you want to stop being mine?" I continue, running my thumb over the collar's lock. "To stop taking my orders? To stop calling me Sir?"

"No." He starts to calm, hopefully seeing my point.

"Good. Neither do I." I grip the chain around David's neck and use it to pull him toward me, claiming his mouth roughly. "Now get on your knees."

There is a look of challenge in his eyes at the gruff order, but David still sinks to his knees once his wrists are released.

Still feeling a bit of fight, then. Good. That I can handle, at least in this context.

David's eyes follow my hands as they start undoing my pants. Inside, my cock is already growing in anticipation of what is to come while I form a plan of attack in my head. As I fish myself out of my underwear, a memory from yesterday gives me pause.

"If there is anyone out there eavesdropping, you may want to leave now." I speak to the forest as I finish pulling myself out, taking aim at David's face. "Because this is not going to be pretty."

David opens his mouth to make a comment of his own, but before he has a chance, I tug him by the hair onto my cock. He mumbles in surprise around my length but does nothing to dislodge me. I still see fire in his eyes as he looks up at me, and with a smirk, I feed him more of my prick, the muscles of his throat stretching around me.

I pull back before he has a chance to get comfortable, just enough for him to take a breath before plunging back in. David catches on quickly that this is not a blowjob, he is getting his face fucked, and the only "job" is to take my dick. All he needs to focus on fighting is his gag reflex, though I certainly do not mind the way it causes him to squeeze me.

I know I used his mouth with Adam only days ago, but that was different. When someone else is involved, it can sometimes feel as though you are putting on a show rather than fully giving over to the moment. Now, I can enjoy every groan, gurgle, and gag—all of the involuntary sounds I force out of David.

My hand still in his hair, I hold him down on my next plunge, forcing his nose all the way against my groin. David half-groans, half-gurgles around me, pushing against me like he has something to prove. When I finally let him pull back, his eyes are red and watery, but he looks no less determined. One of his hands moves to his crotch, and I quickly and lightly kick it away before he has a chance to give himself a squeeze.

"Who said you could touch my property?" I warn him, getting only a whimper as an answer.

I continue to roughly fuck my pup's face for another few minutes, drool starting to run down his chin from the corners of his mouth and onto my green and heavy sack. Still, David takes everything I give him and even tries to massage the bottom of my cock with his tongue while I use him. *Such a good pup...*

Pleased with his efforts, I push David off and quickly pull him to his feet. I kiss him hungrily, uncaring about the mess I have made of his face. I growl into his mouth as my hands roam his body, grabbing and squeezing at the flesh of his back, shoulders, and ass. He whines as I nip at his bottom lip, my free cock grinding against his clothed one.

Without warning, I take him by the shoulders and flip him around, pushing him forward to brace himself against the tree. My hands go to his waist, sliding around to the front to unbutton his pants and sliding them and his underwear down just enough to expose David's rump. I hump my length against him, teasing his cleft with the wet head of my cock.

I wish I had anticipated this happening because my bag is still back at camp—meaning so is our oil, charm, and anything else we might use for preparation. That does not deter me, as we have been doing this regularly for long enough that I know David can handle it. Plus, we both know he likes things a little on the rough side.

I spit in one hand, bringing it down and rubbing against his hole. After ensuring it is slick enough, I insert my index finger into his hole. He mewls as I stretch him open, though still pushes back against me. I spit in my hand again and repeat this with two fingers, forcing even more whimpers from his mouth.

I spit into my hand for a final time, this time running it over the length of my cock, slicking me as best I can. With my other hand on his hip, I poke between his cheeks and take aim at his hole, pressing inside. I groan low as David whines high, my hands gripping him as the tight heat squeezes around me. *Spirits, he feels good.*

I allow David a few moments to adjust to being filled, his body clenching and unclenching around me. He gasps when I run my hands under the bottom of his shirt, reaching up to pinch his nipples and scraping the blunt of my nails over the skin of his stomach. I flex my cock on instinct, David whimpering at the added pressure.

Moving both hands to his hips, I pull back before slowly thrusting back in. Things are dryer than usual, a little rougher, but it is not an unpleasant feeling. Even while no doubt feeling the sting of my entry, David still pushes back for more. I am very lucky to have found such a natural bottom.

Once I am fully seated, I wrap my arms around David's chest, pulling him to stand with his back against my chest. Bending my knees, I start to fuck with quick, short thrusts, barely pulling out before refilling him, my pubic hair scratching against his ass each time. I don't have the time to use all my skill and finesse to take him apart, but something fast, rough, and dominating is all we need right now.

I breathe heavily against David's ear, my tusks scraping over his neck. We are both hot, sweat building under our clothes from the exertion. I bite along his neck and shoulders, growling as I worry the skin between my teeth, further mixing the pain and pleasure. As I bring one hand up to wrap firmly around David's throat, he whimpers, grabbing me by the wrist—though not to pull me away.

The longer we fuck, the more animalistic we become, rutting like animals against the base of the tree. I can hear little over the rumbles of my growls and the slap of my skin on his. David cries out weakly as I fuck him through an anal orgasm, his inner walls convulsing around me. Nearing my own end, I tighten my arm around his chest and hand on his throat.

After just a few more thrusts, I tip over the edge, slamming our bodies together. David cries out as my cock expands as I cum, and then again when I bite into his shoulder, unable to stop my body from shuddering with each shot. After all the exertion, it's all we can do to keep our balance against the tree.

I release David's flesh from between my teeth once I have finished unloading, admiring the bright red bite mark. Making sure he is steady first, I carefully drag my hips back, pulling out but otherwise leaving our bodies connected. David leans against me, still shaking with sweat on his brow. For a moment I just hold him, nuzzling against his neck until I am ready to let him go.

After the perspiration has cooled on our skin, I finally release him, helping to adjust his pants and tucking myself away. Turning him around, I am pleased to see that he looks thoroughly well-fucked, a warm look behind his eyes. I try to straighten his hair, but it just ends up sticking to his forehead and I give up, pulling him to my chest.

"Still doubt that I want to own you, pup?" I ask with a kiss to the top of his sweaty head.

"No, Sir," he answers, grinning against my chest. "I'm just glad we're on the same page again."

"I am as well." I separate, meeting his eyes. "Just because I might have some reservations about the way our relationship started—"

"What?" David's head jerks back as he cuts me off. "That is *not* the page I am on."

"Then what did you think I was saying?" My shoulders sag. "That you didn't have any reservations at all anymore?" He looks annoyed.

"Just because I..." I sigh, feeling like I'm talking in circles. "David, that isn't a realistic expectation of *any* relationship."

"What do you mean?" He looks at me, defiant. "*I* don't have any reservations."

"It's a natural thing to feel," I try to explain. "Even without the more unfortunate circumstances of how it began, I would have these feelings about our relationship."

"Oh, so now you doubt our entire relationship?"

I feel my blood pressure rising in frustration. "That is not what I am saying!" *Why is he so determined to take this as negatively as he possibly can?* "They are not a reflection on you, or me, or our relationship."

"What kind of things make you doubt us?" He is just ignoring me now. "I wanna know."

"So you can get more upset over nothing?" I challenge.

"*Tell me*," he grits out.

"Fine." *I know I am going to regret this.* "What about things like our eight-year age difference? Or the fact that we come from two *completely* different cultures? Or that this is not just your first relationship with a man, but your first real relationship at all?"

"You think I'm too young for you?" *Spirits, I should have just kept my mouth shut.* "You think I don't know what I want? Or that I'm not really gay, like Mike thinks? That's the kind of stuff you worry about?"

"They are not things I am *worried* about." I struggle to not let my frustration show in my voice. "They are just things I take into consideration when...spirits, things like *this* come up."

"Whatever you say." He turns away from me, arms still crossed. "*Sir.*"

I sigh to myself. We are not going to get anywhere tonight, not with him so intent on being angry. With everything else going on, I am exhausted trying to continuously explain myself. Maybe after things settle down some, we will be able to speak more calmly about this.

"Perhaps we should head back to camp?" I suggest after we both stand there silently for a moment.

"Fine," he replies, not turning around to look at me before he starts walking in the wrong direction.

"Camp is that way, David," I correct, pointing toward where our companions are camouflaged and making him look at me.

"I knew that!" he snaps, forced to quickly turn and look at me for the right direction before stomping off.

When we re-enter camp a minute later, we get a few looks of curiosity, especially from Liss. I return it with a frown and a slight shake of the head, taking a seat on one of the bedrolls. After divvying up the watch shifts, everyone settles down around the fire. There is not much talking, most people too exhausted or emotional to do little more than wait for sleep. I am surprised when David comes to lay with me, squeezing together on the single bedroll.

"You're lucky you're comfortable," he grumbles, facing away from me as he uses my bicep as a pillow.

"I suppose I am," I say, mostly to myself, happy when he does not stop me from wrapping my arm around his waist as we wait for sleep to take us.

Chapter 9

"**We should arrive soon,**" I announce behind me, the terrain ahead starting to look familiar.

We are in the northern forests, with large trees obscuring all but a hundred or so meters of the path at a time as it winds through. It has been quite some time since I have been this way, but there is something about this place that is so familiar. Just a little longer and the trees will break to reveal a clearing with a trading post. There are a few homes and a small inn, but the main "attraction" is the market, where traders from all around will set up shop.

We run some risk by traveling in vehicles belonging to the Blackbriar Guild. There is a chance someone will recognize the coloring or other markings and suspect something. But as long as we are quick, we should be alright. Before we left camp this morning, everyone was supposed to prepare a supply list so that only a few of us have to leave the carts to restock.

"You sure this place will have everything we need?" Elisabeth asks me from inside the cart.

"As long as everyone keeps things simple." When you are limited to whatever the trader is able to carry in his cart, you cannot afford to be very picky. "We should still be able to—"

I cut myself off as the trees give way earlier than expected. Instead of the forest clearing, we are greeted by the sight of a half-constructed wall, with dozens of buildings behind it, some of them fairly large. One appears to be some sort of colosseum, and...is that a *castle*? *What happened here?*

"I thought you said it was just a small trading post," Liss says, taking in the scene next to me.

"It is. Was." I look around, dumbfounded. "None of this used to be here."

I continue forward, our carriages slowly rolling through the streets of this new "city." Looking at the other people around us, I start to notice that they all have something in common: fair skin, the same as David and the others. In fact, I see almost no one that looks like they might be from the local area. The buildings themselves are wood and stone but are in an architectural style I am unfamiliar with. I feel a small amount of relief when the familiar-looking inn comes into view, parking our carriages one after the other in an empty alley behind it.

"This place seems pretty busy," Adam comments to me as everyone exits their caravan and congregates between them so we can speak with privacy.

"It has been several years since I have been here, but these changes are extreme..." How did they manage to build a town—a *castle*—in the middle of the forest? "They have to have been recent, otherwise news would have traveled south before now."

"That's why I told you I needed your help." Several of us jump at the voice of our fairy friend, who is now standing behind David, along with what appears to be another fairy, this one female.

"You have *got* to stop doing that," Michael complains, as one of the people who jumped.

"Who's this?" David asks after stepping to the side. "And what's your name, anyway?"

"You can call me...Robin." *Obviously not his real name.*

"I'm Petal." *Another fake name.* "Can I have yours?"

David looks at her confused. "Uh, it's—"

"*Don't!*" I cut David off before he has a chance to fall into Petal's trap.

"Why would you do that?" Robin looks at her annoyed.

"It is not very *kind* to try and trick the people you claim to need help from," I warn the fae.

"Oh come on, you can't be mad at me for that. He set me up!" she defends with a grin, though it is doing nothing to win me over. "Besides, *he's* the one who wants your help, not me."

"Never tell a fairy your name when asked for," Riley warns David. "It can give them power over ya."

"I hate fae magic," Nathaniel grumbles to himself.

"What did you want our help for?" Adam tries to move the conversation forward.

"What do you mean?" Robin looks between the group, confused. "Look around. None of this is right!" The boy gestures at our surroundings, echoing my earlier words.

"You mean like...the town?" David asks.

"Yes, the town!" Robin stomps his foot, frustrated. "And the forest they cut down to build it, and all the stupid people walking around it, and that *hideous* fucking castle!"

"He is right," I tell the rest of the group. "This entire area used to be a densely packed forest. They must have cut it all down to build most of these homes. That would have displaced many, many animals."

"No kidding." Petal crosses her arms, looking at the ground angrily. "More than half of the ones that survived have fled."

"Spirits, that might explain why we have been seeing so many out of place animals over the past few months," I say to myself as much as to the group, thinking of the feral boar, the trio of black wolves, Sona, and the bear.

"What exactly happened?" Adam asks next. "Where did all these people come from?"

"Like you don't know." Petal rolls her eyes.

"What do you mean?" Michael looks confused.

"You didn't notice?" Liss starts. "The way everyone looked and what they were wearing? They could all be from Lutheria."

"Perhaps it is a new colony?" *One that is far too inland for my tastes.*

"I know it's been a while, but I don't remember hearing about anything," Adam answers.

"That's because it's not a colony." Robin looks annoyed at his unhelpful friend. "Like four months ago, some guy showed up at the inn asking to buy the land around the crossroads from the owners. With gold."

"How much?" David looks around at the size of the new "town."

"I don't know, a lot?" Robin shrugs. "More than I'd ever seen before. Enough to get them to agree to sell the land."

"Land that wasn't theirs to sell to begin with!" Petal stomps her feet.

"Was it your land?" Corrine asks.

"It's not *anyone's* land," Petal responds with a huff.

"She is not wrong. As far as I am aware, no one has ever made a claim to the surrounding land." Though I am not sure I can fault them for accepting what sounds like a life-changing amount of money. "What happened after that?"

"It was two months later, when humans just started... showing up. Like, an army of them," Robin continues to explain. "They started chopping down the trees and building everything. Fast."

"Whoever paid for the land also paid for a bunch of construction mages," Petal interjects. "It's been almost nonstop. They just completed the 'castle' a week ago, and they're supposed to finish work on the arena in a few days."

"How do you even know all this?" David asks suspiciously.

"Eavesdropping, how else?" Robin looks at him unimpressed.

"Look, I know it's not great, but why exactly do you care so much?" David continues to question.

"Because it isn't right?" Robin looks at him, incredulous. "They destroyed the forest and the homes of so many animals! They even built that stupid castle right on top of one of the entrances to the fae-realm!"

"So you can't get home?" Corrine questions with some concern. "Where are the other fairies? Are they all trapped?"

"No, we can get in and out just fine," Robin admits. "It's just annoying."

"He's the only one who wanted to ask mortals for help." Petal huffs, rolling her eyes.

"What exactly do you want *us* to do about it?" Adam returns Robin's incredulous look.

"Get rid of them!" Robin nearly shouts.

"How?" Liss stares at him, annoyed. "You want us to just walk up and ask them to leave?"

"I'm not even sure they really did anything wrong," Adam admits reluctantly.

"As despicable as I think their actions are...I am afraid I agree." I sigh unhappily. "I am not sure they have broken any laws, and I am not even sure who we could report them to if they did. Who is the person in charge of all this?" Knowing that information may at least help.

"Some guy who insists on making everyone call him a prince." Robin huffs. "Prince Calvinson."

"Calvinson?!" Liss almost reaches for her sword.

"Do you think it's the same guy?" Tsula wonders aloud.

"A rich Lutherian with that last name throwing his money around?" David summarizes. "Has to be."

"So we're even *less* safe here than we thought we were," Piper complains aloud.

"Look, apparently we're being hunted by the person you want us to fight," Adam starts to let the two Jogah down. "Even if we somehow could help, we don't have the time."

"I told you this was pointless." Petal rolls her eyes, crossing her arms.

"So that's it? You're not going to help us at all?" Robin grits his teeth.

"I'm sorry, but no." Adam shakes his head "We have to keep moving."

"I can't believe I actually helped you." Robin glares at us with disdain and disappointment in his eyes. "I thought you were supposed to be heroes."

Both fairies fade from view, leaving the ten of us between the two carts, anxiety growing among us.

"Adam, we can't stay here," Nathaniel pleads, his voice filled with worry.

"You sure?" Liss asks, eyeing him with an annoyed look. "Seems like a great chance to finally give Calvinson a piece of my mind."

"Is now *really* the best time to get revenge?" Adam asks her in return.

"If we take him out, then there's no one to collect the contract on Nate," Liss explains her reasoning.

"So now we're going to *murder* him?" David is taken aback by the suggestion, as are most of the others.

"We're wasting time..." Adam wipes a hand down his face.

"Does everyone have their supply lists ready?" I decide to take charge so we can move things along.

"Yes, I gathered ours together." Piper hands over the lists of everyone riding in her carriage.

"Great." Adam straightens his posture before pointing to myself and David. "Khazak and David, the three of us are going to go get everything while the rest of you wait here. Nate, get into the cart and *do not* come out until we are out of the city. Okay?"

Everyone agrees with that plan with no complaints, though Liss does not necessarily look happy about being told to wait back. I am not sure if that is because Adam is worried about her going off on her own and enacting whatever revenge plan she has cooked up, but the fewer of us there wandering around, the less of a chance we have at being noticed. Not to mention how hard it could be to round up ten different people in an open market.

I lead the way to the market. It is not far from the inn, seeing as it used to be one of the only other structures in the area. What used to only be a few stalls and carts has turned into a bustling marketplace. With the addition of the surrounding homes, it is not that dissimilar from the market in V'rok'sh Tah'lj.

The majority of what is on our lists is food, so that is what we move to take care of first. We split the lists up according to what is the most similar, taking care not to wander far from each other as we search for our purchases. David picks out a selection of fresh fruits and vegetables, storing them in my spacious satchel after paying.

The increased size of the market means a greater variety of goods. We do not have any issues finding most of what we need, and even point out other useful items to each other—like replacement bedrolls. As I shop, I notice that many items seem to be more expensive than I am expecting and cannot help but grumble.

"Has business been good?" I ask the halfling selling freshly caught fish.

"Incredible," she tells me, wrapping my purchase in paper. "With all the new customers, I've been able to cut my travel in half, which means not arriving home so late in the evenings."

"That does sound nice." I nod at the woman, fetching my coin purse. "And what do you think of all the other changes around here?"

"Well, I do miss some of the forest scenery," she admits. "They may not have the best choice in aesthetics, but these people aren't so bad. Although..."

"What is it?" I ask when she bites her lip rather than continuing.

"Well, a friend of mine in Rakatune told me he had a cousin who was coming to visit him from up north." She frowns to herself. "He was supposed to pass through here, but my friend said he never showed up."

"Really?" That is concerning. "What do you think happened?"

"I'm not sure." She shrugs. "I haven't seen anything odd myself."

"It is always good to keep your eyes open," I encourage her to stay alert.

"Very true." She nods and finishes tying a twine string around the wrapped fish. "That'll be five gold."

"Thank you," I sigh, keeping the information that the fish used to cost half that—and come pre-cleaned—to myself as I hand over the money.

"I think I gotta agree with what everyone is saying," David tells me when I rejoin him. "That castle looks really out of place."

"Yes, extremely." I look toward the eyesore on the hill. "Do all castles look like that in Lutheria?"

"We don't really have castles in Lutheria, other than a few old ruins." David shakes his head. "I don't know if that's what they used to look like. If they did, maybe it's a good thing that they're mostly rubble now."

"Is it just me, or does it almost look...smaller as it gets towards the top?" I squint, unsure if my eyes are deceiving me.

"It *does* look kinda weird." David joins me in squinting.

"*Guys*," Adam whisper-yells behind us. "On your left."

David and I both look to the left and are frozen in shock at the sight before us: Kez. She is obviously searching for us and appears to be very angry and very tired. The dark rings around her eyes are visible even at this distance. If she and the others have already caught up to us, I doubt they have slept at all.

"Shit!" David spits out as we both jump back, out of her potential eyeline.

"If she's here, then the others probably are too," Adam points out. "We have to get back to the carts and get out of here."

"While making sure to avoid being seen by any of them." I try to think of how we are going to hide the carts. "Did we at least manage to get everything on our lists?"

"Mostly? I think we missed some of the smaller things, like snacks." David frowns. "A few people wanted some clothes too, like new socks for Corrine. And still no new tents or bedrolls."

"We will have to make do with what we have a little longer." I sigh unhappily.

We start our trek back to our friends, moving as fast as we can while (hopefully) not drawing attention to ourselves. The three of us cannot help but watch everyone around us suspiciously, paranoid that another Blackbriar may appear at any moment. We are barely out of the market when that paranoia pays off, two Briars visible in the road ahead of us, looking just as frustrated and exhausted as Kez.

"Shit!" David curses as we duck behind a home. "More of them?"

"They must have gotten here right after we did," Adam growls, frustrated. "The rest are probably here too."

"How'd they get here so fast?" David complains.

"Other than not sleeping?" I point out the obvious. "It would have only taken one of them to figure out how to pick the locks on the cuffs. Which they have likely done before."

"What?!" David glares at me. "Then why did we leave them there like that?!"

"I assumed it would have taken them longer than *this* to catch up with us," I defend myself. "What would you have had me do instead? Kill them?"

"Guys, maybe argue about this later?" Adam looks between us. "We need to figure out how we're going to get to the others before they do."

"How are we supposed to sneak around them?" David leans against the building, crossing his arms. "It's not like we have disguises or anything."

"Well, there is that." I reluctantly point to some robes hanging from a clothesline in the yard of the home we are hiding behind.

David and Adam both look at the clothes, then me, and then each other and shrug. I sigh to myself. *I guess we are doing this.*

The two of them have no problems fitting into the robes, but they are all too small for myself, and I end up wrapping them around my head like a shawl. After a silent prayer to the Three that this will be enough, we step back out onto the street. We start to shuffle down the road, trying to avoid catching the Briars' attention, only a few blocks from the inn. Just when I think we are in the clear...

"Hey, you three!" *Shit.*

"Run!" Adam yells, the three of us taking off at top speed.

There are confused noises all around us as we rush through the crowded street, our arms still full of our supplies. Behind us, I can hear the Briars shouting for their compatriots to give chase. I abandon the makeshift shawl, throwing it to the side as it is doing me no favors. We run around the inn and into the alley, stopping right in front of Riley, who is tending to one of the horses.

"What's wrong?" He takes in our current state, confused.

"The Blackbriar Guild—they're here," Adam tells him, already handing off some of the goods to Liss, who has been standing guard. "We have to go *now.*"

"Oh shit." Riley's eyes go wide as do Liss's.

We immediately start to climb back into carriages while loading our purchases, hopeful that we can take off before the Briars catch up, but it's no use.

"*You!*" I turn at the sound of Kez's voice to see her pointing at us.

"Go," I tell the others, making a split-second decision. "I will hold them off and meet up with you later."

"What?" David's head pokes out of the cart at my statement. "I'm staying with you." He jumps down, standing at my side. Sona is right behind him, jumping down and placing herself between us and Kez with a growl.

I hear a groan of frustration from the other cart before Michael exits. "I'm staying too." He stands near us, looking unhappy. "You're a fucking idiot, but you're still my brother."

"Guys, are ya sure ya want to—" Riley starts.

"We don't have time for this. *Go!*" Adam urges the redhead.

The horses start to gallop, the carts turning the corner too sharply and almost skidding as they take off. Kez immediately shouts for her subordinates, four of them giving chase while the rest of them surround us. Which cuts the group in half and evens our odds, at least a little.

"These guys wiped the floor with us *before* they outnumbered us." David scans our approaching attackers. "What advantage do we have now?"

"Hopefully a lack of sleep deprivation," I comment wryly. Admittedly, the recklessness in my decision to send the others off without me is a bit more like David's style of doing things.

"You're hoping they're more *tired* than us?" David doubts my strategy.

"It's not a bad idea," Michael begrudgingly agrees. "Their mages wouldn't have had a chance to rest."

"And they likely used whatever magic they had left to catch up to us." I have noticed a distinct lack of spells or magical attacks.

"You both need to jump when I tell you to," Michael tells us in a low voice, making us look at each other. "NOW! *Commoveo!*"

As David and I leap into the air, Michael slams his foot into the ground, creating a shockwave that ripples out through the ground around him. Kez and most of her remaining friends fall as they lose their balance, and I am happy to help Rax, who manages to keep his, with a well-placed shoulder check. A second later, David jumps over his prone body.

"Come on, if they're so tired, then we're really gonna make 'em work for it," he shouts back over his shoulder.

Michael and I follow him down the road, and then again when he turns sharply down another, and then another. David has no problem taking the lead, but I worry Michael may have trouble keeping up, so I keep him ahead of me. He is not normally as involved in fighting as we are, but the weeks on the road seem to have done him some good, as he doesn't seem to have any issues. The Briars are right on our tails, but that gives me an idea.

The next time David turns a corner, I slip into a small alley between two homes and press myself flat against the wall. As David and Michael continue on, I watch Kez and her three companions run by without seeing me, and then I rejoin the chase, now right behind the four of them. Before they have a chance to notice me, I close the distance between us and take out the human at the back of the pack, throwing him through a wooden fence and into a ditch.

His scream of surprise and pain is enough to alert Kez and the two remaining mercenaries, Rax and the halfling mage. David and Michael also run out of road, coming face to face with the wall of the coliseum. There is a stone well in the middle of the three-way intersection, and when the people gathered around pulling water from it see the six of us looking for a fight, they quickly abandon their buckets.

"*Coroka!*" the halfling shouts as he directs a fireball at the two brothers.

"*Aquamurum!*" Michael extends a hand toward the bucket of water before arcing it above him, forming a wall of water between them and the fire.

The fire hits the water with a *hiss*, filling the air with a heavy fog of steam. Intentional or not, I use this new cover to rush forward to grab the mage—who is not even a third my weight—and throw him from the battlefield. I hear him land somewhere with a crash. As the fog starts to clear, the others finally notice my presence, particularly Rax. He stares me down with a menacing smirk as he reaches for the club on his back.

"Khazak!" I look to my right and see David, who tosses me his scabbard. I pull out the sword as the brute comes at me, using the indestructible blade to cleave clear through his club. The top half falls to the ground with a heavy thud, Rax staring at it and then me in shock.

"Fuck this." He throws the handle of his ruined weapon down. "I quit."

As he turns and runs away, I hear David dealing with Kez behind me.

"What are you going to do without a weapon?" she sneers, holding her axe.

"I dunno. What are you gonna do without your friends?" David counters. "Besides lose. Again."

"Has anyone ever told you you're an annoying brat?" She swipes forward with her weapon.

"A few people, actually." David dodges back once, and then again.

"Do you *always* talk this much?!" she growls as she comes at him again.

"Only when I'm being a distraction." At that exact moment, I strike her in the back with the heavy head of Brute's wooden club, the weight and my strength making her topple forward. Before anyone can do anything else, Michael runs toward her, placing his hands on the ground next to her.

"*Syrtes!*" The ground beneath Kez suddenly becomes malleable, the bottom half of her body sinking down and trapping her. Once Michael removes his hands, it is once again solid.

"Come on. We have to..." David trails off as he looks around us with wide eyes. "Uh oh."

I follow his gaze and see the armed guards blocking each of the three roads around us, their weapons drawn as they slowly approach. *Uh oh indeed.*

Chapter 10

"**Do not move,**" one of the guards tells us as they slowly begin to close in, swords drawn. "Drop your weapons to the ground and put your hands in the air."

We are greatly outnumbered, and I can already see some of the other guards locking cuffs onto the incapacitated Briars. After sharing a look and seeing we have no other choice, the three of us obey the man's order, dropping our weapons and raising our arms. His armor looks slightly more embellished than the others, so I would wager he is in charge.

As they start to approach, I notice the guards all seem to be human and mostly men at that. Their iron armor shines in the midday sun, appearing so unblemished that it must still be new. The only marks on any of them are a stylized letter "R" engraved into each shoulder. The lead guard, a man that appears to be no older than myself, has black hair poking out from under his helm, and a black mustache on his upper lip.

"Call off your pet." He gestures to Sona, who is still in an attack stance.

"Down, girl," I tell her with some regret. It is my fault she is in the city with us.

<*Not friends,*> she responds, still growling.

On our left, a guard holding a catchpole aims it toward Sona.

"Wait!" I try to stop him.

It is no use, and he quickly loops it around her neck. She thrashes and barks as the noose tightens around her neck, trying to reach for the pole with her mouth. I do not even have time to try to defend her before a mage among their number is rushing forward and putting her to sleep, and then the man holding the catchpole moves forward to lift her unconscious body onto a small two-wheeled cart.

"Where are you taking her?!" My shouted question goes unanswered as the cart is led away from us, though I am shocked that they did not simply attack her.

"The three of you are under arrest," the leader tells us as the others draw our arms behind our backs to lock cuffs around our wrists.

"On what charges?" I question, grunting at the rough way my arms are yanked back.

"Assault, reckless endangerment, and destruction of Richardton property to start with," he lists off.

"Richardton?" Michael sounds skeptical, and I agree. *Is that the best they could come up with?*

"More like Dicktown," David grumbles, earning a snort of laughter from Michael. One of the guards laughs too and gets smacked on the back of the helmet by one of his compatriots.

"We were only fighting to defend ourselves!" Michael tries to argue. "They attacked us first!"

"That's what they all say," one of the guards arresting David comments.

"Who is 'they?'" I question, though none of them particularly seems like they want to answer me. "This city did not even *exist* a few months ago."

"Shut up," one of the two men behind me says with a shove.

"We're gonna need the extra-large cuffs for this one, sir," the other guard at my back tells his superior.

"Then get them." He sounds frustrated. "I want them in a cell in the next twenty minutes."

Better prepared than the Briars were. As the large set of cuffs is locked around my wrists, I feel my magical abilities drain away. *Anti-magic.* While I am sure I feel less naked without my magic than some of the others, I do not like how it cuts off my connection to Sona, not even allowing me to sense her presence. *I swear if they do something to hurt her...*

Once we are all secure, we are marched toward the castle. That includes Kez and her companions, whose complete silence does strike me as a little suspicious, even though remaining silent during an arrest is generally a good idea. We are not brought through the main entrance but instead a side door, then down some stairs to an apparent dungeon. After confiscating our weapons and other items, the three of us are placed in one cell, while Kez and the others are placed in another across from us. All either group can do is sneer at the other, no one willing to actually discuss our circumstances aloud.

The room we are in is round with eight barred cells lining the walls They are split into groups of two with another row of bars separating them. Between each set of cells is a stone wall, three of which hold a door. One of them is hiding the staircase we entered from, and I saw a second staircase behind another when the guards exited, but I am not sure where it or the third door lead.

There is something about this "dungeon" that feels *off*. We do not have dungeons in V'rok'sh Tah'lj, so I am really only familiar with them from stories, but it all feels a little too exact. Almost fake. Maybe it is just because of how new the structure is, making it seem more clean-cut and well-maintained. I actually have to test the bars on our cell because I am half expecting them to bend or snap off. Sadly, they do not.

Now that the immediate danger has passed, David and Michael are back to not speaking, and I am too tired and stressed to attempt to resolve anything right now. Kez and her lot are almost equally silent, speaking low amongst themselves and glaring daggers at us from their cell. With a sigh, I take a seat against the far wall, on the opposite side of David. *At least the others made it away.*

That hope is dashed when the doors we came in through open again and a long procession of people are brought down the stairs—both our friends and Kez's. They are put into the other cells, three or four at a time, our group split between three. Everyone is cuffed and none of them look happy as their items are taken.

"What happened?" I ask Elisabeth, who is shoved into the cell next to ours with Corrine, Piper and Tsula.

"We were about halfway out of town when one of those assholes," she nods her head towards the cell containing the other three Briars, "decided to set the back half of one of the carriages on fire."

"You did *what?!*" I hear Kez shout at the cell next to hers. "I told you to take them alive!"

"I thought we only had to take the thief and the bird-lizard thing alive," the dwarf says after flinching.

"And what if they were in that carriage?!" Kez grits out, walking closer to the bars separating her cell from the other man.

"I figured it was a one-in-two chance." He shrugs but still looks nervous as he answers.

Kez growls and throws herself against the bars angrily, making the man jump back. Liss sighs and shakes her head as we watch the display. The longer I spend time with the Blackbriar Guild, the more I question all the boasting of their supposed skill I heard in my youth.

"Are you okay?" Michael asks Tsula through the bars.

"Yes." Tsula nods. "We got off right away. It wasn't exactly subtle."

"Was anyone injured?" I look over everyone, though Riley, Adam and Nathaniel are in a cell farther away and are harder to make out.

"Some scrapes in the fighting, but nothing too serious." Piper shakes her head.

"Where's the..." David motions his hands squeezing together, indicating something small—the cockatrice.

"They already took it," Nathaniel calls out from the far cell dejectedly.

"Did it seem like they knew what it was?" Michael asks in a low voice.

"I'm not sure, but it certainly seemed like they knew where to take it," Piper answers.

"Do you think Calvinson knows we are already here?" I ask worriedly.

"Oh he *definitely* knows we're here," Nathaniel gripes. "Seeing as Liss shouted his name about a dozen times while we were being arrested."

"We wouldn't even be in this mess if it wasn't for—"

"Seriously, you two?" Adam groans loudly, wiping his hands down his face. "Can you just...*not* right now?"

The two exes stop spitting their venom and instead silently glare at each other as the dungeon falls silent. The tension in the room is thick as the full extent of our troubles starts to sink in. However, something I do not understand is why the other group is being held here if they were working for Calvinson. Perhaps he hasn't been informed of their presence yet.

The silence is broken by the doors opening once more, with more than a dozen guards filing down the stairs. They unlock one of the cells, a guard stepping in and grabbing Riley by the shoulder to pull him out. Then they move to repeat with Nathaniel and Adam.

"Where are you taking us?" Adam demands to know as they escort him out and unlock the next cell.

"To see the prince," the lead guard answers.

One by one, we are pulled out of our cells and marched up the stairs, even the Blackbriars. We are led through the castle halls in a strange procession until we reach what I assume is the throne room—mostly due to the large, pretentious throne at its center. Large purple tapestries are draped along the walls and ceiling, each bearing the letters "R" and "C" in a stylized monogram.

We are separated into our two factions and made to stand in a straight line facing the throne, with guards at the ready behind us, and all around the rest of the room as well. The room is silent except for the shuffling of boots as the guards all move to stand in formation. It takes long enough that I suspect this is fairly new to most of them. Once everyone is finally still, a short, well-dressed human standing on the throne's platform steps forward and begins to speak.

"Now presenting His Royal Highness, Prince Richard Gregory Calvinson III!" the man proclaims to the room.

As the man finishes speaking, a set of double doors on the back swings open and a young man walks into the room flanked by two more guards. He has fair skin with short, curled blonde hair, and dark brown eyes. He is dressed in a great deal of finery: a red ruffled shirt over a pair of deep-purple slacks, both made of shiny silks. There is even a cape and a small golden circlet atop his head. I am confused by his appearance. How could someone so young be responsible for running a criminal empire?

"That's not Calvinson." I turn my head at Liss's statement. *What?*

"No, it's his son," Nathaniel says, sounding equally surprised.

"So, these are the troublemakers causing problems in my city?" Richard asks as he sits on his throne. His accent is... strange. Not like David's or any of the other Lutherians. As if he is adding some false layer of haughtiness.

"Yes sir." The lead guard steps forward. "They were arrested in two different groups for fighting in the streets. They caused damage to a number of homes and roads, and even set a carriage on fire."

"Oh my." He leans forward. "Were there any injuries?"

"Only to each other," the man assures him.

"I am glad you and your men were able to act so quickly, Captain Foster." The "prince" stands, approaching the captain and the rest of us. "You no doubt saved the citizens of Richardton from having to endure any further destruction these villains would have no doubt caused."

"Hold on, are you being serious right now?" Kez's sudden decision to speak has everyone turning their heads. "I was fine going along with the arrest until we saw you, but you know who we are. Tell them to let us go."

"Excuse me?" Richard walks past Captain Foster to where our two groups are being held. "I didn't realize that 'knowing' you meant I was granting you the freedom to destroy parts of my city."

"All we were doing is what you *hired* us to do," Kez shouts back angrily. "We've been tracking your mage and that damn creature for months, finally found them, and brought them right to you!"

"I've seen nothing of the sort." Richard looks down his nose at the woman. "From where I am standing, it was *my* men that captured your targets and brought them to me. All you and yours seem to have done is cause problems for me and my subjects."

"Listen here, you poncy little prick," Kez growls out. "You better uncuff and pay us what you owe *now*, or there will be hell to pay."

"And now you are making threats?" The man pretends to be offended. "No, I don't think I will. Guards, take them to the dungeon."

"Is this some kind of a fucking joke?!" Kez snaps as the guards begin to roughly pull her and the other Briars out of the room. "You're going to regret this! Wait until the guild finds out!"

"I knew hiring them was a mistake." Richard shakes his head as the doors to the throne room are closed. "Now then, which one of you is Nathaniel Carter?"

"I thought your last name was Smith," Liss deadpans to the mage, blowing his cover.

"I..." Nathaniel looks nervously between his ex and our captor.

"So I have *you* to thank for adding the cockatrice to my collection." Richard looks at him appreciatively.

"You're...not going to give it to your father?" Nathaniel hesitates as he asks.

"That *was* my intention when I originally hired the Blackbriar Guild to find you." The would-be prince starts to pace as he talks. "However, Father and I have had a falling out since then, and I see no need to bolster *his* collection any further."

"Are you still going to kill it, like he was?" Nathaniel asks next.

"Can it be safely raised without harming anyone?" Richard questions, stopping in front of the man.

"Yes!" Nathaniel nods. "With the right training, it's possible to—"

"Then I have no reason to follow in my father's barbaric footsteps," Richard cuts him off with a smile.

"Does that mean you'll let the rest of us go?" David decides to risk asking.

"Oh no, I'm afraid that will not be possible." He doesn't sound at all disappointed when he says it.

"Why the hell not?" Liss follows up, annoyed.

"Because I am the ruler of these lands, dear," he tells her condescendingly. "I have a duty to my people to see that justice and fairness prevails."

"It has been a while since I've been home, but I am certain there is more to becoming royalty than simply declaring yourself to be a prince," Piper tells him, voice full of skepticism. While Lutheria does not have any kings or queens, her home country of Albion still does.

"Yeah, ya can't just buy some land and call yerself king, boyo," Riley adds just as skeptically.

"Can't I?" Richard gestures to the room around us. "Besides, I've only called myself prince. I won't be king until after tomorrow's coronation."

"Even if you bought their land, that does not give you the right to call yourself their king," I protest, not caring for his sly attempt at technicalities.

"You sound just like my father," he tells me with a smirk. "It's people like you that helped push me to follow my dreams and build this amazing city."

I roll my eyes at the ridiculous statement. "*Inventing* a kingdom is not—"

"It was five months ago that the idea first came to me." The man ignores me as he pushes forward with his story.

"Father's men had tracked Mr. Carter to Westport, where he boarded a ship for Nova Mundus. He was willing to leave it at that and write the whole thing off as a loss, but I am not someone to give up so easily. I sent some scouts of my own on the next boat out to follow him. I thought I would capture the man myself and present him to my father as a gift."

"You had people crossing the ocean to follow us?" Adam questions as he realizes the full extent of how they were tracked.

"I cannot speak to how difficult it was, but it certainly wasn't cheap," he both complains and brags. "In the time it took them to reach land, I had my falling out with Father. We eventually came to an understanding: he decided on giving me my inheritance early, and I decided it was time to strike it out on my own. After some very carefully worded spell-o-grams to my scouts, I managed to get in contact with the Blackbriar Guild so that Mr. Carter could be located. Then it was time to build my kingdom."

"You cannot just purchase land and call it a kingdom," I repeat myself.

"I am not referring to the land. Except for that drabby old inn and a few other things, it was my craftsmen who built everything around us." He gestures with both hands to the room. "Work on the Coliseum is due to finish today, and soon Richardton will be a shining beacon of wonder and prosperity. Still, there is a lot of hard work to be done—work that I am a group of young adventurers like yourselves will be happy to help us with. I think that will serve as a fitting punishment for your crimes after you defaced our new home so readily."

"We are *not* working for you," Liss spits out almost immediately.

"Yeah, there's no way—" Nathaniel starts to argue next.

"Oh, no, Mr. Carter, I apologize. I did not mean *you*," the "prince" interrupts. "I would actually like to offer *you* a job."

"You... You would?" Nathaniel, and the entire group, is taken aback.

"Yes, of course. As I said, I am building a collection of my own, and I am going to need someone to help me look after it. In fact, I just came into possession of a baby cockatrice." He grins cockily. "Would you be interested in the position?"

"I... I..." Nathaniel looks from our captor to the rest of the group, a sea of disapproving faces. "I'll do it."

"Dude!" Adam shouts.

"You fucking traitor!" Liss screams.

"Excellent." Richard claps his hands together. "Guards, if you could uncuff Mr. Carter and show him to his new quarters."

Nathaniel cannot even manage to look up from the ground as his arms are released and he is led from the room.

"I knew we couldn't trust him," David mutters with a shake of his head.

"Now, where was I with the rest of you?" He grabs his chin as if lost in thought. "Which one of you is the leader?"

"That would be me." Adam stands as tall as he is able.

"I see." The man finally steps off the platform, approaching our group. "Do you make it a habit of regularly adding thieves to your group?" *As if he did not just hire the thief himself!*

"Do you make it a habit of hiring bounty hunters to attack travelers in the middle of the night?" Adam stands firm.

"The Blackbriars were a means to an end," Richard admits. "A drawn-out, unsatisfying one at that. Perhaps hard labor is *not* the right punishment, at least for some of you, but something must still be done."

He turns away, putting some space between us. The man starts to walk down the line of us, stopping to look each of us over. He mostly seems uninterested, only reacting when he gets to me, reaching a hand out toward my chest and dropping it with a chuckle when I jerk away from him. He repeats this on David at my left, with his inspection even starting to seem suggestive. As a look of interest passes over his face, he grabs David's chin to get a look at his eyes.

"Unhand him!" I warn, ready to jump to my pup's defense even if it means dragging the guard behind me.

"Are these the two of them?" Richards asks the man who announced him over his shoulder, pointing between me and David.

"Yes sir, I believe so," the man answers with some weariness in his voice.

"Are we *who*?" David demands to know.

"Well, the Briar's reports were filled with all sorts of interesting little tidbits about your group. Though they failed to mention how attractive some of you were." Richard's eyes flicker over to David for a moment and then to me. "And I can certainly see the appeal of some of your more exotic members."

"Gee, thanks," David deadpans. *Is this man really hitting on us right now?*

"Now then, if I cannot convince you all to work for me, perhaps there is something else you have to offer." He strokes a hand down David's chest.

"I told you to *keep your hands off of him*," I growl.

"Come now, I have it on good authority that I am hardly the first person to put their hands on your property." David's face glows red as the man speaks. "The affection you hold for your slave is endearing. I can certainly see why he has captured your heart."

"What are you suggesting?" I ask, hoping it is anything other than the painfully obvious.

"That in exchange for letting all of you go, I get to have your pet in my bed for the night." He looks at us innocently.

"*Absolutely not.*" The words cannot come out of my mouth fast enough.

"Hell no!" I can hear the others making various noises of disgust as David vocally turns him down.

"Come now." He looks between us, disappointed. "Surely someone like *you* is used to taking things in trade. I am merely attempting to come to an arrangement that benefits us both."

"There is not going to be any sort of arrangement because *you have no right to hold us here*," I tell him through gritted teeth. *Or the Briars, technically, but I am not going to say that out loud.*

"I beg to differ. My land, my laws," he states firmly, as if the alliteration has made a point.

"That's not how that works!" David shouts, then turns to me and asks more quietly. "Is it?"

"No, it's not," I say with my eyes narrowed at Richard. "There is more to establishing a city and laws than simply declaring them to exist."

"Well, I am afraid we are just going to have to agree to disagree on that." He fixes me with a fake frown. "Perhaps some more time in your cells will help you to see things my way. Guards!"

"Wait!" David calls out as the guards start to manhandle us to the back of the room.

Richard holds his hand up, stopping his men. "Change your mind?"

"I want to talk with these two, first." David nods to myself and Adam. "Alone."

"Feisty, aren't you?" Richard rakes his eyes up and down David's body appreciatively, then looks to me. "I suppose you do not have him as well-tamed as I assumed. But alright. Take them to my study."

He points to our guards and then the door behind him with a nod. As three of the guards lead us out of the door, I see David staring at the floor, avoiding eye contact with anyone else—namely Michael. The door leads to another hallway, where we are led through *another* door into a medium sized study room. The walls are lined with bookshelves, a fireplace and easy chair against one wall, and a large desk under a single window against another. After bringing us inside, the guards stand there, watching us.

"I said *alone*," David eyes the guards still in the room, annoyed.

With a huff, the guards exit, no doubt waiting on the other side of the door.

"David, we are *not* making any sort of deal with that man!" I tell him as soon as the door is closed.

"Seriously, David, no." Adam cannot even believe we have to have this conversation.

"Look, I'm not saying I *want* to sleep with the guy," David defends, rolling his eyes. "But if it gets us out of here, why not?"

"Because he's an opportunistic creep?" Adam responds incredulously.

"Honestly David. His choices are either that he gets to sleep with you or he holds us prisoner indefinitely." *Why would he even consider this?*

"Again, not something I *want* to do," he repeats with some frustration. "It's not like he's the first person you've 'lent' me to."

"Gee, thanks," Adam says flatly, both of us sharing a look at David's use of air quotes.

"You know that's not what I meant," David tries to walk it back.

"The difference between now and any of those times is we had an *actual choice* then." I try to get David to see things my way.

"So now you're saying I *did* have a choice back then?" David turns the conversation toward our other recent discussions.

"You *know* that is not what I meant." *Of course we would run into a situation that would do nothing but agitate the issue.*

"Guys, maybe this is another conversation to save for later?" Adam watches the door nervously.

"Do either of you have a better idea?" David crosses his arms over his chest.

"Maybe we could try to fight our way out?" Adam offers hesitantly.

"Except we have no idea where they have taken any of our weapons, and our spellcasters are all cut off from their magic," I point out. "We also do not know how many guards he has working for him, except that we are already outnumbered."

"We've barely been surviving the last few days," David tells us next. "I know it's not great, but it's just sex. If I do this, then we can leave without fighting. Without anyone getting hurt. Okay?"

"How do we know we can trust him?" Adam tries to change David's mind. "He could be lying about letting us go."

"What other choice do we have?" He looks between us. "Seriously. I'm all ears."

I make eye contact with Adam, who looks unhappy but resigned. However, he will not be the person to make the final call here—as David's lover, owner, and in my pup's words, boyfriend, he is leaving that to me. And I really,

really do not want to make this choice. Not when it feels like my hand is being forced by this prick of a man.

"For the record, I really, really, *really* do not like this, David," I finally start to answer with a sigh. "But alright. We can tell him we accept his deal."

"Okay." David nods his head. "I think you should do most of the talking. He seems to be really into the whole master and slave thing. Maybe leaning into that will get him to play nice." He sounds more like he is talking through a battle plan instead of his body being used as leverage for our freedom.

"Fine." I sigh unhappily. "Was there anything else we needed to talk about?"

"No." David shakes his head, both of us knowing that we need to do exactly that, and that this is likely to only set us back further. Hurt and disappointed, David and I search each other's eyes for something before Adam breaks the silence with a cough.

"I'll get the guards." Adam leaves us to our awkward moment, knocking on the door with his elbow.

The guards lead us back through the halls to the throne room. The others are still standing while Richard has taken a seat on his throne. Rather than being brought to the others, the three of us are stood in front of the throne at the bottom of the platform.

"So," Richard leans forward, clasping his hands together. "Do we have a deal?"

"One night," I start, "and then you will release us and return *all* of our items and equipment." There are noises of shock and anger behind me, but I ignore them.

"That sounds acceptable to me," Richard sits up, looking pleased.

"If you harm even a single hair on his head, I will——"

"Is now really the time to be making threats?" He cuts me off with a look of challenge. "Worry not, I will take good care of your pet. Guards, take the rest of the prisoners back to their cells for the night." He stands, closing the distance between himself and David, stroking a finger down his face. "You and I are in for a wonderful evening, my dear."

David looks to me as we are led away, worry and regret in his eyes. I find that I am regretting a few things myself, like not taking the time to tell him how much I loved him while I had the chance. As soon as we are back together, I am going to do just that. Right before I spank him.

Chapter 11

David

I **can't bring myself to make eye-contact with anyone as** I leave the throne room with Richard and his guards. Not after agreeing to whore myself out for our freedom. *At least this time I won't have to fight anyone before I get fucked.*

"Now then, beautiful, I am afraid I never learned your name," Richard says as we come to a stop in the hallway.

"It's David." I don't bother giving him my full name.

"Well, David, the two of us are going to have a very pleasant night together." I resist the urge to roll my eyes.

"Yeah, sounds great." Knowing this guy is me and my friends' key to freedom, I guess I better start at least pretending to like him.

"You must be feeling exhausted after your long journey." He looks me over thoughtfully, maybe thinking that's the reason for my attitude. "Frederick, could you please show David to a bath? I am going to prepare a few other things for tonight."

"Yes sir, right away," Frederick, the guy who made the announcements before Rich here entered the throne room, answers with a nod.

"See you soon." Richard takes my hand and kisses the back of it, and I have to resist another urge—this one to wipe it off.

"Please follow me," Frederick requests, turning and walking down the opposite end of the hall.

We walk past many other doors, taking several turns until we come to a stop at a room at the end of a hallway. Frederick goes first, holding the door open for me and revealing a bathroom. Stepping inside, my eyes are immediately drawn to the large stone tub at the center of the room, steam rising from the already-heated water.

"You may disrobe here." He points to a bench next to the entrances, then he walks to the tub, gesturing to a small table filled with glass bottles and potions. "You should find all the necessary amenities on the table." He walks back toward me and the door.

"Thank you," I tell the man as he moves to the exit.

"When you are finished, simply ring the bell, and I will collect you." He points to a bell attached to the chain next to the bench and exits, closing the door behind him.

I let out a sigh of relief once I am finally alone, taking a moment to inspect my new surroundings. It's not huge, but still bigger than any of the bathrooms I've been in recently. The smooth stone walls are painted with images of blooming red and pink flowers. The tub itself also has swirling lines and patterns carved along its surface, and its four feet resemble a furry animal's paw. One corner holds a tall mirror, and another is blocked by a tall wooden divider, which I peek behind and see is hiding a toilet from view.

The room actually reminds me a *lot* of the one I was in right before my fight with Khazak, the Ritual of Steel & Thunder. That room makes a lot more sense now that I know what was actually supposed to happen after the fight. All the soaps and perfumes, things you wouldn't really think about using before a fight to the death. *At least you know what is coming this time, David.*

I take a seat on the bench and pull off my boots. I do briefly consider skipping it and just ringing the bell now, but I have a feeling Calvinson won't like that. Plus, I do kinda need a bath. But as I am lowering myself into the warm water, I can't help but feel guilty that I am once again up here living the good life while my friends are locked in a jail cell together.

I close my eyes, leaning back in the tub and trying to relax. *Remember, you're doing this to get everyone out. Besides, this would all just go to waste otherwise. Although... Why did he have a tub of hot water all ready to go? Was it for him? Or does he just always keep a tub filled with hot water around in case the need arises? Gods, I hate rich people.*

After a few minutes of lying there, I reach for the soap and start to scrub the weeks of travel from my skin. It feels so nice to dunk my head under the water and run my fingers across my scalp. Still, reality is calling me, and with a regretful sigh, I pull my body out of the water and dry off with a nearby towel.

Once I'm dry, I turn to get redressed, but when I look for my clothes, I find them and my armor gone. Instead, hanging from a hook on the wall above the bench is a fluffy dark-blue robe. *Great.* I sigh, unhappy that they've taken more of my stuff. How did I miss them coming in and swapping them for the robe anyway?

I pull on the robe, not liking the way it covers barely half my thighs. No longer naked, I stare at the bell I'm supposed to ring for a second before trying the door anyway. *Of course, it's locked.* I didn't actually expect to be able to wander around the place or anything, but I still wanted to try. With another sigh, I pull the chain, the golden bell ringing through the room.

It's not even a full minute before Frederick has returned to gather me, holding the door open as I exit. We walk down more halls until we enter a dining room with a single, very long table at its center. Despite having maybe dozens of seats, there are only places set for two people, one at each end. Frederick leads me to the closest seat, pulling out the chair for me before leaving me there alone.

"There you are." *Not for long, though.* Calvinson Jr. enters the room, dressed the same as he was earlier, taking the seat opposite from me. "Did you enjoy your bath?"

"Uh, yeah. It was fine." I have to kind of awkwardly raise my voice to answer him, seeing as he's sitting so far away. *Is this really happening?*

"Excellent." He smiles with fake warmth. "Then I believe it is time for dinner." He reaches for a bell I didn't notice on his right. (There's like seven kinds of silverware and two wine glasses. I was a little distracted.)

Two more men dressed like Frederick enter, each holding a covered tray that they place in front of us. They lift the lids to reveal steaming bowls of soup before walking away. I don't want to be here, but it's not like there's anything else I can do. Might as well eat. I don't even try and guess which spoon is the right one to use; he'll just have to be happy that I'm not slurping or anything.

Shortly after we start eating, another dressed-up man enters, this one with a wine bottle that he uses to fill a glass for each of us. I eye it warily before taking a sip. As much as I'd like to, I don't trust this guy enough to be getting drunk tonight. After the soup, we're brought a salad, and after that some kind of baked chicken dish. All of the food is good, if not a little rich for my tastes. Still, there's something about it that reminds me of home. It feels like forever since I've eaten anything so familiar.

"Are you enjoying the food?" he asks, finally breaking the silence of the last fifteen minutes.

"Yeah, it's good," I admit with a single nod. "Do you usually treat your prisoners to dinner like this?"

"Only the sexy ones," he flirts, actually getting me to blush a little.

"Thanks," I say before taking an angry bite of chicken.

"So what brought *you* to this part of the world?" he asks next, holding out his wine glass as one of the butler-dudes refills it.

"Oh, you know. Fun and adventure," I answer flatly.

"Well from what I have been reading, it certainly seems like you found it with that large green brute in my dungeon." He sips his wine before cutting into his own chicken. "With an owner like that, I am sure you have been through quite a lot."

"He treats me just fine." I get defensive, not needing yet another person telling me things about my own relationship.

"I am certain he does." He chews and swallows some food before continuing. "Tell me, is it true that you were killed?"

"I... Yes." I'm a little stunned at the bluntness of the question. "Why?"

"Merely wondering why he did not protect you." He shrugs a little.

"He had nothing to do with that. He was almost killed too." I put down my silverware, my appetite vanishing rapidly.

"I apologize. I did not mean to offend." He's not even trying to sound sincere. "I only meant to say, if I were to possess someone like yourself, I would do anything in my power to protect you from harm."

"You know I'm already going to sleep with you, right?" *Could he lay it on any thicker?*

"That you are." He grins, all teeth. "Are you ready for dessert?"

"Not really hungry anymore," I grumble-shout across the long table.

"Well that is a pity, but I will not force you to watch me eat." He stands, having barely eaten anything himself—but he is on glass-o-wine number *three*. He walks around to my side of the table, holding out an arm. "Come, let us move onto the next portion of our evening."

Holding back another eye roll, I take his arm as he helps me out of the seat. We leave the room together, once again passing a number of halls and doors. *How big is this place?* I'm expecting to be led to the bedroom, so I'm surprised when I feel a breeze coming from around a corner, right before we step through an archway leading outside. The sun has set, the only light coming from the moon and a few lit torches above us as we stand in some sort of garden.

Nope, not a garden. A zoo. Or the start of one at least. Strewn among the plants and flowers are at least a dozen cages. A few are empty, but most have an animal occupant. Some I recognize, at least I think. I've never actually seen them in person, only drawings and paintings, but there's a lion with a furry brown mane around its neck in one, and an orange-and-black striped tiger in another. Then you have some I don't recognize at all, like a giant bird with translucent blue feathers, and a lizard with rainbow-colored scales that seem to shift and move in the moonlight. There's even a large tank of water with something that looks like an umbrella with long strings hanging off the brim, twirling around inside periodically.

"What is this place?" I move toward the lion's cage.

"My collection. Or part of it." I think he confused my tone as interest instead of disgust. "This is where I keep my favorites or my newer additions. I may need to expand the place soon."

"This is where you're gonna keep the cockatrice?" I watch the large, sad-looking cat behind the bars.

"Once it is old enough, perhaps." He laughs like I told a joke. "Poor thing would just slip right through the bars at the moment."

I ignore him, my attention pulled to something furry and black—*Sona!* She seems to notice me too, standing up on all fours as I rush over to her cage. She whines, pressing her head against my hands when I stick them through the bars to pet her.

"Hey, girl." She doesn't look hurt, but it's easy to tell she's unhappy.

"Is she yours, then?" Richard's voice from behind almost makes me jump. "She has a beautiful coat."

"I... Yes. She's ours." I guess technically she's Khazak's, but I don't feel like that distinction is gonna matter.

"Is she magical?" Sona tenses under my hand when he steps up to the cage, watching her with interest.

"She..." I hesitate to answer, worried he's planning to keep her. "She's coming with us when we leave."

"Of course." He acts like he wasn't even considering it. "Merely curious at how my men had managed to acquire her. It is not every day you see a wild animal traveling with a group of adventurers." I have no idea if that statement is true or not, and I doubt he actually does either.

"I'll be back, girl." I give Sona one last scratch behind the ear as Calvinson leads me away.

Alright, maybe I had some issues with her when we first met—Khazak and I nearly got mauled to death by three wolves who looked exactly like her—but the fuzzball has grown on me over the last few weeks. She guards our camp, helps with hunting, and has backed us up more than once in a fight. She's always waiting for us outside the tent in the mornings with her tail wagging, and she likes to curl up with us when we're sitting by the campfire at night. There was even one time it was raining and *I* was the one to insist she sleep in the tent with us.

Richard continues to show me around the rest of his "collection," pointing out different creatures and explaining what they're called—and how deadly they are. It would be cool if each of the animals didn't look bored and depressed to all hell. I did get a kick out of the lion pacing back and forth, watching the other man like it was looking for the chance to tear out his throat. *You and me both, buddy.*

Eventually, he has enough of showing off and takes me back inside, once again intertwining our arms. This time we walk up a wide staircase to the second floor, and then another to the third, where there are fewer halls and we don't wander long. He brings us straight to a set of double doors—his bedroom.

The first thing I notice after the door opens is the giant four-poster bed on the opposite end of the room. There's a low table and some lounge chairs in another corner, and a large desk covered in papers in another. One wall has an open archway that looks like it leads into a private bathroom, and the closed door I see is probably a closet. There's also lit candles *everywhere*, on almost every surface, like out of a cheesy romance novel.

"Nice bedroom," I say awkwardly after standing there in silence just a little too long.

"I'm glad it is to your liking." Richard steps close, slipping a hand into my robe and rubbing against my chest. "May I undress you?"

"Sure." Not sure why he's asking permission now, but the hand moves down, tugging at the tie on my robe until it's loose and falling open. His eyes rake up my naked body, stopping at my chest. "Is that from the—?"

"Yes." *Is everyone going to ask me about the scar?*

Silently, he slips the robe from my shoulders and has me stand naked before him. He walks around me once, wine glass still in one hand. Unfortunately (Or fortunately? Not really sure.), being on display does to me what it always does, making me feel half-embarrassed and half-turned on.

"Wonderful," he says, mostly to himself, as his eyes wander down to my partially plumped-up prick.

"Thanks." I blush, not knowing how to take the compliment.

"Why don't you lay on the bed while I get comfortable?" he tells me while gently pushing me toward it.

I hop up, sliding back to sit against the headboard while Richard downs the last of his wine and starts to undress. He lays his coat over the back of a chair before removing his circlet and setting it on a desk. He takes off each layer of clothing slowly, deliberately, like he wants me to watch. It's all so much that I can't take it seriously.

"You know, you don't have to try to impress me or any-thing." I don't tell him it's because he *can't* impress me. For someone who negotiated to borrow someone else's "slave," this really isn't what I expected.

"I...apologize." He stops for a moment, looking *actually* embarrassed for probably the first time tonight. "You can thank my father for that habit."

"What do you mean?" I don't know a lot about his dad, other than his reputation for being a dangerous piece of shit.

"My problems with Father date back far longer than this past year." He continues to undress, though it's all perfunctory now. "Ever since I was younger, I always felt the need to impress him."

"Like, you wanted to make him proud?" *Of course* he wants to open up and tell me his life story. *Can't we just fuck and get this over with?*

"Like I had to prove that I was worthy of being his son," he deadpans, before turning to face me, down to just his pants. "Sorry, I'm sure you don't want to hear about this."

"I...kind of get that, actually," I admit. "Having a dad that you never really felt good enough for."

"It seemed like no matter what I did, it was never enough to make him happy." He slides them down his legs, revealing a purple set of underclothes (*must be his favorite color*), right above a hairy set of thighs. "He criticized everything I did even *before* I showed an interest in the family business."

"Do you have any siblings?" *Why am I asking this?*

"No, why?" Down to just his underwear, he starts toward the bed.

"I've got an older brother who I get compared to constantly," I explain, bitterness bleeding into my voice. "No matter how hard I worked, if it wasn't better than Joseph, it didn't matter. My dad didn't care. He used to do the same to Mike, but as soon as he showed a talent for magic, Dad stopped pushing him the same way he did me."

"Who is Mike?" Calvinson asks.

"My *other* brother, who you have locked up downstairs," I say with a slightly bitter edge.

"I'm not sure if that sounds better or worse." He sits on the edge of the bed near me, ignoring the last part of my answer. "I'm...not sure my father ever really *liked* me. Tolerated me, perhaps. But then..."

"What happened?" Why *did* he decide to just up and leave?

"The rift between us had been growing for a while, but as my attraction to men became more and more of an open secret, he decided he'd had enough." I can hear the pain behind his words. "Told me as much."

"I'm sorry." I can't help myself and place one hand gently on his back. "I'm... I'm worried mine is going to react the same way."

"Well, I think we can both agree that fathers are the worst." He chuckles, turning more to face me. "May I kiss you?"

I nod silently, and he closes the gap between us, slotting our mouths together. He's soft, almost sweet, as he slides his hand down my back. He keeps kissing me while he climbs onto the mattress until we're both lying on our sides at the center. It's only then that he finally decides to slip his tongue into my mouth.

He's gentle, but he catches me off guard enough that I automatically open and he slips his tongue between my lips. He tastes like wine, but overall he's...not a terrible kisser. I still can't shake the thought that this isn't what he had in mind when he demanded to sleep with me. Which is fine! I'm not disappointed or anything. I'm just saying, I was expecting something rougher out of all this.

His hands start to wander lower, down my side and then over my hip, before daring to venture back and actually grab my butt. He squeezes my cheek as he deepens our kiss, gently at first before getting rough. He pulls me toward him, rubbing our crotches together and pulling one of my legs over his.

His kissing starts to match his hands, nipping at my bottom lip. He rolls us over, slipping between my legs as he lays me on my back. No longer able to grab at my ass, his hands start to wander over my chest and shoulders, through my hair, finally landing on my wrists. His mouth slows down as he tentatively brings my hands above my head, opening his eyes to look for my reaction as he pins them down.

Once he's happy that I won't try to move them, the kissing resumes at normal speed.

"Now... There is something I have always wanted to try," he starts to tell me, sitting up after finally breaking apart. "Would you...allow me to tie you to the bed?"

"Huh? Yeah, okay," I answer, still a little breathless from the kissing.

With a pleased grin, he shuffles back from me and slides off the bed. He enters his closet again, and after some noisy rummaging, comes back out with his arms full of chains. Like, heavy duty iron chains. There's even a set of metal cuffs for my wrists attached to one end.

"Oh wow, you meant with actual chains." I can't help my surprised tone as he dumps the metal on the bed.

"Is that alright?" He starts to separate the two, laying them out straight.

"Sure." I mean, I guess it doesn't really matter what he ties me up with. It still seems weird that he's even asking.

Happy with that answer, he locks a cuff around each of my wrists with a *click*. Then he pulls my arms apart by wrapping each chain around one of the bedposts behind me, locking the chains to themselves with heavy padlocks. I don't see a key, but I assume it's in the closet or something. It better be, because with the canopy over the bed, the only other way these chains are coming off is by breaking the bedposts.

"Well, I'm happy to see that I'm not the only one enjoying this," Richard teases me as he plays with my cock, which got even harder as I was chained.

I don't say anything, just smile bashfully before he leans back in to capture my mouth again. What can I say? I like getting tied up. And me not hating this whole ordeal is not the worst thing in the world. I can feel guilty about it later.

"Sit back against the headboard," he orders next, first kneeling and then standing on the bed.

As I sit up, Richard's hands dip into the waistband of his underwear, pulling them down. His cock springs from its confines as he steps over my legs until he is only inches from my face. He's average sized (*I dunno, maybe six inches?*), not that I indicate anything one way or the other. He's also got dark brown, neatly trimmed pubic hair—that I am just realizing does not match the blonde on his head.

I open without needing to be told, allowing Richard to guide himself inside my mouth with his hips. It's not that difficult to take him without gagging, having spent the past few months practicing with a significantly larger and greener cock. I feel his fist in my hair after I take him all the way down and massage the bottom of his shaft with my tongue.

He's not holding my head tightly or pushing me against the bed, so I'm able to bob up and down on his shaft as I please. After a little while though, Richard starts humping forward each time I suck him back in. He never quite reaches the level of face-fucking that I'm used to, but if I'm being honest, there's something nice about dealing with a cock that isn't going to leave my jaw sore when we're finished. It feels like I could do this for a lot longer than usual. Richard's had enough though, pulling out of my mouth after maybe ten minutes of oral activity.

"Wait right there." I can see him laugh silently at his own bad joke as he leaves me cuffed on the bed, stepping into the closet once more. He steps back out, holding two familiar sights—lube and a cleansing charm. I actually think it's *my* cleansing charm for a second before I see that it's a different color—solid black.

"I love those things," I tell him as he crawls back onto the bed.

"Handy, aren't they?" He wastes no time in holding the charm against my stomach. "I've known about them for some time but had to have them imported. Couldn't even find a cleric who knew the spell." *Must be nice to be rich.*

After the charm has worked its magic, he tosses it to the side, landing somewhere on the floor with a *thud.* He pulls me down on the bed, spreading my legs and shuffling between them. He uncorks the vial of oil and pours a very generous amount onto his hand and fingers, not caring about the extra that spills onto the sheets. Before I can even blink, his slick fingers are poking at my hole, making me shudder in surprise.

He spreads the slick around the outside of my hole with the pad of his thumb, using a finger from his other hand to press inside. He uses his lube-covered hand to grab my dick, stroking me slowly from root to tip and back down as his finger pushes farther inside. I groan at the dual sensations, my hips not sure which way they want to go as he rubs over my prostate.

He keeps on teasing me, his hands swapping places as he pushes two fingers inside me next. He starts to stroke me faster as he slides in and out of my hole just as fast, and my eyes close as I start to enjoy it. I spread my legs wider, even lifting them up a bit to give him better access. *Okay, maybe I do know what I want. What? I accepted that I'm a bottom a while ago.*

Eventually I realize Richard's had enough of that too when I feel him lifting my legs even further. Looking down, I see his lubey hand stroking over his cock only for a moment before he's aiming for my hole and pushing inside. Our thighs are touching in an instant as he bottoms out in one quick stroke, making me gasp at the sudden intrusion. It's a good thing I'm used to bigger dicks than his, or that might have hurt.

Any thoughts of this guy having finesse fly *right* out the window when he starts pounding away with no further warning. I don't voice any complaints, but I can tell you that most of the noises I'm making aren't out of pleasure. *Not that he seems to notice a difference.* With nothing else to grab onto, my hands grasp at the chains connected to the bedposts.

With some concentration and breathing techniques, I manage to relax enough for things to *actually* start feeling good. His dick might not be huge, but it's still big enough to hit all the right spots. I sigh happily as my prostate is prodded, my own dick lying flat against my belly. It of course hasn't minded any of the roughness so far whatsoever, the traitor.

"Gods, you feel so *good*," Richard mumbles above me, though I don't think he's actually talking *to* me.

At least that makes two of us now. I bite my lip, keeping all of these thoughts to myself. We might have opened up a little to each other, but I haven't forgotten that this guy is holding my friends hostage and is forcing me to do this. *Don't you dare think about how hot that makes to you, David.*

He does slow down at one point, but only so we can change positions, rolling me half onto my side and lifting one of my legs onto his shoulder. He tests this new posture with a few long, slow strokes, but once he's satisfied goes right back to slamming me hard and fast. I groan over the sounds of our skin slapping together, his cock aimed right at my prostate by the new angle.

He fucks me harder and faster, squeezing my thigh against his chest with the arm he's got wrapped around it. I can feel him pushing against me with his whole body, sliding me up the bed on each in-stroke. Just as I feel a much-missed pressure starting to build in my hole, Richard's body gives a sudden jerk, forcing his cock as deep as it will go.

When I feel a familiar warmth starting to spread inside my body, I understand that he just came.

I look up at his face, his eyes closed and his brow covered in sweat. So is the rest of him, actually. I'm like medium-sweaty, I guess. That was nice, but uh, I didn't really have a chance to get going there. Not sure I should be disappointed by that. Richard pulls out of me as silently as he came, and I look down at my neglected cock, wondering if he'll get any more attention now that Richard seems to be done.

"That was...simply marvelous, dear." He tells me with a final kiss, rolling over and sliding off the bed. *Guess not.*

"Yeah, it was pretty great." *It was fine. I've had better.*

"I'm going to need to freshen up before we go again," he half-jokes as he steps into his closet, returning as he pulls on a robe—one longer than mine.

"Yeah, me too," I agree, nodding. "So, do you think you could..." I hold up my hands and shake my wrists.

"Now, why would I do a thing like that?" He pretends to be surprised by my question.

"Look dude, it's your bed. I'm just trying to be polite and not leave a wet spot." I shrug as best I can with my arms spread.

"Why would I untie you at all, David?" He's smirking now.

"I mean, I'm gonna have to pee eventually?" *What the fuck is he getting at?*

"I suppose I will have to devise some sort of bathroom system..." Now he's lost in thought.

"What are you talking about?" I'm instantly on edge, not liking where this is heading.

"The stupid ones really are so precious." He looks at me like a pet who tried and failed to do a trick. "I'm not letting you go, silly."

"What?! Why the hell not?" I shout, pulling at my chains and trying to launch off the bed. "That was the deal!"

"Why would I actually agree to something like that?" he asks mockingly. "What do I stand to gain?"

"Me. For the night," I grit out. "That was the fucking deal."

"Well, I've decided the deal no longer suits me." He turns to look at himself in the mirror.

"Too fucking bad! You already agreed to it!" I say it like I have some sort of way to force him to comply.

"Look at it this way: wouldn't you be much happier here with me than roughing it out on the road?" he asks while straightening his hair and clothes.

"*Fuck you*," I snarl. "I swear to god, the second I'm out of these chains, I'm gonna—"

"Ah-ah-ah." He turns around and cuts me off. "Need I remind you that I have your friends *and* family locked up in my dungeon."

A flare of anger runs through me, but I go silent.

"That's better. See, this can be nice and easy for the both of us." He stands at the foot of the bed, smirking. "Or, if you want to continue making things difficult, we can do this the hard way, and I can hurt one of them."

More anger builds, and I wrap the chains around my hands and pull, tugging at the hard at the bedposts. "Uncuff me, *now*."

He sighs unhappily and turns away. "Well, I suppose I *was* going to have to decide what to do with them anyway. I'm sure some can be put to work, but most of them seem like troublemakers."

My body starts to get hot as the rage inside of me grows, and I continue to pull against the chains with all my strength.

"The easiest thing to do would be to just get rid of a few of them." He paces slowly in front of the bed, talking like he can't hear the periodic *thunk* of metal against wood. "I guess I could be sporting and let you have a say?"

He's trying to make it sound like murdering my friends is no big deal. I'm so furious I'm actually seeing red. *I'm gonna kill him. I'm* really *gonna fucking kill him.* I yank faster, and harder, and I swear I can hear the wood start to splinter.

"So, since I don't need to keep both of them, who would you rather I kill first?" He stops and turns to face me. "Your brother or your lover?"

His answer is a loud *crack*, not even giving him time to scream before the chains break through the bedposts, snapping them like toothpicks. He turns and runs for the bedroom door, throwing it open and pulling it shut as I leap off the bed, taking the chains with me. I don't bother with the knob, barreling through the wood with my shoulder.

I hear another scream at the crashing sound of my exit, letting me know which way prey has run. I rush down the hall in pursuit, roaring loudly in anger as I catch a glimpse of purple in the distance. There are more screams and some loud babbling, but I can't understand what he's saying and I don't care. *He's a dead man.*

I chase him down a flight of stairs to the second floor, where all the racket alerts his staff. Frederick and some other butlers and maids poke their heads out of their rooms only to slam them shut with a scream of their own as I fly past. Several guards rush out to greet me head-on, but I don't pause for even a second. I knock the feet out from under the first, delivering a swift punch to the side of his head as he goes down. The second has his shoulder dislocated after I wrap one of my chains around it and pull, and I kick the third right out of a second story window, not bothering to check where he lands before I start to run again.

I reach the wide staircase we first used to come upstairs, Calvinson already at the bottom of it and still moving.

He screams again when he sees me, more guards already marching up the stairs in his defense. Rather than fight this out, I leap onto the closest man, jumping off of his shoulders and landing on the large rug at the center of the foyer with a slide.

The guards all turn to rush back down the stairs after me, but I'm already in pursuit of Calvinson down another hall. Guards come pouring from gods know where to come at me, but none of them are a match from my speed. I blow past most of them, and any that try to actually stop me find themselves slammed into a wall as I run by, never looking back. I know there are at least a dozen of them chasing me now, but I don't care. I've only got my eyes for one man right now.

He takes a turn through another doorway, this one leading to another familiar set of stairs. Dashing down, I slam through the door at the bottom and find myself back in the dungeons. Calvinson is on the other side of the room, cowering against a wall, and I rush him. He screams, ducking out of the way of my fist, which goes right through the stone wall behind him.

"David!" my master shouts as I pry myself free.

While I'm distracted, Calvinson runs to the only door I haven't seen used yet, flinging it open and escaping down a dark corridor. I growl as I continue my chase, rushing past my friends in their cells without so much as a glance. I'll be back for them, right after I finish killing this asshole.

After a pursuit down a long hallway, I follow him into a dark room barely lit by torches on the walls. There are more cells here, a maze that seems to turn and stretch in every direction. Lucky for me, I have a guide, my eyes locked on the terrified man in purple ahead of me, who is rapidly losing ground. He shrieks when I finally catch up with him, attacking with the chain on my right arm to wrap around his legs and send him tumbling to the ground.

I don't give him a chance to get his bearings, yanking him toward me and pulling him up before slamming his back against the wall. I grab him by the neck, squeezing as I lift him and cutting off his air supply. His eyes go wide when realizes he can't breathe, both hands grabbing at my forearm and trying to dislodge my hand. As his face goes red, he reaches toward my face—but my arms are longer, and I'm not the one being choked to death.

"David, stop!" The shout comes from my left, from my *kyrios*, who has apparently rushed here with several guards at his side.

"<He threatened to kill you and my brother,>" I tell him, keeping one eye locked on the struggling man in my grip.

"He's choking him!" the lead guard says, pulling out his sword.

"Don't. You won't stand a chance," my master warns the man from taking action. "David, please. You have to let him go."

"<Why are you trying to help him? He was going to kill you! To kill all of you!>" I shout back, squeezing Calvinson's neck a little tighter and making his eyes bug out.

"You don't want to do this," he starts to plead, forcing me to look over. "This isn't you. Come back to me, puppy."

"I... I..." *What... What am I doing?* I turn back to look at Calvinson, at my hand still squeezing his neck, and release him in shock, pulling back like I just touched a hot stove. Calvinson falls to the ground, coughing and sputtering as his guards rush forward to help. All the energy and anger I had moments ago is gone, and I stumble backward as the dimly lit room starts to spin, right before it all goes black.

Chapter 12

Khazak

I can feel Michael glaring at the back of my head as we're marched from the throne room back down to our cells. While I would not call any of the guards "polite," there does seem to be a distinct lack of roughness one would expect given the circumstances. Instead, they seem oddly thoughtful of our limbs and appendages as they place us back in our cells.

They leave us without another word, seeming unsure of what to do themselves. It's only when the last of them turns up the stairs that I realize the cells across from us are empty—the Blackbriars were not brought back down like us, apparently. While that seems like it should be good news, I can't help the nagging feeling that something sinister is going on.

"So...what just happened up there?" Liss breaks the silence with a rhetorical question.

"That asshole sold my brother is what happened!" Michael shouts, pointing at me accusingly from the other cell.

"That is *not* what happened," I grit out, clenching my hands at my side and fighting the urge to shout back. Both because I do not think that will actually solve anything and to spare David from embarrassment by not detailing how he came to the decision.

"We were all there. We saw and heard it ourselves!" He gestures to everyone else, most of whom are looking at the ground uncomfortably. "Don't pretend like you don't still think of my brother as your property!"

"David decided to take that fucked up deal all on his own," Adam elects to explain. "Khazak and I *both* tried to talk him out of it."

"Adam, you do not need to—"

"No, Khazak, if he's gonna make a decision like that and ignore everything the two of us were trying to tell him, then he can deal with the fact that the others are gonna find out about it." I grimace but find it hard to argue with the sentiment.

"So what, you just *let* him—"

"Would you give it a fucking rest already?" Adam growls in frustration. "You've been around us for *weeks*."

"So what?" Michael fires back.

"So you've seen how David and Khazak are with each other." Adam gestures to me as he speaks. "Do you seriously think something bad is going on between them? That his friends would just sit back and let that happen? That *he* would let that happen?"

"I don't know what he's doing anymore." Unable to argue but refusing to concede, Michael sits down in a huff and turns to Tsula. "Can you believe this?"

"He's right, though." Tsula shocks Michael *and* me by agreeing with Adam.

"What?" Michael is having a clear problem processing this.

"I won't claim to know or understand every aspect of their relationship," she admits, "but I've been around them long enough to see that they're happy together and they love each other."

"But you heard how they first met, right?" Michael tries to clarify.

"I know I wasn't there, and they were, so maybe you could just listen to the two of them instead of coming up with your own story?" She grimaces. "Also, I'm pretty sure you can't *make* someone gay."

"But he admitted—I wasn't trying to—Ugh!" Michael turns away from her and crosses his arms, clearly unhappy that she disagrees.

The room is tense after that. I appreciate Adam coming to my and David's defense, but it hardly does us any good. We are still stuck here until Calvinson is finished with David, which means I spend the entire night wondering and worrying about how he is and what is being done to him.

"Would anyone like to talk about how Nathaniel seemed comfortable *immediately* siding with our captor without so much as a goodbye?" Piper tries asking.

"A piece of shit agrees to work for a piece of shit," Liss replies stonily. "What's there to talk about?"

"What do you think happened to the mercenaries?" Corrine asks next, gesturing to the empty cells across from us.

"Maybe they were moved somewhere else?" Tsula offers from the other cell.

"Yeah, 'moved.'" Liss rolls her eyes with a huff, sitting against the back wall.

I would like to ignore those dark implications, but she may be right. Like I told David, this man cannot be trusted. We know next to nothing about him, except for who his father is and that he has been hunting for the group for months. We have no guarantee that he will uphold his end of the bargain. He could—

I stop, taking a deep, silent breath and leaning back against the wall. Working myself up is not going to help anyone. I take a seat on the floor like most of the others, calming myself and clearing my head. I grumble about the anti-magic bindings on my wrists, wishing I could reach out to Sona to know she is okay.

We are mostly left alone the rest of the night, though no one is really in the mood to talk given the circumstances. A guard comes down periodically, walking around the room of cells as if there were more to look at than us and then leaves. If they are following some sort of schedule, I cannot to determine what it is, and my internal clock is fairly accurate.

We are brought dinner about two hours after we left the throne room, a meal that consists of bread and water. I sigh unhappily, picking at the half a loaf I'm given. Before they leave, Piper makes a request to use the restroom, which is followed by several others. Right then is when the guards seem to realize that none of these cells have latrines. Possibly because they were not meant to hold prisoners long term, but it could just as easily be a poor design given how quickly the building was constructed.

So, two by two, they take each of us from the cells and bring us upstairs to the bathroom in the guard barracks, which are immediately above the dungeon. Certainly better than using a bucket in the corner, which was what I was concerned would be their original solution. As it is, I get some petty pleasure out of making the guards work.

While being led back downstairs, I can see the clear night sky through a window. Back in the cell with the others, the exhaustion of the past few days finally starts catches up with me. It looks to have caught up with the others too, Adam yawning in the other cell and triggering Riley, Liss, and myself to yawn in response. No one bothers asking for a pillow or a blanket, just trying to find a comfortable position against the wall or on the ground. A few people, like Michael and Tsula, and Riley and Piper, huddle together for warmth.

I lie back against the wall, closing my eyes but not expecting to sleep. Even if this were comfortable, there are *far* too many things for me to stay up for hours and stress about. I laugh silently at my own joke when a crash of thunder can be heard in the distance. Then I jolt upward when a shriek rings out somewhere in the castle above us, too far for any of the others to have picked up. That is quickly followed by a crashing sound and another scream, this one alerting Tsula, who as an elf has her own naturally enhanced hearing.

"What was that?" she asks me, causing everyone else to look around confused.

"What was what?" Corrine looks between the two of us.

Her question is answered by the sounds of shouting and feet stomping, as the guards above us mobilize toward whatever this new threat is. I stand when there is more shouting, the screaming now close enough that the others can hear. The door at the top of the stairs is thrown open, and a few seconds later who should come stumbling down the stairs but Richard Calvinson III. He looks completely terrified as he fumbles with the door's lock, attempting to barricade it with a chair. I don't think I have seen someone that terrified since... *Oh Spirits, no.*

"What is wrong with him?!" he shouts, approaching our cell and pointing frantically at the locked door.

"What's wrong with—" Michael starts.

He is cut off by a loud crash as the locked door is blown off its hinges, splintering as it slams to the ground and confirming my fears. There are several screams, though none louder than Calvinson's. *David.* Though from his rage-filled expression, he is not himself at the moment. What he is is completely naked, save for a pair of metal cuffs around his wrists, each attached to a chain long enough to drag on the floor behind him.

He stalks into the room with a snarl, his gaze moving to Calvinson, who cowers against the wall between cells. David rushes the frightened man, who only just manages to duck the fist that strikes with enough force to punch clear through the stone wall behind him. If that had hit, I do not think Calvinson would have survived.

"David!" I shout, recognizing the familiar rage from his temple rampage.

He looks at me questioningly as he extracts his arm from the wall, just for a moment, but it is enough to allow Calvinson to run through the closed door at the opposite end of the room. David growls in frustration, ignoring all of us as he chases Calvinson through the same door. Unable to follow, my eyes are instead drawn back to the wall David punched through. The stonework is odd, hollow, with criss-crossing wooden beams inside of it. *What?*

"What the hell was that?" Riley asks first in regard to David.

"What was wrong with him?" Michael asks next. "Why was he naked?"

"I feel like that's the one question you *should* know the answer to," Liss comments dryly.

"The temple... The ritual..." *Where do I start?* "It's the same trance he fell into after he was resurrected."

"The one where he slaughtered a room full of people?!" Piper asks with panic in her voice.

"What the hell did you let that guy do to my brother?" Michael shouts at me through the bars that separate our cells.

"I had nothing to do with this!" *I didn't the first time either, for that matter!*

Before we can continue yelling, more people rush downstairs—guards, including Captain Foster. As Foster continues toward the other door, the other four guards lag behind, stopping to catch their breaths. Or maybe just stalling.

"What are you doing!?" he shouts at them. "We have to protect the prince!"

"How? You saw how he tore through everyone upstairs." The man points upward.

"I'm not getting paid enough for this," a female guard, one of the first I've seen, wheezes.

"You need to let me out," I tell Foster before he has a chance to take off.

"What I need to do is stop that *thing* before he hurts the prince!" He points at the door, his men already moving toward it.

"Which *I* can actually do." I point at myself. "So unless you want to crown a dead prince tomorrow, you need to let me out *now*."

With a frustrated grunt, Foster grabs the ring of keys on his belt, stomping to my cell and unlocking it while his subordinates look on. He only allows me out before relocking it, and as soon as my cuffs are off I run for the door Calvinson and David ran through. Foster and the other guards are following me, with no time to waste.

This room, or rather hallway, is much more poorly lit than the dungeons, with the torches placed very sparsely on the walls. Some of them aren't even lit. The hall stretches on for some distance before bending to the left. It's the only way David could have gone, but all that greets me when I turn the corner is an even longer hallway.

At least I think I can make out David chasing Calvinson in the distance, though catching up is a different story. I can hear them as well, though that is mostly Calvinson's sounds of terror. The hall seems to stretch forever, far longer than the length of the castle. I have passed a total of zero doors, and seeing as we are underground, this is really more of a tunnel than a hallway. But to where?

I notice the change in smell first, like an animal. Several of them, as well as a few more unpleasant scents. The end tunnel opens up into a dark room filled with rows and rows of cages and cells. I quickly lose sight of David in the maze, but Calvinson is still easy to track by sound. Foster and the others are somewhere behind me, completely in the dark.

Most of the cells look empty as I pass them, though a few are occupied by some very miserable looking people. I don't have time to examine anything closely, though I do find the animal cages. *Are those lions? What is this man doing down here?*

The sound of someone choking is what finally leads me to David and Calvinson. David has the other man by the throat against the wall, fury radiating off of him in waves. Calvinson is frantically hitting and pulling at David's arm, his face already turning red from the lack of oxygen.

"David, stop!" I call out as the guards finally catch up with us.

"Απείλησε να σκοτώσει εσένα και τον αδερφό μου;" he growls back, and I have no idea what that means.

"He's choking him!" Foster points out, though he and the others are far too frightened to actually approach and do anything to help.

"Don't. You won't stand a chance," I warn, trying to spare them David's wrath. "David, please," I plead, stepping closer. "You have to let him go."

"Γιατί προσπαθείς να τον βοηθήσεις; Θα σε σκότωνε! Να σας σκοτώσω όλους;" He is speaking that strange language again, just like in the temple.

"You don't want to do this," I continue, as he still seems to understand me fine. "This isn't you. Come back to me, puppy."

I can see the fingers around Calvinson's throat twitch, and just as I start to wonder if I will have to try and physically remove them myself, David's whole arm starts to shake before, with a frustrated grunt, he releases the other man, letting him fall to the floor. When Calvinson hits the ground, I have the sudden idea to grab the man and use him as bargaining chip to free me and the others. Then I see David start to stumble, and I drop that idea without hesitation to rush forward and catch him when he collapses. *Unconscious like last time, though hopefully not for four days.*

On the floor, Calvinson gasps deep lungfuls of air before having a coughing fit, his own hand coming up to clutch his bruised throat. With David safely in my arms, Foster and one of the other guards come forward to help their "prince" stand up. They then attempt to help him straighten his clothes, but he swats their hands away, looking furious.

"Sir, I am so sorry," Foster starts, glaring at his subordinates, who quickly attempt to fall in line.

"Is this what you and your men have been spending all that time 'training' for?" Calvinson asks, his voice hoarse. "To *not* be able to protect me?!"

"We had no way of knowing that he was capable..." Foster tries to explain before trailing off after Calvinson gives him an angry look. "I will double the guards' training sessions immediately."

"See that you do," Calvinson orders raspily, then turns to look at me, or more specifically, the naked and unconscious man in my arms.

"What did you do to him?" I growl accusingly.

"What did *I* do to *him*?!" he croaks out, furiously gesturing to his bruised neck.

"The last time he acted like that was right after somebody *murdered* him," I grit out. "So again I ask, *what did you do to him?*"

Calvinson narrows his eyes at me. "Captain, I want that one brought back up to my bedchamber." He points to David.

"Sir?" Foster looks alarmed and confused. "I am not sure that is safe."

"Not to worry." He finishes straightening his own clothes. "Contact Dr. Cromwell, and also the enchanter from town, the one who helped with our 'special project.' After my injuries are taken care of, it should not be too difficult to... hobble some of those talents, with the right magic."

"Why would I even *consider* handing him back over to you?" I clutch David to my chest. *What does he mean by "hobble?"*

"Because you have no weapons, no allies, and your friends are still in a cell under my castle?" As Calvinson speaks, the guards catch onto his words and finally pull out their swords, surrounding me.

"And what should we do with him, sir?" Foster asks, referring to me.

"Well seeing as we are already down here, I think we may have found another challenger for coronation day." He smiles at me sinisterly. "Throw him in a cell. I'll deal with his friends once I can actually speak again."

I understand where we are now: under the coliseum. The guards close in, holding me at swordpoint and wrestling away David's unconscious body. I watch angrily as he is carried away by two of the guards with Calvinson following. I do not know how he intends to hinder David's abilities, but I can only hope that it doesn't work.

I still have no idea what even happened to cause him to attack like that, except to guess that Calvinson did something to enrage him. *Is anger the trigger?* David was ready to kill him. As Foster and the other guards start shoving me toward my new cell, I wonder if I should have let him. *No, he never would have forgiven himself.*

"Khazak?" A familiar voice calls out on my left as I am marched forward.

"Kignun?" I turn my head in shock to see Kignun Hazatin, a dwarf and ranger from V'rok'sh Tah'lj, locked in a cage.

"<What are you doing here?>" he asks me in Atasi so that our captors will not understand.

"<What are *you* doing here?>" He should have reached Manamequohi by now.

"<I rode into town less than a week ago.>" His voice sounds like he has been through hell. "<I got into an argument with a guard, and they arrested me for 'disturbing the peace' and threw me down here.>"

"<For what? Why are they keeping you here? When are they releasing you?>" *Are they running a prison down here?*

"Hey, shut up!" one of the guards behind me shouts with a particularly rough shove.

"<I do not know. They will not say. Most of the others locked up here have the same story as me. Aside from the animals.>" Kignun continues before I am led farther away. "<Whatever they are planning, it is not good.>"

"I said *shut up!*" the guard shouts at the dwarf.

I am shoved into my own cell after that, though unlike Hazatin's, mine is a room with four stone walls rather than a barred cage. The only way in and out of the room is a large metal door with a small barred window at the top and a strange looking indentation on the bottom. It is also the only way for light to enter, and since the outside room is already poorly lit, the room is very, very dark. There is no furniture, though I do have a bucket now. I am not sure that qualifies as an upgrade.

After being walked halfway around it, I know that the room outside is circular, confirming to me that we are in fact under the arena. The far wall, as well as the center "column," both have doors for more rooms like mine, and the space between is filled with rows of barred cells like the one holding Hazatin.

Some of them are smaller, more like cages on wheels, which seem to be filled with animals, like the lion I saw earlier. I can see more cells from my door's window, along with other creatures, like a giant bird with two long legs and a longer neck, and another large feline with orange fur covered in dark stripes. *Is this a prison or a zoo?*

I slam the bottom of my fist against the metal door, the loud *bang* spooking several of the animals outside my cell. I lean back against the wall and sink to the floor of the dark room. How did everything become so hopeless so fast? It was only a few days ago when the worst thing I had to worry about was someone walking in on me and David having sex in the forest. Now I am stuck in a locked room while that bastard does spirits-know-what to my lover and his friends.

My stomach ties itself into knots thinking about Calvinson "hobbling" David. How does he plan on doing that? I am not positive, but David's abilities are not exactly magical in origin—he may have received them from a magical ritual, but he is not casting a spell himself, so anti-magic bracers or an anti-magic field would have no effect. There was mention of an enchanter, who could theoretically sap his strength, but it can be dangerous to make changes like that to someone's body long term, and I doubt Calvinson is planning on releasing him any time soon. And I cannot even begin to wrap my head around whatever that "special project" he mentioned might be.

And what about the others and myself? What is he going to do with the rest of us? Maybe a cell like mine is in their future, but that still does not explain what he is holding us here for. Not just us, but all the others he is keeping locked up. Staring at the stone wall, I recall when David's fist went through the wall near our first cell. *Maybe...* I stand and face the wall I share with the outside room. I am not as strong as David was, but if these walls are hollow... I start to pull back my fist.

"I wouldn't do that if I were you." I look up to see Robin on the other side of the door. "These walls are a lot more solid than that cheap hollow crap in the castle."

"What are you doing here?" I approach the door.

"I'm not here for *you*." He rolls his eyes, walking away from me and toward a caged lion. "I'm just visiting my friends."

"I do not suppose you would be willing to help me out of this cell?" I try to appeal for his assistance.

"Like you helped me?" He rolls his eyes. "Pass."

"I am sorry, but we spoke to the person you wanted us to anyway and still wound up locked in a cell." He ignores me, sticking his hand in the cage to stroke over the lion's paw. "This is pointless." I shake my head and start to walk away from the door.

"Even if I could help you out, what do you want me to do?" He's still petting the lion, who has moved closer to the cage's side. "Iron doors, iron bars, iron locks; I can't even help my *actual* friends out of here."

"What is he doing with all these animals?" *I may at least try and get some information out of him.*

"I'm not really sure." He frowns, still petting the lion. "They don't belong here. They're so far away from their homes. And this isn't even all of them. He's got some sort of zoo set up in one of the castle courtyards." His voice drips with disdain. "I think those are his favorites. They're treated a little better, I guess. That's where your wolf is. But down here, the cages are too small, they're barely fed enough, and there's no sunlight. I even feel bad for the *people* down here, and I can't stand most of you."

"Thank you for telling me about Sona." *At least I know she is alive.* "How many people are down here?" I only saw a handful as I was brought to my cell.

"A dozen? Maybe more?" He shrugs.

"Why are they being held at all?" Hazatin said the reason they gave for his arrest was "disturbing the peace."

"I dunno. It's not like I've actually tried to talk to any of them." He rolls his eyes. "...I *did* notice one thing, though."

"What is that?" I lean against the door, waiting for him to continue.

"None of them are Lutherians." He bites his lip. "They're all people from other nearby cities, who were just passing through."

"*Wonderful*," I say with a sigh. That is exactly what I was worried about. "I suppose we can add racism to the 'prince's' list of crimes."

"Why, are you gonna do something about it?" He huffs and turns away, clearly still upset at us for turning down his request for help earlier. "At least *these* people can get your sympathy."

"Robin... I am sorry did not help you before," I apologize to the fae, largely out of hope that he will help us. "Even if we could not do anything right now, we could have promised to come back, or send someone else who could help. We were panicking that the Blackbriar guild would catch up to us...which they did."

"It's okay," he admits with a small sigh, though he is still paying more attention to his lion friend than me. "I know I was asking for a lot, and you barely know me. Plus you got arrested like, *immediately*."

"The last few days have been very trying," I admit, happy to have garnered some sympathy. "We are only—"

The sound of a door slamming shut cuts me off.

"Someone's coming." Robin looks around panicked. "I have to go."

"Wait!" I stop him before he has a chance to disappear. "I know you cannot help me, but can you find David and make sure he is alright? I am worried about what Calvinson is planning to do to him."

"Okay, I can do that." He nods, and with a final wave, vanishes into nothingness.

"Get your fucking hands off me!" Liss's familiar voice rings through the circular room before I see her being marched forward by two guards, followed closely by Adam and another two guards.

"Liss, Adam?" I call out as they are led past my cell.

"Khazak?" Adam looks over at me, surprised. "What happened? Calvinson and his guards walked in with a knocked-out David before separating me and Liss from the others."

"Calvinson went back on his deal." I can hear an unsurprised huff from Liss. "I do not know what—"

"Hey, shut up in there!" a guard shouts at me while slamming his fist against the metal door with a *bang*.

"We will find a way out of this!" I try to assure them, no longer in my line of sight. *I am not sure even I believed that.*

I can hear the sounds of cells being unlocked and then closed in the distance but have no idea where exactly Liss and Adam have been locked up. Why did they only bring in those two, and what are they doing with all of the others? The fact that they are keeping everyone separated down here cannot be a coincidence.

A moment later, a familiar face steps up to the window of my door—Calvinson.

"What do *you* want?" I glare at the man through the bars.

"Just wanted to make sure you were settling in alright," he jokes cockily.

"Why are you doing this?" It's mostly a rhetorical question. The man is clearly insane and compensating for something. "What are you doing with David?"

"Come now. Is what I'm doing with him really all that different from you?" He tries to sound perfectly reasonable.

"Yes!" I almost shout the obvious answer.

"Really? So you didn't take advantage of him by forcing him into bondage after beating him in a fight he was tricked into?" He says it as though he has caught me in a lie. "I know *all* about your journey together so far."

"If you hurt him, I will *kill you*," I growl, my hands clenching into fists.

He rolls his eyes at my threat. "The way I see it, Khazak, you and I are the same kind of monster. I'm just much better looking."

"I am *nothing* like you," I spit out. *First Michael and now him?*

"You're right. I'm also not the one locked in a cell," Calvinson tells me with a sneer. "Better rest up. You're going to need the energy for tomorrow."

"What happens tomorrow?" *Besides more of this mess.*

"My coronation," he answers ominously before walking away, leaving me.

I sit back down in my dark cell, unable to do anything for myself or the others and our predicament. Without being able to see the sky, I have no clue what time it is, other than the middle of the night. Eventually, I manage to fall asleep, leaning on my side against the wall, a ball of stress and worry growing in my stomach.

Chapter 13

"<Do you always have your boy here modeling the underwear?>" *Brull's new customer asks at the store's counter.*

*"<Oh, the avakesh is not mine.>" Brull shakes his head. "<He
belongs to this man.>"*

*"<Just having him try on a few new things.>" I pat the pile of
underwear next to me.*

*"<Really? You should consider hiring him,>" he tells Brull, then
looks at me. "<He has me considering trying some on.>"*

*"<I think he might still be a little too new for something like
that,>" I say with a smile. "<But perhaps we could arrange a private showing sometime.>"*

*We all have a little laugh as Brull starts to add up the cost of my
purchases. There is a lot between the underwear, toys, harness, boots,
and collar, but it is all worth it. David looked fantastic in everything,
even if he does not think so yet. But I have plenty of time to convince
him otherwise.*

*"<Alright, all together that will be...>" Brull's voice trails off, his
gaze somewhere behind me as his eyes go wide. "<Shit.>"*

*I turn to see what the problem is, only to find David gone. The
shop's open front door is only meters away from where he was standing.
It would have been very easy for him to slip out unnoticed. Shit indeed.*

"<I teased him too much.>" Brull sighs, looking disappointed.

"<No, it is my fault. >" I shake my head. "<I have pushed him a lot in the past twenty-four hours. >"

"<Come on, we have to go after him. >" Brull rounds the counter.

"<Go left. I am going to take the back door. >" I nod toward his back room. "<Meet me in the alley. I have a feeling we can cut him off. >"

Knowing what I do about him so far, David will try to get off of a public street as soon as possible, and the alley that runs behind Brull's shop would be the closest option. I am upset, but more with myself than David. I should have known our little underwear show would be too much. I will have to think of a gentler way to correct his behavior once we find him.

"What the hell is this?" I ask after picking up the flimsy piece of cloth and fur from the floor.

"Your uniform," the guard on the other side of my cell's door tells me.

"I am supposed to *wear* this?" I turn it over in my hand, seeing it is little more than a loincloth. "I am not sure it will even fit."

"Whatever." He shakes his head before turning away from my door. "Just have it on by the time I come back."

I toss the *garment* against the wall, ignoring the guilty feelings the memory of David's underwear show stirs up. I have been awake for several hours, doing little more than staring at the wall and listening. They have given me more bread and water, but I would kill for some meat right now. Orc diets require more protein than other species, so I've really only eaten enough to stave off hunger pangs. Outside of my room, several of the smaller cages cells were moved, the animals within growling their complaints as they were taken somewhere else. I also heard the occasional growl of what sounds like a much larger beast somewhere farther away.

Above me, a crowd that has been steadily increasing for the last hour is filling the colosseum's seats for the coronation. I still do not know what exactly Calvinson has planned, but given our location, it is easy to assume that a battle may be involved. One in which I am sure to be at a disadvantage, given the "uniform" I was given.

With nothing else to do, I try to think of a plan for when the guard returns to retrieve me. If there is more than one, overpowering them will not be easy, as I have very little to work with. But I have to think of something, a way to rescue David and the others, and—

"There you are!" A voice I did not expect to hear, possibly ever again, has me looking toward the door.

"Nathaniel?" I step forward. "What are you doing here?"

"What do you mean?" He holds up a large ring of keys. "I'm here to bust you out."

"You are?" I try not to sound shocked.

"Of course," he continues, confused. "Why else do you think I agreed to work for Calvinson?"

"Well..." I trail off, not wanting to spell out that the group assumed his betrayal.

"You all thought I was really abandoning you," he says, dumbfounded, having come to that realization. "I only said yes because I figured if I wasn't locked up with the rest of you, I might actually be able to help."

"I think given your recent track record, none of us anticipated your words being a ruse," I tell him honestly, hopeful that he will not change his mind and leave me here.

"I guess I deserve that," he replies with a sigh. "Let's get out of here."

"Where did you get those?" I ask as he starts trying individual keys on my lock.

"It wasn't easy," he answers, trying another key. "Calvinson had two guards posted outside of my door all night, and they were following me around this morning, too."

"How did you manage to get away with their keys?" It makes sense that Calvinson would not trust him either.

"I kind of...knocked them out with magic and then put their bodies in a broom closet." He blurts out the second part of his sentence. "So we need to move fast."

He manages to try three more keys before I hear a door opening in the distance.

"You have to hide," I tell him quickly, gesturing in the direction of the sound. "Someone is coming."

"But what about you?" He looks where I pointed nervously.

"I will be fine, for now," I tell him and hope I am not lying. "Adam and Elisabeth are somewhere down here as well. Free them and then find the others. Then you can worry about me."

"Okay." He doesn't seem to like that plan but nods and turns to find a hiding place nonetheless.

"I thought I told you to get dressed?" The guard who dropped off the loincloth scowls as he looks into my cell. "Put it on."

"No," I answer flatly, crossing my arms.

"Just put it on, man," a second guard behind him implores. "We can't let you out until you do."

"How wonderful to be so dedicated to your craft." I roll my eyes, still not moving.

"We're supposed to threaten you until you do," the third guard tells me frankly. "So just...do it and make this easier for all of us, okay buddy?"

Despite the casual tone the words are said in, all three guards reach for their swords. My hands clench, and I glare at the piece of clothing on the floor. *Am I really going to...*

Godsdamnit. With a huff, I bend over and snatch the loincloth from the ground. Before I can second-guess myself, I start stripping, forcing two of the guards watching me through the window to turn away. *Because* they *are the ones who should be embarrassed...*

Once I am naked, putting on the loincloth is no easy task. It has ties that meet at my hips, and the shape forces me to check which side is the front before I attach them. There is a small pouch that is supposed to house my "package," as David would call it, with a flap over the front of the garment's "belt" that does a poor job of hiding the bulge underneath, and a flap on the back that does an even poorer job of covering my ass. I have never thought of myself as someone with body image issues, but this is making me feel a little self-conscious about my weight.

"There. Happy?" I ask once I am done adjusting things, reaching for my boots to start putting them back on.

"Better." The first guard nods. "Leave the shoes."

"What?" I look down at my naked feet. "Why?"

"Because I said so." The same guard makes it sound like he is arguing with a toddler. "My orders say you're not supposed to be in anything but the loincloth. So no boots."

I leave them as requested with plenty of grumbling, setting my boots and the rest of my clothing in a pile in a corner of the room—opposite the one with the bucket.

"Great." The guard is happy to be finished with that. "Now, put your chest against the far wall and your hands behind your back so we can cuff you again."

"I don't need to tell you what happens if you try anything, right?" The third guard says, sword already drawn.

I roll my eyes instead of answering and move into the position requested, pressing my chest to the wall and moving my arms to my back. I hear the lock on the metal door click before it *screeches* open and the guards cautiously enter. I growl when one of them blindly reaches for my wrist to attach the cuff and misses and grabs my ass, making him yelp in fear. After they finally manage to get the manacles around my wrists, they step back and out of the room.

"Okay, you can turn around," guard number one tells me, and I lift off of the wall. "Now, you're gonna walk out of that cell and come with us. You move exactly where we tell you, or else."

"Understood." I roll my eyes again. I wish I were as dangerous as they seem to think.

"Alright, come on." Guard number three points at the ground after all three step back to clear a space for me.

"Donaldson, you go in front," guard one tells guard two.

"What?! Why do I have to take the lead?" he squawks back.

"Just do it!" guard three implores. "If we're the reason this thing starts late, we're all getting thrown in a cell."

"Fine." Donaldson huffs, turns, and starts to walk away.

"Follow him," guard one orders. "The two of us will be right behind you."

At least I can take some amusement in their fear of me. *Especially in this outfit.* I follow the guard ahead of me, who nervously looks back over his shoulder every few seconds. He leads me around the outer edge of the circular room to a ramp to the ground floor, where just as I suspected, the cages containing the animals were moved.

"Khazak!" Adam calls out as we unexpectedly pass his cell just as I start to climb the slope.

"Adam!" I yell back even louder, intending to alert Nathaniel to his location.

"Keep moving!" Guard three shoves me forward. "Why are they always doing that?"

I am led up the ramp to a similar looking if not slightly smaller room located right under the colosseum's audience. There's more light, thanks to the large wooden gates along the inner walls leading outside. I can hear the stomping of people's feet as they walk to their seats. Do they have any idea what is going on beneath them? Around me, I can see a row of lion cages lined up against the far wall. The man I am following takes an immediate left toward the nearest gate, where three other men are waiting.

"This is it?" The man standing at the center of the gate asks as we approach.

"Yep," Donaldson confirms with a nod as the others close in behind me.

"Alright." The man looks me over briefly. "Let's get him out there."

The center guard gestures to the other two to open the gate, which has to be done manually. As the gate swings open, I see the open field ahead of us, a round, even patch of dirt. The ceiling of the tunnel out is low, with the stone walls of the arena appearing equally low. Low enough that I could probably climb over them...

The man starts to lead the way out but stops after taking a single step. "Don't forget the—"

"I got it," the first of my original guards says as he reaches for a spear leaning against the stone wall.

I can feel my heart start to beat faster as I am finally brought outside, suddenly worried this is an execution. I can barely even hear the noises from the crowd at my appearance, a small smattering of cheers and boos, but most people just seem confused. I do not have the time to wonder if I should be offended, too worried that I am about to be impaled to death.

I'm brought toward a set of chains on the ground, both attached to a metal hook embedded within the earth. They make me stand in place over it, and I jump when the guard carrying the spear plants it in the ground at my side, pointing down. On the chains underneath me, each chain has a cuff attached, which are latched to my wrists. As the first set of cuffs linking my wrists together is removed, I feel my magic return to me—the new set is not anti-magic.

After triple-checking my bonds, all of the guards make a quick exit back inside the gate, leaving the spear in the ground next to me. I breathe a sigh of relief—not an execution then. Still, that leaves me here alone in the center of the arena with *hundreds* of curious faces watching on. There are more people here than there were at me and David's *Nagul Uzugor*. Red and purple banners are held high on wooden poles, each bearing Calvinson's monogrammed initials.

A series of horns blares out, the signal sending the crowd into an uproar. I follow their eyes to another part of the audience, a section that is higher than the rest with walls on all sides. Several guards are placed along the edge, with two chairs at the center beneath a fabric awning providing shade. Once the horns are finished, a familiar-looking man steps out of a door behind the seats, the same one who made the announcements in the throne room. He walks to the edge and brings a megaphone up to his mouth.

"Presenting," the man starts, his voice amplified by the magic bullhorn, "His Royal Highness, Prince Richard Gregory Calvinson III, and his new consort!"

New consort? The crowd breaks into cheers at the announcement, the doors opening again to reveal Calvinson...and David. The crowd is just as confused at his appearance as I am, which isn't helped at all by his clothing. Calvinson is dressed in his usual finery, but David is barely wearing more than myself. He has a loincloth of his own, red and long, extending much farther down, the fabric billowing slightly in the breeze. His chest is bare, and from here I can see some sort of marks along his collarbone. He also still has my collar around his neck, which I am pleased but confused by—I would have expected Calvinson to have removed that right away.

As the two of them walk to their seats, I notice that something is off with David. His movements are unsteady, and he almost clumsily falls out of his seat when he tries to sit down. There's a smile on his face, but his eyes seem unfocused, flitting between the people in the crowd, Calvinson, and the guards around them. *Is he drunk?* I glare at Calvinson, who watches me with an evil smile on his face, reaching over to pet a hand along my pup's exposed thigh.

"We would like to welcome you all to the inaugural Richardton Gladiatorial Games!" The horns trumpet again at the man's words, once more riling up the crowd. "We have prepared a number of exciting combat exhibitions for you all. At the conclusion of the games, the coronation ceremony will be held, and our prince will be crowned our new king! Guards, bring out the first round of gladiators!"

The horns blare and the crowd cheers as the wooden gate on the opposite side of the coliseum is opened. Six men are shoved out, four humans, an elf, and a dwarf—Kignun. Just as Robin suggested, none of them look Lutherian, almost certainly citizens of a neighboring village. They all look tired, and probably hungry too, assuming they have been treated the same way I have. They also look confused, wielding short swords and dressed in leather armor that is oddly revealing, almost like a costume, though still not nearly as revealing as mine. The guards behind them block any potential exit, forcing them onto the field with me while the gate closes.

"The first gladiator to slay the green beast will earn his freedom!" *Green beast!?* "Begin!"

As the horns signal the start of the "match," the shackles on my wrists hum with magical energy before opening of their own accord and falling to the ground. My wrists free,

I look at the spear in the ground at my side. I am surprised they would give me a fighting chance, though I suppose it would not be very interesting to watch otherwise.

Kignun and I share a look of exasperation. All any of the others can do is stand there looking puzzled, likely because most of them have never been thrown into a fighting ring and told to fight. I am sure even David received more information than this when we had our own bout in the arena. The energy of the audience dies down at our inaction, clearly expecting more to happen than this.

"I hope you all realize we can simply choose not to do this," I shout at the men across the field, making no attempt to reach for my weapon.

Proving my point, Kignun drops his sword to the ground, standing defiantly with his arms crossed. While some people in the audience begin to jeer, the elf and human at his sides look at him, then myself, and do the same thing. The other three humans, however, continue to anxiously clench their weapons. Then, with an angry yell, one charges at me.

The man is not a warrior, his form all wrong, running with his sword held over his head. I sigh, not wanting to do what has to happen next, but having no other choice. I side-step the man and pull the spear from the ground, using the blunt end to trip him as he passes me. Tumbling to the ground, he loses his grip on the sword, and I take the opportunity to kick it away.

"Stay down," I tell him before planting the spear back in the dirt and turning back to the others.

My quick thinking with the spear earns me some cheers from the audience, but those quickly die down when they see we are back to a stand-off. After seeing what I did to their friend, the other two men quickly throw their swords on the ground and join Kignun and the others in refusing to fight. The boos start up quickly, some people throwing bits of bread and other food into the arena.

I look up at Calvinson with a smirk, pleased that I have ruined his plans. His face is tight, but I can see his hands clenched on the armrests of his seat. He angrily calls over his man-in-waiting, animatedly saying something that makes the other man go still, before switching to speak with Captain Foster. That man looks equally nervous, nodding before he disappears through the doors behind them to take care of whatever it is Calvinson has requested next.

I get my answer a few minutes later when the gates behind the would-be gladiators open again. But other than the two people pushing it open, all I see is a row of cages. Six of them, containing lions. After the two men scurry back inside, the cages are pushed forward and onto the field. *What are they...?*

"Over here, quickly!" I shout to the other men, some of whom have already retreated to my side when the beasts first made their appearance.

Unfortunately, most of them forget their weapons, though Kignun manages to grab two swords before joining me at my side. I help the man I tripped stand, the seven of us standing together as the carts come to a stop. The animals inside appear restless, agitated, and hungry. The audience, however, is extremely happy to see them, roaring in approval.

"As these so-called warriors have regretfully chosen not to fight, we are moving on to the next exciting match of the evening," the well-dressed man announces. "Man versus beast!"

"What the hell are they thinking?!" Kignun asks me, gripping his sword tightly.

"They are not thinking at all," I reply as I watch in horror as the gates on each of the cages are lifted with magic.

As the lions stalk out, fear and worry fill my chest. That fear is not just for myself or the others here on the arena floor, but for the entire crowd. I am no expert on lions, but I have had run-ins with bobcats and the occasional cougar, and I know that if there are two things big cats are good at, it is jumping and climbing. The lion farthest on my left moves toward the arena's edge, drawn in by some of the thrown food. As the nearby crowd watches with excitement, I realize these people have no idea how much danger they are in.

"We have to calm them before they hurt someone," I tell Kignun without taking my eyes off the predators.

"Are any of you a druid?" Kignun asks the other four men. "Or can use nature magic? Any magic at all?"

Everyone shakes their head, meaning I am the only one with said magic at my disposal. I am glad that they took off the anti-magic bracers, but this is still far beyond my capabilities. I might be able to calm one animal, but six? I step forward, hand outstretched to draw their attention as I attempt a casting.

I try and focus on a single lion, the one that is closest, trying to link my aura to theirs. When we finally connect, I feel a rush of anger flood my mind at being taken, caged, and starved. I do my best to try to push past that anger with my own feelings of calm and peacefulness, but it is difficult. As soon as I make some headway, the next lion on his right stalks forward, forcing me to switch my focus. I might be able to calm them now, but if any of these creatures decide to start acting on their feelings, it will be impossible for me to do anything to change their minds.

"Khazak!" I look behind me to see Adam's face through the slates in the gate, Elisabeth at his side.

"Perfect timing," I tell them before turning back to the pride of hungry lions.

"Unless any of you wants to stay and help, make your exit now," Kignun tells his fellow captives as the gate opens enough for Adam and Liss to slip out. All of them do.

"Where is Nathaniel?" I ask when Adam steps up to my right, and I see now that he is wearing a similar costume to Hazatin and the others.

"We showed him the tunnel back to the castle so he could free the others," he tells me quickly. "How did you both manage to get out here?"

"Punched first, asked questions later," Liss comments on my left, still in her original armor. "I can't believe they got you to wear that."

"When Nate and I found her, she was using her costume to choke one of the guards through the window on her cell's door. Made it a lot easier to knock the rest out," Adam adds as he watches the cats nervously. "What exactly are we doing here?"

"Trying to stop them from attacking anyone." As I tell him, the lion on the outskirts starts to crouch down, readying herself for a leap into the stands.

I let out a roar, the best imitation of a bobcat that I can muster. It serves its purpose, drawing the cat's attention away from the crowd and onto myself, but it undoes nearly all the progress I've made with the others. They are once again agitated, watching us as they prowl back and forth.

"So this seems bad," Elisabeth comments from my left. "Maybe we should bail?"

"If we leave, there is nothing to stop them from jumping into the crowd." Hazatin shakes his head. "Idiots don't even realize."

I spare a glance up to the box with Calvinson and David. Calvinson looks angry, no doubt because we have continued to spoil his fun. David still looks like he is drunk or high, or both, with no idea about what is actually going on. I have not been paying them much attention, but as much tension as the lions have brought to the field, the crowd still seems a little bored.

A snarl from one of the lions draws my attention back. I don't think I will be able to stop them completely, but if I can just hold on long enough for—

Another, deeper, and much louder growl emanates from behind the north arena gate to our left. It gets everyone's attention, even the lions, many of whom react with *fear* and scurry back behind their brethren. As the gate opens, a single cage is pushed out, containing a hulking mass of a creature. It is covered head to toe in black fur, thick muscles rippling across its entire body. With sharp claws on its hands and feet, and its canine looking head, it is impossible not to know what this creature is.

"Is that a...?" Adam starts.

"Werewolf," I finish.

"It's the middle of the afternoon!" Liss exclaims, pointing at the sun in the sky.

"Some werewolves are able to shift even during the day," Kignun explains, readying his weapon. "But they usually have to be very in control of themselves to do that... I think there is something wrong with this wolfman."

He is certainly a man, his cock and balls hanging between his legs as visible as a black rabbit in snow. From the way he is crouched over, he must be nearly two and a half meters tall. I can see what look like burn marks wrapped around his limbs and torso, like they were caused by a chain or rope. It is impossible to read anything other than rage on his face, and if I were not certain about this man being held captive and tortured here, I might think he was rabid.

A sudden growl on my right brings my attention back to the other danger at hand: the lions. While most of them are too preoccupied being afraid of the werewolf, the others have not taken kindly to the fact that we now seem to be encroaching on what little territory they had. My eyes flick back and forth between the two, trying to decide what to do next. I am not even sure if my abilities would work on the werewolf, so I will have to focus on the lions, but if help does not arrive soon, retreating back inside may be our only option.

"I got 'em, big guy." *Thank the Three!* I sag in relief when I hear Riley's now-familiar voice as he and our other friends run out into the arena. "Holy shit, is that a fuckin' *werewolf?*"

At Riley's exclamation, the werewolf slashes his claws against the bars of his cage with a roar. Not even a second later, the door on the cage starts to lift. With my internal alarms blaring, I look up into the crowd, catching the sadistic grin on Calvinson's face before the werewolf leaps from his prison, landing with a roar and sending the entire arena into chaos.

Chapter 14

The werewolf's roar sends the lions into a full-blown panic. A few cower and run for cover behind their abandoned cages, but it's the two that turn toward the audience that have me the most worried. The people in the stands above them barely have time to register the danger when both lions leap up, their claws catching on the ledge as they try to escape the danger behind them.

That sends the *audience* into a full-blown panic, everyone screaming as they scramble for the exits. All the noise and commotion draws the attention of the werewolf, who turns toward the crowd to find dozens and dozens of new targets trying to flee. The spectators finally understand the level of danger they are in, but in their terror, I have no doubt that even more people will be injured.

There is no visible response from any of the Richardton guards. In fact, when I look through the stands, I see several of them fleeing along with the citizens. Calvinson looks frozen in his seat as the chaos and destruction unfolds before him, while at his side David is smiling and swaying his head to music that only he seems to hear. Finally, at the urging of Captain Foster and his footman, Calvinson stands, barely remembering to grab David as they are ushered through the door for safety. My blood boils with anger as he makes his exit. *He is not getting away.*

"Adam, Calvinson is escaping. I have to go after David," I inform the man of my intentions, prepared to leave whether I have his blessing or not.

"I'm going with you," Michael says without a hint of animosity.

"Go get our boy back." Adam nods in the direction of the fleeing Calvinson.

"Wait!" Nathaniel calls out before we can leave, handing me the ring of keys he stole from the guards. "Those should help. The cuffs the guards all carry use the same key, this small silver one." He points out the universal cuff key before returning to Adam and the others.

"Riley, do what you can to get those lions in check. Tsula, I want you to help anyone trapped in the crowd while Corrine focuses on healing the injured," Adam hands out the orders. "The rest of us will worry about keeping the werewolf occupied. You're sure that's a person?" He directs his question to Kignun.

"Yes, somewhere in there," the dwarf confirms.

"Okay then, that means we try not to kill him." Adam nods to himself. "Let's go!"

With that, we break and rush toward our respective assignments. My focus is now solely on the door that Calvinson absconded through with David. I don't slow down as I approach the arena wall, using my momentum to jump and grab the lip of the wall and pull myself up. I turn around to help Michael up behind me, but before I can, he jumps, thrusting both of his palms down and expelling a magical force that sends him flying through the air to land next to me in the stands.

The people around us panic at our sudden appearance, but most are already running for the exits. Calvinson's private box is up ahead and will require some climbing to get to. We move through the rows of seats, Michael right behind me, when an armor-clad man decides to step into our path.

"Not so fast, monster!" a guard, who has apparently decided to play hero, shouts on my left. "You're not going to... AAAHH!"

The man is blasted in the chest by a green bolt of arcane energy, sending his body crashing backward into the stands.

"Keep moving," Michael tells me from behind, eyes and hand still glowing green. "I've got your back."

Good to see that neither of us is holding back. With a nod, I continue forward, stepping over the guard's prone body. When we reach the wall that raises Calvinson's box above the rest, I step onto the rampart along the back of the coliseum to get the height needed to reach up. Michael uses his jumping spell again, and I help pull him the rest of the way up after he grabs the edge of the box.

We rush through Calvinson's escape door to find...a staircase leading down. Following that brings us to another door, which leads out under the coliseum, right where I started. I look left and right, seeing no signs of the escaping Calvinson, David, or any of his guards. Frustrated, I slam the bottom of my fist against the wall with a growl.

"Over here!" Robin's voice calls out from deeper in the arena's catacombs.

"Isn't that the fairy kid who robbed us?" Michael points at his figure in the distance.

"Yes." I hurry toward the boy, who only grins and starts to lead me away.

"They went this way," he says as leads us around the circular room, coming to a stop in front of a blank section of wall. "There's a door around here somewhere."

He starts to swipe his hands along the wall, looking for a switch or trigger. I reach out and do the same, both of us feeling along the smooth stone in search of a way in. A hand on my shoulder gets me to stop.

"Move." Michael tells us both, pushing us to the side and placing both hands against the wall. "*Recludo.*"

A pulse of green light extends from his hands, sinking into the lines and cracks of the stonework and spreading out until the glowing outline of a doorway is formed. The light pulses brightly for a second before there is an audible *click*, and it dissipates. A second later, the outlined portion of wall swings inward, revealing a dark hallway running along the inside of the coliseum's outer wall.

"They went that way." Robin points to the now-open passage.

"How did you know?" *He had to have been following them to find something like this.*

"Enh, you asked if I'd watch David for you." He tries to shrug nonchalantly. "I just *happened* to catch them going this way. That's all."

"Thank you," I tell him honestly, then remember his connection with the caged lions. "You know, some of your friends from earlier are loose in the arena and could probably use your help."

"Yeah, I guess I should go keep them out of trouble." He sighs, looking toward the gate. "See ya later."

After the fairy vanishes once more, I turn to Michael. "Ready?"

"Let's go." He nods once, following me inside.

The secret passage is dim, the walls almost too narrow to run, but we press forward. My naturally enhanced vision is able to pick up on a dim source of light somewhere ahead of us, but much more prominent are the voices. One of them sounds like Captain Foster, and I start devising a plan of attack.

"I can hear them," I whisper behind me after coming to a brief stop. "I do not know how many there are, but I am going to rush forward and take down the lead guard. Can you focus on the other guards that may be with them?"

"Yeah, I can do that." Michael nods, his hands glowing softly as he prepares a spell.

We run forward, the light getting brighter and the voices growing louder. I hear Captain Foster speaking again and lock onto his voice, the man a more dangerous target than the others. His back is to us when we reach the room, allowing me to crash into him shoulder-first and smash him against the far wall with a shout of surprise.

"*Somnus!*" I hear Michael call out as he rushes past me and places his hands on Foster's prone form, taking advantage of his shocked state to put him to sleep.

There are five other people in this room with us: David, Calvinson, his footman on one side, and two guards on the other. The guards draw the swords, and I drop into a fighting stance with my own. It has been some time since I took on two armed opponents at once, but I *have* done it.

"Drop your weapons," Michael orders angrily on my right, his hands glowing bright with arcane energy. "Or I drop *you*."

To prove he is serious, he fires a bolt from one hand just to the right of the guards' heads, chiseling away some of the stone and leaving a dark scorch mark. After sharing a look of fear, both men drop their swords to the ground and raise their hands above their head.

"What the hell do you think you're doing?!" Calvinson cries at the sight of his men surrendering so quickly.

"*You!*" I growl, turning to the man responsible for this mess.

"Hi Khaz! Hi Mikey!" David with a bright smile and a happy wave just behind him.

"Hello, David," I say as calmly as possible, before closing the distance between me and Calvinson, grabbing him by the shirt collar with both hands, and slamming him into the wall. *"What did you do to him?"*

"Frederick!" He turns his head to the right to call to his footman. "Would you *do something?!*"

"I-I..." the grey-haired man stammers.

"Yes, Frederick. *Do something,*" I taunt. "Make a wager that my friend won't blow your head off as well."

The older man's eyes go wide at the threat, looking between myself, Michael, and then the floor, falling silent. Still in my grasp, Calvinson scoffs at the perceived cowardice, glaring at me in silence. When it becomes apparent that I will not be getting an answer to my question, I slam him into the wall again in frustration.

"Michael, watch him while I handcuff the guards," I say while dropping Calvinson to the floor.

"On it." The wizard aims his left hand at the man while keeping his right on the guards.

I quickly grab one of them and shove his chest against the wall. Relieving him of his cuffs, I lock his arms behind his back, then repeat this on the other man, entwining their arms so they are forced to stand back-to-back. As I bend over to do the same with the unconscious Captain Foster, Calvinson lets out another scoff, and I pause.

"Are you honestly just going to let them—?!" He is cut off when a glowing green palm is shoved in his face.

"Dude, I am literally *begging* you to give me a reason to fuck you up," Michael warns him, voice dripping with contempt.

The immediate danger passed, I take a moment to look around the room. It's small, feeling more than a little cramped with seven of us in here. There are a few chairs along the wall with a small cot in one corner, and in another is a set of shelves so tall it almost reaches the ceiling, filled with glass jars containing what looks like food and other perishables. Nothing of interest, meaning I can finally give David all my attention.

"Are you alright?" I ask while looking over his body for marks and injuries.

"Uh-huh." He nods with a smile, his eyes glassy and unfocused.

Seeing my collar around his neck soothes me, though the rest of his outfit is still completely ridiculous. I am not sure if it is less or more revealing than my own, and I probably take a little longer than necessary inspecting it to try and figure that out. He doesn't appear to be hurt, but all around his collarbone are black symbols, like a language I can't understand. That combined with his strange behavior makes me think he must be under some sort of spell or enchantment.

"What is on his neck?" I ask Michael, pointing out the markings.

"Runes of some kind," Michael informs me, looking as close as he can while keeping Calvinson in his sights. "I don't know many specifics, but there are enchanters who can use paints or dyes to apply enchantments to a person's body."

"What did you do to him?!" I repeat my question to Calvinson.

"I did what I wanted to with *my* property," the man sneers as he picks himself up from the floor.

"That isn't an answer," Michael warns him through gritted teeth.

I turn my gaze on Frederick, who is unable to meet my eyes, and I doubt the guards know anything useful.

"We don't have time for this!" I growl, frustratedly kicking over one of the chairs. "Thanks to your recklessness, your citizens are currently causing a riot as they flee for their lives from the *hungry and dangerous predators you released* while our friends are doing what they can to keep the *werewolf* I know you have been *torturing* from going on a murderous rampage! Answer me, dammit!"

"They're supposed to make him quiet and easier to handle," one of the guards surprises me by answering.

"What are you doing? Shut up," the other guard warns him to stop.

"*You* shut up," the first guard tells him with an eye roll. "I *told* you this job was too good to be true. I don't care how high the pay is. The shit they've been having us do is insane. Hell, they said this orc was supposed to be some kind of a monster, and he speaks Common better than either of us. I'm *done*." He turns back to me. "The enchanter came and painted them on him last night. He was supposed to come back today and make them permanent with a tattoo."

"You were going to *tattoo him!?*" I am once again lifting Calvinson off the ground by his clothing.

"What? Did you think I would allow something so *dangerous* arou—"

There are a few gasps and a shout of worry from Frederick when my fist connects with the side of his face before he can finish, his body crumpling in a heap. Even I am taken aback by my reaction, the burst of angry possessiveness overtaking me after hearing that he intended to mark *my* pup, *my* David, like that. *Almost.*

"Damn," Michael comments, his hands no longer glowing. "I'm kinda bummed it wasn't me."

After checking that he is still breathing, I use the final set of cuffs I find on Captain Foster to lock one of his wrists to Calvinson's, threading the chain through the slats of the cot to make things that much more difficult for him. The only person still free is Frederick, but we are out of restraints, and time. He does not strike me as a fighter, and as terrified as he is, the smart thing for him to do would be to wait here until the danger outside has passed.

"Michael, we need to get back to the others," I say as he attempts to communicate with his brother.

"Are we just going to leave David here?" Michael asks with a frown.

"He is in no condition to fight," I admit with a sigh. "I am not even sure he would realize we *were* fighting right now."

"Alright." Michael nods, hugging his brother before we have to leave, who happily hugs him back.

"David." I take both his hands, looking him directly in the eye. "It is not safe outside, so I need you to stay here until we come back, okay?"

"Okay!" he agrees with a smile and a nod.

"We will be back as soon as we can." I hug him myself and turn to leave with Michael. As soon as we start to walk away though, David tries to follow.

"Ugh." I sigh.

"What do we do?" Michael confers.

"I have an idea, but neither of us are going to like it." I take David by the shoulders and stand him in front of Frederick, who is currently kneeling on the floor next to Calvinson and attempting to lay his unconscious body in a more comfortable position. "*You.*"

He jumps at my voice, but turns around, shaking slightly in fear. "Y-yes?" he asks, his voice quaking.

"You are going to watch him and make sure he does not leave this room." I point to David, who is now inspecting the items on the shelves with interest. "If *any* of you are not here when I return, I promise that you will all suffer for it. Am I understood?"

"Y-yes, sir." The gray-haired man nods frantically, as do the guards.

"Good." I reach for David, pulling him away from the shelf. "Stay with Frederick. I will be back soon." I kiss him on the forehead after giving him another hug.

This time when David tries to follow us out, Frederick catches him by the wrist before he can leave. This does not seem to phase David, who waves goodbye with that same glassy-eyed smile that leaves me feeling cold. *I will undo whatever they have done to you, pup. I promise.* Back in the circular room under the coliseum, Michael turns and places his hand on the part of the wall that swung open, closing it with a low, "*Claudo.*"

"We make a pretty good team," Michael admits as he dusts off his hands.

"I would have to agree." I nod with a begrudging smile. "Now let's help the others."

"Have you ever fought a werewolf?" Michael asks as we head for the gate outside.

"Plenty of wolves, but no werewolves," I confess. "My friend Kignun seemed knowledgeable, so he may—"

"Hey!" Yet another familiar voice shouts for my attention, my ears leading my eyes to an arm frantically waving out of a cell window. "Over here!"

"Kez," I confirm with a sigh, the woman's face greeting us as we detour toward the cell against my better judgment. Behind her, I can see several other Briars crammed into the same small room.

"It's good to see a familiar face," she tells me in a tone that is *far* too comfortable for her to be using with either of us. "Wait, what are you wearing?"

"Is that really your most pressing question right now?" I ignore the embarrassment I still feel over my current outfit.

"You gotta help us out, man," Rax, the bulky club-wielding man implores from the cell next door.

"Yeah, we need you to let us out of here, please." She grabs the bars of her window for effect.

"Ha!" I laugh loudly in her face. "Why would we do that?"

"Because after stealing our stuff and leaving us locked in a cart like that, you owe us!" Rax insists.

"*Your* stuff?!" Michael's pitch goes high in anger. "You destroyed our entire campsite and then kidnapped us!"

A roar of anger from outside interrupts our conversation.

"Let me make something clear to all of you: we owe you *nothing*, nor will we be apologizing." I narrow my eyes at Kez. "As far as I am concerned, you can rot in here. Now if you will excuse us, we need to go help our friends."

"Wait, please," Kez calls out when we turn to leave. "I don't know what's going on out there, but we can help too. I swear."

"Why would we trust you?" Michael counters. "What's to stop you from just leaving, or going back on your word once this is over?"

"Look, what do you want from me?" Kez inquires. "Money? A favor? What do I need to do to get us out of here?"

"Are we negotiating now?" I cross my arms, considering the possibility that she might be serious.

"If that's what it's going to take," Kez accepts, completely serious.

"Alright." I stop to think through everything we require right now. "I want full assurance that the Blackbriar Guild will not be coming after anyone in my group, and that includes Nathaniel and the small creature you were after. I do not care if you say the contract was completed, or that he is dead, but *none* of us are to be your targets any longer."

"Okay." Kez nods. "I can do that."

"Are you sure about this?" Michael asks me with a side eye, unsure of whether we can trust them.

"I am," I assure him. "I am certainly not a fan of the Blackbriar Guild, but they are supposed to be good for their word."

"We are," Kez agrees. "So, the contract on Nate and the little bird-lizard will be taken care of. Is that all?"

"No," Michael jumps in, now fully into the spirit of things. "You're also going to replace the tents and bedrolls you destroyed before we leave town."

"What?!" Rax complains.

"Shut up," Kez warns him with a growl. "Fine, we'll replace your camping equipment. Anything else?"

I share a look with Michael, both of us considering what else we might ask for, but the sound of stomping of feet and cries of terror above us remind us that people are in danger.

"That is all," I tell Kez. "We have a deal?"

"Deal." She sticks her hand out through the window again, reaching for mine in an awkward attempt at a handshake.

"Alright, just a moment while I figure out which key to use." I retrieve the ring Nathaniel gave me, sighing at the amount I have to go through.

"Screw that." Michael aims a palm at the part of the wall to the right door's lock and handle. "The doors are anti-magic but the wall isn't. *Dissolvere.*"

A ray of light fires from his hand at the door, the stone surrounding the area hit disintegrating into dust and allowing the door to swing open. He repeats this on the other door, freeing both groups. Getting the bracers off everyone is a quick affair, and the mages are especially happy to be free of the anti-magic metal.

"So, what can we do?" Kez asks as she and the rest of the Briars stretch their free limbs.

A howl rings through the air, loud enough to echo through the room we are standing in and sending a chill through us all.

"Have any of you ever fought a werewolf?"

Chapter 15

With Kez and the other Briars in tow, Michael and I
rush out onto the field to find everything in disarray.
The stands are almost completely empty, save for a few
stragglers still enraptured by the terrifying action. The lion
cages have moved, some seemingly tossed onto their side,
though the two that are still upright are once again holding
lions, the metal gates closed shut. But the real point of concern is our friends and the werewolf.

They are huddled together against the far wall, beneath
a translucent purple-colored dome of light. A magical wall
of force, which from the color I would assume was cast by
Piper. The werewolf stands on the outside, continuously
attacking the dome with his claws. Each time they scrape
over the wall, purple sparks fly off, leaving a slowly fading
trail of light in its wake.

"I think your friend is hurt," Kez comments as we take
in the scene.

"Shit, that's Adam," Michael confirms.

They are right. Within the dome, I can see five figures. Piper with her arms stretched above her as she main-
tains their defenses, Nathaniel assisting by doing the same
next to her. Behind them, Kignun clutches his sword while
Adam sits on the ground with Liss kneeling by his side. He

is holding his stomach, and though it is hard to tell because of the wall's color, he appears to be bleeding.

"I'm not sure Piper can hold that for much longer," Michael adds with worry.

"We need to get him away from them," I state the obvious.

"Tak, Pim, Rax, distract it so we can get to the others," Kez orders without hesitation.

"You want me to fight that thing? Without a weapon?" Rax asks, his voice far more fearful than sarcastic.

"Len, you go instead of Rax," she orders with a sigh. "You have *got* to get over your fear of dogs."

"That thing's no dog..." Rax grumbles to himself.

We watch the three requested Briars run ahead onto the field. I recognize one as the halfling mage I kicked before being arrested, another as the dwarf woman who David tricked into following him in the forest, and the third is one of the two men we caught following us. The three move along the arena's edge, away from us and the werewolf.

As the mage begins to glow with magic, the human darts forward to grab one of the discarded swords. At the same time, the dwarf's body begins to change, growing and morphing into a large brown bear. *Another druid.* Now armed and in position, the mage fires off a bolt of energy, striking the werewolf in the back and getting him to stop his rampage against the purple dome, at least temporarily.

As the werewolf prepares to switch to its new target, the transformed druid rushes forward with a roar, the two near-animals clashing when they meet at the center of the arena. As they fight, the mage prepares another spell while the man with a sword inches closer, waiting for an opening. With the werewolf preoccupied, the rest of us are able to walk along the arena's walls toward our friends unnoticed. When we approach, Piper drops the magical shield, allowing us to actually speak.

"Where's David?" Adam asks from his spot on the ground, still bleeding.

"And what are *they* doing here?" Liss adds, gesturing to Kez and the Briars.

"David is safe," I tell her. "And they are here to help."

"Trust us. David's in no condition to fight right now," Michael assures them. "What happened to you?"

"He got mauled by a werewolf is what happened!" Nate exclaims.

"We managed to push it back far enough with our magic to rescue him, but it kept us boxed in like that until you returned," Piper explains.

"I'm fine," Adam groans unconvincingly. There is a bite mark visible on his shoulder and a series of deep red slashes on his stomach.

"Dot, heal the kid," Kez instructs one of her people, a human woman.

"You got it." She rubs her hands together as she kneels down next to Adam, palms already glowing as she places them over his open wounds.

"Great, can you do something about the werewolf infection, too?" I freeze when I hear Liss's half-serious request, only just realizing the implication of Adam's bite mark.

"It's a curse, not an infection," Kignun corrects her. "One that can only be passed on during a full moon. He will be fine."

"Oh thank god," Piper says out loud what several of us were feeling. "I was *not* prepared to travel with a werewolf."

"Where are Corrine, Tsula, and Riley?" I ask after our other companions. "What happened to the other lions?"

"They escaped into the city," Nathaniel reveals. "The others went after them before they could hurt more people."

"There are *what* loose in the city?" Kez looks toward the cages with the two recaptured lions.

"The werewolf is shrugging off every spell that mage is throwing at it," Michael comments as he watches the Briars on the field.

"Werewolves are naturally resistant to magic," Kignun informs him. "They heal quicker, too, so regular weapons will not do much damage."

"Then how are we supposed to fight it?" Piper questions, looking over nervously. "I would kill for my wand or a focus right now."

"Well, if we can knock it out, it should revert to human form," Kignun says, not sounding very confident.

"What do you mean: 'should?'" Liss questions.

"The man is clearly not in his right mind," he tells her. "I have no idea what else might be going on with him."

"I know they are weak to wolfsbane," I try to refocus the conversation on what we do know.

"Great. Got any on you?" Liss asks sarcastically.

"What if we locked it back in the cage it came out of?" Nate offers up next.

"We would need to get it inside first," Kez points out.

"I am not even sure it would hold; it looks to be just iron and wood," Kignun comments as he looks over the cages. "If we had some silver, that would be a different story. In fact, that is probably what the burns on its neck and limbs are from."

"Your friend is all healed," Dot interrupts to tell me. "But he's lost a lot of blood. He needs to rest."

"I'm fine. I can still fight." Adam stands up wobbly, convincing no one.

Before anyone can argue, there is a loud crash as the sword-wielding Briar is thrown through one of the wooden gates. With one of his attackers now off the field, the werewolf is able to focus all of his attention on the bear he's once again forced to grapple with, who is starting to look rather haggard herself. Behind them, the mage is starting to look nervous as he prepares another spell.

"Dot, get blondie inside and find Len and patch him up, too." She grimaces as her friend in bear form is forced to retreat behind the mage, who throws up a shield of his own. "And then maybe find someplace safe to hide."

"Wait, inside!" Kez and Hazatin's words both get me thinking. "They have to have been holding the werewolf in another cell. It must contain silver or some other item they were using to keep him under control."

"Not a bad idea," Kez agrees, then turns to her companions. "Alright, Vuk, Dot, and Boz, you get the injured kid inside and find Len, then start looking for that werewolf's cell."

"Yes, ma'am!" Dot tells her as she and who I think is Vuk help Adam inside, followed by Boz.

"What about me, boss?" Rax questions nervously.

"You're one of the strongest fighters here, Rax," Kez tells him straight. "Time to put on your big boy pants and fight."

"Okay, since none of us can do much damage to it as it is, our best plan here is to keep it distracted." With Adam out of commission, I take charge of the situation. "Split into groups of two or three and spread out. Mages, keep as much distance as you are able, and the rest of us, find a weapon and only approach if you are prepared to retreat just as quickly. The more confused we keep him, the better."

After sharing a look of agreement, our group breaks up. There are enough discarded swords left for those of us still on the field, and I also make a point to grab the spear I was given, which is still sticking up out of the ground. Kignun and Michael both join me, and together we inch around the side of the arena and wait for an opening.

Nathaniel, on the opposite side of the arena, finds his and lets loose a large fireball. It strikes the werewolf with a sizzle, singing some fur and drawing his attention. That grants me my own opening, and I run toward it, throwing the spear with my right arm which lands in the creature's shoulder. As it howls in pain, I land a few quick slashes with my sword along its back.

Now fully aware, it turns to face me so fast that the spear is dislodged and flung to the ground. I am very quickly put on the defensive, dodging and deflecting his swiping claws. I can barely withstand the force of his blows, being slowly forced backward, when a glowing purple whip wraps around the werewolf's ankle, stopping it in its tracks. The weapon glows brightly as it is overcharged with energy, causing the beast to howl in pain as it crackles against its skin thanks to its new attacker: Piper.

The sorcerer is caught wide-eyed, her summoned weapon still in hand as it turns to face her. For a second, I worry for her safety and prepare myself to once again draw the monster's ire, but he is intercepted, this time by Kez and Rax at the same time. The two mercenaries deliver a series of sharp sword blows on either of the creature's sides, making it difficult for the werewolf to focus between them.

Continuing in this pattern of attack, the now-recovered Briar mage sets off a series of small light explosions around the werewolf's head, Kez and Rax retreating in their wake. They do not make it out unscathed, Rax taking a shallow slash along his arm from one of the wolf's claws. The werewolf temporarily blinded, something brown rushes in from my left as the dwarfen druid engages him in another wrestling match. The two roll around on the ground in a blur of fur, claws, and fangs until the werewolf forces the bear away.

Despite Rax's injury, I am still feeling very confident about our chances here. Michael attacks next with his own arcane bolts, allowing Liss a chance to use her blade, and then we are back around to Nathaniel, who creates another opening with his fireball spell. This time, Kignun leads the charge with me right behind him. We continue in this pattern for a while, and I am actually impressed with how well we are doing despite acquiring the occasional injury.

I know this cannot last forever, and bad luck strikes during our fourth rotation. That, or there is still enough of a person inside for the annoyances to have built up and push the werewolf over the edge. After Piper attacks with a lightning-based spell, Rax and Kez rush in for an attack, but the wolf, eyes still locked onto Piper, quickly knocks the both of them away and advances on the sorcerer.

She screams, running for cover behind the toppled lion cages. The creature roars as it pursues her, swiping its claws through the gap in an attempt to reach her. Without a second thought, I rush forward and stab at his back with my spear, over and over, determined to get his attention. I succeed after the tenth or so jab, but with the cages surrounding us, none of the spellcasters are able to clearly aim, and none of the fighters can get between it and me.

I retreat back as fast as I can as the werewolf angrily advances on me, but bad luck strikes again when I trip and stumble. The werewolf's shadow overtakes me as I hit the ground, and though I try to scramble backward, he is already on me. I bring up my spear, lodging the wood between the wolf's jaws as they snap at me, splintering the wood. I try to push it away as I slide back, futile as that may be, and am shocked when I realize the wolf is not following me, but is sinking into the ground instead. *Michael!*

The wizard, who has just saved my life, is barely ten meters away, his hands on the ground behind the werewolf as he casts his spell. I exhale in relief as I put more distance between the two of us, Michael doing the same. As the wolf struggles, cracks appear in the earth around it, making it apparent that this will not hold him long. *I do not know how much longer we can keep this up.*

"We found it!" someone shouts behind me.

I turn to see Vuk and the other Briars coming out of the destroyed gate, sans Adam. In their hands and thrown over their shoulders are metal chains, the silver shining brightly in the sunlight. Seeing that the werewolf is about to escape his trap, they surround him.

Just as he frees himself from the ground, the Briars strike, wrapping the first of the chains around his neck. The wolf howls in pain, an audible *sizzle* coming from the metal as it touches his skin and fur. More than just hurting him, the silver actually makes him weaker, forcing the creature to his knees. The others quickly wrap their chains around his limbs, the wolf crumpling to the ground in pain.

Seeing that he is fully restrained, and recalling Kignun's words, I pick myself up from the ground. Sword still in hand, I approach the weakened wolf. He watches me, eyes still full of anger, but also a little fear.

"I am sorry about this." I bring the pommel down on the back of his head with a heavy *thud*, knocking him out.

The wolf's unconscious body slumps the rest of the way to the ground, the chains pulling taught. His body starts to shift and change, fur being slowly replaced by skin, limbs twitching and spasming (as much as they are able) as he returns to human form. Even without enhanced hearing, the sickening crunch and scrape of bone on bone is audible. It sounds *painful*, almost stomach-turning. When he is finished, we are left with a nude man lying on his stomach.

"Alright," Kez starts as she approaches. "Let's see who we're dealing with."

All of the others, seeing that it is now safe, gather around as Kez flips the man onto his back. Her fellow Briars are at the ready should something happen, though I expect the chains to hold without issue. The man revealed to us is fairly attractive, with lightly tan skin and dark black hair that matches the color of his fur in his other form. He has a scruffy looking beard, right above a set of runes along his collarbone—much like David's.

"Do any of you know who this is?" Kez directs her question to everyone.

"Don't think so," Liss comments.

"I cannot say that I do," I add. "Those symbols on his neck though, Calvinson put similar ones on David. These look like tattoos, though." *Like what he had planned for David.*

"Not the only one, either. Look." Kignun points to his shoulder, where I can see another tattoo on his deltoid muscle.

"What does it mean?" I look closer at the image of a stylized wolf head over a pair of crossed swords.

"That he is a member of the Litkalaa Royal Guard," he finishes, still inspecting the symbol.

"And what does *that* mean?" Piper asks next.

"That Calvinson may have gotten more trouble than he bargained for," he answers with a sigh.

"Litkalaa is an island to the north. The royal family are all werewolves," I explain. If this man is a member of the royal guard, Calvinson may have caused a far bigger mess than I could have anticipated."

"We found the cell they were keeping him in," Dot, the healer tells us, already moving to assist the druid in taking care of everyone's injuries. "Silver bars and all the chains. The walls were covered in claw marks. That's where we left Len with your friend."

"What should we do with him?" Liss asks, looking over the naked man.

"Though I hate to say it, because we do not know how in control of himself he will be when he wakes up, locking him back in his cell may be our only option." I grimace as I look over the man's scarred body, and the way the silver chains still sear his skin on contact. "Then we probably need to help the others with the lions still on the loose."

"Oh gods, I totally forgot about those," Kez says with some alarm. "Pim, you head out there now. The rest of us will meet up after we're done here."

The druid agrees, transforming into a bird and flying out of the arena to find the ferocious felines. Next, Rax and I lift the werewolf by the shoulders as Dot leads the way inside the arena and then downstairs, where we find Adam and the previously thrown Briar waiting. After setting the man down in his cell, which is as bleak as it was described, I lock the door using the ring of keys which miraculously managed to not fall out of the ridiculous costume I am still wearing.

"So what now?" Adam asks, eager to rejoin the fight.

"Well, the others are still dealing with the wild animals on the loose, so I would say most of us should assist with that," I tell him, and the rest of us gathered. "However, we also have Calvinson, his footman, and the captain of the guard restrained in a small room on the other side of the arena. That is where David is, so I will be going there."

"Wait, you did *what?*" Kez has to make sure I am not joking. "I'm coming with you."

While most of our two disparate groups head out to the city to help contain the chaos that spilled out of the colosseum, I bring Adam, Michael, Kignun, and Kez to where the hidden door is located. First though, I make a quick stop by my cell to grab my original clothes, having had enough of this flimsy cloth wrapped around my groin. After I am redressed, Michael uses his magic to reveal the passage to the inner panic room and leads the way inside.

Before we are even halfway to the room, I can hear an angry voice—Calvinson's. When we enter the panic room proper, I see him struggling with his wrists still attached to the cot, glaring at Frederick, who hovers over him with a grimace, not actually attempting to help. Upon hearing our entrance, both men turn to look at us wearing vastly different expressions.

"I-I swear, I haven't, I wasn't—" The man stumbles over his words in fear.

"Where is David?" I see Captain Foster still asleep on the floor, and the other two guards still sitting in the spot I left them, but not—

"Hi Khaz!" I look up toward the ceiling to find David at the top of the very, very tall shelf—upside down, hanging by his legs.

"David," I try not to let the worry enter my voice, "could you come down here, please?"

"Okay!" David lifts his legs, and I almost shout when he allows himself to slide off the shelf—only to flip backward as he falls, landing gracefully on his two sandal-clad feet. "What's up?"

"I just...wanted to make sure you were alright." I share a look with both Michael and Adam over David's mental state, as well as the dangerous stunt he just performed like it was nothing. "Can you wait down here with me and your brother?"

"Sure. Hi Mikey, hi Adam!" David hugs his brother and friend happily.

"What's wrong with him?" Adam asks after noticing the strange behavior.

"I am not sure, but I think it has something to do with the symbols around his neck." I indicate the runes. "The werewolf's tattoos were similar. I assume the work of the same enchanter. They were planning on making David's permanent as well." I can feel the anger rise at the memory.

"That's him," the more talkative of the two tied-up guards agrees. "He was due to come back after the coronation."

"Yeah, before everything went to hell," the other guard adds.

"Would you two *shut up*!" Calvinson decides now is the time to speak. "You there, Blackbriar. Help me to safety, and I will *double* your fee."

"Oh, so *now* you're gonna pay us?" Kez replies with a predatory smile. "Sorry, I'm afraid I've already accepted a better offer."

"What *exactly* is it that you think you can do to me?" he sneers from the floor. "What have I even done wrong!?"

"Besides holding over a dozen people against their will and making them fight for your amusement?" Adam questions sarcastically.

"All lawbreakers within my city!" I can tell by his tone of voice that at least *he* believes that.

"I wonder if the King of Litkalaa will feel the same when he finds out that you've been torturing a member of his royal guard," Kignun tells him plainly.

"I've done no such thing!" Calvinson defends.

"He's talking about the werewolf, you idiot." I can hear Michael's eyes roll.

"I am not sure what you thought you were doing here, but I can assure you that King Samoset has more influence, money, and firepower than you ever could," Kignun warns the Lutherian human, who is starting to realize how deeply he has messed up.

"And I doubt he will like hearing about what you were doing to your other 'prisoners' either, nor will the leaders of *their* homes," I add on, enjoying the growing look of fear on the cowardly man's face.

"It was all Captain Foster's idea!" Calvinson blurts out after a few moments of panicked silence. "He and his men are the ones responsible!"

"You *would* try to blame the guy who's asleep," Kez mutters behind me.

"You mean to tell me that Prince Richard of Richardton was taking orders from his subordinates?" I fake shock. "Very believable."

"I do love when they start to turn on each other," Kignun says to me with a sly grin, no doubt thinking back to one of the many interrogations he conducted over his years as a ranger.

"For the record, none of the rest of us meant for anything like this to happen," the chattier guard says. "We were just following orders."

"Oh, well I suppose that makes locking me in a cell and then trying to convince six strangers to *murder* me alright then," I growl, turning to glare.

"Right now, the only chance *any* of you have at receiving any sort of leniency is by cooperating with us while we work to clean up your mess," Kignun says less sarcastically.

"We can do that!" the other guard quickly agrees.

"Traitors!" Calvinson shouts, still locked to the cot.

"What *is* the plan here?" Adam asks. "What do we do next?"

"First, we need to contact the homes of each of the victims and request assistance." I start preparing a mental list. "It will take a few days at least, and until then we will need to fortify our position, seeing as we are still vastly outnumbered by the city guard."

"Yes, it is probably best to keep our little 'coup' a secret until reinforcements arrive." Kignun looks over our captives.

"Unless we can find a way to clear out the castle's guards and staff, we may be stuck down here for the time being."

"Oh, I'm sure Frederick here will be more than happy to help us with that." Michael walks over to the cowering man, who looks up nervously. "Won't ya, buddy?"

"I-I..." he starts to stammer.

"Don't you *dare* help them!" Calvinson spits out.

"Sir, I am sorry, but this has gone too far," he says with more confidence than I thought possible, before turning to me. "I will help you however I can to restore order and right these wrongs."

"Good man," Kignun tells him, pleased. From what little I have seen, I think Frederick has a large hand in running and organizing things around here. "You can start by clearing out the castle and securing us a safe location to hold our prisoners until aid can arrive."

"I can take Freddy back to the castle and get started on that," Kez offers.

"I will go with you as well," Kignun decides.

"We can help with the other guards!" one of the men tied together blurts out.

"Yeah, we outrank most of them, so they have to listen to us," the second man adds, eager to find a way to lessen their inevitable punishment.

"Something to keep in mind, but until the others get back here, I am not comfortable letting more than Frederick out of the room," Kignun explains his very reasonable hesitancy.

"We can look around the rest of the arena while we wait," Adam suggests next. "I know they've got more people locked up down here."

"Yes, we should free any of the other prisoners, and if we can, locate those who were on the field with us earlier," I add, recalling the fearful looks in their eyes as they were ordered to fight. "I know many of them will want to return home immediately, but we should at least ensure they are able to make it out of the city safely first. Especially with the lions still on the loose"

There is a sudden gasp behind me. "You saw the lions too?!" David asks excitedly. *Uh oh.* "They were so cool looking!"

"I think we need to add finding the enchanter responsible for...*this* to the top of the list." I try to give David my least-worried smile.

"I can help with that as well, sir," Frederick says without hesitation.

"Does loyalty mean nothing to you?!" Calvinson is practically frothing at the mouth.

"Do you want me to gag you?" Michael threatens, shutting Calvinson's mouth.

Adam starts the search for his other victims while Frederick leads Kez and Kignun out of the panic room. I remain here with Michael to watch David and our prisoners, having a seat on the cot while Calvinson writhes angrily on the floor. As happy as I am to feel him cuddling into my side, I am eager to have my normal, mouthy, trouble-making pup returned to me soon.

Chapter 16

"**David, please stop trying to climb the shelf.**"

"Aww." He pouts but obeys, taking a seat on the cot next to me.

"Tell me something." I turn to Michael on my other side, who has been waiting with me for the others to return. "Has he always been so...athletic?"

"Yeah, he was always wanting to wrestle or roughhouse." Michael nods. "My parents signed him up for football as soon as he was old enough. They signed me up too, but I only lasted a few games before I quit."

Good information, but not exactly what I was looking for. Though the image of a much younger David and Michael playing on a rug'bal field is adorable. "What about climbing? Anything out of the ordinary?"

"Hmm." Michael thinks on it. "I mean, he was always climbing up trees and stuff. There was this one time he got all the way up on our roof once when we were only three years old. He got so mad at me for telling Mom and Dad... but come on, we were *three*. I thought he was going to fall off and die or something."

"Was he ever injured?" My questions must seem odd, but Michael may be the only person who can answer them.

"No, I guess he was always pretty lucky." He shakes his head. "Never got all that sick either. None of us kids really did."

"Hmm. Thank you." The information Michael has given me only further strengthens my hypothesis that there is something special about David that existed before that night in the temple ruins.

"So look, I know we have this truce going on right now, but I still don't like you very much because of what you did to my brother," Michael tells me honestly. "Right now, I'm having a hard time seeing the difference between you and that asshole." He nods toward the silently glaring Calvinson.

You and me both. Before I can say anything, the faint sound of footsteps can be heard echoing down the corridor. "I think some of the others are back."

"Go on and check it out." Michael nods toward the entrance. "I'll keep watch here."

"Thank you. I will be right back." I stand and walk down the dark and narrow hallway that leads back into the colosseum's basement. Just as I exit, I see Adam, Liss, Kignun, and Kez returning with almost a dozen other former prisoners behind them.

"This is everyone we could find on both floors," Kez starts.

"We did our best to explain what was happening to everyone," Kignun continues for her. "But they are understandably nervous."

"We only found three of the five that were on the field with you though," Adam says next. "The other two must have made it out into the city."

"Hopefully they are safe." They will most likely attempt to return home, but without the proper rest, food, and other supplies, I worry they may not make it.

"Any sign of the others?" Adam questions.

"Not yet, I—" I pause, hearing a door opening and...
Was that a growl?

I turn to face the noise and see sunlight streaming in through an open door to the outside, along with several figures, mostly people. Once they are closer, I can make out Riley, Tsula, Corrine, Piper, Liss, and even Robin, along with the other Briars. There are also three lions walking calmly behind Robin, whom none of the others seem particularly worried about.

"It is good to see you all," I tell them as they approach, only now making out the mixed emotions on their faces—Riley and Robin in particular.

"Weren't there four—" Liss tries to count.

"We weren't fast enough," is Riley's depressed-sounding answer.

"It took us a while to find all of them out in the city," Tsula explains. "People were being attacked and had to defend themselves..."

"I am so sorry." My apology is largely directed at the druid and fae. "Was anyone else hurt?"

"Two people were killed," Corrine answers sadly, and I'm just noticing the blood on her robes. "A few others were injured, but they'll be okay."

"It's not fair," Robin spits bitterly. "They were scared, and hungry, and only doing what their instincts told them to. They shouldn't have even been here."

"I am very sorry, Robin. I know they were your friends." I also know that they are still wild animals, whose presence is making several of the civilian victims uncomfortable. "Would you and Riley mind returning them to their cages?"

"What? You want me to lock them back up?" Robin looks decidedly nonplussed.

"Just temporarily until we can get a few other things settled," I try to assure him.

"I'm not putting them back in those tiny cages!" He points toward the arena's center.

"Then are you willing to babysit them?" I ask, half-serious. "Because they can't just be allowed to roam free."

He glares at my response and huffs. "*Fine.*" He turns on his heel, making a gesture with his hand that has the lions following him, Riley right behind them.

"What's going on here?" Corrine asks those of us who stayed. "What happened to Calvinson and David?"

"Khazak and Michael managed to catch up with them," Adam explains, nodding to the open passage behind me. "We've got Calvinson and some of his guards tied up in there now."

There are a few cheers from some of the Briars and other prisoners—and one man who spits on the ground at the mention of his captor's name.

"Michael is there with them and David," I continue explaining. "We are just waiting for Kignun to return with Frederick to tell us if it is safe to move everyone into the castle."

"Is David alright?" Corrine asks next. I appreciate the concern.

"I am not entirely sure," I answer honestly. "It might be better for you to see for yourself."

"Okay." She nods.

"Be right back," Adam tells the others as the three of us enter the passageway.

The panic room is as I left, the three guards and Calvinson still restrained and on the floor. Michael is sitting next to David, who jumps up when he sees us enter and rushes to give me a hug. As I return his embrace, I feel his hands start to snake down my back, pinching my ass and making me jump in surprise.

"He has been very *affectionate* since returning to us, among other things." I take him gently by the wrist and pull him away from my body so that Corrine can see the symbols on his upper chest. "I believe these are the cause of his behavior."

"I've seen some of these before." She steps closer as she inspects his skin, pointing to some of them. "Enchantment runes. This one alters your perception, these sap your strength, and I'm pretty sure this one lowers intelligence. I'm not sure about the others."

"Can you remove them?" I ask, hopeful.

"I can, but I'd need to figure out exactly what they all do first," she confirms with a caveat. "If you're not careful with the order you remove or apply them, the wrong spell effect could be triggered or amplified."

"Frederick, Calvinson's footman, is supposed to be retrieving the enchanter responsible," I inform her, feeling a small bit of relief. "They should be able to tell you everything you need to know." *They had better.*

"I will never forgive that traitor for what he's done to me." Calvinson picks that moment to pipe up from his spot next to the cot.

"*You!*" Corrine turns, voice dripping in venom. "Do you have any idea what you've done? Two people, two of *your citizens*, are dead because you released a pack of wild, bloodthirsty animals loose without a single thought for anyone's safety!"

"I haven't a clue what you're talking about, dear, but you certainly seem upset." He somehow manages to look down his nose at her even from the floor. "Is it that time of the month?"

"What did you just say to her?" Adam takes an angry step toward him, making him flinch.

"He's not worth it, Adam," she tells him with her hand on his shoulder, then looks at the sleeping Captain Foster on the floor. "Is he okay?"

"Yeah, just sleeping. Probably for a while," Michael tells her, scratching the back of his head. "I...might have hit him kinda hard with a sleeping spell."

"Hey everyone." I turn with the others to see Liss coming down the passage. "Kignun and that butler guy are back, and they say we're okay to start heading into the castle."

"Alright," Adam tells her with a nod, then turns to look at me and Corrine. "So, how are we doing this?"

"I can carry the unconscious one," I offer with a sigh.

Riley rejoins us after recaging the lions, and it takes us about an hour to get moved into the castle. Neither of the guards put up a fight, and Captain Foster is unable to do anything more than snore, but Calvinson is another story. Rather than make things easier on himself, he elects to screech and wail as soon as we grab him. That lasts all of five seconds, which is when Liss presses a sword to the skin of his neck and dares him to continue. In the end, he comes along quietly.

Frederick has dismissed most of the castle's staff for the day, leaving us free from worrying about running into an odd maid or butler. The guards, however, are not under his jurisdiction. Thankfully, the castle itself seems to be void of them after the chaos of the coronation. Still, with their barracks attached to the ground floor, I am careful while carrying the unconscious body of their leader.

We claim the top floor for our own purposes, setting up a base of operations in a spacious bedroom we deduce is Calvinson's from the way he immediately begins complaining about us "messing it up." The double doors leading in are wooden and appear to have been broken with fresh planks hammered over a hole near the center. I also notice that two of the bedposts are broken, the canopy above sitting at an odd angle. I pull David closer, ignoring the feelings of rage I feel building when I see the bed.

Tsula and Corrine help Calvinson's other victims settle into some of the many spare bedrooms on the third and second floors while Kignun works on writing the letters to contact each of their homes. The guards, Captain Foster, and Calvinson have all been separated into rooms of their own, with Calvinson currently bound and gagged in his bathroom's tub. The two guards have been very willing to cooperate, but where Foster's loyalties will fall are still a mystery. I want to be there when he wakes up. Without his "prince" whispering in his ear, I am hoping he will be more open and truthful with his answers.

"Alright, so, what comes next?" Adam asks once we're all in the room.

"What do you mean?" Liss is confused by the question. "We won."

"Yeah, the fight, but what happens now?" Adam points toward the bathroom. "We have the leader of the city tied up in a bathtub."

"Yeah, what happens when people start asking after 'im?" Riley inquires, sitting on the edge of the bed.

"The people in the castle are going to wonder when they can come back to work," Tsula points out. "Not to mention the guards."

"You mean the guards that hightailed it out of there once shit started going down?" Liss scoffs. "Barely saw any in town when we were trying to catch the lions. Probably hiding in the forest."

"What happens after we leave, for that matter?" Piper questions next. "Not to be rude, but we are on something of a tight schedule."

"And several days behind," I add with a sigh. "Kignun and I considered that when we started drafting the letters."

"That we did," he responds, still bent over the desk and writing. "There is no guarantee, but each letter also includes a request for assistance in setting up a provisional government here. With the amount of people living here, I think it best to ensure that our would-be royalty is not able to wrest back any power."

"Assuming he's not in a prison cell," Kez adds with a smirk. She and her Briars have remained helpful, acting as guards and escorts for our prisoners.

"*Just* him...right?" Nathaniel asks, having been nervously avoiding Kez's gaze since entering the castle.

"Don't worry, stretch." She looks from Nathaniel to me. "You and your friends are safe."

"Kez and I came to an agreement," I tell him and the others. "In exchange for their freedom, you and the cockatrice are no longer one of their targets."

"Oh gods!" Nathaniel jumps to his feet. "I gotta go find the little guy!"

"Would somebody please go with him?" I ask aloud as the mage rushes out the bedroom.

"I'll make sure he stays out o' trouble," Riley offers.

"While you are with him, could you please locate Sona as well?" I've felt her presence somewhere in the castle since returning from the arena but have not been able to pinpoint her location.

"You got it!" The druid gives me a small salute before exiting.

"Okay, so it's great that help may be on the way, but what do we do until then?" Kez asks after they leave the room.

"I don't think people are gonna just accept us telling them that Calvinson decided to 'step down.' Not to mention the soldiers."

"I am hoping that Captain Foster will be more cooperative with us in that area," I reply.

"But what if he's not?" Corrine asks, sounding worried.

"We could always pretend?" Michael suggests. "Have Frederick relay messages as if they were from Foster or Calvinson?"

"That might work short term, but eventually someone's gonna wonder why they haven't actually seen either of them," Adam points out, leaning against the wall.

"What about illusion spells?" Tsula turns to Michael and Piper. "Like the ones you made of David and Riley when they left Rakatune ahead of us."

"Is *that* how you managed to get the drop on my guys?" Kez sounds impressed.

The two mages look at each other nervously before Michael speaks up. "I mean... We could try? But making an image of someone is one thing, copying their voice is a lot more complicated."

"Not to mention things like their mannerisms or personality that can't be mimicked," Piper adds, sounding disappointed. "As much as I hate to admit it, I do think that might be out of our skill range, and it still would not matter after we've left."

"Looks like it's up to me to save you all again," Robin remarks from a corner of the room, his sudden appearance making several of us jump.

"Robin!" except David, who happily throws his hands in the air when he sees the fairy.

"How exactly is this one going to help us?" Kez looks him over, unimpressed.

"Like this," Robin replies, equally unimpressed, before his body begins to grow and shift until he resembles Calvinson, clothes and all.

"Okay, that's pretty impressive," Liss admits. "But can you act the part?"

"My dear, I have spent the past few weeks doing nothing but following this man around and plotting his downfall." When he speaks, his voice is that of Calvinson's. He looks over his fingernails, uninterested. "Trust me, I know my lines."

I pull David to my side, smiling to myself. With Robin's help, I think we may actually have a decent plan worked out. We just need to make sure all the individual moving parts work the way we need them to. A small knock on the room's doors draws our attention.

"Excuse me, sirs and madams." It's Frederick, along with his two Briar escorts. "The enchanter is here. I have them waiting in the castle's infirmary."

"Perfect." I turn to Corrine, who is already walking toward me and David. "Take us to him, please."

The six of us make our way downstairs as quickly and carefully as possible. With the possibility of running into a guard or other castle-worker in the air, I want to get this done fast. Frederick navigates the halls with ease, leading us straight to the infirmary's doors.

"Halt!" *Dammit!* We freeze at the shouted order behind us. "Who's there? What are you—Oh, Frederick." The first of the two guards questions, his hand dropping from the sword at his side.

"What are you doing here with these prisoners?" the second guard asks, hand still on his sword hilt. "And isn't that the, uh, new consort?"

"Ah, well, you see," the older man nervously stammers, "Prince Calvinson asked that I bring them to the infirmary."

"He...asked you to bring prisoners to the infirmary?" The second guard's eyes narrow. "Personally?"

"I... Yes, he——"

"Is there a problem here?" The addition of *another* voice makes even the guards jump—particularly when that voice belongs to *Captain Foster*.

I stare in shock as the man who *should* be upstairs, unconscious and locked in a room, walks toward us. The two guards are just as surprised, saluting quickly upon seeing him. He comes to a stop in front of them. I am confused at how calm he seems, then I catch the captain's eye—or rather, *Robin's* eye in disguise.

"Sir!"

"Sir!" they say in unison.

"It's a relief to see you, sir," the first guard starts. "Things have been out of control since the coronation. After the animals broke loose, we've been doing what we can to keep order in the city."

"We've been unable to locate all but one of the lions," the second guard explains. "Some citizens were saying they possibly saw them being brought back to the arena? We haven't had a chance to follow up. Half the men have deserted and ran for their own homes in the chaos."

"Is everything handled with the..." The first guard pauses, looking around and dropping his voice like he's sharing a secret. "Werewolf?"

"Yes, the lion and werewolf situations have both been handled," Robin-as-Foster assures them. "They are safely back in their cages at the arena, but make sure people stay away from the area regardless."

"Yes, sir. What are your other orders?" the first guard asks. "Should we start rounding up the deserters?"

"No, I don't think that will be necessary." It is small, but I catch a flash of nervousness on his face as the questions continue. "In fact, I think with everything that happened today, you've all earned the next few days off."

"Sir?" The second guard is clearly surprised by the order.

"Go home. Be with your families. We all came close to death today." *Some of us much closer than others...* "Now then, is there a reason you've stopped Frederick from completing his task?"

"Sorry, sir, we just wanted to be sure everything was alright," the first guard apologizes.

"We thought it was strange for him to be escorting these prisoners by himself," the second guard explains.

"Well, let me assure you then that this is exactly what he was told to do," Robin-Foster says with confidence. "I just left Prince Calvinson's bedroom after escorting him there myself. Are you questioning his—and my—authority?"

"No sir, not at all!" the first guard blurts out, shaking his head.

"We were just being cautious!" the second guard adds quickly.

"It is alright," Robin-Foster says with a fake sigh of understanding. "Just make sure you share my orders with the other men. The prince would like a few days to himself, so let's keep traffic inside the castle to a minimum."

"Yes sir, right away!" Both men salute again before turning and walking the other way down the hall.

"That was very quick thinking, Robin," I whisper as soon as the guards are out of earshot.

"How did you know we would need your help?" Corrine asks softly.

"You always need my help," Robin whispers back in his normal voice. "Besides, I've been dying to try that one out."

"Shall we...continue?" Frederick asks, still confused but seeming to understand some of what just happened.

As we finish our trek down the hall, I hear one of the guards in the distance talking to the other. "See? I *told* you the captain was fucking him!" *What!?*

I do not get a chance to share that information yet, as Frederick is already opening the door to the infirmary.

"I am so sorry, your highness. After what happened before the coronation, I was not sure you still needed me today," the enchanter says after hearing the door open. He appears to be a middle-aged Lutherian man with graying hair, facing away from us as he removes items from a leather bag and sets them on the table in front of him.

"I'm afraid the prince is indisposed at the moment," I alert him to our presence and Calvinson's absence, and he turns around in surprise.

"Who are you?" He looks nervously between the seven of us. "Frederick, where is the pri——"

"I would not worry about the prince right now." I step toward him menacingly as the two Briars block the exit. "Now, would you care to explain what you have done to our companion?" I point my thumb toward David, standing with Corrine.

"I... I only did w-what was asked of me," he stammers out.

"So, you were totally fine with doing all of this," Corrine gestures to the two long rows of runes below David's collarbone, "to someone and didn't question it at all?"

"I-I didn't realize he——" he tries to explain.

"Was he even conscious at the time?" I have no interest in his excuses and already know the answer, but he still nervously shakes his head no.

"I can undo it!" he quickly offers. "It's not permanent."

"Unlike what you did to our lycanthropic friend in the dungeons?" I bring up the werewolf, as I assume he is responsible for the man's tattoos and subsequent rage-filled disposition—Calvinson's "special project."

"...I can undo that too." He sounds less confident about that.

"And you will, but first you help my friend." Corrine fixes the man with a stern look as she approaches with David. "You are going to remove each of these runes, and you're going to explain exactly what each of them are for while you do it. Understood?"

"Yes ma'am." The man nods quickly.

After some cajoling, we get David to lie back on the examination table at the center of the room. Ignoring the tools he had laid out, the enchanter pulls a bottle of clear, blue-tinged liquid from his bag, and a cloth rag. Dampening a portion of the rag with the liquid, he begins to methodically wipe away the runes under Corrine's watchful eye. The man explains that the rune paint is made of a special pigment that allows enchanters to apply longer lasting enchantments to directly to a person's body, and that the pigment can also be made into a tattoo ink that can make them permanent.

I listen to what the man tells Corrine as he works, describing the effect of each rune, but most of my focus is on David. He is happy enough to lie there as requested, but he cannot seem to stop wriggling because, as he says, "it tickles." It takes about twenty minutes, but eventually the man finishes, wiping the last of the enchanted paint from David's skin.

"Just give him a few minutes for the effects to fully wear off," he informs us, recorking the blue liquid.

"Thank you," I tell him flatly. David is still lying back looking dazed, but at least he is no longer giggling. "Now, about the werewolf and his tattoos."

"I can't just remove them," he admits, still nervous. "I don't have the right equipment. There's a special kind of oil..." He trails off, seeing that neither of us are impressed with his answer.

"Then what *can* you do?" I growl, not happy with the answer.

"Counter-runes!" he blurts out. "I can paint on runes that would cause the opposite effects, so they would cancel each other out. At least until they can be removed permanently."

"I guess that's as good a solution as we're gonna get right now," Corrine accepts with a sigh.

"We can escort our new friend down to the dungeon to take care of that in a short while," I tell Corrine, looking towards the Briars as well. "For now, would you mind bringing him up to the master bedroom so we can regroup and go down together?" The werewolf should still be subdued by the silver, but I would like to get him out of that so the man can start recovering.

"Sure thing, Khazak," Corrine answers with a smile. "Come on, let's go so we can fix your other mess."

Corrine and the Briars march the enchanter and Frederick from the room, leaving me alone with David as he regains his full awareness. I pull a chair up to the table and take a seat, reaching for his hand and stroking my thumb over his. After a few minutes, he makes an attempt to sit up with a low groan. His hand moves to his forehead before trying to rub the non-existent sleep out of his eyes.

"Are you back with me?" I ask hopefully.

"I think so," he answers, looking at me and then around the room. "What happened?"

"A lot, but the most important thing is that Calvinson has been deposed," I tell him with a smile as he swings his legs around to the side of the table to face me. "What can you remember happening after you left us in the throne room?"

"I was brought to a bathroom so I could clean up, where I think they stole my clothes. Then we had dinner at this *really* long table, then he showed me around his weird little zoo where—" He stops mid-sentence, eyes going wide. "That's where Sona was, in a cage."

"Riley and Nathaniel are looking for her right now." I squeeze his leg, happy for the knowledge. "What happened next?"

"Well, we went up to his bedroom to uh, do the deed." He looks away as he says it.

"Did he do anything to hurt you?" I feel the sudden urge to inspect his body for bruises.

"No, nothing like that." He shakes his head. "It was... fine? Nothing rough or even that kinky. The craziest thing he wanted to do was tie me to the bed. Then he..." His eyes narrow as recalls the night's events. "He said he wasn't going to honor our deal, then he started threatening you and Mike. He was *gloating* about it. I remember getting angrier, and angrier, and then..." He pauses, still looking at the wall. "It happened again, didn't it?"

"It did." I nod. "Though I only saw the end of it."

"I can remember chasing him through the castle, and then down into the dungeon, and...I had him up against the wall?" He looks me in the eye. "Did I hurt anybody?"

"You crushed his windpipe slightly, but he recovered," I answer honestly. "Other than that, maybe just a few people's pride after seeing you naked."

"*Oh gods.*" He blushes, covering his face with his hands for a moment. "Wait, what the hell am I wearing?"

"You will have to ask Calvinson about that." I leer down at his exposed thighs. "Though I have to admit it is not exactly *un*appealing."

"Is *that* why you haven't bothered getting me dressed yet?" He rolls his eyes at me.

"Oh, we tried, but you were not exactly cooperative in your previous state." *It was like babysitting a small child.* "When you had Calvinson cornered in the dungeon, I found you, helped you to stop, but then you passed out. Can you remember anything after that?"

"Kinda? It's all a little fuzzy." He scratches the back of his head. "I get flashes of faces, mostly Calvinson's. I can remember feeling angry again, I think he tried to take off my collar, but then something scared him, and I don't think he really touched me much after."

"He had an enchanter paint runes on your chest that affected your mind and body." I look at the clear skin beneath the shining metal collar, smiling at the thought of an incapacitated David refusing to remove it. "More than a dozen. He was afraid of your strength, and I'm not even sure he was very confident they would work."

"Thanks for getting me back to normal." David grins, before biting his lip and looking down. "I'm, uh, sorry for taking the deal, even when you told me not to."

"While I am not prepared to say that it is alright, I understand why you felt it was our best option. And if I am being honest, were the offer to come from a more trust-worthy source, I could see myself making the same choice," I admit. "What bothers me more is the comparison you made between what Calvinson was doing and our own relationship."

"You know I didn't actually mean any of that," he half-mumbles, looking recalcitrant. "I was just...being an asshole."

"You were not the only one to note the similarities," I start, remembering the man's words to me under the arena. "Calvinson thought we had a lot in common in the way we treated you. Part of me would like to think he was trying to convince himself of that more than me, but he had a point. After all, we both captured you and forced you into our beds."

"You two are nothing alike!" he defends, loudly. "Those are completely different situations. I committed *actual* crimes in the temple outside of Tah'lj, not to mention the way Redwish was manipulating the both of us."

"There is only so much we can blame on Redwish without also considering the choices I *did* have control over," I speak softly, knowing I am treading on a touchy subject. But it is one that needs to be touched, now more than ever. "And criminal or not, your 'punishment' should not include forced servitude and sexual assault. Could you imagine if we weren't attracted to each other? If I were a crueler man, the things I could have done?"

"I don't understand you." He shakes his head, standing and pacing around the table. "I thought we settled all this months ago. It's like you *want* me to be angry with you!"

"Because maybe you should be! At least a little." David meets my eyes again, looking confused and a little hurt. I lean forward to take his hands in mine. "Just, listen to what I have to say, please."

"Is our relationship important to you?" I ask, waiting for his silent nod. "It's important to me too. Possibly the most important thing in my life right now. And because of that, it feels wrong to not be honest with myself by putting all of the blame on Redwish to rationalize things I know were wrong. Can you truly say that I am blameless?"

"I mean... It isn't..." He huffs and looks away, frustrated. "No. I can't. And if I think back, I can remember how scared I was. I didn't know what was happening, or who you were. I'd never even had sex before. And when I think about it being anyone but you..." He has a full body shudder.

"I am sorry, David." I squeeze his hands gently. "I won't try to justify my actions because of the anger or frustration I felt at the time because that does not matter. It was wrong, and I've been carrying the weight of that guilt around since the day I met you."

"It's just...hard," David says, looking me in the eye. "I get that it was wrong, but if things hadn't happened the way they did, we probably wouldn't be together. So it's hard for me to pretend like I wish things were different, because...I don't."

"I understand that." I squeeze his hand again. "Even though I know part of the reason we are together is due to the unique circumstances of how we met, I still wish your introduction to this world had been gentler."

"I hate that you've been feeling this way for months." He grimaces. "I don't want to be the reason you feel guilty."

"This might sound strange, but I am actually *glad* that I feel guilty." I chuckle at the confused look he makes in response. "What kind of person would I be if I didn't? Someone without remorse, or compassion, or humility. Someone who would have no business being your owner."

"But it's not like I still feel angry at you for any of it." He squeezes my hands back. "I mean, yeah it sucked, but there's also a part of me that *liked* that you were forcing me. If I was ever *allowed*, I'd probably have jerked off thinking about it a few dozen times already... Does that mean there's something wrong with me?"

"There's nothing wrong with you, David," I reassure him. "I am not saying it is a story I want to tell to our children, I just want us to be able to look back on how we met and not be filled with guilt or resentment, or to let it affect us doing those things we like again in the future because of the memories they are attached to."

"You...want to have kids?" David asks with a bewildered smile.

"One day, yes." I am suddenly much more nervous about my next question. "Do you?"

"I mean, I kinda always figured I'd have kids, at least before..." He gestures back and forth between us. "But I never really gave it much thought. How do two men even have children?"

"There are options like adoption, or relationships like the one between my fathers and aunts." I feel myself warming quickly to the idea of starting a family with David. "My point is, whatever our future together might be, I don't want something from our past and our inability to be honest about it to hold us back. It's not that I think you are too young, or too inexperienced, but not taking those things into account sometimes will only hurt us. I want to talk about the things that worry us. That is all I was ever trying to say."

"I understand now." He gives me a tentative smile, sitting up straight. "Though I don't think my brother will."

"Yes, he may still be a problem." I sigh, releasing his hands and sitting up. "And I cannot exactly tell him his feelings are unjustified."

"Maybe you won't have to," David says as he stands, offering me a hand. "I'll handle it. Not in a 'I'm doing this without you' way. I'll talk to him. Make him understand."

"And I will be there to support you however I can." I take his hand and stand.

"At least we're *actually* on the same page now." He pulls me in for a hug. "You know...I kinda like the idea of having a kid with you."

"I do as well," I speak against the top of his head, trying to hide exactly how much I like it.

"So what's going on with Calvinson and everything?" he asks as we break apart. "You said he was 'deposed?'"

"We have captured and restrained both him and the captain of his guard while his footman has agreed to work with us to try and fix this debacle," I start to explain. "We have a tentative plan in place to help his other victims and ensure he cannot do something like this again, but I can explain the rest on our way to rejoin the others."

"Can we also find me some clothes? Because this really isn't gonna cut it." He gestures to his long flowing red and gold loincloth.

"Yes, we can find you some clothes," I tell him with a chuckle before pulling him against me by the ass. "Though you can absolutely expect to wear this for me later."

"Yes, Sir," he agrees with a grin. *There's my pup.*

Chapter 17

"We can't... Are you able to speak in Common?"

Honestly, these humans invade our territory and then expect us to speak their language? I huff in frustration before responding in Common. "Who—"

"IGNI!" one them shouts, releasing a massive fireball that singes Rangers Deepfist, Firedrum, and Lowtusk as they jump out of the way.

"Dammit!" The blonde male cries out, right before he pulls his sword and charges at me.

He strikes me with an overhand swing that I block with my own longsword, returning with a swing of my own. He is strong, but I am stronger. We continue to trade blows as a battle unfolds around us, these humans giving my rangers far more trouble than I expected. Lowtusk has fallen, having taken more of the fireball than it first appeared, and a sudden scream has us all looking to where Ranger Stonearm is chasing one of the humans around the back of the room. Crafty they may be, they are still outnumbered, and one by one me and my rangers manage to pin them to the ground.

"I was willing to hear your explanation, but after attacking us, you and your lot can rot in a cell for the rest of the day," I growl as I start to pull the blonde man's arms behind his back.

"Hey!" I turn my head to see the only human still standing shout, just before he runs toward me.

He's a scrawny looking thing, and when he leaps at me, I brace myself, bouncing him off my armor. He falls to the floor, the sword sliding from his hand. He reaches for it as he climbs off the ground, and I drop the blonde man in my grip and rush my new attacker, slamming into him with my shoulder and sending him flying toward the center of the room, the back of his head striking the stone altar with a loud crack. Spirits, I did not mean to hit him so hard.

With my men finishing the other arrests, I stand over the injured human, who can only look up at me with unfocused eyes before passing out. A combination of anger, guilt, and annoyance all flood my mind as I bend over to pick up his unconscious body. I hold the slight man to my chest, feeling his neck for a pulse. He is still breathing but is otherwise out cold, and I brush some of the black hair from his forehead to get a better look at his face. There is something about him that I cannot help but find attractive, and I shake the thought from my head. Rounding everyone up, we bring the arrested humans back to the city, where we can take the injured from both sides to the healer. None of this had to happen.

"Go back to the part where they made you wear a loin-cloth too."

"Mine was much smaller, I can assure you."

I spend the walk back to the room filling David in on the rest of what he missed while he was "out." There was a righteous flare of anger in his eyes as I recounted the events of the Richardton Gladiatorial Games, though I could do with a little less interest in what I was wearing. Seeing as this is now the third time David has fallen unconscious, I could not help but think back to the first and how we met. And how glad I am now for everything to have gone so wrong. By the time we are standing outside the bedroom's double doors, he has been brought up to speed with our current plans.

"I'm just saying, maybe I'd like to see it." He looks me over as if I were wearing it now.

"Your interest has been noted," I respond dryly, knocking twice on the doors before entering. Things are as they were when I left, with the exception of the enchanter sitting in one corner under guard.

"David!" Michael stands from the bed to quickly meet us by the door. "You back to normal?"

"Yep, back to normal." David nods with a smile as he hugs his twin.

"Good to have you back, man," Adam greets him next, the rest of our friends gathering around for their turns.

"It's great to see you all, seriously," David tells them as he is circled, "but could someone please give me my clothes?"

"We haven't actually figured out where they're keeping our stuff yet," Liss tells him.

"Oh, I bet Calvinson has something that will fit!" Piper says excitedly as she takes David by the wrist. "Come with me."

"That is one problem taken care of," Kignun says to me as we watch the two of them disappear into the closet. "We were just about to bring the enchanter downstairs to paint the counter-runes on the werewolf, but I thought you'd want to go with us."

"Yes, we should bring as much muscle as possible. A few mages as well." I know he is restrained in the silver chains, but you cannot be too careful. "We can..."

I trail off when I feel an excited presence in my mind, right before something begins scratching against the door. As soon as they open, a blur of black rushes in with a whine—*Sona!* She pounces on me when I crouch down, scratching the fur around her ears and neck as she licks my face in greeting.

<Khazak!> She yips happily, running around me in a small circle. *<Happy to see friend!>*

"It is good to see you too." I smooth her ruffled hair with my hands. "I am sorry that you were taken away."

"She asked about you nonstop on the way here," Riley tells me as he enters the room behind her.

<City bad.> She gives a small huff. *<Cage bad. Miss forest.>*

"We will be leaving soon, I promise," I assure her with another scratch before turning to Riley as I stand. "Thank you for finding her."

"No trouble at all," the druid responds with a shake of his head. "She didn't belong in that cage. None o' those animals do."

"Were there a lot?" Robin and David both mentioned something about a zoo.

"Too many," Nathaniel comments, the cockatrice held against his chest. "And I'm not sure any of them are being taken care of properly."

"That's what I said!" Robin concurs with excitement. "So you're with me when I say we should just go and let them all out of their cages now, right?"

"What? No." The wizard is taken aback, clutching his creature more closely. "Half of them wouldn't stand a chance in the wild, and the other half would completely destroy the local ecosystem. And that's not even taking into account that some have probably been in captivity for so long or since they were so young that they might not even know *how* to survive on their own."

"...Fine." Robin narrows his arms and crosses his arms with a huff. "But we need to figure something out, it's not fair to keep them in there."

"Perhaps the two of you could work on a solution together?" I suggest. Aside from Riley, they seem like the most qualified. I also think it is in our best interest to keep Robin occupied.

"Yeah, we could do that," Nathaniel agrees with a nod, right before his face lights up. "Oh! You could do some shapeshifting and tell all the caretakers they have to listen to me!"

As the two of them begin discussing plans, Piper exits the closet with a fully dressed David. He's wearing a pair of tight, dark-brown leggings, and a white ruffled shirt with long sleeves. He fills them out well, but they are very refined compared to his usual style—too refined.

As soon as she sees him, Sona hurries over to David, greeting him with a light *yip*.

"Hey, girl." David crouches down to greet her like I did, petting over her fur. "It's good to see you." The sight of the two of them having bonded brings a smile to my face.

"Now that everyone has returned and is wearing clothes," Kignun walks up behind me, putting a hand on my shoulder, "perhaps we should take care of our werewolf problem?"

While we are safe on the upper floors, there is still a risk of running into the odd guard or other staff on the bottom. So, as much as I would like to have everyone with us, it is only Kignun, Kez, Michael, Adam, Corrine and myself that escort the enchanter through the dungeons. The older man tries to stumble his way through excuses for his actions on the way down, but we make it clear we expect silence from him until we reach the beast's cage.

The werewolf is awake when we approach the cell, but other than no longer being in his human form is otherwise just as we left him, bound in silver. Between his movement being restricted and the silver weakening him, there is little he can do but wriggle on the ground. He is barely able to growl over his whimpers of pain, and as we get closer, I can hear his skin burning against the metal.

"How do we do this?" Adam asks, the six of us standing outside of the cell.

"I imagine he will need to be as still as possible," I say, the enchanter confirming with a nod.

"He should already be pretty feeble, but I'll see what I can do." Michael cracks his knuckles as he prepares to cast.

"He's weak enough that I should at least be able to make him drowsy too," Corrine adds.

"I-I'll also need a clear patch of skin to apply the paint," the enchanter stutters nervously outside the cell.

I sigh to myself, my pocket knife still missing along with our other belongings.

"Does it matter where?" Kez asks, kneeling down and pulling a small blade from the bottom of her boot.

"N-no." The man shakes his head. "Anywhere will do."

"Alright, you three wanna hold him steady while I shave a spot on his back?" she asks me, Adam, and Kignun.

The three of us share a look before agreeing with a nod. After waiting for Michael and Corrine to cast their respective spells, the four of us enter the cell slowly. The werewolf's head swings toward the door unsteadily, tongue lolling out of his mouth after sluggishly snapping at us, Corrine's spell taking effect.

There is not much effort involved in keeping him still, Adam and I each grabbing one of his arms as Kignun sits on his legs. Kez moves in on his left side, knife in hand, and uses it to remove a swatch of fur from the wolf's lower back. The revealed skin beneath is a light tan, though I can already see what looks like stubble coming through, meaning the enchanter will need to work fast.

The man kneels over the werewolf's other side, already dipping his brush in the small pot of paint. He paints with the quick, measured strokes of a professional, albeit with very questionable ethics. Each rune shimmers briefly after it is completed before sinking into the skin.

"Finished," the enchanter announces with relief, leaning back on his heels.

Almost immediately, the body underneath me begins to move and shift. It starts slowly, with his body hair receding, but then his torso gives a sudden jerk that almost makes me jump off him in surprise. We all back away when his limbs are next, twisting and wrenching in different directions, even tied as they are. The whole process appears incredibly painful, but when it is finally done, we are left with a bound, naked, unconscious man before us.

"Still a pretty big guy," Adam comments, looking over the man's body.

"Though significantly less intimidating," Kignun adds. "I suppose we can get the silver off of him now."

"Is that really safe?" Kez asks next.

"This man was as much a prisoner as the rest of us," I respond. "I felt terrible that we had to take things this far just to protect ourselves."

"I won't keep him locked up and in pain any longer," Corrine states directly. "Even magically enhanced healing has its limits."

"Khazak and I can carry him back upstairs with us," Adam volunteers for the two of us.

I cannot help the stab of guilt when I see the burns left on the man's skin by the chains as we release him. Adam and I lift him from either side, his arms thrown over our shoulders. Getting him back to the castle is a series of trial and error, particularly when we try to negotiate him up the spiral staircase in the holding dungeon. We manage to get him to the top floor of the castle and into one of the extra bedrooms, laying him as gently as we can on the mattress. After asking Kez to post two of the Briars outside of his room, we leave him to rest and return to the master bedroom.

"Great, you're back," Liss tells us as we enter, standing from her spot leaning against the wall. "Foster is awake."

"Excellent, we can interrogate him next." I push the enchanter farther into the room. "Would someone mind making him comfortable with our other 'guests?'"

"I-I'm not free to go?" the enchanter asks nervously.

"Ha! Good one," Liss mocks, slapping him on the back. "You still got plenty to answer for, bub."

"Kignun, would you care to join me?" I ask the dwarf ranger.

"It will be just like old times," he replies with a smile.

"I'm coming too!" David says as he slides off the bed where he was lying down. "Tired of sitting around doing nothing."

"That is fine, but no one else," I tell the room. "He may feel less inclined to speak if too many of us are in the room."

The three of us walk together to the bedroom holding Captain Foster. The Briar standing guard outside gives us a nod but otherwise does not move from his post as we enter. Now that they are on our side, I have to admit I am impressed with their professionalism.

The room we are holding Foster in is one used by the castle's servants for storage with shelves of linens all along one wall, and brooms, brushes, sponges, and other cleaning supplies on another. Just like the still-unnamed werewolf, Foster is exactly as we left him, tied to a chair with his arms cuffed behind him. His head shoots up when we enter, glaring angrily but otherwise remaining still and silent. I stand on one side of him while Kignun stands at the other with David leaning against the wall behind us. It reminds me a little of home and running interrogations at the station.

"Good morning, Captain Foster," I start.

"Or should we say good evening?" Kignun follows. "Glad to have you back with us."

"Where is Prince Calvinson?" he asks with undeserved righteous anger. "What the *hell* do you think you're doing?"

"Probably a better job than you ever did..." David mutters behind us.

"*Richard* is doing just fine." I make sure to sound as casual as possible. "We were hoping you could answer a few questions about the past few weeks."

"You won't get away with this," Foster says cooly, sitting up straight.

"Get away with what?" Kignun asks him. "We are not the ones illegally detaining and abusing over a dozen people."

"I don't know what you're talking about." The way he says it, I actually almost believe him.

"Really? Because I know you weren't there when he was *fucking* me," David spits, pushing off from the wall to stand between me and Kignun. "But there was also the blackmailing, the threatening to murder my friends and family, using magic to trap me in a prison of my own mind," David counts off on his fingers. "And that's just me."

A strange series of emotions passes over Foster's face when he hears David: disgust, hurt, anger, and fear, before finally returning to the stony glare he wore when we first came in. "Maybe *some* things got out of hand, but——"

"You tried to have us kill each other today," I cut him off before he can continue his feeble excuse. "Me, specifically, before you unleashed dangerous predators to hunt us *and the rest of your city's population.*"

"I... I didn't know they would——" he tries anyway.

"We figured as much," Kignun is quick to say. *Spirits, I missed this, this rhythm.* "I am assuming you also did not know that the werewolf you were torturing is a knight from the royal court of Litkalaa." He pauses, then looks to me and speaks with his voice low, "The more I say that, the more it feels like I am trying to convince everyone that I have a famous friend."

Still, Kignun's words have the desired effect, Foster's complexion paling significantly. "I... I don't believe you."

"None of us cares whether you believe us or not," Kignun states flatly. "And I doubt King Samoset will either."

Foster doesn't have a snappy response to that, his eyes cast down to his lap as he considers our words. "What... What do you want from us?"

"Information," I answer first. "And for you to assist us in ensuring things remain peaceful while the future of the township is decided."

"You can't expect us to just hand over the keys to the city!"

"Dude, if you can't run a city without kidnapping people so they can fight to the death gladiator-style, then I don't think you get to run a city," David counters, bringing that strange pattern of emotions back to Foster's expression.

"No, I mean... There are so many people living here. Families with nowhere else to go and with little money left after traveling so far." He sounds reasonable for the first time tonight. "You can't just get rid of them."

"I agree that *most* of the citizens here in are innocent in this," Kignun concedes. "I do not have anything against Richardton's existence, but that does not negate the fact that its current leadership has been a *catastrophic failure*. Your best chance at ensuring all of those innocent people can continue living their lives is by cooperating with us."

"Although you really should think about changing the name, 'cause otherwise I think Dicktown's gonna stick," David adds.

Foster goes quiet again, mulling over our words and his decision. "I want to see Richard. I'm not agreeing to anything until I know he's safe."

"We can do that," I nod. "Only for a moment, and then you will tell us what we need to know."

"Alright." He nods his agreement.

Kignun and I untie him from the chair, David watching to ensure he does not try and escape. With his arms still cuffed, we help him stand and march him from this room to the master bedroom. We get a few strange looks from the others when we enter, but no one objects verbally as we bring him into the bathroom with the bound and gagged Calvinson.

"I want to talk to him," Foster demands, seeing him struggle in the large tub.

Wearily, I sigh to myself but agree to the request if it will move things along faster. Leaving Kignun and David with Foster, I move around to the other side of the tub, kneeling down behind Calvinson and pulling the gag from his mouth. He sputters angrily once it is free, glaring up at me indignantly.

"Richard, are you alrigh—"

"Do I look alright?!" he screeches before Foster can finish. "Where the hell are the rest of your men?!"

"They had their orders, but after all the chaos, *you* became my highest pri—"

"You said they were trained!" Now that the ability has been restored, he won't stop talking. "Or was all that time and money wasted on nothing?"

"They *are* trained, but you—"

"Why aren't you—"

"*Would you shut up?!*" Foster finally snaps. "Do you have any idea what's happened? What we've done? People are dead because of us! And we almost killed even more!" He grows more somber. "What happened, Rich? None of this is like what we talked about."

"I should have known you'd turn traitor like everyone else." The disgust that fills Calvinson's voice makes me want to smack him in the back of the head.

Foster winces at the word "traitor" but otherwise does not respond. "I'm done here," he tells us instead.

Calvinson sputters angrily when I pull the gag back between his teeth. He tries to spit out some sort of curse as we lead Foster from the room, struggling as he falls back in the tub. We bring the former captain back to his original room, letting him sit without being rebound, for now.

"It wasn't supposed to be like this," he says with a shake of his head.

Kignun and I share a look, making a silent decision to use his sudden urge to be talkative to our advantage. It is much easier to get information out of a willing subject. The more we can learn without a fight, the better.

"What was it supposed to be like?" Kignun asks the first leading question.

"I don't know. Just...better." He sighs.

"How did you come to work for Calvinson?" I question next.

"We grew up together," Foster answers with a small unhappy sigh. "My father worked for his."

"Did you also work for his father?" Kignun follows up.

"No, my father didn't want me to." He shakes his head. "I used to think it was because he didn't think I was capable, but now..." *What is it with Lutherian fathers and bad parenting?* "After school, I enrolled in the knight academy."

"As in the Northlake Academy of Knighthood?" David asks in shock. "I fucking *knew* you looked familiar!"

"You two know each other?" I look between the two humans in surprise.

"No, not really," David denies. "He was a few years ahead of me, I just knew about him in passing. Does the last name 'Cerano' mean anything to you?" The question is directed to Foster.

Foster stares at David for a moment before realization crosses over his face. "Oh my god, you're Joseph's little brother." If it was possible, he seems even more annoyed with David's presence than before.

"Yep," David confirms with a grimace.

"If you were already training to be a knight, what made you decide to leave and come here to found Richardton?" Kignun gets the questioning back on track.

"With the way Richard talked about it, the plans he had, I thought it would be a chance to prove myself." He finishes with a small laugh at his own reasoning.

"And at what point did you decide throwing innocent people in a dungeon and making them fight for your buddy's amusement was a good way to 'prove yourself?'" Even *I* wince at David's wording.

"At what point did *you* decide to start fucking your way out of trouble?!" Foster snaps back, and I see all that strange hostility for David I previously saw rise to the surface.

"What is your problem with me, exactly?" David moves to stand between me and Kignun. "Are you jealous?"

I expect Foster to deny it, but instead, he looks away when David tries to meet his eyes, face turning red.

"Spirits, you and Calvinson *are* fucking," I mutter, remembering the guards' whispered conversation outside the infirmary. As if to confirm, Foster's face turns an even brighter red.

"Whatever we once were to each other, we aren't anymore. Haven't been for a long time. He's not the same person I used to know," Foster says with conviction, finally meeting our eyes. "I want to help fix the mistakes we've made. However I can."

I am happy to have his cooperation, but there is a part of me that feels sorry for the man and his apparent romantic woes. But seeing as we have it, we spend nearly an hour going over what we have planned. Frederick should have already sent out the letters Kignun wrote, and though he expects a response in the next few days, it may be over a week before anyone dispatched can reach the city.

Having Foster on our side will allow us and the other prisoners to move more freely through the city and castle without worry. The captain does his best to defend the men he has been leading, leveraging his cooperation to try and ensure any punishment they receive is lenient, but the best we can do is promise that whatever happens will happen fairly. "They were only obeying orders" has its limits.

When we are finished, we leave Foster in his quarters and return to the others in the master bedroom. Before the doors are even fully open, my nostrils are hit with the scent of something delicious, and I remember that I have not had a decent meal in days. While we took care of the werewolf and Foster, Frederick and some of the others made it down to the kitchens to prepare dinner. Apparently quite the feast was prepared for the coronation celebrations, meats and cheeses and all sorts of baked sweets, so there is plenty to fill our too-empty stomachs.

After we have all eaten—including the prisoners, except for Calvinson who silently and angrily refused his—it is late. With our plan of action in place, there is nothing left to do but sleep. Though a few of us still have to share, the castle thankfully has no shortage of empty bedrooms, and after divvying up watch shifts with the Blackbriars (even with things going our way, you can never be too careful), everyone retires for the evening.

"I can't get over how weird it is," David says wistfully.

"That you and Foster knew each other?" I ask, standing over a small wash basin Frederick filled with warm water.

"Yeah. That he and Calvinson came from the same town as most of us," David continues, lying back on the bed. "I can't believe I didn't recognize him sooner."

"We were all a little preoccupied." I finish washing and drying my face and hands. "He mentioned your brother, Joseph. Were they friends?"

"Doubt it. He would have been a couple of years behind him," David informs me. "Joseph was just a really big deal there, same as my dad." The unspoken "same as me" hangs in the air.

"He seemed to have some issues with his own father," I tread carefully into the potentially-volatile subject.

"Yeah... I know what you're getting at." He sits up and turns to me with a sigh. "I mean, my dad's not a crime lord and doesn't work for one but..." He pauses, worrying his lip. "It's hard not to see the similarities. Maybe not as much with Calvinson, but Foster and I basically had the same life. If I was a few years older, I could have easily done the same thing he did."

"Perhaps." I would like to think my pup has a stronger moral compass. "We are often victims of our circumstances. Does it...make you feel any differently about your family?"

"You mean, does it make me want to talk to my father?" he responds wryly. "Maybe. I think I'm kind of done talking about family stuff for a while."

"Then perhaps you would instead like to discuss the punishment you'll be receiving for bartering with *my* property yesterday?" I approach the bed with an amused smirk. "As well as the way you spoke to me just a few days ago in the forest the *first* time we tried to have that conversation."

"I'm...still getting punished?" His expression is caught somewhere between hesitant and hopeful. "Not that I'm not trying to get out of it, I mean like, in general. After our earlier conversation, I wasn't sure if that was still going to be a thing, and I guess I didn't really know how to—"

"David," I cut off his nervous rambling, taking a seat next to him. "Do you *want* to change that aspect of our relationship?"

"No." He shakes his head, pausing to gather his thoughts. "Okay, so for the record, I am not saying that I *want* to be punished, but I did always kinda like that I didn't really have a say in the matter. That there would be consequences when I disobeyed you."

"I like that aspect too," I agree.

"But isn't that kind of at odds with everything we talked about earlier?" I can hear the shame in his voice.

"Not necessarily." I stroke a hand over his upper leg. "We needed to have that conversation so that we know how the other person *actually* feels, instead of working based on assumptions. As long as we are open and talk about things, I see no reason why we cannot continue as we have been."

"Does that mean we're going to have a whole conversation any time we want to do...anything?" He asks it like a teenager being told to finish his homework, and I don't hold back my laugh.

"Do you remember our 'performance' outside of Brull's shop in Tah'lj?" I ask, my own memory of that afternoon a very fond one. "The safeword I gave you?"

"'Jailbreak?'" he responds with a grumpy smirk.

"Yes, jailbreak." I squeeze his thigh. "If you ever use that word, no matter what we are doing, we stop. That doesn't mean we can't talk about things when we need to talk about them, but outside of that signal, you are mine, my property, my avakesh, with all the rules and restrictions that come with the title. Does that sound alright to you?"

"Yes." He nods. "Yes, Sir."

"Good." I smile, leaning over to give him a quick kiss, then pat my thigh. "Now, get over my lap."

"...Right now?" he asks coyly. "I just...think the walls are kind of thin."

"Thin *and* hollow," I correct. "Which means you will have to be quiet about how much noise you make."

With a silent grumble, David unbuttons and pulls his pants down past his thighs before crawling over my lap. I smile as his furry cheeks come into view, palming them as he settles into place. Despite my taunting, I am not actually planning on being terribly rough this evening. There are plenty of other ways I can punish my pup back on the road. And as our room is not being flanked by his brother, I am less concerned about making noise than David.

I start with a few light smacks to both cheeks, just warming them up. David whimpers but still makes sure to keep his ass propped up for me. It has been far too long since we've done this; he can deny it all he wants, but me and my pup both know he enjoys being disciplined. Frankly, a brat of his caliber would benefit from regular maintenance spankings. Ragnar has a standing appointment with Nylan's rump every Astraday before bed.

And if I am being honest, I need this too. Having him here with me, under my hands, where I know he is safe, helps me feel grounded. I know we have barely spent time apart in months, but not knowing where or how he was for the past day and a half was difficult. Even as capable as he is at taking care of himself, there are many dangers I would prefer to face together.

I continue to pepper each side of his ass with light, full-handed smacks, slowly turning the pale flesh pink. I do not have a particular number in mind, but with every strike, I can feel both myself and David sinking into our respective headspaces. With each spank, David lets out a small whimper, his body still flinching slightly in reflex, but then relaxing further over my legs.

I look over his body, his back shiny with sweat and his muscles slack, trying to let go of the anger I still hold toward Calvinson for taking him from me. At David for putting himself in danger. At myself for not protecting him. With each strike, the skin of his rear ripples, going tense for a split second. Even as my palm starts to sting, I press on with the spanking, the rhythm almost therapeutic in itself.

I lose track of the hour by the time we are done, stroking my hand across David's back. I wipe my brow, both of us panting from the exertion and intensity of the punishment. Still over my lap, David turns his face to me, his eyes rimmed red with silent tears. When I reach up to tuck a sweaty lock of hair behind his ear, his hand quickly darts out to take mine, pressing his lips to my palm in a quick kiss.

For a while, I just bask in the comfortable silence, gently petting my spent pup. Well, not entirely spent, if the half-hard erection poking into my thighs is any indication. Feeling playful, I use my fingernails to lightly scrape over the inflamed skin of his ass, pleased with the gasp I force from his lips. I continue to tease and play until he is squirming on my lap, both of us hard and rutting against each other.

With some quick maneuvering, I have us on our sides, facing each other. One hand on his bruised bottom, I pull him in for a searing kiss, knocking one of my tusks into his cheekbone in my urgency. As David returns my kiss hungrily, I start to delve my fingers between his cheeks, seeking out his hole. He gasps into my mouth when I make contact, and as I continue to tease him, a thought crosses my mind.

"David, do you know where your cleansing charm is?" I reluctantly ask, already knowing the answer.

"...Godsdamnit," he answers with a frustrated groan. "No, and we forgot to ask Foster where they're keeping all our stuff."

"I was worried about that." While it's not the end of the world, it does at least mean having to change my plans for the night.

"Calvinson had one somewhere in his bedroom. I could go look for it, maybe?" David offers with hesitation.

"That is alright. I do not feel like putting my clothes back on either," I tease. More to the point, I am not sure how I feel about using any of that man's sexual aids. I like even *less* the fact that he was the last person to touch David like that—a problem I will be remedying as soon as possible— but for now...

I tighten my grip on David's ass, crushing our crotches together and capturing his mouth in another kiss. I growl into his mouth as our hard cocks grind against each other, using the hand on his ass to encourage David to hump against me. As usual, my pup is already leaking like a faucet, and I am not far behind, a dual set of sticky spots on each of our stomachs.

Figuring out my plan, David finds his rhythm, throwing an arm over my waist to hold himself steady as he humps and grinds. Feeling drier than I'd like, I spit into one hand and reach down to slick us both as best I can, easing some of the friction. David sighs happily against my lips when I lean in for another kiss, his hips never stuttering.

As our not-so-dry humping continues, our movements grow more frantic. Our kissing gets more intense as we drive each other closer to our goal, until we are practically growling into each other's mouth, all teeth and tongue. I can feel David reaching the edge first, his eyes screwed shut in concentration when I open mine. Feeling generous, I break our mouths apart to spit in my hand again, reaching down to take a hold of him.

His reaction is instant, his eyes shooting open as he involuntarily bucks into my hand. I start to work my fist up and down his length, revealing the slick head of his cock peeking out from his foreskin. When he starts to moan and whine, I press our lips together in a soothing gesture, never letting up as my hand becomes a blur of green over pink. The muscles in his thighs start to tense before, with a low groan, David cums, spraying over my own stomach and groin. While I slow my hand, he continues to hump forward, the final shot spilling over my fist.

With one of us finished, it is my turn. I run my hand over my slick stomach, gathering as much of David's seed as I can before smearing it over my cock. Then, after capturing David's mouth in yet *another* kiss, I roll him onto his back and slot myself between his thighs, pressing my chest to his and pinning him to the bed.

I roll my hips, my slick cock finding the groove of his inner thigh and snapping down. I growl into his mouth as I savor the feel of David's soft skin as I chase my own orgasm. I am already close, and without thinking I grab both of his wrists and pin them above his head, squeezing them just as I reach the precipice. After a handful more forceful thrusts against him, I explode, burying my face in David's neck and shuddering as I unload all over his crotch and belly.

"That was...awesome," David says between breaths, finally finding his voice.

"Yes, it was," I pant in return. "And you should enjoy it while you can."

"I'm going back in the chastity cage, aren't I?" he half-asks, half-whines.

"For a *long* time," I tell him with a smile and a *boop* on the nose.

I lie there, nuzzling against his neck, both hands now tangled in his sweaty hair and petting him gently. His own hands free, they come up to wrap around my back, squeezing the muscles of my shoulders and making no attempt to push me off. As we lie there, breathing, relaxing, I start to doze, until we are both asleep, his body covered by mine.

We are awoken by a knock on our door sometime later. I am not sure how late it is, but it feels too early for our watch shift. After carefully and somewhat painfully extracting ourselves from each other (never fall asleep with semen drying in your pubic hair, especially when it is tangled with someone else's), I hastily pull on my pants and stumble to the door.

"Khazak." It's Kignun, looking tired and stressed. "Sorry to wake you."

"Is everything alright?" I ask, not moving from the doorway to spare David some dignity.

"Yes, just my damned memory getting away from me," he explains, looking frustrated. "There is something I needed to tell you."

"It is alright. You have been through a lot." Even more so than us. "What is it?"

"Redwish," he answers with a grimace. "He was here before I was arrested."

Chapter 18

"**And how long ago was it?**"

"Almost two weeks, at this point."

"Did they have any other information?" Adam asks next.

"I am afraid not." Kignun shakes his head with a sigh. "Only that a red-haired orc was seen passing through town, headed for Manamequohi."

"Damn," Adam curses after hearing the early-morning retelling of his news regarding Redwish.

Shockingly, David and I did not have the easiest time returning to sleep after the dwarf's late-night revelation. In fact, as soon as he heard Redwish's name, David was up and out of the bed, completely forgetting that he was both naked *and* covered in the dried remnants of our earlier romp in bed. He only got dressed at my urging, saving him and Kignun from an embarrassing eyeful.

After we were presentable, Kignun came in and told us the whole story—not that there was much to it. After we last saw him in Pákannon, Kignun continued to track Redwish's location, one of my final orders as Ranger Captain. He followed his trail all the way to Richardton, where he learned that an orc matching Redwish's description had been seen at the inn. The innkeeper confirmed, stating that he was only there for a single night, did not talk to anyone, and left early the next morning. After asking a few more people around the market, Kignun learned that Redwish appeared to have left town to the north—which is when he ran into trouble with the local guards and was unfairly arrested.

Kignun felt terrible, apologizing profusely for not remembering to tell us sooner, though I did my best to assure him it was alright. The last few days have been stressful to say the least, and the poor man spent longer than any of us being locked up, mistreated, and underfed. Last night was the first chance for any of us to get some real rest since this began.

It was still very late, and neither myself nor David wanted to wake anyone up to deliver the news—we were not going to leave to chase him in the middle of the night. We tried to sleep but largely just laid next to each other while tossing and turning until finally giving up and leaving for our watch shifts early. We shared the information with some of the others during shift changes, but the rest of the group is only learning about it now.

"I cannot tell you how sorry I am for not remembering to tell you sooner," Kignun apologizes again.

"It's really okay," David repeats what we told him last night. "I'm not sure we could've really left any sooner anyway."

"It is nice to have a reminder about what we were doing before all of this happened," Corrine agrees, gesturing to the room around us.

"It also means that I'm not sure we have the time to stick around and help clean all this up," Adam adds with a grimace.

"I agree. You do not," Kignun tells him. "The good news is, with everything we have managed to accomplish so far, I should be able to handle the rest here without you."

He pauses, turning to look at Kez. "Can I continue to count on you and your compatriots for support?"

"If we get paid, we can stick around as long as you need us to," the mercenary tells him with a cocky smile.

"I am sure something can be arranged," Kignun responds wryly.

"Alright, so what's the plan, boss-man?" David rhymes with a grin.

"The first thing we need is supplies—old and new," Adam starts.

"Foster should know where they are holding our belongings," I point out.

"Oooo, I can take care of that. Been wanting to give that guy a piece of my mind," Liss volunteers as she quickly exits the room.

"Cory, will you—"

"Go with her to make sure she doesn't hurt the guy?" the blonde cleric finishes. "On it."

"Thanks," Adam tells her with a nod of his head. "That still leaves the supplies we needed before we got here—I know we picked up a few things, but since we're not being chased out of town, I'd like to try and get anything we missed."

"Kez here promised to replace the camping equipment they destroyed," Michael informs the others with a grin.

"Just bring me a receipt." The woman rolls her eyes but doesn't disagree. "I'll reimburse you when we find my wallet."

"I can handle the shopping!" Piper happily volunteers. "Though I may need some help carrying things back."

"I would offer, but I think I might draw a little too much unwanted attention." I frown.

"You and David both," Adam agrees. "Riley, Nate, would you go with her?"

"No problem," the druid agrees, all three spellcasters exiting together.

"What next?" Michael asks now that half our group has been given assignments.

"Well, if we can get everything together fast enough, we could leave in a few hours," Adam suggests. "Manamequohi is still a week and a half away."

"Sir, if I may," Frederick, who has been left untied but not unmonitored, offers from a corner of the room. "The castle has a fleet of horses and carriages. I could have some prepared for you, if you'd like."

"Not that it doesn't sound good, but how would we return them?" Tsula asks timidly.

"You could consider it a gift?" The man is obviously trying to please us in exchange for leniency, though I am not sure if that is for himself or his former charge.

"I won't turn down something that'll make our trip easier," Adam says, considering the offer. "They will need to be able to hold ten people—and one wolf—comfortably."

"Of course." Frederick nods his head. "I can have them ready for you in—"

The man is interrupted by a crashing sound followed by shouts that are either angry or confused. All of us share a look of worry, but before anyone can take so much as a step toward the doors, they open and one of the Blackbriar guards pokes his head in. He looks equally worried.

"Hey Kez?" he starts, nervously. "That werewolf guy is awake, and uh, he doesn't seem very happy."

Without any further prompting, we rush from the room, following the Briar back to the bedroom. As we turn the corner, I notice two of the other Briars standing in the hall, looking into the room's open door with apprehension. Before we can ask them anything, a sound somewhere between a shout and a growl comes from the room.

Standing behind the Briars, I see the man inside looking half-feral. I am not being facetious; there is hair sprouting from his face and neck, his eyes have yellow tinge to them, and his teeth resemble fangs—he is mid-transformation. Not wanting things to escalate, I step forward with Kignun.

"Please, wait." Kignun holds both of his hands up. "We are not your enemy."

"Why would I believe that?" the wolf-man growls.

"We are not the ones who imprisoned you," I try to tell him.

"Then why am I being kept in this room?" he points out, still looking understandably distrustful of us.

"We know you were being held here against your will. So were the rest of us," Kignun starts to explain. "We recognized your tattoos and sent word to King Samoset regarding your condition and requesting assistance."

"We are not trying to hold you here," I say next. "We understand if you do not wish to wait for a response, but we only want to help."

He looks between everyone gathered outside his room, still anxious but at least dropping his aggressive stance. "You've really contacted my king?"

"Yes," Adam assures from behind. "We really just want to help you and the other people being held here however we can."

"Like, maybe by getting you some pants?" David points out the man's nakedness. "Or some food?"

The attempt at humor forces a small laugh from the man's mouth as he looks down and realizes his nudity, cutting some of the tension. "A meal and some pants would be nice. Thank you."

"We can get those!" Tsula offers, taking Michael by the wrist as she walks toward the kitchens.

Fewer people in the hall might make him feel less boxed in, so Kez calls back the Briars who were keeping guard and leaves us to handle things. The werewolf happily accepts the clothes and food that Tsula and Michael return with, dressing quickly before he tucks in. When his eating finally starts to slow down, he seems ready to talk.

"We never got your name, friend," I start with the obvious. "I am Khazak, and this is David, Kignun, and Adam," I finish, referring to those of us still in the room.

"Hebert. Achak Hebert, royal guard of Litkalaa," he answers with a sense of formality.

"How did you come to be here, Achak?" Kignun asks next.

"What's the date?" Achak asks after swallowing another bite.

"The 16th of Cancea," Kignun responds.

"Gods, I've been gone over a month now." His eyes grow wide in worry.

"You've been here over a month?" David asks in shock.

"No. I've been here about three weeks," he corrects with a shake of his head. "I was first captured two weeks before that, north of here."

"Manamequohi?" Adam asks next.

"No, much farther," he corrects. "Natathoda."

"What was Calvinson doing all the way up there?" Adam wonders in surprise.

"It wasn't him," he corrects again. "Slavers. The kind that were specifically looking for people like me."

"Werewolves?" David asks.

"And other magically enhanced people," he says with a sigh. "They were prepared. They originally talked about selling me to some mining operation out west, but then Calvinson offered them double what they wanted. I was on my way here the next day."

"Do you remember much about your imprisonment?" I question.

"Only the first week or so." He pauses, searching his memory. "I can remember everything up until I met that enchanter. The runes he used forced me to shift, and something else kept me angry and aggressive. Things are less clear after that."

"You still have those tattoos, by the way," David informs him.

"We had the enchanter apply counter runes to nullify them until you can have them removed," I explain.

"Thank you for that. Tattoo removal sounds fun." He grimaces before straightening his posture. "Now tell me about these plans you've made."

We spend the next hour going over the events of the past two days and the current situation. Achak is happy to assist in maintaining order while waiting for reinforcements. The current plan is to utilize Captain Foster and a shapeshifted Robin to keep things running as smoothly as possible. Robin will announce that the city is establishing diplomatic ties with some neighboring cities, so as to lessen panic and suspicion when the requested backup arrives.

We assemble near the castle's rear gate just after noon. It is technically called a postern, but when I use that name everyone except Frederick stares at me in confusion. Elisabeth seemed disappointed with how easy it was to get the location of our belongings while I am just surprised to find that none of it was picked through. Even the other captives' belongings were left alone. Piper's group returned with our supplies about a half an hour ago, and we immediately brought them here to load into the carts.

The two carriages we have been given look much more extravagant than those we commandeered from the Blackbriars, at least on the outside, painted white with red and purple embellishments. The spacious but barebones interiors contain two rows of padded benches, which will suit our purposes just fine. We now also have four horses to care for, so I make sure each cart is loaded with plenty of feed. Seeing me raiding the stables gives David his own idea, grabbing my satchel and rushing off to the kitchens.

"I do not feel right leaving you here to handle all this on your own," I tell Kignun as we finish loading things onto the second carriage. "It is not what I would do if I were still captain."

"Then I guess it is a good thing you are not captain anymore," he says with a laugh as I step down. "Someone has to take care of it—and someone else has to catch Redwish."

"It was good to see you again, even if it was under these circumstances," I tell him as we clasp each other's wrists, pulling one another in for the Tah'lj version of a handshake and hug. "I know it is somewhat distant, but please, if anything happens, send word to us in Maname."

"You do the same, sir." He salutes me when we break apart. "And try to keep that boy of yours out of trouble."

"Good luck with that," Adam jokes as he hops down from the back of the other carriage. "I think that's everything. We can leave once David gets back."

"Actually, I need to talk to you all about something," Nathaniel starts to say, pausing to take a deep breath. "I'm not going with you."

All of us are stunned into silence, not sure what to make of the statement.

"What do you mean?" Adam asks after sharing a particularly long look with Liss. "I told you, we worked everything out with the Blackbriar Guild. You're safe."

"Yep!" Kez confirms happily. "Nathaniel Carter died in a bear attack, and that egg was destroyed."

"A bear attack?" The wizard shakes head, bewildered. "It's not that. There are a lot of animals here that need to be taken care of, and I just...think I can do some good."

"I could certainly use the help," Kignun comments. "I do not know what to do with half of those magical beasts, and I am not sure I trust that fae's intentions."

"Are you sure staying here is the safest thing for you to do?" Corrine asks hesitantly. "I mean, Calvinson's son founded the city...and he's still here."

"She's right," I step forward to agree. "There is no guarantee his father will not still come looking for you or for proof that you are truly dead."

"Well, maybe I'm also tired of running," Nathaniel replies confidently. "I've made up my mind. I'm staying."

"Wait, really?" David, who has reappeared with my bag thrown over his shoulder, asks in surprise.

"Yeah." Nate nods with a straight face as David approaches.

"Damn." He puts a hand on the other man's shoulder. "I was just starting to like you."

"Wish I could say the feeling was mutual," the wizard replies with a roll of his eyes, though his begrudging grin says differently.

Most of the group has only known him for a month, and even I have not gotten terribly close to the man, so our goodbyes are short. But for Adam, David, Corrine, and Elisabeth, things are a little more somber. Even if they did not always get along, they are losing a teammate.

"It's been fun traveling with you, Nate," Corrine tells him with a hug. "Stay safe, okay? And take good care of that little guy."

"Thanks, Cor. I will," he says as they break apart. "Try and keep everyone out of trouble."

"That'll be a lot easier without you around setting everything on fire," David tells him, reaching out to Nate's extended hand and using it to pull him in for a hug. "It's been an adventure, man."

"Yeah well, try not to die without me." He pauses. "Again."

After David, the only person left to say their goodbyes is Elisabeth. Sensing that they may want a little privacy, me and the others say our goodbyes to Kignun, Kez, and the Briars. Even Frederick wishes us well as we climb into the carts to allow the two humans to finish their farewells in peace. And while I certainly don't *intend* to eavesdrop, I cannot help if I have above-average hearing, can I?

"So... I guess this really goodbye," Liss starts awkwardly.

"I guess it is," Nathaniel agrees. "I just want you to know how sorry I am. For lying to you, for hiding my past."

"I know," she responds sadly. "I get why you did it, but I still don't think I can forgive you for it."

"I understand." Nathaniel sounds just as sad. "The past four months have been some of the craziest of my life, but you were definitely a highlight. You're an amazing woman, Elisabeth."

"Take care of yourself, Nate," she says, and then I hear the rustle of a hug and maybe a small peck of a kiss before the back door of our carriage opens, and Liss climbs inside to take her seat.

"Alright, let's get a move on," Adam says, allowing his friend to stare a hole into the wall.

With a nod, I move up to the front of the cart, once again taking up the reins. Our group is split into groups of five, with David, Adam, Liss, and Sona with me, and Riley, Tsula, Corrine, Piper, and Michael in the other carriage. I have not seen the two brothers interact much since David rejoined us, and I suspect they are still avoiding one another.

With my cart in the lead, I take off from the castle, waving goodbye to Kignun and the others as we pass. I get a few strange looks as we pass the guards stationed at the half-constructed wall, but no one tries to stop us. As soon as we are past the city's borders, Sona comes up through the driver's compartment and leaps into the forest from the seat next to me.

<Forest! Run!> She barks happily as she exits the cart. I worry for a second that she may be leaving us altogether, after being captured the way she was, but then I feel her keeping pace with us, and I relax. *Poor girl just needs to run on her own for a while.*

"So you were just gonna leave without saying goodbye?" I startle when I hear Robin's voice just behind my head.

"*Stop doing that!*" David shouts.

"Whatever." I hear his eyes roll. "I just wanted to say bye. And even though you only helped me *after* you were in trouble, I still wanted to thank you."

"Everything worked out in the end," Adam tells him. "I'm glad we were able to do something."

"You *are* still gonna help Kignun and the others even though we're leaving, right?" David asks, worried.

"Whatever it takes to get them to tear down that cheap ugly castle," Robin grumbles in agreement.

"Thank you for your help, Robin. We would not have been nearly as successful without it," I say behind me. "And good luck at getting back your forest."

"Good luck to you too," he responds with a final nod. "I hope you can figure out whatever is going on with your boy." And then he's gone.

We make excellent time that first day, stopping only briefly so that David can pass out some of the food he stole from the kitchens for lunch. Free from the fear of being pursued, we are able to set the horses at a leisurely pace, pushing on until the sun starts to set and we decide to camp for the night. While the others set up our site, I tend to the horses with Riley, ensuring they are fed and watered for the evening.

"Is this tent larger than our previous one?" I ask as I enter, David just finishing with the tent poles.

"I might have told Piper to get the biggest one she could find." He shrugs with a sly smile. "Bedroll, too. Not like I can't afford it."

"I believe it was Kez who afforded it, but as you like to say, 'I'm not complaining.'" I smile. It is not a large difference, but enough that I am looking forward to stretching out tonight.

"It was literally the least she could do." He shuffles over to me on his knees for a kiss.

"Mmmm." I hum happily against his lips. Dinner tonight will be more of what David took from the castle kitchen, but before we rejoin the others, it is time to broach a touchy subject. "Have you spoken to your brother at all, yet?"

"...Nope." He turns and tries to make a quick exit, forcing me to follow him outside.

"*David*," I scold as I grab his arm. "Unless our plans are waylaid again, we only have a few more days before your brother and his friends are supposed to leave us. Is this really how you want it to end?"

"No," he says with a sigh. "But can't we just skip the parts where we have to talk about our feelings?"

"Avoiding an awkward family conversation?" Riley, who has stepped out of his own tent, asks after overhearing. "Ya know, I might have somethin' that'll help... Hold on."

After turning to grab something inside his tent, he motions for us to join him by the fire, where a few of the others are already gathered. Taking a seat next to him on the grass, I see what he's holding is a glass jar, containing a small wooden pipe, matches, and what I think is cannabis.

"Is that weed?" David asks what I am thinking, using a slang term I've heard Nylan use before.

"Yep, been savin' it for a rainy day," the druid replies as he opens the lid of the jar. "And after all that nonsense in Richardton, I think it's lookin' pretty cloudy."

"Count me in," Liss announces from across the fire, the first words she's said since we left Richardton.

"Are you okay with this?" Riley asks me as he packs some of the green plant matter into the pipe. "I know you used to be a lawman."

"I may hold off so that at least someone remains sober in the event of an emergency, but why would I have an issue?" I am confused by the question.

"A lot of drugs aren't illegal where he's from," David explains to Riley from my other side.

"Really?" The redhead pauses, looking lost in thought for a moment. "Maybe I should consider moving."

I have heard of cannabis being illegal in other places, but I cannot say I fully understand it. In V'rok'sh Tah'lj, we call it tro'kla or relaxing weed. It is also used for medicinal purposes, and the fibers are excellent for making rope or certain types of clothing. While hardly a frequent consumer, I have enough recreational experience to know the effects are much milder than other narcotics or even alcohol.

"I'm gonna pass," Adam says with a wave of his hand. "I don't like the way that stuff makes my head feel."

"Me as well, I'm afraid," Piper also declines.

"Thank you anyway!" Corrine concurs with a smile.

The six of us who will be smoking move away, forming a second circle on the grass downwind of the campsite. After lighting the pipe with a match, Riley inhales first before passing it to me, and then it moves on to David, Liss, Michael, and finally Tsula. There's a fair amount of coughing between us, but most of it comes from Tsula, whose face is teary and red when she's finished.

"First time?" Michael asks with concern over his face.

"Was *cough* it that obvious?" she asks, drying her eyes with her sleeve.

"Oh boy," Liss comments with a grin. "You're in for some fun."

We pass around the pipe once more, Tsula skipping her turn the second time around. I can already feel the effects starting, so before we are too far under, I nudge David, looking toward his brother when he meets my eye. With a silent sigh, he stands.

"Hey, uh, before we get all giggly," he starts to say to his twin, "can we talk?"

"Yeah, okay." Michael nods, standing and dusting his hands off on his robe as the two of them step away from the group, far enough so that people cannot hear. Well, *most* people.

"So, about what happened a few days ago..." David starts.

"Let me go first," Michael insists. "I'm sorry about some of the things I said. I think you were right. I was just lashing out because I don't like that things are changing. That we're changing. I know it's not a bad thing, but it does seem like other people know you better than I do now."

"I don't really think I'm *that* different," David responds. "But I understand."

"David, the stuff about you and Khazak," Michael continues. "You have to understand that the way your relationship started, the way he treats you, it's not right."

"Look, I won't deny that the way it started was fucked up. He and I both know that." *Well, we do* now *after finally talking it through...* "But it isn't like that anymore and hasn't been for a long time."

"David, he makes you wear a chain locked around your neck," the brown-haired man points out.

"The only things he 'makes' me do are things I'm generally interested in doing to begin with," my pup defends me and our relationship. "And those 'things' aren't really any of your business anyway. Or do you want me to explain how I get turned on when he ties me up and spanks me?"

"Nope. No. I don't— You don't—" Michael stumbles over his brother's excessive information, shaking his head vigorously.

"Then trust me when I tell you that this is what I want," David says with a gentle tone. "Trust that I'm happy. That when I say I love him, I really do love him."

"...I'll try," Michael answers after a beat of silence.

"Thanks." I hear the familiar clothes-rustling sound of a hug. "I know I can't make you like him, but I hope you can at least learn to get along because I don't think he's going anywhere. Not if I have a say in it." *Me neither, puppy.*

"Like I said, I'll try." Another hug. "Love you, D."

"Love you too, Mikey."

Finished with their family chat, the brothers rejoin us as Riley is packing the last of the cannabis into his pipe. David offers me a smile as he retakes his seat next to me, leaning over for a kiss, as if to prove a point, but I do not deny him. The pipe is passed around again, and I start to feel the familiar relaxed, slightly elated feeling that comes with ingesting cannabis. When all that's left is ash, we return to the fire and the others.

It is interesting to see how getting "high" can affect different people in different ways. For her first time, Tsula is understandably talkative, a trait she and Michael share, the two of them chatting about magical theories far too complicated for me to understand at the moment that I'm willing to bet that neither of them will remember come morning. Riley is much quieter, and if he is anything like myself, very introspective. David is predictably hungry, and I have to stop him from devouring everything he raided from the kitchen in one night, and I am not sure what I expected from Liss, but sitting quietly with Sona and petting over her fur was not it.

The rest of the evening is quiet and relaxing, a nice change of pace from our last time on the road. After sharing dinner around the fire (and waiting for a few of us to sober up), we split up the watch shifts for the night before taking care of washing or anything else that is needed before bed. As we enter our tent, David pounces on me, having moved on from hungry to horny.

"Someone is in a mood," I tease as he chases my mouth for a kiss. "I hope someone also remembered that now that I have my bag back, they have a date with a certain chastity cage."

"Of course I remembered, Sir," he responds as he pulls off his shirt and lays down on our bedroll. "But I have a feeling you're gonna make it a pretty memorable date."

"Mhmm. Finish stripping," I order with a smirk as I turn to my satchel.

I retrieve the cage as expected but also a few other items: two black handkerchiefs and a bundle of soft, cotton rope. David spots them when I turn back to him, watching my hands with curiosity. I set them to the side, near his head, as I lower myself to capture his lip. Slotted between his thighs, his arms and legs wrap around me, and I grin against his mouth at the instinctual reaction. I squeeze his upper arms before taking him by the forearms and pressing them to the bedroll beside his head. His legs only clutch my waist tighter in response, and I fight to keep the growl I respond with low.

"Onto your stomach, hands behind your back," I order quietly after we break apart.

It looks like David might argue with me for a moment, but he complies when I kneel up, watching me over his shoulder as I straddle his legs. I take him by the arms again, pressing his wrists together at the small of his back with a silent instruction not to move. He strains his neck when I reach for the rope by his head, trying to follow me.

"You're gonna tie me—mmff?!" David's quip is cut short by the handkerchief I shove between his teeth, tying it behind his head.

I undo the rope bundle's coil, wrapping one end of David's left wrist, and then moving on to his right. I continue alternating as I weave a long band of rope along the length of both forearms, tying the two ends together in a simple overhand knot with a bight. Sturdy enough to keep his arms in place, but simple enough to undo when I am finished. I watch as David tests the rope's strength, pleased when there is no give.

After finishing the ties on his wrist, I flip David onto his back, careful of his bound arms beneath him. I fold the second handkerchief into a thick strip of cloth I tie around David's eyes as a blindfold, who makes a soft sound of confusion when things go dark. With him bound, gagged, and blinded underneath me, I take the opportunity to tease his naked body, lightly trailing my fingertips down his chest and over his nipples. At first he fights against chasing the fleeting sensations, but when I tickle over his stomach he struggles to remain silent.

Next, I move down to his cock, thick and heavy between his thighs. He is already hard and leaking, his length twitching as I tease him with my fingers, tracing them up to his head, and then back down to the base. I roll his sack between my fingers, enjoying the light feeling of fuzziness in my palm, and the way it causes even more pre-cum to leak from his cockhead.

But tonight is not about David's cock.

"*Waruk*," I whisper to myself, wrapping my hand around his shaft.

There is another muffled noise of confusion followed by what I can only describe as *almost* a shriek, after my hand suddenly grows cold. *Very* cold. I may not use it often, but a small temperature spell is simple enough for a spell-caster of my caliber. I hum thoughtfully as the appendage shrinks in my hand, David whining and trying to wriggle out of my hold. Once he is soft enough, I slip the base ring of the chastity cage down his shaft and under his testicles before guiding him into the metal sheath and locking the two together. Placing the small key to the side, I wonder if I should just keep a copy around my neck next to the one for his collar, what with all the use it's been getting lately.

I play with his upper body a little more before rolling him back onto his stomach. After checking the rope and his arms to verify everything is as it should be, I slide back, leaving David alone and exposed to the air. As I strip off my own clothes and retrieve a few final items from my bag, I watch him lie there, bound and waiting for me. I take more than a little pleasure at the way he jumps when my hands finally return to his body.

Straddling his legs again, I take his ass in my hands, squeezing and kneading the fuzzy flesh. Spreading them apart, I run my thumbs along the inner seam of his cheeks, just outside the tight ring of muscle at the center. I repeat this, moving farther in each time, barely ghosting over his entrance. My own cock twitches at the way David presses his ass back against me, fighting for more contact. He sighs in pleasure when I finally appease him, licking my thumb before rubbing it in firm, slick circles against the outside of his hole.

Before we go any further, I take the cleansing charm in hand and slide it under his belly. After its work is done, I uncork the bottle of oil, dribbling some down the crack of his ass and over my cock before tossing both items to the side. I return to his now-slick ass, slipping a finger into his hole. David sighs happily into his gag, spreading his legs wider and pushing backward.

I use my finger to open his hole, sliding it deeper before slipping out, and then back in. After a few more shallow strokes, I add a second finger, David's ring clenching around the intrusion. I sink them in deep, rubbing the pads of my fingers against his inner walls and teasing his prostate. I grip my cock with my other hand, slowly stroking the oil up and down my shaft as I stretch my pup open. By the time I can add a third finger, I am rock hard in my fist and ready for what comes next.

With David still on his stomach, I press my wet cock along his crack. He squeaks happily, wriggling his hips as it rubs against his hole. Gripping myself in one hand, I point my cock down as I cover David's body with my own. Feeling for his entrance with the head of my prick, I push my hips downward and press inside. I grab David by the hair with my free hand, turning it to the side and nuzzling my face against his neck as I slowly sink into the hot, warm, opening. Moving from his neck to his ear, I tease the outer shell with my tongue before sinking my teeth into his lobe.

"I would be careful about the noise I make, if I were you," is the only warning I give before I start thrusting.

"Thrust" may not be the right word to use, as I take care to keep my movements as slow and steady as possible. Despite my puppy's predilection for humiliation, I am not trying to make our tent the center of attention by having it rock back and forth in the light of the campfire. So with that in mind, I carefully roll my hips as I lay atop David, sliding the length of my cock in and out of his ass. David writhes underneath me, the fingers on his hands twitching in vain against my stomach as I work my cock in and out of him. Given my slower pace, I am not sure David will get the friction or strength needed to reach an anal orgasm, the only type he can expect with the cage on. Shockingly, this does little to change anything about what I am doing.

He does come close, though. After almost fifteen minutes of enduring the agonizingly slow thrusts, his hole starts to flutter, the muscles pushing out around my cock. Unfortunately for him, those fifteen minutes have been more than enough for me to near my own end, the hand in his hair tightening as I cross over the edge. I growl low against his ear, muttering an Atasi curse to myself as my cock starts to unload inside of him. It has only been a few days, but it feels like one of the biggest of my life, filling his hole to the brim with how overstuffed he already is.

David lets out a small whine of frustration as I nuzzle against his sweaty neck. I slip my free arm under his chest, feeling his heartbeat against my palm as I come down from my orgasmic high. I only allow myself a few moments of respite before lifting off of David's body, reaching down to untie the rope from his wrists. He rolls onto his back to stretch his limbs as I undo the blindfold and gag next.

"Thank you, Sir," David surprises me. I was half-expecting at least a little begging after he was ungagged. Instead, he is perfectly content to cuddle, his eyelids already looking heavy as I pull him to my chest, and we fall asleep.

Chapter 19

We have two more days of pleasant travel before we finally reach the shores of the city, the scent of salt-water in the air. Manamequohi, often shortened to Maname or simply Mana, is a large, globally recognized city-state located on the northeastern coast of Avural Ug'dol. Though it is not actually on the mainland, instead occupying an island in the middle of a large natural harbor. The island is easily five times the size of V'rok'sh Tah'lj with close to ten times the population.

Travel in and out of the city is strictly regulated, and every boat that docks there is inspected and registered. Without your own boat, the only way on (or off) the island is via ferry departing from one of the four docks located along the mainland's coast. Over time, small townships grew around each of these docks, forming their own small communities outside of the city proper. We are approaching the southernmost of these, Venzor, where we will board a ferry to reach the city proper.

"So the city's on that island?" David asks, sitting next to me at the reins. "What's that green dome around it?"

"The city's version of a security system," I tell him as we enter the town. "It is a spell that scans everyone who enters. If you are not properly registered within a few minutes of docking, the city's authorities are alerted to your location so that you can be apprehended."

"That sounds complicated," he comments offhandedly.

"Less complicated than a series of illusion and alarm spells in a forest that has to be patrolled almost around the clock," I point out. "That strict control is exactly why a place like this can offer sanctuary to those in need."

"How do you even power a spell that big?" His eyes scan the sky above the island, trying to gauge how large the dome of light is.

"There, off the right side of the island, separate from the rest." I point to a lone island a little farther out to sea. "Do you see that statue?"

"Is that a gnome?" His eyes squint. "With its hair on fire?"

"That it is," I answer with a nod. "The statue is called the Testament of Unity. It is built on top of a leywell, which it draws from to power the spell."

"Okay, but why is its hair green?" He is still squinting at the statue.

"Because that is the color of most Pukwudgies' hair," I answer with a shrug. "The security spell is a more recent addition; the statue itself has been around for centuries or longer. It is quite large."

"Like, large-large, or large for a gnome?"

"Large-large," I confirm with a chuckle.

Before we can embark on the ferry, the first thing we will need is a stable to board our horses and store our carriages. This won't be too difficult; Venzor is only a few blocks wide, made up largely of businesses with a few small homes sprinkled throughout. There are several inns, taverns, and even a few equipment stores, but they are all outnumbered by what I can only describe as "tourist stands," small shops devoted entirely to selling small objects and trinkets relating to the city—things like a small wooden version of the Pukwudgie statue or a carving of the city's skyline. There is even one that sells green, dome-shaped lamps.

I bypass all of that, heading straight for the docks. As I expected, once we get closer, I see a number of signs advertising their boarding services. After settling on one with decent rates and a reputable sounding name, I turn, following the arrows to the stable in question. Riley pulls into the grounds behind me, and while I take care of the boarding with David, Adam gets everyone and our belongings out of the carts.

They will be charging us a few gold a day with the first three days covered in advance. The rest will be added to a tab to be paid on our return, which David insists on paying with the earnings from his time as my assistant. While I am fine with that, I do not know how long we may actually be here and costs can slowly add up.

"Worst comes to worst, we sell the horses," David says as we exit the building, having finished negotiating with the stable's owners. Two stable hands follow us out, assessing the horses before climbing up and taking the reins so they can move the carriages closer to where they will be stored before stabling the steeds.

"So you said we need to get registered and take a ferry?" Adam inquires as the carts are led away.

"Yes, they can handle all of that at the docks," I say, leading the nine of us from the stable yard, our packs on our backs. "There is something I need to take care of first. I will be right back. This will only take a moment."

On the street, the docks are to our left, but I turn right, toward the forest. I scan the tree line, looking for the black fur that matches the presence I can sense. Once I am far enough from the town, Sona slowly pads out of the brush, coming to stop at my feet.

"I hope you've enjoyed being back outside." I drop to one knee, petting over the fur of her head. "I am so sorry again for getting you locked in a cage."

<Forest good. Cage bad.> She leans into my hand. *<Not Khazak fault.>*

"It is, a little," I say, despite knowing she likely will not understand. "We are about to travel to that island on a boat. We will be gone for at least a few days."

<Sona wait here.> She stands, turning around in a circle and facing the forest. *<In forest.>*

"Are you sure?" I ask, fully prepared for her to leave and return to her own life. "Do you want me to remove the collar?"

<Collar stay. Forest big. Happy wait,> she insists, huffing.

"Alright." I smile, petting over her head. "I will try not to be too long."

<Friend stay safe.> She licks my cheek before turning back to the forest.

"That wasn't like a permanent goodbye, was it?" David asks when I rejoin him and the others.

"I do not think so," I answer honestly. "Though there is always a chance."

"I think she'll stick around," Riley assures me. "She would have left already if she wasn't attached."

I nod at that, silently hoping he is right, and then turn and lead the others toward the docks. They are much like I last remember them, perhaps a little larger. There are six piers, twice as many as I remember, and what was once a fish stall is now a fish market, the smell of fresh seafood in the air. Between the dock workers and tourists, the place is cramped with other people, and I head straight for the large ticketing and registration office.

A sign next to the entrance written in multiple languages indicates a ferry departs for the island every twenty minutes. There are two guards on the inside of the doors, a human and a gnome, watching over the proceedings. Expectedly, there is a fairly long queue of people ahead of us, but the five clerks manning the registration counters have it moving fast. After waiting in line for barely fifteen minutes, it is my turn.

"Name and date of birth, and reason for visiting?" The gnome woman asks as I step up to her booth.

She is older, though similarly to elves, age can be hard to gauge on a gnome. Her forest-green hair is pulled back into a ponytail, and her green eyes sit behind a pair of round spectacles. As she speaks, she holds her right hand up, projecting a blue light out from her palm toward me: a scanning spell. The light moves up and down my body, providing her with information on how much I weigh, how tall I am, and my approximate age, which she begins to fill in on the paperwork in front of her.

"Khazak Ironstorm, Scorpius 27th, 4012, and I am here with my companions to visit a family friend as well as do some sight-seeing in the city," I make sure to answer loud enough for the others to hear before they are called up by their own clerks, so we can all be sure to give similar reasons. After what happened in Richardton, I think it is in our best interest to keep as low a profile as possible.

"Thank you," she says automatically, scribbling in the information required. "Alright, if you'll just take this and proceed to the back, one of the customs officers will finish your registration." She hands me the paper as she points to a hall leading to the customs office.

"Thank you very much, ma'am." I bow my head to her as I stand.

The hall leads me to a large open room where there are three rows of desks divided by short wooden walls. When I enter, a guard directs me to one of the desks, where two gnome officers wait to receive me. One of them takes the registration paper from me, reading it over quickly.

"Please remove any weapons, bags, and any other items and place them on the table," the officer not reading the paper tells me.

I remove my sword, bow, and quiver, as well as my pocket knife, and place them on the table with my satchel. When I am finished, the second officer steps up (literally, on a small stool) and casts another scanning spell, this time on each of my belongings. To my left, I see David approaching his own set of officers and preparing to do the same.

"How long were you planning on visiting Maname, Mr. Ironstorm?" the first officer asks, finished with his reading.

"I am not sure exactly. At least a few days, possibly longer," I answer honestly.

"Not a problem, but if you plan on staying longer than a month, you will need to re-register at one of our offices." He adds some of his own scribbles to the sheet.

"Steel sword and knife, wooden bow and arrows, nothing magical," the second officer tells the first, who continues writing. "The magic satchel's contents are...camping supplies, clothing, and...a lot of loose food. Bread, fruit, and... is that four whole cooked chickens?"

As the officer looks at me for confirmation, I look over the cubicle wall and sigh loudly at David, who grins sheepishly in return. "That is correct, sir."

"Sounds like you packed well," the first officer notes off-handedly, signing the bottom of the sheet. "Alright, everything seems to be in order."

The officer holds a hand out, casting a spell similar to the scanning spell, though this time the light is green. It lingers on my body a moment, marking me approved for entry.

"You are free to carry your weapons, but keep in mind that all violence in the city is prohibited and will be met with immediate expulsion from the island," the second offer tells me.

"Yes sir, understood. Thank you." I return my sword to its scabbard and bow to its sling as the man explains Maname's deportation policy. As I prepare to exit the room for the ticket counter, where I can regroup with the others, I overhear confusion from one of the officers dealing with David.

"Where'd you get this sword, kid?" The first officer, a human, looks over David's Harpe. "Not even sure what kinda metal this is."

"The scan's not telling ya?" the other officer, a gnome, asks.

"No, just that it's magic." He picks up the weapon in confusion. "Too heavy to be mythril."

"It was a...gift," David lies. "I'm not sure what it's made of. I just know it's really old, and magic like you said."

"Alright, well, none of the enchantments seem dangerous. Just make sure you keep an eye on that thing." The second officer gives his approval while the first finishes signing David's paper before casting the same "marking" spell. "Enjoy your stay."

After David gathers his items, we exit the room and proceed to the ticketing area with the others slowly joining us. This is the largest room of the three, almost as big as the other two combined, with multiple counters for purchasing tickets, each with their own queue. The back half of the room is a waiting area for people as they await the next ferry, many of the seats already filled with other visitors.

Tickets are one silver per person, so it does not even cost us a full gold to get ours. The next ferry is only a few minutes away from docking, so rather than wait inside, we proceed back out. There are already a few passengers gathered around the dock, the ferry visible out on the water. We move to stand with them, looking out across the bay at the island.

"Those buildings look like they might be pretty big," David notes.

"Just wait until we are closer," I respond, the statement feeling much more ominous to myself than it probably sounded to the others.

A bell on the boat rings as it approaches the pier, alerting the dock workers who are already making sure people clear the immediate area for its docking. Once it has been secured, a ramp drops from the side, and the captain gives the order for the current passengers to disembark. Once it is empty, the dock workers give us the okay to begin boarding, checking our tickets as we pass.

The ferry is medium size, made of dark wood with a high railing around the edge, and a leather awning above to protect passengers from the elements. It is propelled through the water by a large rotating paddle on its back, which is powered by a steam engine and at least a little magic. There is enough room for around a hundred people, with most of the seats filling up quickly.

Once everyone is on board, another bell rings and the boat pulls away from the pier. As it turns toward the city, many passengers move to the front to get a better view of the island, including us. The waters around us, a mixture of saltwater from the ocean and freshwater from the rivers emptying into the bay, are dark and no doubt freezing this far north, despite the summer sun. Leaning over the railing, my companions watch with awe as the light of the green dome passes over us. On this side of the dome, the green light is invisible save for the glow of the statue's flaming hair, letting you see the city in all its glory.

"You weren't kidding about the buildings," David says on my right as we approach the island's shores.

"I was not." I chuckle. "Some of them extend as high as ten stories into the air." They are (thankfully) not nearly as tall as the tower in the Karthani ruins, but they put Richardton's castle to shame.

"They take down the information of everyone who enters, right?" Adam asks, moving to stand at my left side.

"I believe the city's immigration office has records dating back centuries," I answer, not quite sure where this non-sequitur is leading.

"Well, they must keep those records somewhere, and I was thinking we could try to use them to track Redwish," he suggests leaning over to include David. "I know he may have given them a fake name, but they'd still know what he looks like."

"That is...not a bad idea." David sounds like he wished he had thought of it himself.

"We would at least be able to confirm if he was here and when." I pause to think, frowning to myself. "I am not sure how we would gain access to them, though. I doubt those records are available to the public. If I were still a ranger captain, I might be able to pull some strings."

"Not to put a damper on your plans, but are offices like that here usually open on the weekend?" Liss asks, reminding us it is Solisday.

"...Alright, so we go check first thing Lunaday morning, tomorrow," Adam corrects.

The ferry's bell rings again as it swings around to pull in, the dock workers zipping in to moor it to the pier. When the ramp is down, we disembark, passing a large group of people who are waiting their turn to leave the island. The docks here are larger than their Venzor counterpart, with additional piers for private boats. There are also a lot more people as families regroup either before or after riding the ferry, so I move to quickly get us out of the chaos so we can collect ourselves.

"What now?" Liss asks as we walk to a small open park across the road from the docks.

"We're supposed to meet your friend Nylan's dad, right?" Corrine asks next.

"Yeah, we should head there first," Adam confirms. "I doubt he can put all nine of us up, but he might be able to recommend a good inn."

"Do you know where we're going?" David turns to me as he did not bother writing down the information from Nylan himself.

"I have an address and a neighborhood," I answer. "But it has been almost a decade since my last visit."

To be safe, I stop someone in the park and ask for directions. Mana is a large city, and it is easy to get lost if you do not know what you are doing. However, the city's roads all follow a fairly strict numbered grid system, so if you *do* know what you are doing, you can get anywhere. The streets are just as busy as I remember them, filled with people and carts of all types. It is difficult to keep a group of nine together, a task made even harder thanks to the distraction that comes with being in a new city. I can hardly blame them though, as Maname is truly one-of-a-kind.

The population of Manamequohi is incredibly diverse with people from all over Terra having come to call it home. The two species more plentiful than the others are those who founded the city, humans and gnomes—the pukwudgies. The humans mostly share their resemblance with the other tribes of humans we have met on our travels, with tan skin and straight black hair, but the pukwudgies bear a very unique look. Their hair—head, facial, and body, from what I understand—is a vibrant green, the color the same shade as forest grass or the leaves on a tree. Some lean into this natural resemblance by weaving flowers and other decorations into their hair, though with visitors from all over the world, people with hair dyed in unexpected colors and making strange fashion choices is increasingly common—I am seeing a *lot* of tight leather for the summer.

Almost all of the buildings are multiple stories tall, with wooden walls constructed around a solid stone frame. While buildings of multiple levels are nothing new to us, the fact that most of these are separate homes and apartments built atop one another is. The entire city is like this, housing any number of businesses, families, and households within a single construction. The truly large towers are located closer to the island's center, but even those here on the outskirts can reach between three and four stories each.

While some of these structures have their outside walls painted, most have the raw wood exposed, only painting the accents or covering them with a simple pattern. All of them have the local flora incorporated into the design with vines growing along the walls and trees sprouting through ceilings. Occasionally, where there should be a building will be an empty lot occupied by a garden or park, similar to the one we entered after first arriving.

Some of these domiciles are clearly intended only for gnomes or other small species, reaching the same heights but with twice the floors. A few of those are literal trees themselves, almost as wide as the treetop homes in Pákannon, although significantly shorter and with most of the interior hollowed out. The architecture reminds me a lot of the ruins of Karthani with the homes stacked on top of each other and the wild vegetation growing everywhere, though obviously with much better upkeep.

All said, it takes us half an hour to locate the home of Nylan's father, Atsadi Adcaryn. His apartment is located in a building near the west coast of the island that is a staggering five stories tall—and of course he lives on the fifth. The doors to the building are already open, leading into a small but tall lobby. A staircase spirals around the room clockwise as it ascends, a landing in front of each apartment door.

Despite my fear of heights, I do not have any problems climbing the stairs—though I do hug the outer wall the entire time. A few of us are panting by the time we reach the top. There are only a few apartments at this level, so it is easy to locate Atsadi's and knock firmly on the wooden door.

"Just a minute!" comes the muffled request from the other side, followed a few moments later by the *click* of a door unlocking and swinging open. "Hello, yes, how can I—Khazak!"

"Mr. Adcaryn, it is so good to see you," I greet Nylan's father, an older human, with a hug. He is about as tall as his son, which means a little shorter than David, with short black hair that is greying on the sides. He shares the same cheeks, mouth, and eye-shape as his son, though with many more wrinkles.

"Please, you've known me for decades. I've told you to call me Atsadi." He moves forward to greet me with a hug, then takes in the group of people behind me. "These must be the friends Ny said you were traveling with... A few more than I expected."

"Yes, we picked up some stragglers along the way," I joke.

"Well please, all of you, come in." He turns and walks back inside waving his hands for us to follow. "I apologize for the mess. I wasn't sure when to expect you."

"We very much appreciate your..." I trail off as I take in the "mess" he is talking about. "Hospitality."

After only a few steps inside what I assume is the living room, I see that every surface of the apartment is covered in stacks of books and papers. Not just the surfaces, but even the chairs and some sections of the floor. Some of the stacks reach all the way to the ceiling. The nine of us are barely able to squeeze inside.

"The library is undergoing some renovations, and I'm afraid I don't trust anyone else to properly store and organize these," Atsadi tells us when he notices us taking everything in. "Before we get to the introductions, I need to know: which one of you is David?"

"That would be me—oof!" David is immediately grabbed in a tight hug by Atsadi.

"I cannot thank you enough for saving my son's life," he tells David.

"I was just doing the right thing," David tries to downplay.

"Not many people would risk their own lives for someone else's," he says as he breaks the hug. "Now, who else do we have?"

The rest of the group individually introduces themselves to Atsadi, who greets each of them warmly. We explain what our journey to the city has been like, leaving out the more violent details. He seems to take a particular interest in Michael, Piper, and Riley's teleportation experiment.

"I had heard rumblings in town that someone had discovered some sort of teleportation magic," he comments after Michael finishes his tale. "I had no idea they'd be visiting my own home!"

"I'd be happy to share notes sometime," Michael offers. "But the reason we're actually here is—"

"Yes, of course, apologies." Atsadi bows his head briefly. "You're not here to talk magical theory; you're here to discover what happened with David in the Temple of Zeus."

"Yes, precisely," I confirm, happy to be back on topic. "We were hoping that as one of the people to originally investigate the temple ruins, you might be able to answer a few questions."

"You were one of the people to write this report, right?" Michael pulls the stack of papers from his bag, which have been folded and creased after being read many times over.

"A different member of the group was in charge of the actual writing, though I contributed much of the information inside," he explains. "I still have my original notes. Let me just grab those and then we can..." He pauses as his eyes drift between all of the book stacks. "Oh, dear."

"What? Is everything alright?" Liss is the first to ask.

"I...may have just realized that I am not actually sure where the notes are in all this chaos." He turns around, an embarrassed look on his face.

"Well, there are nine of us, so maybe together we can—" David starts, reaching toward one of the stacks.

"*No!*" Atsadi shouts, quickly grabbing David by the wrist before he can move anything. "Sorry, these are just in a very specific order at the moment, and I do not want to risk jumbling them up."

"Okay..." David slowly moves his hand away from the stack. "Then what *can* we do to help?"

"I can find the notes. I just need a little bit of time," Atsadi assures us. "A few hours."

"We can do that," Adam decides with a nod. "Could you maybe direct us to a decent inn for the night?"

"Oh, we could visit the market as well, get a start on finding the reponiam for our trip home," Piper suggests.

"That sounds like an excellent idea," Atsadi says, clasping his hands. "In fact, if you head in that direction, there is an excellent inn on 34th street just a few blocks down from the market. The Moonbright Inn."

"Sounds as good as any." Liss shrugs.

"When should we return?" I ask Atsadi as we start moving to the door.

"Let's say 5 o'clock?" he suggests. "That should be enough time for me to find them and clear out some sitting space."

"I think that will work for us. We will see you then," I tell him back out in the hallway. "Thank you again, Atsadi."

"Thank *you*, Khazak and David." He hugs each of us, lingering for a moment on David. "After everything that happened with my wife, I don't know what I would have done if I lost my boy, too."

"Your son is an amazing person," David tells him as they break apart. "I'm happy to be able to call him a friend."

"He says the same about you." Atsadi smiles warmly. "Now then, I need to get to work and find that report. I will see you later this evening!"

With a final goodbye, our group marches back down the stairs and out of the building.

Time to explore the city.

Chapter 20

It is not a long walk from Atsadi's apartment to the Moonbright Inn, only another twenty minutes or so. It is not a boring walk either, not in a city like Maname. In addition to the amazing architecture, the people we see along the way are their own characters. On almost every corner, we see someone trying to sell cheap looking jewelry or questionable smelling food. There are people of all species wearing all manner of dress: leather, cotton, silk— some in styles which I have never before seen. We pass one woman walking her two dogs whose fur is colored blue and orange respectively, and another walking a *cat*.

The inn, like most of its neighbors, is in a tall building, this one seven stories tall. The outside of it is painted so that each level is a different color of the rainbow, starting with red at the top and leading down to violet on the ground. Entering through the double doors in front, I see that the entire first floor makes up the lobby and common areas of the building. There is a kitchen and dining room to the right, and what appears to be bathrooms and showers to the left.

We request five rooms when we check in, splitting as we did before the events of Richardton. The smells from the kitchen are tempting, the dining area full with other residents. We haven't eaten since breakfast, so we have a quick meal of grilled sea bass, freshly caught in the waters bordering the isle. With decently full bellies, we leave the dining area together.

"Okay, I know we're all exhausted, but we still have a lot to do," Adam turns to us as we reach the staircase. "So let's say forty minutes to relax and grab a shower, and then we meet back down here and head to the market."

With the showers on the ground floor, our group is split between those who want to use them now, and those who want to go up to their rooms first. David and I are in the former group, finding the showers divided into two rooms by gender. At least in the men's room, there are two long rows of showerheads along each wall, a set of smooth stone dividers separating them into stalls. David and I use two next to each other, drying off quickly with the provided towels before finally making our way up to our room.

We are on the fourth floor, which is as high as I can be comfortable with considering we will be sleeping here later. The room is small, with little more than a bed and small nightstand. A mirror is on the wall in one corner over a small empty wash basin, a simple (and hopefully magical) chamber pot behind a wooden divider. There is a window on the far wall, which David moves to close the shade on before I even shut the door.

"Thank you," I tell him as I lean my pack against the wall. "Now then, what should we do with our remaining free time?"

"I bet you can think of something, Sir." He bites his lip, already disrobing.

I cannot help the lecherous smile I flash at him in return, reaching for my own clothes. Once we are both naked, I push David toward the bed. Sitting on the edge, he watches as I reach into my satchel and pull out three items: his cleansing charm, a bottle of oil, and the magical plug

Brull made us. With my hands full, I walk to the bed, urging David to move over so I can sit next to him.

"It occurred to me that I never explained to you how this toy works, did I?" I ask, holding up the toy in one hand.

"No, you didn't..." David's tone is hesitant, but his eyes are intrigued.

"No time like the present." I grin and move us up the bed before pushing him on his back and spreading his legs, dropping my items between them on the mattress.

After situating myself at his side, I reach for the first tool of the evening, the charm. I lay it above David's groin, allowing it to work its magic before moving it out of the way on the nightstand. Next, I uncork the oil, lifting David's testicles with my free hand and moving them up, back, and out of the way of my other hand, which dribbles some of the oil along his perineum.

Putting the oil to the side, David's breath hitches as I reach down to spread it on his skin. I take my time, teasing him as I slide my slippery fingers down across his hole and then back up, before slowly circling it with my fingertips. I start to play with David's entrance, barely inserting my finger to the first knuckle before pulling away completely, a whine on his lips. He is torn between wanting to lift his legs and push his ass down onto my hand.

"Patience," I taunt, reaching for the oil again as well as the plug.

After ensuring it is slick, I bring the toy to David's hole, holding it against his entrance with enough pressure to keep it in place, but not push inside. I lean over and capture David's mouth in a kiss, grinning against his lips at his whine of frustration. When I decide he's had enough, I finally push the toy past his ring of muscle, making David whimper and then sigh as it sinks into place.

"Better?" I ask, breaking our kiss.

"Yes, Sir." He nods with a smile.

"Now, when you want to turn it on..." I reach between his legs. "You just tap on the base three times."

David jumps as the plug springs to life, vibrating steadily inside of him.

"To speed it up, you circle your finger around the base clockwise..." David moans as the vibrations grow more intense. "And you slow it down by circling the other way."

"Okay, that's... Wow." David takes a moment to catch his breath as the toy slows. "But how were you doing that when we walked down the mountains? I was fully clothed, and your hands were nowhere near my ass."

"That would be thanks to this." I reach for the final object on the bed, the rounded stone that acts as a controller. "It works the exact same way."

I demonstrate all the same gestures, making David squirm as the plug alters its intensity repeatedly. Satisfied with my thorough explanation, I spend the next few minutes testing limits: David's and the toy's. I take one of David's nipples into my mouth as I use the remote to speed the plug up. Latching on gently with my teeth, I continue to increase its power, David writhing and bucking as his prostate is toyed with. Given enough time, I could probably make him climax like this, but sadly, that time is not today. So as we near the time to meet with the others downstairs, I slow and then stop the plug's vibrations.

"That toy is amazing," David says breathlessly, sprawled on his back.

"Adam thought so as well when I let him play with it." I meet his eyes with a lecherous smirk, sliding off the edge of the bed.

"*Adam* used it?" I cannot decide if he sounds more surprised or offended.

"The remote," I clarify, still smirking and offering him a hand up. "Who do you think was playing with it while we were talking that day?"

"Should've known you'd get someone else involved." He shakes his head as he stands.

"I think involving Adam in things has paid off." I wink and reach for my clothing.

"Yeah, 'cause it means you have someone else to help with your torture," he complains without any real bite, watching me dress. "So...are you going to take out the plug before we leave?"

"I am not." I grin, handing David his pants.

We find the others already in the lobby, their excitement palpable. The Magic Market is only a fifteen walk from the inn, located next to a large park at the center of the island. It is actually only one corner of a much larger marketplace, selling food, weapons, tools, art—just about anything imaginable. The already-busy streets grow even more crowded once we enter with bright and colorful advertisements everywhere we look. Most of the shops and stalls at the very least have one sign in front of their business, though some take things a step further. Large placards sit atop many storefronts, and the outside walls of many buildings are painted with brightly colored images and logos.

"What is this place?" David asks as he stares in wonder at an enchanted advertisement for a soup-based restaurant that has been animated, broth dripping from a spoon above a steaming bowl.

"You should see it at night," I tell him. "It looks entirely different. Everything is illuminated with magic."

"We'll have to come back later, then" he says as we step farther into the marketplace.

Manamequohi was founded centuries ago, and in the time since has grown into an internationally recognized port, welcoming visitors of all species who come here to seek fame, fortune, and adventure. While the original inhabitants of the city were humans and gnomes, there are also plenty of elves, dwarfs, halflings, and orcs—the six species make up the majority of Terra's population.

It is obvious that many of them are from other parts of the world, such as the elven woman with bronze-colored skin running a vegetable cart or the dwarf with eyes such a piercing light blue that they almost seem to glow. The dwarf is also using a large dog as a mount for some reason, which entertains many of my friends to no end, but what draws my own eyes are a pair of orcs with large white horns sprouting from their heads. One has skin colored a vibrant red, while the other's is dark blue. I saw similar looking people during my last visit—*oni*, originating in a far-off island country known as *Taiyohito*.

People of all sentient species can be found here. We pass many goblin-run storefronts selling different sorts of gadgets and knickknacks, the short, green-skinned species known for being as mechanically inquisitive as gnomes. A booth of merpeople, or at least part-merpeople, their skin tinged with blues and greens and gills visible on their necks, advertises underwater tours off the island's coast. And sitting in a long row at a food stall are a group of beastkin, a species originating from a nation I have only heard referred to as "Dreamland." The men and women all appear to have feline features, though I understand it is an incredibly diverse species even within itself.

After navigating through the crowd, we are able to enter the Magic Market proper. There are several entrances, and the one we use is marked overhead with a sign against an awning, the words "Magic Market" in glowing white text underneath the image of a long magic wand. Periodically, a shower of colorful sparks will spray from the wand's tip, a flashy display from the proprietors within.

Much like the rest of the marketplace, the streets here are filled with vendors selling from their carts and stalls. The difference is on what is being sold: potions, spell reagents, and all sorts of magical items and weapons. I must admit, I am just as fascinated with my surroundings as my companions, having not been here in such a long time.

A trio of witch sisters are selling "brew it yourself" potion ingredient sets, and a halfling with dark skin offers fashionable accessories for your pet or familiar. There are stalls with wands, robes, and one that *only* sells crystal balls. Between the flashy signs and shouted slogans, it is a bit overwhelming, so when I see a familiar looking storefront, I guide our group inside.

Hadawako's was founded over a century ago by a family of the same name. Originally nothing more than a simple cart centered around the crafting of high-quality wands and quarterstaffs, the store now occupies almost an entire city block. As the business has grown, so has its selection of items, covering just about any magical item you could want, though it has also had the added effect of lowering the overall quality. Still, the group is in awe at the store's interior, particularly the magic users.

"Look at this place!" Michael almost shouts in wonder.

"Yeah, this place is..." Liss pauses, her eyes drawn to a wall housing dyed animal pelts. "A lot."

"They carry so many different kinds of spell components," Piper notes, peering into a glass display case containing all manner of geodes, gemstones, and metal ingots. "Look, reponiam!"

"Do ya think they'll have enough for us to get home?" Riley looks over the small smoke-colored crystal.

"Only one way to find out!" Michael and Piper both take off in search of a clerk.

"Alright, well, while they're taking care of that, the rest of us can look around," Adam says after watching them leave.

"Try not to break anything!" Corrine tells everyone as the group splits up.

"No promises," David says before taking me by the wrist. "Let's see what kind of weird stuff they've got."

"Sure, but first..." I reach into my pocket and tap on the control stone, smirking when David's body jerks as the plug comes to life. "There. Shall we?"

David grumbles under his breath and tries to glare, but it is undercut by the smile he is fighting. As we wander the store together, I continue using the control stone to tease David, who impressively manages to take it all in stride. Well, everything except a small *squeak* of surprise that escapes near the racks of robes, causing another shopper to turn toward us in confusion.

There is nothing in particular I am looking for as we traverse the store, content to just browse. It does occur to me that there should be an "adult" section that might be worth looking through, but for David's sake, I will save that for later when it can be just him and me. We are on the far end of the shop, looking over a selection of different bones to be used in various magical rituals, when something catches David's eye.

Against the wall is a wooden counter, on top of which are a large number of leather-bound books in a variety of colors, but with the spines all blank. Two of the books are opened, set on reading stands at the center of the table, the others lined up at their sides. A single pen sits in a pot of ink between the two, and the presented pages are covered with random text and scribblings. In fact, they almost look identical.

"What's with the books?" David asks a man stacking things behind the counter.

"The pages in these journals are made from enchanted vellum." The human runs his hands along the edge of one of the books.

"I've heard of this." I step up to David's side, inspecting the journals closer. "What you write in one appears in the other."

"Yes, exactly." The shop clerk nods his head, then gestures to the pen. "Please, see for yourselves."

Needing no further prompting, David picks up the pen and scribbles a quick "hi" in the left book. The same words immediately appear in the second book, stroke by stroke. Seeing this himself, David begins excitedly writing more words and even doodling, although when he starts to write the word "fuck," I temper that excitement by driving up the speed of his plug.

"How much are they?" David asks the clerk when he's finished glaring at me.

"Twenty gold for a set of two." He points out the book pairs are of matching colors.

"What do you think?" David asks me.

"Expensive, but certainly useful," I tell him, knowing who he is likely to give the other journal to if he plans to keep one.

David bites his lip in consideration before nodding to himself. "I'll take a set."

After he selects a pair of journals with green covers, David and I return to the front of the store. While he pays for them, I join Tsula as she looks through a bookshelf near the entrance. There are a few beginners spellbooks, some journals on magical theory, and a few biographies on famous spellcasters. As I am perusing the titles, I notice something outside that seems familiar.

"Whatcha looking at?" David asks as he joins me, his purchase completed.

"A memory, I think." I turn to Tsula one shelf down. "Would you mind letting the others know I am taking David to that shop there?" I point to the shop in question across the street.

"Sure thing," she agrees with a nod before turning back to the bookshelf. "I'm still trying to decide if I should get a new spellbook..."

"What's over here?" David asks me as we exit Hadawako's.

"If I am not mistaken, this is where I purchased my magic satchel," I reply as we approach the store with a sign reading "Bearfoot Brothers Tinkering & Enchanting" above. "I thought you might like one of your own."

The store is much smaller than Hadawako's, sandwiched between two other storefronts. Combined with the multiple stalls others have set up out front, I almost can't make out the sign's text. The inside of the store is equally as cramped, with half-finished mechanical projects hanging from the walls while smaller (and presumably completed) items line the shelves. It all looks familiar, though I am not sure I recall it being so disorganized last time I was here.

At the back of the room is a large wooden desk. A gnome sits behind it, hunched over with a white glowing stone at his left. He's wearing a pair of glasses, a small metal tool in his right hand while his left holds the object he is working on steady. Sweat has matted his short green hair to his forehead, and his expression is one of deep concentration. I feel a little bad, but when he does not acknowledge our entrance, even after approaching him, I clear my throat to get his attention.

"Oh, hello!" He looks up at us with a surprised smile, putting his things to the side and smoothing his hair with his hands. "Welcome to Bearfoot Brothers, where the enchantments are so strong, you'll feel like family!"

"Hello, Mr. Bearfoot," I reply once he has finished with his slogan. "We were passing through the city, and if I am not mistaken, this is where I purchased this." I place my bag on the countertop.

"A Spacious Satchel!" He takes the bag in his hand and looks it over. "Yep, this is one of ours. We——"

The sound of a door opening and slamming shut cuts him off as someone stomps down the stairs behind him. It is another gnome, presumably the other Bearfoot Brother. He has green hair like his sibling, though the top of his head is bald with only a crown around the edge, flowing downward into an equally green mustache and beard. He is also wearing nothing more than a towel around his waist, which proves that his body hair is *also* green.

He shouts something as he comes down the stairs in a language I do not speak, pausing only when he notices me and David. Then he speaks angrily in the same language to his brother as he clutches his towel tighter. After a little back and forth between the two, the second gnome stomps back up the stairs, still looking angry.

The first gnome shouts up in the same language after his brother before the door is slammed and he turns back to us. "Sorry, he has a problem remembering that we have business hours. My name is Onas. It's nice to meet you two. Well, nice to meet *you* again, I suppose." He pats the top of my satchel with a chuckle.

"It is nice to meet you as well. My name is Khazak, and this is David." I return his warm smile. "This satchel has served me well for almost ten years, and I was hoping you might still sell them."

"We do!" He hops down from the tall stool he was sitting on and walks around the counter and toward the shelves. "They should be right over...hmm." He pauses, scratching his chin. "Maybe they're in the back."

"You guys have a lot of weird stuff here," David says as he inspects what looks like a dragon made of iron and steel hanging from the wall, covered in scorch marks. "I don't mean that in a bad way," he quickly adds.

"Ah, that old thing." Onas looks up at it wistfully. "It was *supposed* to fly through the air and deliver a spectacular fire and light show, but we could never get the furnace working quite right. Kept breaking through the defensive enchantments and bursting into flames."

"That sounds like quite a problem." I can hear old alarm bells ringing in my head at the *flying fire hazard.*

"That sounds fucking *awesome!*" David cheers—I know, big surprise. "What are you working on now?"

"Nothing *that* spectacular," Onas says as he walks back around the counter that doubles as his bench and climbs his stool. "But you might be able to help me with it."

He reaches over to the object he had been working on when we came in. It is a small, thin piece of metal, the shape resembling half of a heart, or a human's ear. Setting it down in front of us, he reaches under the counter for a second object, encouraging us to inspect them. Up close, I can see extremely small symbols have been etched into the metal with a very fine tipped tool—what he was doing when we came in.

"What are they?" David asks, running his finger along the runes.

"Translators," Onas answers simply with an excited grin.

"Really? How do they work?" I try not to sound skeptical.

"They attach around the outside of your ear." He moves his finger behind the shell of his ear to demonstrate.

David looks at me, waiting for a nod of approval before we both slide them on.

"Is it...working?" David asks, unsure.

"<You tell me,>" Onas repeats back in perfect Atasi—though the sound is delayed a moment, not matching the movement of his mouth.

"What just happened to your lips?" David looks at him suspiciously.

"I think that means they are working," I attempt to clarify. "Though I am still curious as to how."

"It's a few different enchantments all working in concert," Onas starts to explain. "One records what you hear being spoken while another translates that into a language that a *different* spell determines is the one you speak the most."

"That sounds intricate." I wouldn't even know where to start with something like that.

"That's not even mentioning the spells to match the speaker's voice and regulate volume." He sighs. "I've been trying to fix the audio delay, but the magic can't figure out what you're saying until you say it, so." He shrugs.

"And they work with any language?" David touches the translator on his ear.

"They should. The enchantments are meant to capture the *meaning* of what is being said, regardless of syntax. I've tested it myself, and it works better than a <boulder washing a fishing rod.>" David and I share a look of confusion at Onas's odd wording. "Okay, so there are maybe a *few* issues when it comes to idioms and turns of phrase, but everything else—"

The door at the top of the stairs cuts him off as it opens again. "I told you to warn me when we had customers," the other gnome grumbles as he comes down.

"And I told *you* we needed to fix the alarm bell on the front door," Onas tells him. "This is Khazak and David. Gentlemen, please meet my brother, Wari."

"Sorry for being so underdressed before," he apologizes, climbing onto his own stool. "What brings you two to our shop?"

"We were actually hoping to get another one of these." David points to my bag on the counter.

"A Spacious Satchel, eh?" Wari looks over the dark brown leather bag.

"Do you remember where we moved those to?" Onas asks a little sheepishly.

"Yeah, they should be back here." Wari hops off his seat and walks toward the alcove under the stairs and after moving a few things around, turns around with several bags in his arms. He passes them up to his brother before retaking his seat. "You know we invented these things, right?"

"Really?" David asks in surprise as he looks through the options. They all look similar to mine, though the shade of the leather varies.

"Yep, about three hundred years ago," Onas confirms, while also revealing the brothers' true ages.

"I'm surprised you don't have them front and center in here." David looks around at the shop's general disarray. "Seems like they'd be a big seller."

"Well, they were for a while, but then other people figured out how to make them and started selling their own," Onas complains.

"Is that what the problem was?" Wari asks, uninspired with his brother's explanation. "Because I could have sworn it was marketing."

"Here we go..." Onas sighs and adjusts his glasses.

"'Spacious Satchel' hardly rolls off the tongue," Wari continues. "*I* wanted to call them Roomy Rucksacks."

"That was your fourth or fifth idea." Onas counters with a roll of his eyes. "If I recall, you were also very fond of 'Boundless Backpack.'"

"That would've been a great option too!" Wari insists. "So, you're just here for the bag?"

"They're also wearing my new translators," Onas corrects with a grin.

"Are you sure they're ready?" Wari eyes his brother skeptically. "The last one almost blew out my eardrum."

"I fixed that problem," Onas replies with a huff. "They're perfectly safe, and besides, they need to be tested by someone other than the two of us. Who better than two world-traveling adventurers?"

"Who said we were world travelers?" David crosses his arms in unneeded suspicion.

"Well, the pale skin kind of gives away that you're not from around here, so..." Onas shrugs.

"...Fair enough," David concedes.

"You were planning on giving these to us?" I touch the translator on my ear.

"I was." Onas nods. "You'd be doing me a big favor."

"For *free*?" Wari scoffs at Onas's suggestion. "Mythril isn't cheap."

"Fine," Onas capitulates. "The satchels normally run twenty-five gold, so together with the translators, let's make it an even thirty."

"Deal!" David heartily agrees, holding out his hand for the other man to take.

After selecting a bag with a reddish hue, David retrieves the pouch holding his gold. As he is counting out the total, I hear footsteps behind us and turn to see Michael, Piper, and Adam entering the store. Although transfixed like we were when we first entered, they spot us at the counter.

"Mikey!" David says excitedly when he notices his brother's presence. "Check it out. I got my own magic backpack." He pulls the bag onto his shoulders and turns around.

"Really? Maybe I should get one too." Adam inspects David's bag, then the others on the counter.

"Were you able to solve the reponiam issue?" I ask, not seeing any visible signs of them having purchased the crystals yet.

"Yeah, they were kind of expecting us," Michael says with a bashful grimace. "Apparently word about our teleportation experiment really has gotten out."

"Unsurprising considering two of the owners' children are students at the Institute," Piper adds. "They say they could have it ready in a few hours. We should be able to leave later tonight."

"You're leaving *tonight*?" David does his best to mask the disappointment in his question.

"Wait, *you're* the kids who teleported?" Onas looks at Michael and Piper in amazement.

"The whole market's been talking about you for weeks," Wari says, impressed.

"It was nothing," Michael downplays.

"It certainly was not nothing." Piper gives him a side eye.

"Just trying to stay humble," the wizard claims, obviously wanting to say more.

Which David ignores. "I thought you could only leave from another elven monument?"

"Well you know the giant statue? The Testament of Unity?" Michael points over his shoulder toward the exit.

"Is the statue the monument?" I can see the gears turning in David's head.

"In a way. The statue was carved from a large mountain of astral obsidian when the city was founded," Piper explains. "Inside that mountain was a small cavern used by ancient gnomes to perform different rituals, with similar architecture as the elven monuments, though the markings are all in ancient gnomish."

"The Great Rending is believed to have affected gnomes as much as it did elves," Michael continues.

"So why does anyone only ever talk about the elves?" Adam posits a very good question.

"Because elves love talking about themselves," Wari grumbles under his breath.

"Gnome communities are known for being secretive, so it's a little tougher to get information on," Michael clarifies.

"We're a private people." Wari crosses his arms and juts out his chin proudly. "Sorry we didn't feel the need to cover the world with gaudy monuments to our greatness."

"Except for the giant one with flaming green hair, of course," Onas counters wryly. "He's not wrong, though. Our ancestors *were* extremely secretive. There might *still* be uncontacted gnome tribes in the hiding in world."

"Are you sure that the gnome monument will work the same as the others?" I ask the two mages.

"Pretty sure, but there's only one way to find out." Michael's tone sounds more confident than his words make me feel.

"Is everyone gonna be cool with you using it for that?" Adam asks, likely remembering how some of the elders in Pákannon reacted.

"We'll just have to see." Michael grins nervously.

"So you're really leaving?" David frowns at the new information

"Gotta get back to school and fix the mess we made," Michael admits with a sad smile. "What? Did you think we were going to have to travel all the way back to Pákannon or something first?"

"I dunno, maybe." David shrugs, trying to hide his disappointment.

"You're going to cast your teleport spell tonight?" Onas asks the group. "Do you think we could watch? I'll give you a free Spacious Satchel."

"*Free?*" Wari complains, only for Onas to give him a smack on the shoulder with the back of his hand.

"I think that'd be okay," Michael agrees with a nod before turning to his brother. "Are those bags what you guys came in here for?"

"Yeah, but check out what else we picked up." David removes the translator from his ear. "It's a language translator. Put it over your ear."

"Really?" Michael slides it on. "How do I know if it's working?"

"<If you can understand this, then it is working,>" I say in Atasi, Michael's eyes growing wide as he presumably hears it in Common.

"That's amazing!" he exclaims and turns to the Bearfoot brothers. "How much are they?"

"I'm afraid those are actually the only two I have finished at the moment," Onas lets him down with a sad smile. "But I appreciate the interest! If you can come back in a few weeks..."

"Maybe not in a few weeks, but I will be back," Michael says confidently as he hands it back to David. "Will you be here later? We can stop by after we pick up our reponiam order at Hadawako's."

"We'll be here," Wari confirms with a nod, apparently on board with the plan despite his complaints. "You can have your free bag then."

"Alright, then are you guys ready to talk with Atsadi?" Adam asks the rest of us.

The walk back to the hotel is quiet, with David and I bringing up the rear of the group. His mood is bordering on somber, no doubt thinking about his brother leaving later tonight. So, being the kind and thoughtful man I am, I take it upon myself to help distract him.

David manages to not jump, but he does look over nervously when I use the control to reactivate his plug. I leave the intensity low at first, slowly increasing it as we make our way through the city streets. Then, when we are only a few minutes away, I turn it up very high, and then quickly very low, going back and forth in a way that I hope makes it feel like it is pulsing. By the time we are upstairs, a sweat has broken out on his forehead.

"Evil...fucking...orc..." he pants when he finally makes it into our room, collapsing over the edge of the bed.

"Aww, having some trouble, puppy?" I tease, turning off the plug and running my hand down his back.

"This isn't fair," he whines as he rolls onto his back.

"Punishment is not meant to be fair." I tap him on the nose. "Now, we have about half an hour before we are leaving to see Atsadi. Strip."

David's mood perks up at the order, quickly pulling off his boots before standing. I take his place on the edge of the bed, watching intently as he removes the rest of his clothing until he is naked, save for the plug and cage. I grin as evilly as he accuses me of being when I see his cock already trying to get hard.

"On your knees," I command as I unbutton the front of my pants.

David's eyes brighten as he kneels, aimed straight at my crotch. I stop him as he shuffles forward to get between my legs, pressing my shin against his chest, my foot right under his encased manhood. He looks up at me questioningly, and I instead guide him toward my cock, his mouth opening automatically as I feed him the head.

I hum happily as the heat of his mouth engulfs me. He flicks his tongue against the underside of my shaft as he sinks down. With about half of me in his mouth, he lays his head against my thigh with a playful look. I give his hair a gentle tug before slowly stroking my thumb along his cheek. He nuzzles into my hand before pulling back so he can swallow me down again.

As he begins to suck in earnest, I grind my ankle against his crotch. Unable to help himself, despite being caged, he humps uselessly against me. Lifting my foot, I feel the area where his groin meets the cage, where the only untrapped portion of his shaft is hard as a rock. I chuckle at the whine of frustration David makes around my cock. He is going to hate what I do next.

His attention otherwise occupied, I stealthily reach into my pocket for the plug's control stone. David's whine becomes a yelp as it springs back to life, my hand in his hair preventing him from pulling away. Glaring up at me, he nonetheless continues to lavish me with his oral attentions.

I use my hand in his hair to guide him up and down, savoring the drag of his warm lips along my length. I use my other hand to alter the plug's speed, enjoying the groans of frustration David makes as his hole is repeatedly tortured. Without warning, I jerk his head all the way down and bury myself in his throat. At the same time, I lift my foot and press against the base of the plug with the toe of my boot. Trapped between the two, I revel in the way he can do nothing but accept what I do to him.

I start to pump his mouth faster and faster on my cock. My sack, slick with David's spit, draw up toward my body the closer I get to the finish. David, now well-versed in the signs of my impending cumshot, wraps his arms around my leg to ground himself as he prepares to swallow. When I finally crest over the edge, I pull my puppy all the way down to the base, my prick pulsing as it fires directly into his throat.

His eyes red and watery, David continues to suckle on me even after his head is released, licking me clean when I am finally free of his mouth. I reach down and pet gently through his hair as he leans against my thigh and catches his breath. Below us, his cock still fights its captivity, a long string of pre-cum dripping from the head down onto my boot.

"It appears you have made a mess of my boot, pup," I tell him when he finally pulls away.

His eyes follow mine down to my shoe, seeing the small puddle left in his wake. He looks back up to me for a moment, a questioning look in his eye, before he steels himself with determination, bends over, and licks the slick spot from my shoe. Without being ordered to.

That was not what I had planned. But in more of David's own words, "Fuck, that was hot." I grab the back of his head and slam our mouths together, tasting the remnants of myself on his tongue.

We may be a little late seeing Atsadi.

Chapter 21

*F*ollowing our late afternoon tryst, David and I meet the others downstairs. After seeing the state of Atsadi's home, we decided that it would be best to shorten the list of who is going to those closest to David and the incident: myself, Adam, Michael, and the only other person actually able to read the report, Tsula. We will update the others when we return in the evening.

The trip there is uneventful and silent. There is a tension in the air, particularly from David, as we wonder if we will finally have answers to some of our questions. I am trying to temper my own expectations; Atsadi is only a human, and it was over twenty years ago that he originally researched this.

"Come in, come in," Atsadi tells us after opening his door. "I cleared off the couch and some chairs. Please make yourselves comfortable."

I breathe a silent sigh of relief when I see that there is in fact enough room for all of us. David takes a seat on the center of the couch with me and Michael on each of his sides while Adam and Tsula use nearby chairs. After we all decline an offer of water, Atsadi finally takes his seat as well.

"Before we get started, I have letters for you two!" Atsadi picks up three sealed envelopes, handing two to myself and one to David. "From Nylan and Ragnar, as well as your family, Khazak."

"Thank you," I respond as we tuck the letters into our bags. Knowing Nylan and Ragnar, it will probably be better to read those back in our room.

"So, I was able to locate all of the original research notes I took with Ahyoka and the rest of the archaeological team." He pats a stack of papers on the short table in the center all our seats. "I also re-read the letter Nylan sent me that described what happened that night, but I would like to hear your firsthand experiences." The request is aimed at me and David.

"Right, well, I guess the place to start would be the first time we entered the temple," David begins. "There was this weird sound coming from the altar that only I could hear..."

David continues with his explanation of what took place during his two visits to the temple ruins, glossing over anything that has to do with our relationship or his crimes. Adam and I will interject now and again with our own observations while Michael and Tsula have already started looking through the stack of notes. It isn't until David finishes describing our capture at the hands of Councilman Murbank that I feel the need to take over for a moment.

"Sir, before we continue, there's something you should know." I feel like a ranger again, having to deliver unwanted news. "We learned shortly after we were captured that we were not actually the cult's intended target. Your son and Ragnar were. Murbank was under the impression that elf blood was somehow the key to activating the altar. It was a theory that he shared with his father for some time."

"Bastards." He shakes his head in disgust. "That damn Fudhag kept trying to push us to experiment with an actual sacrifice."

"Murbank's dad's name was *Fudhag*?" David snorts under his breath.

"I think that may be the reason for your wife's death." I pause, not knowing how he will feel about what I say next. "I believe Murbank, his father, and members of their original Order of Zeus kidnapped her with the intention of sacrificing her. Instead, she sacrificed herself before they were able to bring her to the temple. I am so sorry, but I hope that might bring you some closure."

The silence that fills the room as Atsadi processes this information feels like it stretches on for an eternity.

"Murbank is dead?" he asks for confirmation.

"Yes." I nod.

"Good," he says with conviction. "To think that I almost lost my son to the same monster that took my wife... I truly cannot thank you enough for saving my boy."

"I'm only sorry he was ever in any danger to begin with," David responds. "They only found Nylan and Ragnar after they interrogated us. Murbank pulled Nylan up to the altar and had the sword out, ready to bleed him dry, when we managed to cause enough of a distraction for me to run up and knock Murbank out of the way. Nylan was able to run to safety, but Redwish—the man we've been chasing here— grabbed me. Before I even knew what was happening, he ran me through with the sword."

"I watched as he bled out, stumbled onto the altar, and died," I recount next. "I do not think it was even a full minute before he was alive again."

"Can you remember anything that happened while you were...gone?" Atsadi asks on the edge of his seat.

"No." David shakes his head. "There are some fuzzy flashes of what came after, but I can't remember anything clearly until I woke up a few days later."

"He was not himself when he...came back." I was the only witness to this part of the night. "He spoke in a foreign tongue and seemed to have had an immense increase in speed and strength. He was able to defeat a room full of enemies in minutes, though after he was finished, I was the only person able to snap him out of whatever trance he was in. He passed out immediately and stayed unconscious for almost five days."

"That sounds like a harrowing event," Atsadi says with unease. "But you were perfectly healthy when you awoke?"

"Yeah, just with this weird scar." David unbuttons the top of his shirt and tugs it down to show the top of this chest.

"Fascinating." Atsadi cannot help but move to take a closer look at the raised, golden-colored skin. "Have you noticed anything else unusual since then?"

"Not exactly," David denies while I think back to some of my own observations. "Though it did happen again a few days ago. The...transformation."

"Really? What happened?" Atsadi returns to his seat but begins to search through his notes.

"Someone was holding us captive for a lot of bullshit reasons," David summarizes. "He started making threats to me about hurting some of the others, and before I knew it, I was breaking down doors and hunting him down."

"Was it like the first time? Could you still not remember anything?" Atsadi takes a pen and begins jotting down something in his notes.

"It was a little clearer this time, but something was still off." David bites his lip, looking down as he thinks. "I was in control, but it's like my body was listening to someone else's instincts. The only real thing I can remember feeling is anger."

"Fascinating," Atsadi repeats.

"Do you know what's happening to me?" David asks, worried.

"Well, I know you've read a copy of our report." He looks around at all five of us. "The simplest explanation is that the altar worked as intended. You were granted the strength of gods."

"But that doesn't make sense." David shakes his head. "I wasn't the one doing the sacrifice, I was the one *being* sacrificed. And even then, it was kind of an accident."

"Was it an accident?" Atsadi's question is full of implications. "I assume you are familiar with the inscription around the altar's basin?"

"'Only blood spilled in sacrifice can restore the strength of the gods,'" Tsula recites from memory.

"That's it...more or less." Atsadi nods, though there is an unspoken question on his lips. "Can I see that section of your copy? I need to check something."

Tsula flips through the pages of our copy of the report, finding the section with the inscription and handing it over. Setting it down next to his own notes, Atsadi flips through, running his fingers over specific lines as he searches. When he finds whatever he is looking for, he sighs.

"Damnit, Ayo, I told you we shouldn't have let Parvat handle the transcription," he mutters under his breath before speaking aloud. "I think I may have found at least part of the problem. Do you know why translations of old or ancient languages often seem long and overly wordy? That's because the translators are trying to capture the specific meaning of what is being said. Dead languages have words we have no direct translation for, and modern languages have words that can have *multiple* meanings."

"The way the word 'sacrifice' is used here," he continues, pointing to a section of our report copy, "is not describing the sacrificing of someone's life. It is a reference to a truly selfless act. By saving my son's life at the cost of your own, I think you did just that."

"So you're saying it was always intended to change the person being sacrificed?" Michael interjects. "But how would that even work? How could anyone set something like that up? If they knew they would be brought back to life with all this power, wouldn't that make the act by definition *not* selfless?"

"I think the other part of the problem is viewing the inscription as instructions, rather than in reference to a specific event." Atsadi sits back up as he explains. "I do not consider myself a religious man, but I do not think that the altar was intended to ever work for anyone but you, David."

"What? But that..." David shakes his head in disbelief. "That makes even less sense. The temple was thousands of years old. How could the people who built it have possibly known that I'd travel halfway across the world and be there at the exact right time to save Nylan like that? It's impossible."

"I think that is how fate works," Atsadi says with a wry smile.

"I hate to admit it, David, but he has a point," Adam admits with a grimace. "I mean, our leading theory is that you're some kind of a demigod."

"Which we also know doesn't make sense," Michael adds. "Demigods are made when a god impregnates a mortal, and we are definitely our father's children. It was our grandparents on our *mother's* side that were Olympian anyway."

"You both have Olympian ancestry?" Atsadi jots down more notes. "Have you noticed any other strange coincidences? Perhaps from before David's transformation?"

"*No*," David denies with force. "None of this stuff started happening until after that night in the temple."

"That is not entirely true." As I say this, David's head snaps around to me with a look of betrayal. "There was the matter of the sound you heard from the altar, which you told me later transformed into whispering once the lead cover was removed. As if it were calling to you. But even outside of that... David, I've seen you jumping and climbing in ways that I'm not sure a trained acrobat could do. The unnaturally fast way regained much of the weight you had lost just as quickly, it is like your body was adapting to the changes in your diet. There was Shaman Bonespirit's comments about your magical aura, and even Robin could sense there was something *different* about you."

"I'm not sure I've ever seen you sick, or tired, or even hungover," Adam adds with a frown.

"Shit," Michael curses under his breath after hearing our list of observations.

"Don't tell me you're buying this crap?" David stands, turning on his twin.

"I just think he might have a point." I am shocked it is Michael who is agreeing with me over David. "You've been good at basically anything physical or athletic since we were kids."

"Yeah, because I worked hard!" David responds, offended, and I think I am starting to understand why.

"I'm not saying you didn't, but think about it," Michael tries to reason. "Whatever transformed you was an Olympian ritual. We know we have Olympian ancestry, and we can safely assume Zeus didn't knock up our mom, so there has to be something to it."

"Then why are these things happening to me and not my other three siblings?" David spits back to one of the siblings in question.

"I mean, it's not like Joseph is a slacker, and just a few months ago, Kira was telling me the magical institute contacted her about testing to become a student," Michael responds with a shrug.

"And what about you, my twin?" David crosses his arms and cocks his hip.

"You mean the magical prodigy who solved a millennia-old mystery about teleportation?" Tsula makes the comment while twirling her hair braid nervously.

"Oh, that's another one: we still don't know why my first teleport spell sent me to the exact monument you happened to be at," Michael adds with a grimace.

David narrows his eyes at the two mages, his hands dropping to his side and clenching into fists. Before he or anyone else can say anything, he turns on his heel and walks out the front door, slamming it behind him. The rest of us remain seated around the table in stunned silence.

"I will speak with him." I sigh as I stand from the couch and exit the apartment. I find David right outside, leaning over the apartment landing's railing.

"Are you alright?" I ask, not quite approaching.

"I'm fine," he responds gruffly.

"That's ten for lying to me," I half-joke. "Do you think you could tell me what made you so upset?"

"I'm not upset, okay? I just—" He shuts his mouth after turning to see the unimpressed look I give him. "I just don't like the feeling that someone else has been making all my decisions for me. That I've never had any say in anything I do."

"I understand that," I tell him, stepping into his space. "If it helps, that is not what I think has been happening."

"Then what do you think?" David looks to me for answers.

"In V'rok'sh Tah'lj, we have a saying. 'The heavens may put the buck in your sight, but it is you who must release the bowstring.'" I watch as David tries to piece together my meaning.

"That's kinda wordy," David points out.

"It sounds more elegant in Atasi," I insist with a laugh. "It means that no matter what circumstances fate might bring you, you are the one who has to follow through with your choices. You are one of the most unselfish people I have ever met, constantly putting yourself in danger to protect others. It is not difficult at all for me to believe that gods, or destiny, or whomever may have decided that you are the person they should grant these gifts to. You will use them well."

I can see my words affecting David, a begrudging smile growing on his lips. "I just wish I knew *why*."

"That is what we will work to figure out next." I pull him into a hug. "Shall we go back inside?"

"Okay." David nods against my chest. "Thank you."

Everyone lifts their heads when we re-enter the overcrowded apartment. Adam and Tsula have moved onto the couch, the four of them in some sort of discussion. Hopefully not just gossiping.

"Everything okay?" Adam asks once the door is closed.

"Yeah, just needed some air." David nods as he sits down. "Sorry for getting a little heated before."

"It's cool." Adam smiles. "We were just coming up with some plans."

"What sort of plans?" I ask next.

"Obviously, we need to take care of the Redwish stuff first thing in the morning, but I figured we could do a few other things while we're here," Adam explains. "Like for starters, maybe help David figure out how to control this new strength of his."

"That would probably be useful," David admits.

"From what you've told me, it sounds connected to your emotions or is a response to a distressed or traumatic state,"

Atsadi offers. "I'm not an expert of biology, magical or otherwise, but I have some friends who may be able to help."

"And once I'm back at school, I'll be able to use their gigantic library to research everything I can about resurrections and Olympian rituals," Michael says next. "I might even be able to convince some other students to help."

"And there's a pretty sizable library here, too!" Tsula says excitedly. "And Atsadi was just about to tell us about some other ruins."

"Yes." Atsadi nods. "You all must have noticed that there is something odd about an ancient Olympian temple thousands of miles and an ocean away from Olympia, that not even they have records of building."

"It is something I have always wondered about," I admit.

"I can tell you that at least three other temples with mismatched geography have been discovered in the last century," Atsadi tells us confidently. "I haven't exactly kept up with all my old friends from the dig-site, so I don't know if there have been any other developments, but I can remember the discovery of a temple to the Aesir in Grimmland, one for the Ennead deep in northern Shiveria, and a shrine for the Kami was located on our own west coast! Though that is still almost five thousand kilometers away."

"Other temples?" David leans forward, immediately interested. "Do you think they're the same as the one we visited?"

"I'm not sure. I've never seen them myself," Atsadi answers. "We didn't even know what the Olympian temple was for, until you."

"Redwish is still priority number one," Adam tells us. "But now we've got multiple leads for what to do next."

"That all sounds well thought out to me," I give my blessing.

"Thanks for doing this, everyone," David tells the room. "I owe all of you."

"Of course we're gonna help you," Michael says to his brother. "But you can repay me by buying the reponiam we need to pick up later."

We make plans with Atsadi before we leave to come back tomorrow before lunch. David and Michael leave to spend time together, walking around the city on their own, meeting us at the inn later that evening where we have one final meal together as a group. After the twins finish trying to embarrass each other with stories from their childhood over dinner, it is almost time to go. We stop by Hadawako's for the reponiam, going across the street to pick up the Bearfoot brothers while we are there. A few of the Hadawako's clerks also wish to witness Michael's sure-to-be flashy exit, so with an entourage in tow, we leave for the Testament of Unity.

"Are you sure you've gotta leave tonight?" David asks as we step off the ferry that has brought us to the monument. "It's so late."

"Yeah, but it's already morning over there," Michael tells him with a sad smile.

"Plenty of time to spend the day getting our arses chewed out," Piper grumbles under breath as she passes.

Testament Island is relatively small, really only large enough to house the monument itself and a few small city offices. This close to the statue's flame, everything is bathed in a sheen of green, people flocking here even at night to take in its glow. There are two entrances to the monument itself that are open to the public, the first (and much more popular) option opens to a winding staircase that takes you all the way to the top of the statue, all the way into its arm just below the torch. The second leads down to the monument's center, where the ritual room can be found. My sister Ayla and I climbed the statue the last time we were here, though she insisted we skip a tour of the ritual room as it sounded "too educational."

An open iron gate marks the entrance to the ritual room, a tunnel which is large by gnome standards, but still forces me to crouch. Torches line the walls of the tunnel, but inside the room new lighting has been added with glow stones hanging from the ceiling. The ritual room is not exceptionally large, much smaller than the Onyx Spires, though at the center there is a similar platform. This one is round with four thin rounded walls along the edge that meet in the center like a dome that has had four large sections of it cut out. There are a few people milling about, mostly looking at the artwork on the room's walls.

"So, you've got everything you need?" David asks his brother as the others say their goodbyes to Piper and Riley.

"Yep, think so." Michael nods, patting his bag. "Piper and I figured out all the calculations before dinner, and we have more than enough reponiam."

"And you are sure you will not overshoot your target again?" I ask the man next.

"I mean, I hope not, but who knows?" He turns to David. "Maybe I'll show up outside wherever Joseph is posted."

"Have fun with that." David rolls his eyes, then frowns. "I'm really gonna miss you, Mikey."

"I'm going to miss you too, D." Michael embraces his brother in a tight hug. "I'm just glad I know you're alright... and I bet Mom and Dad would be too."

David pulls back at the mention of their parents. "Really, dude?"

"David, they're worried that you might be *dead*," Michael implores his twin to the seriousness of the situation. "Please, can't I at least let them know you're alive?"

David does not answer for some time, furrowing his brow and crossing his arms.

"Fine," he finally answers. "You can tell them you got a letter from me. That it came in while you were gone, but you don't know from where. You tell them that I'm alive, and that I'm okay, and that's *it*. Got it?"

"Got it." Michael nods in relief. "Thank you. Now I just wish we had a better way to stay in touch."

"Oh crap, that reminds me, I have something to give you!" David says with realization, reaching into his new magical bag and pulling out one of the green journals. "I have the other copy. It's a magic journal that'll let us write to each other."

"Enchanted vellum!" Michael grins, eagerly accepting the gift and then hugging his brother tight. "David, this is great. We'll be able to talk whenever we want."

"Now there's no excuse not to keep in touch," David says after releasing his brother. "And...be careful with all this. However you do that with teleporting."

"I'll let you know as soon as we arrive at the institute," Michael promises before turning to me and extending his hand. "Khazak, it's been...mostly good getting to know you."

"It has been good getting to know you as well." I shake his accepted hand.

"Take care of my brother," he warns.

"I will," I promise. "I hope you and your friends travel safely."

"Thanks." With a smile, he turns to say goodbye to the others while Riley makes his way over to me and David.

"It has been quite the adventure travelin' with you folks," the redhead says as he gives us each a hug. "And I'm doubly sorry we never got to have that roll in the hay we've been building up to," he tells me with a wink.

"You have been a pleasure to travel with and an excellent fishing partner, Riley," I compliment, ignoring the blatant proposition.

"Yeah, and thanks for the weed, too," David jokes.

"If you all are ever in the Eire, you be sure to let me know," he tells us both. "I'd love to show you around some time."

"I'm sure you know all the best hay-rolling spots," David flirts. "You thinking of heading home next?"

"Yeah, after all o' this, I could use some downtime. And if I'm being honest, I kinda miss my own family," Riley admits.

"I am thinking of doing the same." Piper joins our conversation as Riley exits. "Thank you for putting up with the three of us after we forced our way into your group."

"Nonsense. Helping you was the right thing to do," I assure her. "Your magical skills have been invaluable on our journey."

"Seriously, you might give Mike a run for his money," David tells her. "Make sure he doesn't do anything stupid, okay?"

"I shall do my best," she answers with a small curtsy. "Now, if he could finish saying goodbye..."

David and I both turn to see Michael and Tsula speaking awkwardly, saddened by Michael's imminent exit. Having never established any sort of official relationship, it sounds like the two are making small talk as if they hadn't spent the last month bonding. Perhaps they just cannot bring themselves to say goodbye.

"It was really great meeting you," Michael tells the girl he clearly has feelings for.

"It was great meeting you too," Tsula repeats. "Good luck sorting out everything with your school."

"Thanks. There's going to be a few unhappy faces waiting for us." Michael scratches the back of his head nervously. "Are you gonna keep traveling with David and the others?"

"Yes, I think so." Tsula nods. "It's been incredible so far."

"Maybe you could write to me?" the male wizard asks nervously. "I mean, I know you'll probably be moving around a lot, but I—"

"I'd like that," Tsula answers with a smile, taking Michael's hand.

"Kiss her!" David calls to his brother from my right, hands cupped around his mouth.

Michael glares at his twin, then turns back to his girl. "So, uh..."

Tsula closes the distance between them, pressing her lips to his. Michael is shocked for a moment before he relaxes into it and kisses her back. David lets out a *whoop* when they finally break apart, earning him another glare.

"I guess it's time to go," Michael says sadly.

"Yes, and with the platform free, we should move now," Piper points out the lack of people at the center of the room.

"Goodbye everyone." Michael and the two other travelers wave as they step onto the platform at the center of the room, our group watching from the sideline.

The three humans move to the center of the platform, standing in a small circle and taking each other's hands. As Michael starts to chant, the room begins to shake slightly and the ancient gnomish symbols etched into the partial-dome covering them begin to glow, starting at the base and rising up. Once it reaches the top, the dome itself begins glowing, and the other people inside the chamber cannot help but notice the light show. A beam of multi-colored light suddenly shoots down from the top of the dome, startling all of the onlookers.

Before it can strike the ground, the light forms a bubble around the three humans. Within the bubble, the bodies of our friends begin to glow as well until it appears they are made of the same light, losing their defined forms completely. The bubble surrounding them shrinks as the light within condenses before the bubble and beam are sucked back into the dome with a rush of air. The room is dead-silent for a moment before the people around us begin speaking in amazement to each other about what they just witnessed. Someone who appears to be part of the island monument's staff, watching the whole situation with wide eyes, rushes from the room.

"We may want to get out of here before someone starts asking questions," Onas tells us as he watches them leave.

"Wait!" David shouts, digging into his bag for his other journal and opening it. He stares at the blank page intently waiting for a sign. Over his shoulder, I watch when a message finally appears on the page, letter by letter.

Made it home safe! Lots of shocked faces, so we better go take care of some stuff. I'll write you later! -M

"Okay, we can go." David closes the book in relief, putting it back in his bag.

We manage to exit the ritual room and get back on the ferry to the main island without any issues. The monument island staff are clearly attempting to discover what just happened, but thankfully, no one was paying enough attention to our group to think we were a part of it. I am not against explaining what happened to anyone, but it has been a long day, and right now, I just want to get my pup back to our room.

It is a quietly somber walk back to the inn, our group now much smaller. It is late when we reach the inn, everyone splitting up to return to their own rooms for the night. Lots to do in the morning.

"How are you feeling?" I ask once we are back in our room, lighting the lamp on the wall.

"I guess I'm kinda down about Mike leaving," he admits, flopping stomach-down on the bed. "But he and I can talk whenever we want now. And it'll be nice not having to worry about him catching us fooling around anymore."

"I'm glad you think so." I step to the center of the room, standing tall and puffing out my chest. "Because I have plans for how the next few days are going to go."

"Sir?" David lifts his body with one arm.

"Attention." I snap my fingers and point at the floor in front of me.

It takes David a minute to realize the order, and then he is scrambling off the bed to stand where I have indicated. He brings his heels together and straightens his back, arms straight down by his side. I keep my face passive as I walk around him, inspecting his posture.

"Good boy," I praise as I step toward the bed, where he can watch as I start to slowly unbutton my shirt. "I know it has been a long month of travel—though I could swear it feels like we left over a year ago—and I was hoping that with your brother gone, we could spend that time re-establishing a few things in our relationship. Any objections, puppy?"

"No, Sir." His eyes are locked on my exposed chest.

"Good." I finish pulling my shirt off. "Strip and prepare yourself with your charm."

There is no hesitation to obey that order, David moving quickly to remove his boots, shirt, and pants. As I am still taking my time, he is nude first and retrieves the cleansing charm from where we left it on the nightstand. He finishes using it and returns to the spot I first instructed him to stand just as I am done stripping myself.

"Kneeling inspection," is my next order, and David sinks to his knees, his hands moving to grasp the back of his neck. "Good boy."

I walk around him, inspecting his body once more as the pose demands. I stop in front of him, my already hard cock bobbing in front of his face. David's eyes move from my face to my cock, subconsciously licking his lips. I bring one of my feet between his spread thighs, rubbing against his caged cock. Then, grabbing him by the hair, I hold him in place as I bring my hips forward, his mouth opening automatically to take me in.

"Mmmmm..." I moan dramatically. "For the next few days, you can expect to follow protocol whenever we are alone."

David whimpers around my cock, his lips stretching wider as I push forward. I slowly sink in with over half of my cock before pulling back, just enough to tickle his throat but not fully gag him. I am not looking to be particularly rough—there will be plenty of time for that later—this is purely about control.

I continue fucking his face and throat with steady, measured strokes. The skin of my cock glistens as it leaves his mouth before his pink lips are once again stretched around my green shaft. After a few minutes, drool starts to escape from the corners of his mouth, dripping down into his beard. Before things get too messy, I take a step back, my cock leaving his throat with a wet *pop*.

"On the bed, ass over the edge, chest to the mattress," I order as I fist my slick cock.

"Yessir," David says with a gasp, finally breaking position to wipe his face on his arm before crawling onto the bed.

Bent over with his legs spread, his ass parts naturally to reveal the hole within, lightly dusted with fur. I kneel behind him, clutching him in both hands and spreading him wider.

His cock hangs between his legs, the metal ring behind his balls shining in the room's light, precum already gathered at the cage's head. I squeeze his cheeks, teasing my thumbs into his crack, before lowering my head and licking over his entrance.

David moans, sinking farther into the mattress as he arches his back, seeking as much friction as he can get. I grin against him, my tusks pressing into his skin as I swipe my tongue over his hole, pushing against his entrance, the wrinkled flesh giving way to the wet muscle. David rocks himself backward as he is tongue-fucked and I growl, reaching down to play with my cock as I lick open his passage.

With a final nibble to his hole, I tear myself away. Standing and slicking myself with oil, I drip some along his crack, lubricating his hole with my fingers. David whimpers as the first digit breaches him, his hole squeezing around me as I sink in to the final knuckle. After adding a second finger, he starts to rock himself back once more, and I know he is ready.

I take myself in hand, aiming at his hole as I step up behind him. The head of my cock presses against him, opening easily to allow me entry. I push inch after inch of my cock inside, his hot passage squeezing me tightly. I grab his hips with my now free hands, holding him in place as I push the last few inches of myself inside, forcing David to gasp.

Rumbling low in my chest out of pleasure, I squeeze his hips before pulling my cock halfway out. The skin around his hole drags with me, and I watch, transfixed, as I push back inside, my cock disappearing into David. As I slowly pick up speed, David presses his face into the bed, using the mattress to muffle his moans. Happy with the pace I've set, I spank his right flank, grinning at the *yelp* he makes in response.

After a few minutes of staring at the sheen of sweat growing on David's back, I pull out, taking him by the thighs and flipping him over. I grip both of his legs behind the knees, bending them back and pressing them to his chest. His eyes bug out when I re-enter him, bottoming out immediately. Grinning, I bend over and catch his lips in a quick kiss.

I start to fuck David at the same pace as before, giving him little time to adjust. Rather than be overwhelmed, David reaches both hands up to grab his own feet, pulling his legs back even farther. A steady stream of pre-cum leaks from the end of the cage, bouncing against his stomach with every thrust. When David's legs start to shake, I look down and watch his hole push as I give him his first anal orgasm of the night, relishing the way he squeezes me.

Of course, one orgasm precedes another, with David soon having them back-to-back. I continue to fuck him through each and every one, pulling my cock almost all the way out before plunging back in. Eventually, David is unable to continue gripping his feet, and his hands fall to the mattress as his eyes roll back in his head sometime after orgasm number seven. Every time it happens, the feeling of his tight, wet hole squeezing around my cock brings me closer and closer to the edge.

When I can feel myself on the precipice, I drop down, bending David in half as I force my tongue into his mouth. Slamming my hips against him one final time, the dam bursts, and I growl against his lips as I cum. My body makes small, involuntary jerks with each volley until I am finished, panting into David's ear, his body still folded beneath me. Eventually, I allow his legs to drop, my cock slipping from his hole as I roll us onto our sides.

We lay there for a few minutes, enjoying the post-orgasmic high as I stroke my hands down David's sweaty back. His prick still strains against the cage that now pushes against my lower stomach, but good pup that he is, David does not beg to be released. With a final kiss to the top of his head, I pull away and stand, wetting a washcloth with my water canteen and wiping us both down.

"Thank you, Sir," David says sleepily as I run the cloth over the backs of his legs and thighs.

"Feeling better?" I ask, now using the same cloth on my sticky cock and balls.

"Much, Sir," David nods sleepily against his pillow. "Though I wouldn't mind being let out of this cage..."

"You still have at least several more days of cage wearing by my count," I tell him with a chuckle as I blow out the lamp's flame.

"Yes, Sir." David sighs, making room for me to join him on the bed. "You know what I realized?"

"What's that, pup?" I ask, flipping David around so I can spoon him.

"It's been over a week and neither of us has had a nightmare." He cuddles back against me, and as we both drift off to sleep, I wonder if that's a positive sign of things to come.

David and I are running through a dark forest. A forest we've been to before... Being chased by something familiar. In fact, all of this is familiar. As the realization that we are in a dream hits me, I come to a stop, David stumbling to his own stop ahead of me.

"What are you doing? We can't stop now. He's right—" David stops as the sky turns black and the strange bells begin to ring their disturbing, discordant tune. "He's here."

With my memories of our previous time here fresh in my mind, I pull the sword from the sheath on David's back, using the magical blade to slice through each of the black tendrils as they rise from the ground to strike at us. With David at my back, I cut each of them down until the forest floor is littered with writhing, inky-colored appendages.

But it isn't over. The still-moving tendrils pool together, melding into three amorphous black blobs. Those blobs start to grow, their features becoming more and more defined, until we are surrounded by three wolves, completely black except for their glowing red eyes. They growl and begin circling us, the black of their fur dripping down like tar.

I grip the sword tightly, digging my feet into the ground as they come to a stop, crouching down just before they pounce—

I wake with a start, finding myself not in a forest, but our room at the Moonbright Inn & Tavern. David is still asleep next to me, and the hints of morning are peeking in through the corners of our window's curtain. I wait for my heart to stop racing, allowing myself a few quiet moments in bed where I at least attempt to go back to sleep. But my mind will not stop thinking about the seemingly updated nightmare, or the fact that David almost certainly hexed me by mentioning the lack thereof before bed last night.

After rolling my eyes and kissing my still-sleeping pup on the forehead, I carefully extract myself from bed and pull on some pants. I may as well see if they have any coffee downstairs. Before I leave though, I dig into my Spacious Satchel, pulling out a forest-green thong that belongs to David—and is one of my favorites. I leave it on the nightstand, on the off-chance David should wake before I am back and decide to put it on—it would certainly be a welcome sight to return to. Quietly exiting the room, I make my way to the dining room, pleased to be handed a steaming mug of my favorite dark liquid. As I reach for the sugar, I notice some of the inn's other patrons gathering near the windows. Then some rush outside.

Curious myself, I follow, mug in hand. Outside it is not just the inn, but people are seemingly spilling out of every building into the streets, all of their gazes locked to the sky. I follow with my own eyes and see that there is *something* up there, hovering over the city. As it draws closer, its image becomes sharper and more visible until...

Is that a *dragon*?

Khazak, David, and the rest of their friends
will return in *Steel & Thunder* Book 5!

Book Club Questions

1. What do you think is the significance of the title?

2. How would *you* have handled Nate's situation with Liss if you were in his shoes?

3. Do you agree with all of Khazak's guilt over his early treatment of David?

4. Should Khazak and David have told Michael the truth even sooner, or do you think they should have tried to keep it a secret even longer?

5. What do you think of the Lutherians who moved to Richardton? Should they have to leave, like Robin wants them to?

6. What would you have done when presented with Calvinson's offer?

7. Do you think the group will be successful in reforming Richardton? What other changes do you think they will need to implement?

8. Do you think Calvinson can be redeemed? How do you think he should be punished?

9. Were you sad to see any of the characters leave? Who will you miss the most?

10. What other sorts of items do you think might be for sale in the Magic Market?

About the Author

Dominic N. Ashen is an author and avid reader with a heavy focus on gay BDSM-themed erotica. After spending his youth in search of books with characters who were more like himself—queer ones, specifically—he decided to start creating some of his own. His stories star queer protagonists, most often gay and bisexual men, and feature heavy themes of dominance, submission, and all sorts of kinks. Dominic loves the fantasy, sci-fi, and horror genres with a penchant for writing longer stories where he is able to weave in the sex and kink right alongside the plot.

Website: https://www.dominicashen.com/

Patreon: https://www.patreon.com/dominicashen

Twitter: https://twitter.com/DomNAshen

Facebook: https://www.facebook.com/dom.n.ashen

Instagram: https://www.instagram.com/dom.n.ashen

MORE BOOKS FROM 4 HORSEMEN PUBLICATIONS

EROTICA

ALI WHIPPE
Office Hours
Tutoring Center
Athletics
Extra Credit
Financial Aid
Bound for Release
Fetish Circuit
Now You See Me
Sexual Playground
Swingers
Discovered

ARIA SKYLAR
Twisted Eros

CHASTITY VELDT
Molly in Milwaukee
Irene in Indianapolis
Lydia in Louisville
Natasha in Nashville
Alyssa in Atlanta
Betty in Birmingham
Carrie on Campus
Jackie in Jacksonville

DALIA LANCE
My Home on Whore Island
Slumming It on Slut Street
Training of the Tramp
The Imperfect Perfection

Spring Break
72% Match
It Was Meant To Be... Or Whatever

HONEY CUMMINGS
Sleeping with Sasquatch
Cuddling with Chupacabra
Naked with New Jersey Devil
Laying with the Lady in Blue
Wanton Woman in White
Beating it with Bloody Mary
Beau and Professor Bestialora
The Goat's Gruff
Goldie and Her Three Beards
Pied Piper's Pipe
Princess Pea's Bed
Pinocchio and the Blow Up Doll
Jack's Beanstalk
Pulling Rapunzel's Hair
Curses & Crushes

NICK SAVAGE
The Fairlane Incidents
The Fortunate Finn Fairlane
The Fragile Finn Fairlane
Us Of Legendary Gods
So We Stay Hidden
The West Haven Undead

DISCOVER MORE AT 4HORSEMENPUBLICATIONS.COM

CPSIA information can be obtained
at www.ICGtesting.com
Printed in the USA
BVHW042010060223
657986BV00004B/45

9 798823 200899